Dear Target Guest:

Thirteen years ago, I adopted my dog from a local shelter. She was nervous and shaking, a rescue from Tennessee with a long, jagged scar on her leg. She licked my hand when I reached into her cage, and in that moment I knew that we belonged together.

Those moments in life are rare—when you just *know* something. You feel it in your bones and there is no explaining it to others. A hidden truth suddenly revealed.

The same thing happened when I began writing *The Twelve Lives of Samuel Hawley*. After hundreds of wasted pages and years of searching for a character to follow, I discovered a tall, rugged man standing on a fishing pier. It was a bit like falling in love. *Ah*, I thought. *There you are.*

His story began in Gloucester, Massachusetts, at a real contest that takes place each summer among the local fishermen: a forty-five-foot pole is covered with grease, attached to a pier and set horizontally above the water. A flag is nailed to the end. The first fisherman to make it to the end of the pole (and capture the flag) wins. I grew up nearby, and know the contest well. At my writing desk, I closed my eyes and tried to describe it. I focused on one of the men on the pier. I watched him remove his shirt and take his first step onto the pole. Then I realized that his skin was covered with scars. And I *knew*.

There are stories behind the scars that we carry. Stories we tell only to the people we're most intimate with. Samuel Hawley's scars were a mystery I wanted to uncover, and his body became a map of the book I was going to write. Through Hawley's restless daughter, Loo, I worked to uncover his hidden past, weaving it together into the present and taking both characters into the future.

The Twelve Lives of Samuel Hawley is about continuing to live, even when life seems impossible. It's about making the most of your time on earth. It's about finding people to love. It's about forgiveness and heroes and sacrifice and secrets. It's about all the blank spaces that will never be filled in. It's about the mysteries we are to one another.

I barely notice the scar on my dog's leg anymore. But on our morning walk, people often point and ask, "What happened?"

"I don't know that story," I say. "It happened in her previous life." Then I scratch her ears and she wags her tail and we continue on. We keep living.

I'm so grateful to Target for making *The Twelve Lives of Samuel Hawley* a Book Club Pick, and to you for choosing to take this adventure with Hawley and Loo.

I hope you share the stories of your own scars. I hope you find some light in the darkness. And I hope that these pages fill you with courage, just as writing them did for me.

Cheers,

Hannah Tinti

Praise for *The Twelve Lives of Samuel Hawley*

• • •

Named a 2017 Notable Work of Fiction by *The Washington Post*
and a 2017 Great Read by NPR

"[Hannah Tinti] knows how to cast the old campfire spell. I was so desperate to find out what happened to these characters that I had to keep bargaining with myself to stop from jumping ahead to the end.... Each [chapter] is a heart-in-your-throat revelation, a thrilling mix of blood and love. Some of these well-drawn characters exist only for a few pages; others rear up again when you least expect them ... A master class in literary suspense."

—Ron Charles, *The Washington Post*

"[A] strikingly symphonic novel ... [Tinti] has a deep feeling for the passage of time and its effect on character.... The story is bound together by memory as a kind of highlight film. Which is to say, by memory as it actually is and not as a neat, banal narrative.... There are surprises.... And diversions. And mysteries.... We read on, carried by Tinti's seductive prose."

—Pete Hamill, *The New York Times Book Review*

"Tinti depicts brutality and compassion with exquisite sensitivity, creating a powerful overlay of love and pain."

—*The New Yorker*

"Can a man be both a violent criminal and a good father? Imagine a Quentin Tarantino movie crossed with a John Green novel, and you'll have a sense of what this coming-of-age novel is like."

—*Entertainment Weekly*

"[T]he book [has] an irresistible velocity that Ms. Tinti sustains to the end."

—*The Wall Street Journal*

"Tinti has established herself as one of our great storytellers. She draws you in with this book, and it's really difficult to get away."

—*Rolling Stone*

"A shoot-em-up, a love story and a mystery, this is one heart-warming feast of a book."

—*People*

"The term 'literary thriller' is almost an oxymoron. It's the writerly equivalent of threading a needle while riding on a roller coaster, requiring attention to character and fine prose while hurtling from one near-disaster to another. Only a few writers can pull it off, and Hannah Tinti is one of them. . . . *The Twelve Lives of Samuel Hawley* is a gripping father-daughter road trip where the bad guys are never far behind. . . . Tarantino-like in its plot twists, action, and violence, the novel sweeps across the country and back and forth in time. Its structure feels as meticulously crafted as a matchstick Taj Mahal."

—*Interview*

"Tinti makes each of her crime scenes wildly different yet equally suspenseful. As skillful as she is, she never romanticizes her bad actors.

What most deeply interests her is the stumbling, fumbling humanity that results in bad actions. . . . She fuses urgent, vibrant storytelling with a keen understanding of broken people desperate to be whole."

—*Newsday*

"Hannah Tinti's beautifully constructed second novel . . . uses the scars on Hawley's body—all twelve bullet wounds, one by one—to show who he is, what he's done, and why the past chases and clings to him with such tenacity. Nearly nine years after *The Good Thief*, Tinti has fused a cowboy-noir action adventure and a coming-of-age tale into a father-daughter love story."

—*The Boston Globe*

"Even before the official release of *The Twelve Lives of Samuel Hawley*, early readers deemed it worthy of excitement. . . . At once a coming-of-age adventure, a love story and a literary thriller."

—*Time*

"*The Twelve Lives of Samuel Hawley* is a miraculous accomplishment in genre-bending: Not only a gripping American-on-the-run thriller, it's also a brilliant coming-of-age tale and a touching exploration of father-daughter relationships. Regardless of what your reading tastes are, there's something here for absolutely everyone."

—*Newsweek*

"*The Twelve Lives of Samuel Hawley* is an adventure epic with the deeper resonance of myth. . . . Tinti exhibits an aptitude for shining a piercing light into the corners of her characters' hearts and minds. Her ability to lay bare their passions, portraying their vulnerabilities and violent urges with equal insight, leaves the reader at once shaken and moved."

—*O: The Oprah Magazine*

"An achingly beautiful story about a single father raising a daughter whom he's trying to keep from repeating his own mistakes. . . . Tinti's language is precise and beautiful. She writes rich and nuanced characters. In spite of his past, there's never any doubt about Hawley's good intentions and the love he has for his daughter. Their story is a poignant one that readers won't want to see end."

—*The Dallas Morning News*

"Tinti's second novel was years in the making, and well worth the wait. It tells of teenaged Loo and her father, a hardened criminal, as they attempt to settle down from a life on the road in a small coastal town that is resistant to outsiders. . . . This contemporary interpretation of the Greek myth of Hercules, whose twelve labors are represented by Hawley's twelve bullet wounds, is at once an American epic, a hardboiled crime story, and an exploration of familial love."

—OTTO PENZLER, *LitHub*

"*The Twelve Lives of Samuel Hawley* is an impeccably crafted novel that will thrill new readers and those who have followed Tinti's work over the years. . . . Set aside a weekend for this captivating novel, because once you start it you won't want to put it down until you reach the last page. And even then, you'll want to start again from the very beginning."

—Minneapolis *Star-Tribune*

"Tinti's second novel skillfully channels suspense, longing and loss . . . [and] has all the elements of an Academy Award–winning film: enthralling action, unexpected love and a close examination of the human condition. . . . The bottom line: Tinti is an excellent storyteller. . . . *Twelve Lives* is a moving, human drama of lives inextricably bound to one another, linked by past and present. It raises essential questions of heroism, family and identity—letting readers seek the answers—and embeds them in a truly magnetic story."

—*The Kansas City Star*

"Hannah Tinti has crafted another masterpiece. *The Twelve Lives of Samuel Hawley* explores a captivating father-daughter relationship, weaving the pair's saga through two narrative timelines. . . . The result is a fascinating literary thriller, with Tinti building the tension as both timelines count down to the final gunshot."

—*Paste*

"Seamlessly transposing classical myth into a quintessentially American landscape and marrying taut suspense with dreamy lyricism, Tinti's beautifully intricate second novel is well worth the wait. . . . Tinti's imagery evokes time, space, the sea, and the myth of Heracles without losing the narrative's sure grounding in American communities and culture. This is a convincingly redemptive and celebratory novel: an affirmation of the way that heroism and human fallibility coexist, of how good parenting comes in unexpected packages, and of the way that we are marked by our encounters with each other and the luminous universe in which we dwell."

—*Publishers Weekly* (starred review)

"[An] atmospheric, complexly suspenseful saga . . . With life or death struggles in dramatic settings . . . and starring a fiercely loving, reluctant criminal and a girl of grit and wonder, Tinti has forged a breathtaking novel of violence and tenderness."

—*Booklist* (starred review)

"What Hannah Tinti knows about fathers, daughters and time could, as they say, fill a book—and truly does. *The Twelve Lives of Samuel Hawley* is bold, exciting, and original."

—MEG WOLITZER, author of *The Interestings*

"*The Twelve Lives of Samuel Hawley* is utterly magnificent—gripping, suspenseful, funny, and so full of heart. Young Loo and her father are contemporary characters with the stature and magnetism of the great heroes of literature. The reader in me was racing through to find out what would befall them, while the writer, awestruck by Hannah Tinti's powerful storytelling, was desperately trying to slow down. This is a book I will return to again and again, for sheer pleasure and to learn how it is done."

—RUTH OZEKI, author of *A Tale for the Time Being*

"One part Quentin Tarantino, one part Scheherazade, and twelve parts wild innovation. Hannah Tinti proves herself to be an old-fashioned storyteller of the highest order."

—ANN PATCHETT, author of *Commonwealth*

"A riveting character-driven thriller, a father/daughter road trip you won't soon forget. Fans of *The Good Thief* who have been waiting for whatever comes next from this gifted writer will find their patience richly rewarded."

—RICHARD RUSSO, author of *Everybody's Fool*

By Hannah Tinti

The Twelve Lives of Samuel Hawley

The Good Thief

Animal Crackers

The TWELVE LIVES *of* SAMUEL HAWLEY

The

TWELVE LIVES

of

SAMUEL HAWLEY

a novel

. . .

HANNAH TINTI

THE DIAL PRESS  NEW YORK

2018 Target Edition

Copyright © 2017 by Hannah Tinti
Reading group guide copyright © 2018 by Penguin Random House LLC

Published in the United States by The Dial Press, an imprint of Random House, a division of Penguin Random House LLC, New York.

THE DIAL PRESS and the HOUSE colophon are registered trademarks of Penguin Random House LLC.

RANDOM HOUSE READER'S CIRCLE & Design is a registered trademark of Penguin Random House LLC.

Originally published in hardcover in the United States by The Dial Press, an imprint of Random House, a division of Penguin Random House LLC, in 2017.

LIBRARY OF CONGRESS CATALOGING-IN-PUBLICATION DATA
Name: Tinti, Hannah, author.
Title: The Twelve Lives of Samuel Hawley : a novel / Hannah Tinti.
Other titles: 12 lives of Samuel Hawley
Identifiers: LCCN 2016021409 | ISBN 978-0-525-51147-2 |
ISBN 978-0-8129-8989-2 (ebook)
Subjects: LCSH: Fathers and daughters—Fiction. | Domestic fiction. | BISAC:
FICTION / Literary. | FICTION / Family Life. | FICTION / Coming of Age.
Classification: LCC PS3620.I56 T94 2017 | DDC 813/.6—dc23
LC record available at https://lccn.loc.gov/2016021409

Printed in the United States of America on acid-free paper

randomhousebooks.com
randomhousereaderscircle.com

2 4 6 8 9 7 5 3 1

Book design by Susan Turner

For Helen Ellis and Ann Napolitano,
great writers and true friends

And for Canada,
for walking me through the dark

With a rapid, nameless impulse, in a superb lofty arch the bright steel spans the foaming distance, and quivers in the life spot of the whale. Instead of sparkling water, he now spouts red blood.

"That drove the spigot out of him!" cries Stubb. "'Tis July's immortal Fourth; all fountains must run wine to-day!"

—HERMAN MELVILLE, *Moby-Dick*

CONTENTS

The TWELVE LIVES *of* SAMUEL HAWLEY

Hawley

WHEN LOO WAS TWELVE YEARS OLD HER FATHER TAUGHT HER HOW TO shoot a gun. He had a case full of them in his room, others hidden in boxes around the house. Loo had seen them at night, when he took the guns apart and cleaned them at the kitchen table, oiling and polishing and brushing for hours. She was forbidden to touch them and so she watched from a distance, learning what she could about their secrets, until the day when she blew out birthday candles on twelve chocolate Ring Dings, arranged on a plate in the shape of a star, and Hawley opened the wooden chest in their living room and put the gift she had been waiting for—her grandfather's rifle—into her arms.

Now Loo waited in the hallway as her father pulled down a box of ammunition from the front closet. He took out some .22 rimfires— long-rifle and Magnum—as well as nine-millimeter Hornady 115- grain. The bullets rattled inside their cardboard containers as he slid them into a bag. Loo took note of every detail, as if her father's choices were part of a test she would later have to pass. Hawley grabbed a bolt-action Model 5 Remington, a Winchester Model 52 and his Colt Python.

Whenever he left the house, Loo's father carried a gun with him. Each of these guns had a story. There was the rifle that Loo's grandfather had carried in the war, notched with kills, that now belonged to her. There was the twenty-gauge shotgun from a ranch in Wyoming where Hawley worked for a time running horses. There was a set of silver dueling pistols in a polished wooden case, won in a poker game in Arizona. The snub-nosed Ruger he kept in a bag at the back of his closet. The collection of derringers with pearl handles that he hid in the bottom drawer of his bureau. And the Colt with a stamp from Hartford, Connecticut, on the side.

The Colt had no particular resting place. Loo had found it underneath her father's mattress and sitting openly on the kitchen table, on top of the refrigerator and once on the edge of the bathtub. The gun was her father's shadow. Resting in the places he had passed through. If Hawley was out of the room, sometimes she would touch the handle. The grip was made of rosewood, and felt smooth beneath her fingers, but she never picked it up or moved it from whatever place he had set it down.

Hawley grabbed the Colt now and tucked it under his belt, then strung the rifles across his shoulder. He said, "Come on, troublemaker." Then he held open the door for them both. He led his daughter into the woods behind their house and down into the ravine, where a stream rushed over mossy rocks before emptying out into the ocean.

It was a clear day. The leaves had abandoned their branches for the forest floor, a carpet of crimson, yellow and orange; crisp and rustling. Loo's father stopped at an old maple, where a rusted paint can hung from a branch. He cracked it open with a knife, used the brush tied to the handle to mark a pine tree at one hundred yards with a small spot of white paint, then walked back to his daughter and the guns.

Hawley was in his forties but looked younger, his hips still narrow, his legs strong. He was as tall as a longboat, with wide shoulders that sloped from the years of driving his truck back and forth across the country with Loo in the passenger seat. His hands were callused from the day jobs he'd work from time to time—fixing cars or painting houses. His fingernails were lined with grease and his dark hair was always overgrown and tangled. But his eyes were a deep blue and he had a face that was rough and broken in a way that came out handsome. Wherever they had stopped on the road, whether it was for breakfast at some diner on the highway, or in a small town where they'd set up for a while, Loo would notice women drifting toward him. But her father would make his mouth go still and set his jaw and it kept anyone from getting too close.

These days his truck wasn't going anywhere except down to the water, where they dug clams and hauled buckets of shells. Quahogs, Hawley called them. But also littlenecks, topnecks, steamers and cherrystones, depending on their size and color. He used a rake to hunt but Loo preferred a long, thin spade that could pierce the surface before the creatures began to burrow. Early each morning father and daughter rolled their pants above their knees and slipped on rubber boots. The shells were pulled from the salt marshes and mudflats, from the sandy bay and at low tide along the shore.

HAWLEY TOOK THE REMINGTON OFF his shoulder and showed Loo how to load the clip. Five bullets slid inside, one by one. Then the magazine clicked into place.

"This is for starters. A practice gun. It won't do much damage. But still," he said. "Keep the safety on. Check your target and what's behind your target. Don't point it at anything you don't want to shoot."

He opened the bolt, retracted, then closed it again, pulling the first live round into the chamber. Then he handed his daughter the rifle. "Plant your feet," he said. "Loosen your knees. Take a breath. Let half of it out. That's when you want to squeeze the trigger. On the exhale. Don't pull—just squeeze."

The Remington was cool and heavy in Loo's hands, and her arms shook a little as she raised the stock to her shoulder. She had dreamed of holding one of her father's guns for so many years that it was as if she were dreaming now. She tried to level the sight as she took aim, pulled the handle in close, lifted her elbow and last, last of all, flipped off the safety.

"What are you going to shoot?" her father asked.

"That tree," said Loo.

"Right."

In her mind she imagined the trajectory of the bullet, saw it going for miles, creating its own history. She knew every part of this gun, every gear and bolt, and she could sense each piece now—the spring and the carrier and the chamber and the pin—working together and sliding into place as she touched the trigger.

The explosion that followed was more of a pop than a blast. The butt of the rifle barely moved against her shoulder. She expected a thrill, some kind of corresponding shudder in her body, but all she felt was a tiny bubble of relief.

"Look," her father said.

Loo lowered the barrel. She could just make out the white mark in the distance, untouched. "I missed."

"Everyone misses." Hawley scratched his nose. "Your mother missed."

"She did?"

"The first time," he said. "Now slide the bolt."

"Did she use this gun?"

"No," said Hawley. "She liked the Ruger."

Loo pulled back on the lever and the casing flung through the air and onto the forest floor. She locked the bolt back into place, and the next bullet slid into the chamber. Her mother, Lily, had died before the girl could remember. A drowning accident in a lake. Hawley had shown Loo the exact spot where it had happened, on a map of Wisconsin. A small blue circle she could hide with the tip of her finger.

Hawley did not like to speak about it. Because of this the air shimmered a bit whenever he did, as if Lily's name were conjuring something dangerous. Most of what Loo knew about her mother was contained in a box full of mementos, a traveling shrine that her father re-created in the bathroom of each place they lived. Motel rooms and temporary apartments, walk-ups and cabins in the woods, and now this house on the hill, this place that Hawley said would be their home.

The photographs went up first, around the bathtub and sink. Her father affixed each carefully so they wouldn't rip—shots of Loo's mother and her long black hair, pale skin and green eyes. Next he arranged half-used bottles of shampoo and conditioner, a compact and a tube of red lipstick, a bent toothbrush, a silk bathrobe with dragons sewn on the back and cans of Lily's favorite foods—pineapple and garbanzo beans—along with bits of handwriting, scraps of paper discovered after her death, things she had needed from the grocery store, lists of activities she had hoped to finish by the following Saturday and a parking ticket with fragments of a dream scribbled on the back. *Old car with hinges folds down into a suitcase.* Every time Loo used the toilet or took a bath, she faced her mother's words, watching the letters bleed together over the years and the ink fade from the steam of the shower.

The dead woman was an ever-present part of their lives. When Loo did something well, her father said: *Just like your mother,* and when she did something bad, her father said: *Your mother would never approve.*

Loo squeezed the trigger. She did it again and again, reloading for over an hour, occasionally nicking bark from the tree but missing the target every time, until there was a pile of brass shells at her feet and her arm ached from the weight of the gun.

"The mark's too small," said Loo. "I'll never hit it."

Hawley pulled a wallet of tobacco from his pocket and shook it back and forth at her. Loo put down the gun. She walked over and took the pouch from him, as well as a package of rolling papers. She slid one thin piece of paper away from the rest, folded it in half with her finger and then tucked some of the tobacco along the crease. Then she placed the filter and began rolling, pinching the ends, licking the edge to seal the fold. She handed the cigarette to her father, and he lit it and settled onto a rock nearby, leaning into the sun. He had started a beard, as he did whenever the weather turned cold, and he scratched it now, his fingers catching in the wiry brown hair.

"You're thinking too much."

Loo tossed the pouch at him, then picked up the rifle again. Her father had hardly spoken during the lesson, as if he expected her to already know how to shoot. She'd been excited when they started, but now she was losing her nerve—in the same way she did in the bathroom surrounded by scraps of her mother's words and cans of her mother's favorite foods and pictures of her mother's effortless beauty.

"I can't do this," she said.

The tide was coming in. Loo could hear the ocean beyond the ravine, gathering strength. One wave after another advancing upon the shore. Hawley tucked the roll of tobacco back into his pocket.

"There's nothing between you and that tree."

"*I'm* between it."

"Then get out of the way."

Loo flipped the safety on and put the rifle down again. She dug a rock out of the dirt with her fingers and threw it into the woods as far as she could. The rock sailed halfway toward the white mark and then crashed into some bushes. Birds scattered. The sound of a plane passed overhead. Loo looked through the branches at the flash of aluminum in the sky. Thirty thousand feet away and it seemed like an easier target.

Hawley's cigarette had gone out as he watched her and now he relit the end, striking a match, the ember glowing once, twice, as he brought it to his lips. Then he crushed the cigarette against the rock. He blew smoke out of his mouth.

"You need a mask." Hawley lifted his giant hands and covered his own face. Then he opened his fingers, framing his eyes and forming a bridge across his nose. It made him look like a stranger. Then Hawley dropped the mask and he was her father again.

"Try it," he said.

Loo's hands were not as big but they did the job, closing her off from the woods and her own disappointment. It was like blinders on a horse. Things got blurry or disappeared when she turned her eyes left or right.

"How am I supposed to shoot like this?"

"Use it to focus, then pick up the gun," said Hawley.

Loo turned back toward the target. The sun was beginning to set. The white spot of paint caught the light and was glowing. What surrounded the tree—the earth, the sky, its own branches—fell away. This was how her father must see things, she thought. A whole world of bull's-eyes.

Just then, beyond the mark, there was a shuffling of leaves. Some kind of movement in the woods. Loo dropped her hands from her face. She held her breath. She heard only the sound of the wind. The rattle of birch leaves flipping back and forth. The distant echo of the plane in the clouds. The scratch of a squirrel's claws as it scrambled up the bark of a tree. But her father was listening for something else. His chin was down, his eyes cutting left. His face tensed and ready.

Hawley was always watching. Always waiting. He got the same look when they went into town for supplies, when the mailman came to their door, when a car pulled alongside them on the road. She heard him late at night, walking the living room floor, checking the locks on the windows. Digging on the beach for clams, he kept his back to the sea. These were small things, but she noticed. And she noticed now, as his whole body became still. He reached behind to his belt, and his hand came back with the Colt.

Loo spun around and picked up the rifle. Her fingers went tight on the grip. She scanned the woods, but she saw nothing. Her father was standing and he was staring in the direction of the tree. At the small white mark one hundred yards across the ravine.

"Loo! Now!"

He shouted her name as if their lives depended on it. And in one movement the Colt pushed through the air like an extension of his arm, and he was firing into the forest, the gun was flashing, blasting over and over, echoing against the hills. Loo brought the rifle to her chest, and she pulled the bolt and fired, pulled the bolt and fired, pulled the bolt and fired, and it wasn't until the fifth pull that she realized her father had stopped and that she was out of bullets. Click, click, click.

Loo lowered the barrel of the rifle, expecting to see—well, she wasn't sure exactly what she was expecting. A monster waiting for them in the trees. A shadow from her father's past. But there was only the narrow pine with a new yellow strip, as if Hawley's Colt had peeled the bark straight from the trunk, and two feet under, in the middle of the white spot he'd painted, three dark holes.

Loo's father jogged over to check the target. He took his knife from his boot and dug out one of the bullets. He walked back to Loo and dropped it into her palm. A tiny piece of metal the color of gold. The bullet was from her rifle, small and shiny and hard and broken. Remade by the impact of hitting its target. Hawley smiled, his eyes bright.

Then he said, "Just like your mother."

The Greasy Pole

LOO HAD SPENT HER LIFE MOVING FROM PLACE TO PLACE. SHE WAS USED to leaving things behind. Hawley would settle them in a town for six months or a year, and then she would come home from school and her father would have the truck packed and they would drive through the night, or two nights or even weeks—living in motel after motel after motel and sometimes sleeping in the backseat underneath an old bearskin rug, with the doors locked. When she was little it was an adventure she looked forward to, but as the years passed it became more difficult to start new schools, to make new friends, to always be the one who didn't get the joke. She began to dread the moves but a part of her also itched for them, because it meant that she could stop trying to fit in and simply slip into the place where she belonged: the passenger seat of her father's truck as they barreled down the highway.

They kept only a few belongings. Her father would bring his guns, and the box of Lily's things from the bathroom, and Loo would grab their toothbrushes and some clean socks; a short, handheld telescope Hawley had bought her to look at the stars; and her planisphere—a circular map about the size of a dinner plate, made of plastic and cardboard, that tracked the constellations. It had belonged to her mother. Hawley had given it to Loo on her sixth birthday. Each new place they traveled to, she would wait until dark, spin the dial, set the right date and time, and the chart would reveal Cassiopeia, Andromeda, Taurus and Pegasus. Even if there were too many streetlights, and only the Big Dipper or Orion's Belt was visible, wherever they were would start to feel like home.

Once they unpacked, her father would buy them new clothes and Loo new toys and whatever else they needed. There was a certain kind of joy in this. And another in cracking the fresh spine of a book that Loo had read three times before. She would not say goodbye to the neighbors when they moved, or to her teachers, even if they were nice to her. She would not say goodbye to her friends, either, if she had friends, which she usually didn't.

Hawley and Loo ate ramen noodles in hot-water cups meant for tea. They opened Campbell's soup with hunting knives and warmed them on cans of Sterno. On special occasions they ordered Chinese. It didn't matter if they were in California or Oklahoma. They could always find a Fortune Palace. Fried egg rolls and wonton soup and scallion pancakes and hoisin sauce were Loo's comfort foods.

On her eleventh birthday they were in San Francisco, and there were so many Chinese food places to choose from that Hawley collected a dozen menus and let Loo pick whatever she wanted. When he came back to their motel room, carrying bags of fried rice and sesame noodles and moo shu chicken, Loo had set up a game of chess on the floor. The board was a birthday gift she'd opened that morning, wrapped in the comics page of the newspaper. They had played checkers all afternoon, but the set also came with pieces for chess.

"You're on your own with that one," said Hawley. "I don't know how to play."

"There's instructions," said Loo. "Each piece moves differently.

The castle goes up and down and side to side. The bishop goes diagonally. The queen moves any way she wants."

"Let's eat before the food gets cold."

Hawley opened a beer and turned on the television. They sat on the beds and dug into the rice and noodles and watched an old Marx Brothers movie together. When it was over, Hawley picked up the food containers and threw them into a bag and Loo sat back down on the floor with her game. Usually they played cards after dinner. Gin Rummy, Crazy Eights or Heads-Up Poker. For chips they used Hawley's spare change, and the winner got to choose dessert from the vending machine. But Loo was ready to do something new. Her eyes had gone toward the chess pieces the moment she'd opened the box that morning. She checked the instructions again.

"Need some help?" Hawley asked.

"I want to figure it out."

"Suit yourself." Hawley tied off the garbage. He tucked his Colt into the belt of his pants and pulled his shirt over it. He took the key and locked the room from the outside, and then she heard his footsteps as he carried the bag down the cement walkway toward the bins.

Loo chose a knight and moved it in the shape of an *L*, two spaces forward and one to the left. Then she got up and went to the other side of the board and sat down. She tried to solve the game like a puzzle. She shifted one of the pawns. Then she got up and went to the other side of the board and did the same thing.

The key slid in the door. Hawley came through and reset the locks, put the Colt on the bedside table, rolled a cigarette and cracked the window. There was a game show on the TV and the audience was clapping. But Loo knew how to drown out noises. She'd been drowning things out for as long as she could remember. And there was something exciting happening on these black and white squares, on this piece of cardboard with the crease in the middle. She'd hatch great strategies while playing the white, and the moment she picked up a black piece those plans faded against the backdrop of this other side that also wanted to win.

She played until the sky darkened outside the motel window and the neon lights from the highway shone across the board and there were only the two kings left and one black rook. She couldn't get the rook close enough to checkmate, and so she was just using it to push the white king across the board. Both kings, black and white, stumbled one step at a time in different directions until Loo lost patience and swept the remaining pieces down all at once with her arm.

The TV was still on. A different game show now. The contestant trying to guess the right answer. A giant clock spinning and clicking off the seconds and the audience holding their breath. Hawley wasn't paying attention. He wasn't even facing the screen. He was sitting in the chair by the window. The ashtray on the ledge was filled to the brim with the ends of his cigarettes, and his eyes had been on Loo the whole time.

"Who won?"

"Nobody," she said.

Loo went into the bathroom and shut the door. She didn't know why she was angry. The game had started full of possibility, but in the end it was as if she were surrounded by empty spaces, taking step after step to nowhere. She brushed her teeth and looked at her mother's things. She spit and leaned closer to a photo strip of her parents taped to the left of the sink, next to the mirror. They were pressed close together in some roadside carnival booth—four pictures snapped in sequence, her mother making faces, her father edging out of the frame. They looked like they were sharing a wonderful secret that Loo would never know.

When she came out of the bathroom the TV was off and the game had been folded up and put away. Hawley had fixed her bed and turned down the covers, as he always did, no matter where they were sleeping, even if it was in the back of the truck. Loo got under the blankets and he tucked her in.

"I know where we're going next," he said.

"Where?" Loo asked.

"Someplace you won't have to play alone."

"But I *like* being alone."

"I know," said Hawley. "But you shouldn't."

THE FOLLOWING JUNE THEY ARRIVED in Olympus, Massachusetts. Hawley told her it was her mother's hometown. Lily had grown up in the ice-cold Atlantic waters, and Loo should have the same experience, ride the waves and hike to the lighthouse, canoe down the Megara River and sail from the Point to Tire Island. A normal life, Hawley said. With a real house and a neighborhood and friends her own age and a school where she could find a place to belong.

They checked into a motel right on the water and went to the beach. Loo made a giant sandcastle, poking windows in the towers with her finger and dripping wet sand to seal the cracks, while Hawley built a wall to hold back the rising tide and then dug a moat so deep that the ocean seeped up and filled the channel. They used mussel shells for the doors and draped seaweed over the ramparts. Then they ate hot dogs and watched the sun go down and when it started to get cold they pretended they were monsters and smashed the castle to pieces, roaring and stomping and crushing the kings and queens and villagers beneath their feet.

The next morning Hawley drove Loo over to meet Mabel Ridge. She was Loo's mother's mother, which meant that she was Loo's grandmother. Hawley was nervous and wore his best shirt. He even made Loo put on a dress and brush her hair, something she rarely did. It had taken nearly an hour to get all the snarls out. The ones she couldn't she cut with scissors, until her hair was chopped and uneven, like an animal had chewed one side.

Mabel's house was near a five-mile stretch of hard rocky woodland called Dogtown, set between Olympus, Gloucester and Rockport. Hawley told Loo that no one lived in Dogtown anymore, but three hundred years ago it had housed Puritan farmers and then fishing widows, freed slaves, outcasts and packs of abandoned, feral dogs that gave the place its name. Now the land was mostly a bird sanctuary, held in trust and crisscrossed with hiking trails, but the dug-out cellars of the old stone houses were still there and drifters still passed through and people still occasionally got stabbed or robbed in the woods.

"So you shouldn't go in there," Hawley said. "I want you to promise."

Loo promised. "How do you know all this?"

"Your mother." Hawley pulled the truck over and parked in front of a run-down house, with slanted stairs and peeling paint and a rusted Pontiac in the driveway.

"Is this where she grew up?"

Hawley nodded and Loo pressed her face against the window. There was an old brass knocker on the door in the shape of a pineapple.

"Your grandmother and I need to talk about some things," said Hawley. "So I want you to stay in the car for now."

"I want to go inside."

"You will," said Hawley. "But we need to be invited first."

Her father got out of the truck and shuffled up the porch steps. He carefully lifted the brass pineapple hanging on the door and let it drop. The knocker seemed familiar to Loo, like something out of a half-remembered dream—the crown of leaves spread out like a flower, the golden color gleaming in the sun.

An older woman opened the door, wearing goggles and wiping her hands on the front of her shirt. She did not seem like the grandmothers from Loo's storybooks. She looked like the kind of woman who could field-dress a deer.

Hawley said a few words. Mabel Ridge said a few words back. Her hand went to the doorknob, but Hawley said something else and it stopped her. She bent and peered around him. The girl and the woman locked eyes for a moment. Then Loo touched her chewed-up hair, and Mabel Ridge slammed the door. When Hawley got back to the truck he punched the dashboard and broke the radio. Loo was too afraid to ask what had happened and they rode back to the motel in silence, Hawley's knuckles bleeding into the cuffs of his shirt.

Back in their room, Loo took off her dress and put her jeans back on and Hawley pulled his bloody shirt over his head and threw it in the corner. They went down to the boardwalk and got some ice cream and sat on the beach in the same spot where they'd knocked down their castle the day before. The tide had washed over everything but there were bits and pieces of shells left behind and the moat was still full of water.

"Do you like this place?" her father asked.

"Sure," said Loo.

"Because we can leave if you want."

"We just got here."

"I know."

Loo watched her father's torn knuckles bend and bleed as he licked his cone. She took another bite of ice cream, and let the chocolate melt on her tongue.

"Let's stay," she said. "Screw that old bag."

"You shouldn't say that," Hawley said, laughing. "Your mother wouldn't approve."

The next morning they started looking for a place to live, and instead of signing a short-term lease, her father used cash from a safe-deposit box in Boston to buy the old Henderson place by the water. The property circled out to the edge of the bay and covered five acres. It was the first time they had lived in a house with stairs. Loo's bedroom was on the second floor, and had two windows and a small roof outside that she could climb out onto. Her father's room was at the end of the hall. At first she had trouble falling asleep with all that quiet, tucked into her new bed, the bearskin pulled across her shoulders. The only thing that helped was listening to Hawley walking around the house at night. A sliver of light cut through the room as he checked on her. She closed her eyes. She tried to look peaceful.

"Faker," her father said.

Then he closed the door and she listened to his footsteps walking away.

Sometimes Loo caught glimpses of her grandmother at the market or heading to the Catholic church on Sundays. If the old woman saw them on the street she stepped into a store and waited until they had passed. When Loo pointed her out, Hawley would say only that Loo looked an awful lot like her mother, and that eventually Mabel Ridge would come around.

"We're family," he said. "Whether she likes it or not."

A MONTH PASSED AND THEN another. Little by little Loo got used to the quiet in their new house, to hearing the floors creak in the middle of the night and the rattle of old storm windows instead of highway traffic. When he was home Hawley cut through the silence, kicking off his boots and shouting her name up the stairs. But her father knew how to be quiet, too. More than once he'd snuck up on her in the kitchen, or startled Loo on the roof outside her window. He would not be there. And then—he was there. Clearing his throat or striking a match and making her jump.

One morning she woke to the sound of a bell ringing outside. She ran downstairs and saw Hawley coasting past on a new yellow bicycle. It was her first. He showed her how to ride it in the driveway. He kept his hand on the back of the seat until she got her balance, running alongside. It took most of the day, but eventually she made it down the street and then around the block. She did not notice when he let go.

Together they went to the marine supply store and picked up waders and tools for fishing and clamming. Hawley had learned how to cast and dig for quahogs from his father, and Loo could tell he was excited to show her what he knew. Just before sunrise he shook her awake and led her through the woods to the shoreline. She had never seen the tide out so far, the water just a streak in the distance. The uncovered sand was littered with shells and crabs and a multitude of tiny, tiny holes.

"Watch this," her father said. Then he crouched and jumped, all six foot four inches, lifting his knees high. His body hung in the air, suspended for a moment, before both of his feet came down with a loud, hard thump. All around them the buried clams released streams of water, squirting straight into the air like hidden fountains. And at that moment Loo knew that they would really stay, that this place was different from all the others: the whole beach springing to life in the early morning, and her father grinning from ear to ear, like he'd just shown her the best thing in the world.

AT THE END OF SUMMER Loo enrolled in the local junior high. Hawley dug out her transfer file—which included past report cards, recent test scores, copies of her birth certificate and records to prove she had all her shots—and brought it with them to the principal's office. Loo had gone to seven schools in seven states. This was number eight.

After her placement test they were told that she'd done well enough to skip a year ahead, and would be joining the eighth grade. The principal was a portly, soft-spoken Swede with hair so blond it was nearly white, and a habit of belching whenever he was nervous. He smiled and shook Loo's hand with his meaty fingers.

"Your mother and I went to school together."

"Here?" Loo asked. "In this place?"

"There've been improvements, of course, but yes, it's the same building."

Loo looked around at the steam pipe radiators, the giant windows, the marble steps and lines of old metal lockers. The students eyed her as they walked by. The boys and girls seemed friendly enough. Maybe eight was her lucky number.

"So you knew her," Hawley said. "Lily."

"We were friends," said Principal Gunderson.

"Tell me something."

"What?"

"About her." Loo's father had stepped up close to the principal. He was at least a foot taller than Gunderson, and she could tell he was making the man nervous. Hawley was missing his left earlobe—the cartilage scarred and twisted just beneath the canal—and the principal was trying not to stare.

When she was younger her father used to tell her that a bird had snatched his ear away. Then it was a horse, then a lion, then a cow, then a dog. Loo would imagine each of these animals, setting their teeth into his skin, then she would pull on Hawley's hair to cover it up.

"She was a free spirit," said Principal Gunderson. "Everyone liked Lily."

"That's not what she told me."

"I mean, well, I mean," the principal released a gush of air, then attempted to swallow it back down. "*I* liked Lily. Perhaps that would be more accurate. I liked Lily very much."

Hawley remained close, looking down at the man in front of him, as if he was trying to figure out a problem. And then he stepped back, and held out his hand. "Thanks," he said, "for taking care of Loo."

"If there's anything I can do to help you settle in, just let me know." The man was relieved now, talking fast. As if he had passed some test of his own. "And you should come by the Sawtooth, my family's restaurant. We've got the best fish and chips in town."

"How about clams?" Loo asked. "Do you sell clams to people, too?"

"Yes, clams too," said Gunderson.

Hawley glanced at his daughter. Then he reached up and tugged his missing ear.

WHEN THE FISHERMEN HEARD THAT Samuel Hawley was selling his catch directly to Gunderson's restaurant, there were complaints, especially from Joe Strand and Pauly Fisk, who sold their shellfish at the weekly market and didn't like outsiders or competition. Joe Strand and Pauly Fisk had grown up in Olympus. Neither of them had ever left. Fisk was on the portly side, and always wore the same baseball cap with the words "Hong Kong" sewn in the front. Strand liked to keep a small patch of wiry scrub at the base of his lower lip, that he credited with attracting the ladies. They both had ex-wives and sons who lived with them that they struggled to like.

Neither of the men picked a fight out in the open with Hawley, but that didn't stop them from spreading rumors about folks getting sick off his oysters, or from pouring bleach down on Hawley's shoreline, either, killing off a whole mess of littlenecks.

Through it all, Loo's father didn't say a word. Not until he came home one afternoon and found his waders gone and his gear fouled. Then he went straight to the Flying Jib and broke Joe Strand's jaw. After that he tracked down Fisk, who was hanging out at the wharf wearing Hawley's waders, and threw him off the pier. The waders filled and dragged the man under. Fisk might have drowned if it wasn't for Hawley going in after him and cutting the straps.

Loo watched all this happen from her father's truck. She opened the door for Hawley as he staggered back across the dock. When he slid into the driver's seat he was soaked through and dripping, blood in his hair and his knuckles swollen. He gripped the steering wheel, breathing hard. His face had taken on a kind of smoothness, as if all the lines of age had left along with his conscience. It was only after they got home, after Hawley had locked himself up for hours with her mother's things, after he came out of the bathroom wrapped in towels and Loo brought him a glass of whiskey, that he looked like himself again.

The fishermen left Hawley alone after that. So did everyone else. But no one besides Principal Gunderson would buy his catch, even though he set up a table at the weekend market. Things got worse as the cold weather drove off the last of the tourists and it was only the locals left selling to each other. Throughout the winter and into the following spring Hawley had to travel four or five towns over—even Rockport and Newbury were too close. And he also had to bring Loo with him to get customers. It was a role she knew well from their time on the road together. Softening up strangers. Asking for things her father could not. Loo would spend the day emptying buckets, sharpening her pocketknife and arranging shells into an intricate, cascading pattern that threaded around their stall. Whenever someone stopped to admire her handiwork, she would stand by Hawley while he offered up a price.

By this time Loo was twelve and a half years old and nearly as tall as a grown woman. She carried the rough-and-tumble look of children being raised by men, but she also seemed clean even when her face was dirty. Living in a small town had not made her life normal, or given her a place to belong. Since her father's outburst, the fishermen had told their kids to stay away from her, and she had grown strange, the way children will when set apart.

It was not long before she became a target.

The sons of Joe Strand and Pauly Fisk started it all. They were both in Loo's homeroom. Pauly junior had been elected the class treasurer, then spent the collected dues on a new guitar for himself, smashing it onstage during the school talent contest. Jeremy Strand sat by the windows, smelling of sauerkraut. Their greatest joy was jumping off the cliffs surrounding the quarry on the outskirts of town. Their second greatest joy was convincing other kids to jump off those same cliffs. The quarries were full of abandoned construction equipment, lost when the granite miners struck water. Occasionally someone would land in the wrong place, and one day Jeremy Strand did. The police airlifted him out with a brain injury, but as soon as he could walk again, he was back, and, together with Pauly junior, continued shoving other kids off the seventy-foot drop.

The boys threw food at Loo during a class trip to the local whaling museum. It made her hair smell like baloney, and after she went to wash it out in the bathroom, they waited outside and tripped her. The rest of the class all saw this and laughed, and no one helped Loo gather her books from the floor, or helped her when Jeremy and Pauly junior tossed her backpack down the stairwell. Instead the boys and girls turned away and snickered and rolled their eyes so that they would not be next. Then their teacher appeared and clapped her hands and made everyone line up for a tour. Loo hurried down the stairs to collect her bag. By the time she caught up, the other students were gathered around a life-size model of a whale's heart.

The whale's heart was made of red and pink plastic, with giant veins and arteries twisting around it like the roots of a tree. The model was as big as a child's playhouse, big enough to crawl inside. There was a sign encouraging children to do so, and after the rest of the class moved on to the next exhibit, Loo did, shuffling on her hands and knees through the tunnel of the aorta, slipping past a valve into the left ventricle. The space was not designed for someone her size, but it was comfortable enough to move around. Even cozy. Loo pressed her back against the flesh-colored plastic. The sides were rippled and full of shadows and echoed as she shifted her weight.

She was relieved to be out of sight for a few moments. To let go of the face she put on in public. It nearly always felt like she was pretending, as if her insides were only full of locked doors. Loo knocked on the wall of the heart with her fist. *Boom. Boom.* She imagined the muscles around her alive and churning, a whoosh of blood pushing through two hundred tons. Their teacher had said that the human heart was the size of both fists together. Loo squeezed her hands tight. Compared herself to the whale. If someone ever tried to climb inside her heart, they'd have to shrink down to the size of a chess piece.

There was a thud outside the shell. A knocking that answered her own. Loo poked her head out and found Jeremy and Pauly junior waiting for her again, right by the vena cava. They'd brought a shaggy boy named Marshall Hicks with them, who was best known for bottling homemade maple syrup that he brought to school and tried to sell whenever the cafeteria served pancakes. Marshall was the one knocking on the heart, and when he saw Loo he seemed confused. They stared at each other for a moment, and then Marshall smiled like a dog before it gets sick, and Jeremy and Pauly junior pinned Loo down and stole her shoes. She'd been taught by her father to never be a rat, so she lied to the teacher that she'd lost her shoes, and spent the rest of the trip in mismatched socks full of holes. On the bus ride home Jeremy and Pauly junior smacked Loo in the head with her own sneakers. Everyone saw, and the next day the rest of the kids started in on Loo, too.

She took it all at first, the cutting remarks, the tacks on her chair, the stolen lunches, the worms in her books, even the clods of dirt and stones thrown at her back on the way home, never quite understanding the reasons but feeling the cause must be some personal defect, some missing part of herself that the others recognized, a rotting, empty hole that whistled when she walked, no matter how quiet she tried to be.

Loo did not tell her father what was happening at school. Instead she moved to the corners of classrooms. She did her homework but refused to raise her hand, even when she knew the answers, and eventually her teachers stopped calling on her, as if they, too, had caught the scent of her strangeness. Soon, Loo could go entire days being nearly invisible.

This disappearing began at her wrists. It was the only part of her body that Loo considered delicate, and she could always feel her skin thinning there first. Afterward it spread to her fingers and up her arms, across her shoulders, ran down each leg to her toes and then back through her stomach—a sense of coming loose, of filtering away into nothing, winding around her neck until her head felt light and empty and she could wander the halls of the school and no one would look at her, and she could walk the streets and people would turn away, and she could go down to the beach and wander the dunes and feel not like a person anymore but a ghost.

At night Loo sat in the bathtub and stared at her mother's pictures. The way she narrowed her sharp green eyes and the way she smiled with her teeth like she was not afraid to use them. The woman who existed in the bathroom wore bright-red lipstick that smelled like candy, wrote her dreams down on the backs of parking tickets and ate peaches straight from the can. Loo's mother had been dead for years but she had never been invisible. If someone put a tack on her chair, she would take that tack and stuff it up his nose.

AND THEN ONE DAY MARSHALL Hicks decided it was his turn to steal Loo's shoes.

He'd been enjoying a brief period of celebrity. Not because he was friends with Jeremy and Pauly, but because his stepfather was on television. An environmentalist, Captain Titus had recently gotten his hands on a decommissioned Coast Guard cutter, and was now using it to ram whaling ships in the Arctic Circle. A documentary crew was filming his escapades. The show was on public television, but still—it was television—and that made Marshall indirectly famous, and made the girls in Loo's homeroom talk about him in nervous, giggly whispers. The other boys, upon noticing this, got jealous. So they spread rumors that Marshall was secretly boning Loo, and that when this sex happened, the two would pour Marshall's homemade syrup on each other.

Marshall was so embarrassed that he stopped bringing in his golden bottles of syrup (that he'd been so proud of and tapped himself from local trees), but the more he denied the claims, the more the other boys teased him. And so, finally, to prove that he was not having sex with Loo, Marshall followed her from school, pushed her onto the sand, took her sandals and threw them in the ocean, so far out she had to swim for them before they were swept away. She got pulled under and dragged along the bottom of the sea and swallowed so much sand and salt water she felt it coming out of her eyes. When Loo finally made it back to shore, her clothes were sealed to her skin, just as her father's were when he had climbed back onto the pier, and after she crawled and coughed and clawed her way free, she was a different person than when she went into the water. She was no longer afraid.

Loo picked up a piece of driftwood and staggered after Marshall Hicks. She knocked the boy unconscious. Then she chose his index finger and bent it backward until it broke. With this snap of bone she sealed her fear away, like sliding a cover over a barrel and nailing the lid shut.

Before she left the beach, Loo took a large, heavy stone, carried it to her house and slipped it into one of her father's socks. She brought it to school the next day in her backpack. She expected some kind of revenge from Marshall, or at the very least to be suspended, but instead he told everyone he'd fallen from a tree. His finger was wrapped tightly in a splint, and a bewildered look crossed his face each time they passed each other in the halls.

At the army-navy store, Loo changed her sandals for a pair of steel-toed boots. On her hands she slid rings with the stones pried out, the sharp metal prongs raised to cut. Loo remembered everything everyone had done to her, wrote each name down on a list. At the top were Jeremy Strand and Pauly Fisk, Jr.

She kept the rock-in-a-sock close and waited for the right moment.

When it came, Loo snuck into the boys' bathroom and hid in a stall. Once she heard Jeremy and Pauly junior's voices at the urinals and knew their hands were busy, she came out swinging the rock and cracked both of them in the face and broke their noses, splattering blood across the mirrors. The boys writhed on the white tile, screaming and cursing, and she propped open the door so everyone passing by could see, and then she went back in and kicked them both in the ass with her steel-toed boots, over and over, just to make sure they were really hurting.

After the incident was broken up, they were dragged to Principal Gunderson's office, where he gave the boys ice packs and then called everyone's parents. Soon the fathers were in the room: Joe Strand and Pauly Fisk, Sr., and also Samuel Hawley. It had been months since the men had fought, but Strand's jaw had never healed properly. He'd recently had a second surgery, and his mouth was wired shut. But Fisk had plenty to say.

"It's the principle of the thing!" Fisk pounded the table. "There's a principle to life and this girl doesn't give a damn about principles. It's like she never heard the word! *Principles* mean not busting people's noses for no reason. *Principles* mean not trying to kill somebody just because he borrowed your waders."

"Mr. Fisk," said Principal Gunderson. "The girl is not the only one at fault here. Your boys confessed to wrongdoing as well. I'm sure we can come to some understanding."

Strand opened his lips and moaned behind clenched teeth. He pointed at the wires in his chin, then gestured at Hawley.

"Exactly," said Fisk. "*Principles* mean paying for somebody's doctor bill when you break their jaws."

Strand moaned again. He pantomimed pouring something into an invisible glass and raised the glass to the ceiling.

"What's he saying now?" Gunderson asked.

"*Principles* mean you at least buy them a drink."

Hawley ignored Fisk's lecture and Strand's grunts. But when Gunderson showed him the rock-in-a-sock that Loo had used, covered in blood, his face grew troubled. And when Jeremy and Pauly junior were finally led to the nurse's office, their nostrils filled with toilet paper, Hawley picked up Loo's rock in one hand and placed the other on her shoulder. He pushed her out the door and into one of the chairs lining the hall.

"You would have done the same thing," said Loo.

"Not like that," said Hawley. "It was sloppy. You got caught."

"Yeah," said Loo. "But now they'll remember."

Her father rubbed his beard.

"Let's move," said Loo. "Somewhere else. Then none of this will matter anymore."

Hawley took in his daughter's boots and chewed-up hair, the blood splatters on her T-shirt. He hefted the rock in his hands. "It always matters," he said. Then he went back inside the office and closed the door.

For the next hour Loo sat in the hallway listening to the men's voices. There was talk about expulsion and suspension and detention and threats and favors, but after a long negotiation, all three teenagers were released with their enrollment and school records intact. The price for this clemency was paid for by their fathers. Strand, Fisk and Hawley were now officially pledged members of Principal Gunderson's Greasy Pole Team.

The Greasy Pole Contest had been an Olympus tradition for nearly a century. Every June, during the blessing of the fleet, a forty-five-foot wooden mast, planed down from a Scotch pine, was covered with inches of lard and grease and set out over the town pier. At the end of the pole was nailed a tiny red flag. The first team that made it to the end of the pole and captured that flag had bragging rights and drinks at the Flying Jib for a year. Sometimes the contest would take hours. Others it would take days. But they would not stop until the flag was captured. The greasy pole started as a drunken contest between sailors, and was now a serious battleground of old neighborhood rivalries, where generations gathered to watch the men of Olympus receive concussions, twist ankles, break arms and slip off the pole into the ocean.

Loo's principal had dreamt of winning the Greasy Pole Contest ever since he was a little boy. Each year he inflicted his obsession on his students, lecturing on the history of the contest and his attempts to build a winning team, driven by decades of ribbing by his older brothers, who spent their time out on the water catching swordfish. These brothers had hairy chests and laughed easily and did not have poor vision or fallen arches or wives who had left them. And so each spring Principal Gunderson would attempt to win the flag, and his students and teachers would cheer him on, until he fell, belching, into the sea.

There were three main tactics for winning the contest. The first was slow and steady—the man tried to walk the mast like a balance beam. This usually got him at least halfway to the end, but inevitably ended badly—too much grease would build under his feet and send him flying. The second tactic was the crawl—the man went hands and knees. This nearly always ended with an inverted hug, the man slipping underneath the pole and dangling for a few moments, the crowd joyfully screaming a countdown, before he lost his grip. The last tactic, the most spectacular, was the slide—the man took the pole at a full run and tried to surf the grease to the end. The slide was a crowd favorite, resulting in the most varied wounds, bloody gashes, broken teeth and absurd-looking pitches into the harbor, face-smacks and groin-holds and every kind of belly flop.

On the day of the contest, Principal Gunderson gathered his team on the old wooden pier and went through each of these methods carefully, using a notebook and pen. He had perfected his own style over the years, which involved a combination of balance, crawl and last-ditch slide. Strand and Fisk sat on the plastic cooler they had brought and watched Gunderson diagram all the ways they could fall. The probable injuries to their bodies (and pride) had dampened their spirits, and they were now trying to raise them with beer. Fisk pounded his drinks. Strand sipped his delicately through a straw.

The other men had stripped down to shorts, but Samuel Hawley kept his shirt and jeans on, as if he might back out at any moment. He remained on the pier throughout the day, quietly observing the other contenders, listening to Gunderson and even sharing a drink with

Strand and Fisk, though he seemed to take no pleasure in the proceedings. It was clear that he was participating in the Greasy Pole Contest for one reason and one reason only: Loo.

Hawley's daughter was on the beach just below the pier. She sat alone in her steel-toed boots, piling rocks one on top of the other until she had balanced six or seven. Small stone monuments along the shore. Around her the crowd whispered; there was talk at seeing Hawley and his old adversaries together. Some people were hoping for a fight. But that morning Loo's father had spent nearly an hour in the bathroom, soaking in the tub and looking at his wife's pictures. He'd watched Loo solemnly as she made breakfast and then pinched her chin before they left, and the girl knew that meant he was not angry—only worried.

By the time Gunderson's team took their places for the contest, the sun was high and beating down on the crowd, the water far below the pier looking more and more inviting. The grease had turned rancid, mixed with the sweat and disappointment of a hundred fishermen, and the tiny red flag still taunted them all, waving at the tip of the mast in the breeze. The whole town had come out to watch the show—the harbor was full of motorboats and sailboats, rubber rafts and dinghies, all strung together into a massive flotilla of drunken men and women, each armed with a boat horn, which they blew in appreciation and regret as fisherman after fisherman slid off the greasy pole into the churning waves below. The rest of the spectators were on the beach, settled in with their lawn chairs and coolers, enjoying crab cakes and lobster rolls and Italian ices while they waited for a winner.

Even Mabel Ridge had come to watch the men fall. She sat on one of the park benches, her hands working a crochet hook. The early-summer heat was sweltering, but the old woman was dressed for a chill, her jacket collar turned up and a roll of bright-red yarn unspooling in her lap. She wound the yarn around her finger, then stabbed it with the hook, drawing the metal in and out and around and then tugging the knot into place. She made another knot and then another. One for each man on the mast. And as each team failed, she spun the square she was making and started a new row.

She was well on her way to a full-size blanket by the time it was Principal Gunderson's turn. He insisted on walking the greasy pole before the rest of his team, too anxious to delay and not wanting to share the glory if he succeeded. He made it past the first ridge, inch by inch, before moving slowly to his knees and pressing his face into the grease, wrapping his arms around the mast and convulsing forward a few feet in an awkward but loving embrace. Then one of his dimpled knees gave out and he was sent tumbling down with a splash.

Strand tried next, grinning with fear, the metal in his jaw drawn even tighter than usual. He'd sipped too much beer and missed the pole entirely, catching his foot before spinning over the edge of the wharf and crashing into the ocean. But he gave a wave when he broke the surface, and stayed with Gunderson, treading water, as was the tradition, until all the members of the team were through.

Fisk turned to Hawley, and then, like a soul bravely facing his doom, he leaned in, whispered something and shook the hand of his teammate. Loo's father looked surprised. They nodded at each other. Then Fisk straightened his Hong Kong baseball cap, made the sign of the cross, took a few steps back and ran full out, screaming at the top of his lungs, trying for a foot-first slide. He made it farther than any of the rest, leaving a trail behind in the grease with his hip, but he lost control and careened over the edge, toes splayed, still screaming, until his body splashed into the water below.

And then it was Hawley's turn. The crowd went quiet as he stood at the end of the pier and untied his boots, peeled off his socks, then began to unbutton his work shirt. Down below, Gunderson, Strand and Fisk bobbed in the waves. Now that Loo's father was following through with his promise, a feeling of genuine camaraderie seemed to wash over the men, and they lifted their arms out of the water and clapped, then watched as Hawley's shirt fell.

Across his body were rounded scars—bullet holes, healed over. One hole in his back, a second through his chest, a third near his stomach, a fourth in his left shoulder, another through his left foot. The scars were dark and puckered in places, as if the bullets that had entered Samuel

Hawley had eaten their way through his flesh. A breeze came and the flag at the end of the pole fluttered and the town stared while Hawley crouched and rolled his pant legs, revealing two more scarred holes—one in each leg.

There was a collective breath, and then the crowd began to murmur. The only person who did not respond was his daughter, still piling rocks by the shore. The marks on her father's body had always been there. He did not show them off to Loo but he did not hide them, either. They reminded her of the craters on the moon that she studied at night with her telescope. Circles made from comets and asteroids that slammed into the cold, hard rock because it had no protective atmosphere to burn them up. Like those craters, Hawley's scars were signs of previous damage that had impacted his life long before she was born. And like the moon, Hawley was always circling between Loo and the rest of the universe. Reflecting light at times, but only in slivers. And then, every thirty days or so, becoming the fullest and brightest object in the sky, as he did now, when he finished rolling his jeans, stood at the edge of the pier, raked his fingers through his beard, stepped onto the greasy pole and started to dance.

At least it looked like dancing. His feet moved so fast it was hard to keep track, knees bobbing up and down and arms flapping to the side. He moved sideways down the pole, as if he were log-rolling, grease splattering out from the soles of his feet. A few times his heel went too far and he fell back and the crowd cried out and then his other ankle swung around and he caught himself and started again with the flapping. He made it past the first notch and then where Gunderson fell and then he reached the last of Fisk's trail. When he moved beyond it he hit a glob of grease, his giant frame contorting in the air, until he caught himself once more, feet flying furiously in a jig, and the town of Olympus roared.

A ball of yarn dropped off of Mabel Ridge's lap as she lifted her crochet hook, unraveling a thin line of red that sped down toward the edge of the water, where Loo was still watching, her pants wet up to the knees. The boats blew their horns and the girl covered her ears. She took a step and then another into the ocean, her eyes never leaving her father.

The flag bounced at the tip of the mast to the beat of Hawley's dancing. He was two lengths away, then one, the wood thinning as he neared the end. His chest and face were splattered with black grease, his body silhouetted by the sun, a man against the elements, a whirligig gone wrong. The prize was right in front of him now, and as he stretched out his hand, he put everything behind it—every part of himself that had been built to keep on living.

And then suddenly it was over. The lunge threw him off balance and he flipped backward, so that for a brief shining moment he was upside down, his feet still madly pedaling the air, and then the full weight of Samuel Hawley crashed down on the tip of the greasy pole, snapping the end of the mast in two, shooting splinters across the harbor, bringing the entire town to their feet, and sending a jumble of wood and grease and man exploding into the sea—followed by a tiny red flag, fluttering slowly past the pandemonium and into the open, waiting, grateful arms of Principal Gunderson.

Bullet Number One

THE JOB IN NEW BRETON WAS SUPPOSED TO BE AN EASY TAKE. THE PLACE was closed for the winter, one of those great houses in the mountains, where magnates brought their summer guests from the city to sit on Adirondack chairs and listen to the loons calling to one another at night and feel like they were a part of nature. In January there was no one for miles, and the lake froze so deep you could drive a truck over it, and there was all that silver unprotected in the pantry, wrapped in velvet so it wouldn't tarnish, and also some jewelry, and maybe a painting or two, and clocks, clocks everywhere—for it was said the fellow who owned the property would get nervous when he didn't know the time. There was supposed to be a clock in every room, and there were a lot of rooms, nearly fifty or more. Who knew what else they might find, if they were lucky.

Hawley was working with a partner named Jove. They'd met on the railroad outside of Missouri. Hawley had been on the run from social services and not much more than a kid at the time, alone and scared, his stomach and his luck empty, stumbling alongside a freight train in the dark. He would never forget how Jove's hand had suddenly appeared from above, thrown out and open, and how he'd clung to those fingers and held on as they lifted him into the boxcar.

They'd pulled a few jobs together already, nothing too large, just enough to tide them over until they moved on to the next place. But Jove had ideas of buying a boat and taking it down the Hudson. He didn't know how to sail but he'd grown up on that river and it was all he talked about now, the lighthouses set along the shore like streetlights, the currents so fast you didn't need any wind. He was older than Hawley, close to twenty-five, with a thick mustache grown out to prove it and three years in prison already under his belt. Hawley wasn't even seventeen then and still unsure of himself and so he let Jove make the decisions.

He should have known, though. He could feel a pinch in his ribs as soon as they walked up onto the grand stone porch, the one overlooking the lake that wrapped all the way around the front of the great house. It was almost as if the bullet were already lodged there in his back, but Hawley was too green and didn't know how to trust his body yet—it was only something that carried him around—and so he just held up the blanket while Jove broke the window and eased his body through the frame and out of the cold.

The furniture in the main hall was covered with white sheets. The shapes were strange and made shadowy figures scattered around the fireplace. In each corner there was a clock. A grandfather with its long golden pendulum by the stairs. Other timepieces hanging on the walls, displaying numbers and phases of the moon. There was a table that ran the length of the room, big enough for more than thirty people to eat at together. Hanging above it all was a chandelier made from antlers, the horns tied together in the middle and reaching out like the roots of a tree.

It was the kind of place built for grand summer parties. Jove had been to one long before with a pal of his from prison, a boxer named King, who'd scored an invitation after taking a dive. It was how Jove knew about this great house tucked away in the mountains, and why he thought it might be empty now. He often talked about that wild night, mingling with rich people from the city and eating caviar and smoked salmon and drinking Champagne. Hawley had listened to the story, shivering in empty railcars and hitchhiking on the highway and swilling crap beer in motel rooms, until he nearly felt like he'd been at the party himself, clinking cocktail glasses with Frederick Nunn, the money launderer who owned the majestic palace with all those clocks. It was hard to believe they were standing in it now.

Jove pulled down a few of the white sheets and revealed some taxidermied ducks mounted in flight by a window seat, a portrait of Nunn with a heavy mustache over his lip like a finger, and, set above the mantelpiece, dangling over yet another antique clock, was the lumpy head of a female moose. Underneath the moose was a small brass plate listing where it had been found and the date it had been killed.

"I guess he bagged that one himself," Jove said.

"Guess so," said Hawley. He crouched down and touched the bearskin rug in front of the fireplace. He was surprised how slick the fur felt beneath his fingers. The bear's glass eyes were hard and fixed, its mouth slightly open. The skin had been cut and glued around the snout, which was made of leather and wax and slightly twisted, as if someone had tried to pinch the nostrils closed.

The men took in the grandness of the room, their cold breath puffing out in clouds and disappearing into the rafters. Then Jove wiped his nose and pushed through the swinging doors to the kitchen. The back rooms were cavernous, built for a team of servants, a stove with sixteen burners and racks of copper pots hanging from the ceiling, four sinks, a walk-in freezer, a butcher block the size of a bed, and rows and rows and rows of knives. In the pantry they found the place settings, and it was better than they'd thought—forks and spoons for a hundred people, and not just in silver but also plated in gold, an assortment of complicated utensils for every type of food—salads and snails and fish and steak and sherbet and soup and even butter.

He filled the bags they had brought. Then he found some pillowcases near the laundry room and filled those. There was a back door, and when Hawley stuck his head out he could see a fenced-off garden and beyond that, a path to the garage. He wondered what kind of cars might be inside, but he was too nervous to check. He dragged the bags of silverware back to the window where they'd started. Then he waited for Jove, who was upstairs rifling the bedrooms.

Hawley pulled the bearskin rug off the floor and wrapped it around his shoulders to keep off the cold. The underside was soft as suede. He tied the arms around his neck. Felt the tips of the claws sewn in. The head flopped on his shoulder. He touched the bear's mouth. The teeth were real, canines yellowed and thick.

Hawley thought of the party Jove had described to him, and imagined the ice and snow melting and the grass beneath springing to life and the dry heat coming back to the floorboards like it was the middle of summer. The house would be full of guests, drinking and laughing, playing cards or listening to music maybe, their chairs pulled around the fire, the windows open and a warm breeze coming off the lake. There would be people outside on the porch, too, smoking and talking in the moonlight. Maybe some his own age. Maybe a girl.

Hawley pictured her there, leaning against one of the pillars like it belonged to her, wearing a silver dress and her hair fixed with a comb. And then the girl turned and caught him staring, and she was slipping through the doors and moving toward him with a low smile, his heart thumping as if he'd swallowed a bunch of birds, and then it grew louder and Hawley realized the sound wasn't coming from inside him—it was the clock on the mantelpiece, on the other side of the room. The one beneath the moose head. It was ticking.

The clock hanging by the kitchen door was going, too, and so was the grandfather clock by the stairs. How did he not notice before? These machines needed to be wound each day. And someone had been winding them. Someone had the keys and was checking every hand in the house, keeping time moving forward through the winter so that not a minute was lost.

Hawley heard a thundering of footsteps overhead, and then Jove rushed down the stairs, the pockets of his coat bulging. "Time to go."

Jove grabbed one of the pillowcases, then turned the lock and threw open the door to the porch. Hawley could hear someone coming in the back entrance, then hurrying through the kitchen. He snatched up the remaining bags and followed Jove outside, the bearskin still tied around his shoulders, flapping out behind him like a cape.

It had started to snow again, the flakes coming down fast and sideways as the two men leapt over the railing and hurried away from the great house. Hawley heard a voice shouting behind them, and then came the blast, and a pain shot through his guts, in the same place he'd felt before they'd broken the window, which made him wonder for a moment even as he was sprinting across the lawn with all the adrenaline of a man being chased for his life, and then the hurt flew up and caught him by the throat and he dropped the bags and crashed into the trees at the edge of the forest.

HAWLEY WOKE UP IN A shed full of goats, strangely warm. It was dark. Jove had him spread out on top of the rug, and was in the process of sterilizing a pair of gold sugar tongs over a kerosene lamp. Hawley could smell the blood.

There were four goats and they were all watching him, their heads between the slats of their pen, somber and still, their ears twitching back and forth, their strange eyes glittering in the amber light. Hawley shifted, and a thunderous ache threaded through his back and crushed his lungs.

"Would have been better if you'd stayed out," said Jove.

"Where are we?" Hawley choked. He moved his hand and grabbed a fistful of hay.

"Not sure. But far away enough, for now."

"I need a doctor."

"I am a doctor—didn't I tell you before?" Jove turned the tongs into the flame. "Certified."

Hawley looked down at his shirt. He'd gotten it for his birthday last year. It was the first time he'd ever bought himself a present. He'd seen it in a store in Poughkeepsie, right after they'd had their first good take, and he hadn't even tried it on, had just brought it up to the register and paid. He'd never felt so good. Hawley and Jove had gone out to dinner and ordered half the stuff on the menu and eaten it all, and then they went to the movies and sat through some half-baked comedy. They laughed pretty hard anyway, they were in such fine moods, and then they went to a bar and there was a pretty girl behind the counter and they tipped her heavily and she filled their drinks and even bought them a round, and then Hawley remembered his new shirt and he brought it to the bathroom and changed and it fit him just right and when he got back to the bar there was a candle stuck in a piece of pie waiting next to his glass and Jove and the girl sang "Happy Birthday."

There wasn't much left to the shirt now. The buttons had been torn loose in front and the sides were soaked through with blood. Jove ripped the seam to get at Hawley's back.

"The bullet's stuck in your ribs," he said.

One of the goats started bleating softly, like its throat was sore. Hawley turned his face into the hay and thought of the girl from the bar. He'd had so much to drink that night he didn't remember leaving. But he remembered her name: Laura. He'd gone back three more times but she wasn't working and he'd been too embarrassed to ask anyone when she did.

It was her face he'd imagined on the porch of the great house. Her smile coming through those doors and crossing the room. Her hand reaching up and squeezing his arm, just as she had that night in the bar, when she leaned over and said, *Nice shirt*, and then asked Hawley what he'd wished for.

That's what he tried to picture now, the two of them here together in the dark with nothing but the glow of the lamplight between them. Her fingers peeling away the cloth and wiping the blood, her breath across his back, her weight pressing hard against his skin, and not the terrible moment when he'd realized all the clocks were ticking.

"This is going to hurt," said Jove. And then he slid the tongs inside him.

The Widows

THE FIRST WIDOW BROUGHT A CHEESECAKE. BUT NOT JUST ANY CHEESE-cake. This one was made from ricotta, the curds gathered and strained and aged by the widow herself in fat little molds. "It's a family recipe. I make it only for special occasions."

Loo stood in the doorway, wearing an old shirt of her father's, her hair unbrushed, her feet bare. They had lived in Olympus for over a year, and no one had ever come to visit. Their porch was covered with buckets of rotting seaweed, the front hall littered with sand. The widow smiled as she handed over the heavy plate, then peered toward the back rooms with a searching glance that made it clear that the cheesecake was not for Loo.

The next widow delivered blueberries from her garden—too much for her to eat, she said, and the bushes kept producing. They didn't stop, even though she was exhausted from picking all day, even though her fingers were turning purple. She could use some help, someone needed to come over with a ladder to reach the higher branches. Someone tall, she said. Someone strong.

Another widow arrived with two children, young boys whose hair was combed but whose faces revealed an inner misery, a misery that grew as they watched their mother pass a box of chocolates, along with a perfumed note tied with ribbon, into Loo's hands.

Some were actual widows, their husbands lost at sea or struck down with heart attacks or smashed into trees while driving drunk, and when they knocked, they were the most apologetic, the most unsure of themselves. The rest were simply fishing widows, left at home while their men followed schools of cod or tuna out to the Bitter Banks, or made their way down the coast after swordfish, for weeks or months at a time. The women all brought food, but Loo thought they were the ones who looked hungry. Her father was caught once in the front yard as he was coming in from the beach, and the woman was so nervous and laughed so high and hard, backing him into a corner, that he started avoiding the house during the day.

A part of Loo felt guilty for closing the door in their faces, though she also hated it when the widows pushed their way inside, their eyes searching for clues while setting their baked goods on the kitchen table, right next to the watermark that Hawley had made over hundreds of nights, polishing his guns and drinking mugs of coffee. When they asked if they could use the bathroom, she didn't even make an excuse. She just looked them in the face and said no.

In his brief, shining moment on the greasy pole, her father had wiped away the town's ill will. The men of Olympus pulled him out of the harbor and carried him away on their shoulders, and the women of Olympus watched the water running down his scarred back and pressed their lips together.

A barstool was now kept reserved for Hawley at the Flying Jib. The fishermen welcomed him into the daily market, where he could sell directly to wholesalers and other restaurants besides the Sawtooth. In the meantime, gossip spread of how he'd earned those scars—as a cop, as a soldier, as a hit man for the mob. Whatever the case, Hawley wasn't talking. And now no one stole his daughter's shoes. Loo didn't even have to do homework. Principal Gunderson gave her a hall pass so that she could come and go as she pleased. The other boys and girls still considered her a weirdo, but a few even made attempts at friendship, which she handled awkwardly, as she did most things. So while her father began to spend nights at the Flying Jib with Strand and Fisk, who had given Hawley a table right next to theirs at the fish market, Loo continued life the same as always, except that she was not fighting. No one in her school would fight her. Not even when she wanted them to.

There was a taste that filled Loo's mouth whenever she was getting ready to hit someone. Tangy, like rust. She could feel it in the glands on either side of her jaw. As if she'd bitten her tongue. The first few times the taste came slowly, but soon it flooded her mouth whenever a situation was turning against her. Then the pull took over her senses, and for a moment she crossed over and became another person—a powerful person—even if it lasted only until someone punched her back.

And for a while they had punched back. After she broke the noses of Jeremy Strand and Pauly Fisk, Jr., there had been a brief hiatus, a summer spent fishing and clamming with her father interrupted only by widows dropping off casseroles. Then in September Loo had returned to school and started fighting again. She learned to swing first, and she usually did, first with Rachel Mirden (hair-puller), Sung Kim (biter), Wanda Gregson (leg-swiper), Katie Jeffries (pincher), Larry Humnack (crier) and Ria Gupta (surprising left hook), until finally Principal Gunderson called her in for another sit-down in his office. Any more violence on school grounds and he'd take away her hall pass. "I've got parents asking for you to be expelled," he said. "Please don't make me do that."

Loo tried to control her temper, but when she got home from school she still felt angry, and the only people she had a chance of fighting now were the widows, who flocked to their house like birds. So far none had taken the bait, or tried to even slap her, no matter how rude she tried to be. Still, whenever she heard the sound of their timid knocks, Loo's mouth would fill with saliva.

Then, on one unseasonably warm day in November, just a few

weeks after Loo had turned thirteen, the knock was different: two quick raps, brisk and assertive. She opened the door, and instead of a widow standing on their porch it was a child. At least, Loo thought it was a child. Then she noticed the Birkenstocks and Indian skirt and unshaved armpit hair peeking out from her sleeveless top and realized the child was a very short, middle-aged woman holding a clipboard. Her skin was weathered, her teeth bright but slightly crooked. And beside her, at the bottom of the stairs, half hidden by a rhododendron bush, was the boy whose finger Loo had broken: Marshall Hicks.

"Is your father home?" the woman asked.

"No," said Loo.

"Well," the woman said. "I'm here to talk about something very important." She held up her clipboard. "Did you know that in ten years, there will no longer be any codfish in the North Atlantic? Unless we create a marine sanctuary in our waters, we're looking at an environmental holocaust."

Loo leaned against the doorframe and peered down at Marshall Hicks. The boy was dressed in a shirt and tie, nicer than she'd ever seen him in school. His forehead was shiny with sweat and he, too, was carrying a clipboard, as well as his mother's jacket. He stared into the heart of the rhododendron bush, as if he wished it would swallow him up.

The woman pressed a pamphlet into Loo's hand. *What happens when the ocean is empty? Stop commercial overfishing at the Bitter Banks. Save the Atlantic cod!* Loo turned the page. There was a photograph of a drift net full of dead fish.

"I need your father's support. This is about saving lives." The woman's lips twitched as she spoke. Her eyes pinned Loo in the doorway.

"He should be back soon."

The woman smiled and stepped inside. "Honey," she said over her shoulder, "why don't you keep going down the block. I'll catch up with you later."

"*Mom.*" Marshall Hicks glared at them from the bottom of the stairs. Loo nearly felt bad for him—for being beaten by a girl, for having to lie to his friends, for having such an embarrassing mother. But then she didn't.

"Bye," Loo said, and closed the door on him.

When she turned around, Marshall's mother was already walking through the living room, looking at photographs, checking the spines of their books. The volumes were stacked from the floor to the ceiling. Hawley had made the bookshelf in their garage, and Loo had taken great pleasure filling it up with science fiction trilogies and textbooks about the constellations.

"Did you bring anything?" Loo asked.

"I beg your pardon?"

"They usually bring something. The women who come for my father."

For a moment Marshall's mother looked flustered. Then she put down her clipboard. She reached into her bag and took out a bottle of wine. "I'm Mary Titus." She held out her hand.

Loo shook it. "I thought your last name was Hicks."

"That's Marshall's father's name. When I got married again, I took my second husband's. You know the TV show *Whale Heroes*?"

"No."

"Well, Marshall's stepfather is the captain of the *Athena*. The boat that rams the Japanese whalers. He's off filming in the China Sea right now. We're divorced." Mary Titus stood there holding the bottle. "Got a corkscrew?"

They settled in at the kitchen table. Mary Titus poured out the wine. Hawley had never let Loo drink before, and she hesitated for a moment before picking up the glass. Once she'd snuck a beer from the fridge and ended up pouring nearly all of it down the sink. The wine looked more promising. It smelled sweet and was the color of honey. Loo took a sip and held it in her mouth while Mary Titus talked about the petition. With five thousand signatures of support from the community, she'd be able to submit her petition to the National Oceanic and Atmospheric Administration for a marine sanctuary to be created at the Bitter Banks, an area of underwater plateaus sixty-five miles off the coast of Olympus, that brought nutrients to the surface and created a massive breeding ground for all kinds of fish, but especially cod. For centuries, fishermen had traveled out to the Banks and brought back massive hauls, but now, with trawler nets and giant commercial boats, the species was dwindling.

"The cod's not as flashy as a whale," Mary Titus said. "But it's an important part of the food chain."

Loo drained her glass. The wine was making her feel generous. And there was something compelling about Mary Titus, who seemed as if she were riding the edge of some great emotion. As she spoke about trawler fishing, the widow's eyes brimmed with tears one moment and then she would bark out a laugh the next. She told Loo she'd seen her father selling his clams at the Sawtooth, where Mary Titus worked as a waitress.

"He looks lonely," she said. "Do you think he's lonely?"

"No," said Loo.

The woman picked up Loo's star chart from the table. "What's this for? Is your dad into astrology?"

"Astronomy," said Loo.

"I'm a Cancer," said Mary Titus. "The crab. Loving but dangerous." She held her hands up, fingers pressed together like claws. "When's your birthday?"

"October twenty-fifth," said Loo.

"Scorpio, then. That means you've got a hidden stinger."

"Stinger?"

"Sex," said Mary Titus.

Loo reached for the bottle and refilled her glass.

Mary Titus did not seem to care that she was drinking with a minor. She ran her palm across the table. A puddle of milk had dried into the wood, and she started picking at it with her nail. "It was stupid of me to come here." She swung her tiny legs back and forth underneath the table. Her eyes brimmed with tears again. "I'm crying because I miss my husband."

"I thought you were divorced."

"From my second husband. I miss my first husband. He was the one I really loved. He died when Marshall was seven."

Loo kept drinking and listened to Mary talk about this dead husband, how he was washed overboard during a storm near the Banks, and how she couldn't stop picturing him lost under the waves, about the fish eating his skin in little pieces, about barnacles and mussels attaching themselves to his bones. She said that after it happened, she rolled a blanket and put it in bed next to her, just to feel the warmth, and sometimes she pretended his hand was touching the base of her spine, his voice murmuring at the back of her neck. She said her skin smelled like him when she woke up in the morning. She said she felt like she was losing her mind.

"And then I met Marshall's stepfather," said Mary Titus, "but he left me, too. For a *whale*." She sighed and wiped her cheeks with the hem of her Indian skirt. Then she leaned her face into the cloth. Loo did not know what to do. No one had ever confided in her like this before. She patted Mary Titus on the head.

For as long as she could remember, Loo had noticed women noticing her father. And when they failed to get his attention, they tried to reach him through her. There was the waitress at the diner outside Kansas City, who took Loo into the bathroom and showed her how to braid her hair. The shopkeeper in New Mexico who helped Loo try on her first bra. The landlord's wife in Virginia who slipped Loo a box of Tampax and a copy of *Our Bodies, Our Selves*. A girl without a mother, the women would say. So sad. So sorry. And they would bat their eyes. And they would lean in close. But their attentions would only send Hawley brooding. And not long after, Loo would come home from school and the car would be packed and they'd be moving on to someplace else. Someplace new. And she would have to start all over again.

She handed Mary Titus a napkin to dry her eyes. "You're not the only person who's lost someone," she said. Then she led the widow to the bathroom and opened the door to her mother's shrine.

The room was still muggy from the shower Hawley had taken before he left, the papers and photographs moist and curled. Mary Titus's eyes went wide at the cascade of memories taped to the walls—picture after picture of the same crooked smile, followed by the letters, the jars of cream and lipstick, the cans of food, the chewed-on pencils, the hospital bracelet, the cashed checks with Loo's mother's signature, the torn-out pages of novels with words underlined and the lock of dark hair pinned by the mirror.

Mary Titus sat on the side of the tub. "Is everything hers?"

"Yes."

The widow took hold of a receipt that was taped to the wall. Loo knew the list of items like she knew her own name: two bars of French lavender soap, bug spray, AAA batteries, a package of Uniball pens, a roll of breath mints and a birthday card. The birthday card had been for Loo's first birthday. Her mother had bought it right after Loo was born. She had died before she had a chance to sign it. The card was taped to the wall next to the receipt. A picture of a cupcake with a single candle. Each year, on her birthday, Loo would open it. The inside was always blank.

Mary Titus tore the receipt off the wall. "He's crazier than I am," she said with a laugh. "Thank God."

All that Loo knew of her mother was in this room. She'd grown so used to the objects piled in the corners and the scraps of paper on the walls that most days she barely looked at them. But Mary Titus had brought the photographs and cans of food back to life, their importance and their details into focus. The Polaroid by Niagara Falls had bled between the layers, so that the plastic was rubbery and her mother's face was stained. There were split ends in the lock of hair by the mirror. The bottle of perfume in the corner was open—it hadn't been earlier this morning—and Loo realized that her father must have been smelling the perfume, that maybe he even took the small glass stopper and slid it down the length of his chin. And suddenly this world of adults seemed much too complicated, and all she wanted was for Mary Titus to stop laughing.

"Quit it," said Loo.

The widow looked at her but she didn't stop, her eyes wet now and her teeth flashing, and before Loo knew it, the taste of rust was crawling up her tongue. The friendship she'd felt a few moments earlier for Mary Titus faded, just like her mother's writing on the walls, and Loo watched as her own hands went up and shoved the widow hard. Mary Titus fell backward into the tub, her short legs kicking the air, her body twisting and her skull cracking against the faucet. The widow's eyes fluttered for a moment before she sat up and touched the back of her head. Her fingers came away crimson, the same color as the ancient lipstick on the counter. Mary Titus shifted her legs in the empty tub and leaned all the way back, as if she were taking a bath in her clothes. There was blood in her hair and down her neck. She was still laughing but now it was more like crying.

And then Hawley came home. Loo recognized her father's boots on the porch, shuffling slowly and steadily the way he did when he'd spent a long day at the market, and she had just enough time to slam and lock the door to the bathroom before he called her name.

"Quiet," Loo said to the widow.

"Is that *him*?" Mary Titus giggled.

Loo pressed her hand over the woman's mouth. If there had been water in the tub she would have drowned her. Hawley moved into the kitchen and she imagined him picking up the bottle, sniffing the top, noticing the two glasses on the table. He called her name again, and this time it was a question.

"I'm in the bathroom," Loo called.

"Who's here?" Her father was on the other side of the door; she could hear him shifting his weight. "Have you been drinking?"

She had never lied to Hawley before. But she did now.

"No."

"What's going on in there?"

Loo knew then that she had made a mistake letting an outsider into their bathroom. Revealed something no one else should see. Mary Titus was struggling under Loo's hand. She kicked her tiny heels against the porcelain tub. And just as Loo was about to answer her father, the widow bit the girl hard and freed herself.

"Sam Hawley," Mary Titus yelled, "you're crazier than me!" Then she fell into another round of hysterics.

For a minute there was nothing but silence on the other side of the door. Then Loo's father tried the knob. When that did not work he broke the lock with a single kick. He stepped inside. There was Mary Titus in the bathtub, rolling back and forth in a pool of blood, and Loo holding her own palm, imprinted with the widow's teeth.

It was a small bathroom, and with the addition of Hawley the last of the air leaked out. Loo watched her father and waited. He was the person she knew most in this world. She had seen him disappointed and angry enough to throw someone off a pier, but she had never seen his face harden in the way it did when the widow pointed at the photos of his wife and laughed.

Hawley's shoulders filled the entryway. He smelled of fish guts and brine, his hands red and rough from handling knives and opening oysters, and he used them to scoop Mary Titus up in his arms. In two giant steps he had tossed her out onto the porch as if she were a dog and shut the door on her. Then he was back in the bathroom with Loo.

"Are you hurt?" he asked.

"No," said Loo but again she was lying.

"Show me," he said, and Loo turned her palm over. Hawley ran his fingers across the bite. He closed the lid of the toilet and set Loo down on top. Then he turned his back and opened the cabinet under the sink and pulled out their medical kit: a bright orange toolbox with a red cross on the lid. The orange box had saved Hawley's life once in Alaska, and after Loo was born it had traveled with them across the country, stocked with gauze and bandages, flashlights, bottled water, freeze-dried meals, tablets of iodine, knives, duct tape, plastic tarps, matches and a crank-powered radio. Whenever one of them was hurt, the answer to fixing them was always inside.

In one quick sweep, Hawley gathered her mother's toothbrush and perfume and the crimson lipstick and put them in a drawer. In the space made he set down the toolbox, opened the latches and took out a bottle of witch hazel and some cotton balls. When he turned around his face was calmer. He sat on the edge of the tub, doused the cotton and pressed it where Loo's skin was broken and swollen. They could both hear Mary Titus, who was no longer laughing. She was screaming and pounding her fists on their front door.

"Did you hit her?" her father asked.

"No," Loo said.

"Too bad."

Loo's hand began to sting. She tried not to listen to the muffled thumps of the widow, and kept her eyes focused on the orange toolbox. Like the photographs of her mother, and the scars on his skin, this box had come into her father's life long before she ever did. For what felt like the thousandth time, she read the words hand-painted across the front: THESE THINGS WE DO THAT OTHERS MAY LIVE.

"I'm a terrible person," she said, and she gestured with the hand Hawley was not holding, at the bathtub splashed with red, at her mother's torn receipt on the floor, at her own drunken state. Now that her father was here she did not know why she had opened the bathroom door, why she'd ever let a stranger inside their world.

Hawley pressed the towel against her palm until it hurt. He shook his head. "You don't know what terrible is."

Mary Titus was shouting now, loud enough for the neighbors to hear, saying his name over and over. *Sam Hawley Sam Hawley Sam Hawley Sam Hawley—open the door! Open the fucking door! I'm going to die out here and it'll be all your fault, Sam Hawley!*

Loo's father got a roll of bandages from under the sink and started to wrap Loo's hand like a mummy's. He peeled off some surgical tape and pressed down the corners, until the hurt was sealed.

Outside, Mary Titus continued to scream.

"Everyone's going to hate us again." Loo watched as her father pulled another towel from the rack and rinsed it with cold water. He twisted it tight as a rope between his hands. Then he started to wash her face, and it was only then that she realized she had been crying.

"Let them," he said.

Bullet Number Two

HAWLEY HADN'T BEEN IN THE DESERT SINCE HIS MOTHER DIED. THAT WAS four years ago, when he was just twenty-one. The hospital had tracked him down with the news, and he'd taken the bus, all the way from Cheyenne to Phoenix. The police made him identify her body in the morgue. The place was dank and cold compared to the heat outside and smelled of chemicals and bleach. He stood underneath the fluorescent lights and they rolled his mother out of a drawer in the wall.

She'd been dead for more than two weeks, and her body was absolutely still, like an animal run over on the side of the road. Her face had sunken in and most of her teeth were gone, but she still had that square chin and those long, delicate fingers, the ones he remembered running through his hair in the dark when he was a kid. He buried her alone in a cemetery near the hospital. Then he'd taken the bus back to Cheyenne.

Hawley had wheels of his own now, an old Ford Flareside. He'd bought it on his twenty-fifth birthday with cash and he enjoyed opening up the engine on the highway, the windows rolled down and the blazing heat channeling in, the sand blowing through his hair and the red cliffs layering hues in the distance. Behind his seat was a twenty-gauge Remington shotgun, a nine-millimeter Beretta, a SIG Sauer pistol, a crossbow tire iron, his father's rifle from the war and seven thousand dollars.

He'd gotten a postcard from Jove, who was working outside Flagstaff at an Indian casino. Jove still had dreams of buying a boat and sailing it down the Hudson, but he also had a bad habit of burning through his money fast. Now he had an angle for ripping off the casino, and he'd asked Hawley if he wanted in.

It was night by the time Hawley crossed over into Arizona. He took Route 191 to 160 and after an hour or more he was the only car for miles. When he looked in the rearview it was nothing but blackness and when he looked out the windshield it was nothing but blackness and all he saw was to the end of his own headlights beaming into the dark. An hour later he was in the middle of a dust storm, tumbleweed flashing past, sometimes hitting the grate and getting caught under the body of the truck. The wind swept down in gusts, shimmying his Ford off the road. It was late and his eyes were already bleary and now he had to struggle with the wheel to keep his tires straight.

After a long while of this he saw a light ahead, a motel standing all by itself at the crossroads. He pulled into the parking lot and got a room. The guy at the desk was a Navajo Indian. He was wearing a red bowling shirt with a white collar and a pair of pins embroidered over the heart. Behind the desk was a back room and Hawley saw another Navajo and a freckled guy at a table playing cards. They looked like they'd been going all night, empty bottles of beer lined up on the floor and ashtrays full.

"You're big blind," the man with the freckles called out.

"Just take it from my stack," said the guy at the desk. "Want to join us?" he asked Hawley.

The men at the table leaned forward in their chairs. The other Navajo gave Hawley the once-over and returned to his beer. But the one with the freckles kept staring. He had hair the color of motor oil, and marks that blossomed across his face and neck like a rash. There was something about those freckles that made Hawley's stomach ache.

"What's the game?"

"Hold 'Em."

Hawley was tempted. He hadn't held cards in nearly a week. He watched as the man with the freckles reached over, grabbed some chips from the desk guy's pile and threw them in the center of the table. The man's wrists were covered with homemade tattoos, the kind done in prison. One was a serpent with nine heads on nine separate, twisting necks that disappeared up his sleeve, the other was the number 187, the section of the California penal code for murder. The ink was still fresh. The edges had not faded.

The clerk slid a key across the counter.

"Thanks," said Hawley. "I'll pass."

He made his way back to the truck, pulling his shirt over his face to keep the sand out of his eyes, then drove around the back of the building and pulled into the parking spot with his room number spray-painted on the asphalt. He climbed the stairs to the second-floor landing, carrying his bag full of guns and the money, which he'd been keeping in a jar of black licorice. The bills were stuffed in rolls down in the bottom and the thin strips of candy were layered on top, like a pile of shoelaces. He hated licorice and he figured most people didn't like it, either.

The motel room smelled like corn chips and cigarettes and there was a hole punched though one of the walls. On the bedside table was a clock, the digital kind with glowing numbers, but he couldn't get it to work. His own watch had stopped in Denver, and he didn't know what time it was. He put the bag full of guns in the closet. Then he unzipped the side pouch and took out his Beretta and set it on the bedside table.

When he was a boy Hawley's mother had taught him how to handle a gun. Take a breath, she told him, take a breath and let half of it out. She'd said it so often that he nearly always breathed this way, even when he didn't have a gun in his hands. He took in what he could and he held half of it back and that's how he kept himself steady, day to day, year to year, every time he squeezed the trigger.

Hawley went into the bathroom and turned on the light. He had a bad case of trucker's tan, his left side all burned from keeping the car window open. He turned on the shower and stepped into the cold water and washed the sand out of his hair. When he got out he wrapped a towel around himself and then he got back into his jeans. He'd just turned on the TV when he heard a knock on the door.

It was a girl, maybe twenty years old. She was nearly as tall as Hawley. She had a black eye, her blond hair pulled back tight in a bun and seven or eight piercings lining the sides of her ears, sets of tiny hoops looped one after the other and a purple feather dangling from the top like some kind of fishing tackle.

"I'm locked out," she said.

Hawley kept his hand on the doorframe. "Can't the front desk let you in?"

"No one's there," she said, "and I saw your light on."

Hawley wondered if she was a hooker. Then he saw that she was carrying a baby. It was about six months old and she had it in a sling with her coat zipped up around it.

"Wait," Hawley said. He closed the door on her and took the licorice jar out of his duffel bag. He made sure it was screwed tight and put it in the toilet tank. He grabbed the Beretta and slid the chamber to see that it was loaded and tucked it into the back of his jeans and pulled his shirt over it. Then he opened the door again. "I'll go check with you," he said.

They went through the storm to the other side of the building. The girl walked backward against the wind, holding up the sides of her coat to protect the baby. The front door to the motel was locked and the lights were out. Hawley put his hand to the glass and peered in. It was too dark to see anything.

"I told you," the girl said.

Hawley banged on the window. He considered busting the lock. The baby started fussing and the girl bounced up and down on her toes. Then another big gust of wind came and they both got sand thrown in their faces and the baby started to cry.

"Let's go back," said Hawley. He put the girl behind him this time and held his arms out so he'd get most of the sand and not her and the baby, and when they reached his room he let them in.

"Those guys will probably be back in a minute or two," he said.

The girl unzipped her coat. Her black eye was only a few days old, still bloodshot, with a streak of dark purple along the nose. "Is it okay if I change him?" she asked.

"Go ahead," said Hawley.

She took the baby out of the sling and put him on the bed. He was dressed in blue pajamas printed with elephants. There were snaps along the side and the girl pulled them open and undid the diaper and then she grabbed both of the baby's legs with one hand and lifted his bottom in the air and slid the diaper out. The baby stopped crying as soon as she did this.

"How long you been at the motel?" Hawley asked.

"About a week," the girl said. "Only ones here, besides that guy from California." She opened her purse and took out a fresh diaper and put it under the baby. Then she took out a tube of white cream and rubbed some between the baby's legs and across his behind before she closed the diaper and snapped the sides of the pajamas up. The baby stared up at her face from the bed and kept waving his arms back and forth and opening and closing his fists, reaching for her the whole time.

The girl rolled the dirty diaper and used the plastic tabs to close it. "You got a trash can?"

Hawley looked around the room. "Maybe in the bathroom. Here." He reached out and she gave the dirty diaper to him and he carried it across the room. It was warm and heavy against his fingers, like a living thing. He put the diaper in the trash and washed his hands. When he came back the girl was sitting on the bed and she had a bottle of vodka on the table.

"You want a drink?" she asked.

Hawley always wanted a drink. "Sure."

"I don't have any cups."

Hawley went back into the bathroom and got the plastic-covered glasses by the sink. He handed her one, and they ripped open the little bags and slid their cups out. She poured a finger for them both. "Cheers," she said.

Usually Hawley drank only whiskey or beer. Vodka was the drink alcoholics drank, because you couldn't smell it on them. It was what his mother used to drink. He remembered the bottles. He'd even saved one for a while, after she'd left, until his father found it and threw it out. This vodka was cheap stuff and it burned Hawley's throat on the way down. The girl swigged hers fast and poured another.

"What's your name?" Hawley asked.

"Amy," she said.

"That's a pretty name," he said.

She looked at him strangely with her black eye until Hawley felt uncomfortable, so he moved farther away, toward the door, and leaned against the wall there. She was still sitting on the bed. The baby had fallen asleep beside her, his face to the side and his arms over his head like he was in a holdup.

"Did those hurt?" Hawley asked, pointing at her ears.

Her fingers floated to the hoops, caressed the purple feather. "The ones up top did," she said. "But now I don't even think about it. I get a piercing whenever something important happens, something I want to remember." Amy poured a third drink for herself. She threw it back like a shot and sighed. "Is that the right time?"

The clock on the bedside table said 4:16 A.M., the same numbers as when Hawley arrived. It could have been 2:00 or even 5:00—there was no way to know because the sandstorm outside had turned the sky so dark and yellow. Hawley took another sip of his vodka. "Probably not."

"I'm so tired," Amy said. She closed her eyes and rubbed them.

"I'll go see if they're back," said Hawley. He put his drink on the table, unlocked the door and stepped onto the landing. The wind was still fierce. He jogged down the stairs and around the building, thinking about the holes in Amy's ears. He wondered if she'd ever want to forget the things that had happened to her. Remove the hoops and let the skin close back over itself.

He tried the motel doors again. They were still locked. He beat on the window but nobody came. He checked for cars. There were two parked in front, a pickup with an Arizona license plate and a brown van from California, but they were both empty. He walked around the corner. His Ford was still where he'd left it. A few spots down there was a blue hatchback with a big dent in the passenger side. Through the window he could see piles of clothes and a few taped-up boxes and a baby seat in the back. He stood in the parking lot and looked up at his room. All the other windows in the motel were dark.

Amy was stretched out next to the baby on the bed when he opened the door. He could tell from the way her shoulders moved that she was asleep. He closed the door gently and then he went into the bathroom and checked the toilet. The licorice jar was still there. He threw some water on his face and then he came out and pushed the bag of guns deeper into the closet. He walked to the other side of the bed and took the Beretta from the back of his pants and put it in the drawer of the table, next to the Bible. Then he slipped off his shoes and sat down on the bed.

The smell of cigarettes still hovered in the corners of the motel room, but all the bed smelled of now was baby powder and apples. Hawley leaned back against the headboard. He could barely keep his eyes open but he didn't feel right lying down with them. The baby made little sighing noises and sucked on air, its mouth moving like it was going at a bottle. The bruised side of Amy's face was against the bedspread, and without the black eye showing she looked even younger. She'd taken her hair out of the bun and it was spread across the pillow. Hawley listened to the girl and the baby breathing. Then he reached over and turned out the light.

When he woke up it was still dark and Amy was kissing him. Hawley didn't know where he was at first and then he saw her face leaning over him in the red of the motel clock. The numbers still read 4:16. She was soft and warm pressed up against him. Hawley was afraid that touching her would end it, so he kept still. She was kissing him slowly and carefully. When he couldn't help himself anymore his hands went to her waist and she moved away. Then after a minute she slid forward again and kept her mouth just out of reach, hovering over his, their faces close and their breath going into each other.

Her hair fell down and brushed his lips and there were the apples— the smell was coming from her hair. He wound his fingers through to her scalp and pulled. His knuckles brushed the line of hoops in her ear, all that cold metal going through her skin. She tugged at his shirt and he threw it off and she ran her teeth along his shoulder. And then they got hold of each other's belts and tried to unlatch them in the dark. She got his done first and threw it to the ground, then pushed his fumbling fingers away and stood up next to the bed and slid her jeans down each of her long legs and stepped out of them, her bare skin glowing in the clock light.

Hawley caught her around the hips and buried his face in her neck and together they fell onto the carpet. He pushed her knees open and she made a sound like it was hurting her. Hawley tried to see her face but she only wrapped herself tighter around him and their bodies spun and he cracked his head on the frame of the bed. And that's when he heard the gunshots. Two quick pops in a row and then silence.

The girl was still panting and shaking beneath him. Hawley covered her mouth with his hand. They waited like that in the dark on the floor of the motel room. And then there was another blast, and the baby woke up and started crying.

Hawley scrambled to the table and pulled open the drawer and took out the Beretta. He went to the window and pushed back the curtain. He couldn't see anything but the two cars. He turned around and Amy was still lying on the floor, staring up at the ceiling.

"Shut him up," Hawley said.

The girl got to her knees and then climbed onto the bed. She pulled the baby to her chest and started rocking. Hawley found his jeans in the dark and then went to the closet. He grabbed some mags and his father's rifle and then he hurried back to the window. The baby was still crying. Every scream screwed Hawley's nerves tighter. The girl was searching through her bag. She found a bottle but her hands were shaking and she dropped it twice and then she got back on the bed and stuffed the nipple into the baby's mouth and the baby was quiet.

Hawley took a deep breath. He told the girl to keep the light off. Then he told her to take the baby and go into the bathroom and lock the door. She cleared her throat a few times like she was going to say something but then she didn't. He listened to her gather the kid and her clothes and then he heard the door to the bathroom click. His eyes never left the parking lot. The sky was paling, just a few stars left. He could still sense the clock behind him, the stagnant numbers like heat, illuminating the side of his face in the gloom.

A few minutes later the brown van, the one from California, eased around the side of the building. It circled through the lot and slowed by Hawley's car, then stopped right before it came to Amy's. A man got out on the driver's side, holding a handgun. It was the man with the freckles. He was wearing the red bowling shirt the Navajo had had on earlier. Hawley could see his tattoos, the nine heads of the serpent winding up past his elbows. The man checked the license on Hawley's truck and peered in the windows of Amy's hatchback. Then he looked up at the line of rooms.

They'd both seen him—Hawley and the girl. If the man had only stolen some money, he might get in his van and leave. If he'd killed the Navajos, he'd probably come after them. The man with the freckles went back to his van and reached behind the driver's seat. He took out a box of ammo, opened the cylinder on his revolver and reloaded. Then he wiped his hands on the red bowling shirt and started up the stairs.

Hawley knew how to read the weather, to compensate for drag while taking his shot. If leaves changed direction, the wind was close to seven miles per hour. If branches began to bend, it was closer to nine. But there were no trees here to tell how fast the storm was blowing, not even a plastic bag caught in a fence. Only the sand that was circling the asphalt below, crossing the desert and pelting the windows with dust.

The man with the freckles climbed onto the landing, then turned and made his way along the row of doors. He took out a set of master keys and fit one into the lock of Amy's room. He slipped inside. As soon as he did, Hawley stepped out onto the landing. He leveled the rifle but the wind swept up and started pushing against him.

Start with your feet, his mother told him. Your heels are already on the ground. Build from there when you lose your way. Hawley eased his weight back. He shook the tension from his calves and loosened his knees. He turned at the waist. He pressed one elbow to his hip and the other high against his ribs. And then he laid his cheek gently to the stock of the barrel and dragged it down behind the rear sight.

Hawley took in a full breath. He let half of it out.

The man with the freckles stepped from Amy's room, not even careful, the red shirt like a target. Hawley could have shot him in the head but he went for the shoulder. The man cried out and staggered and then lurched for the stairs, but before he made it down he turned and fired off all the rounds he'd been holding. Hawley stepped back too slowly and felt a burn through his right side, and suddenly his arm couldn't support the rifle anymore. It was falling and it fell and he watched it fall and then he was scrambling for the Beretta. He staggered over to the edge of the balustrade with the handgun. There was blood; it was streaming out over the walkway and his head was spinning. He looked from the pool of red to the man struggling into the van below, the bowling shirt catching air and fluttering sideways, clocking the speed of the wind. Thirty miles per hour, Hawley decided. Then he raised the gun and took the shot.

When Hawley tried to stand, his lungs weren't working—it was like there was a sponge at the back of his throat. He crawled across the landing on his knees. The concrete was cold and unforgiving. He called Amy's name and pushed open the door. When she came out of the bathroom she was fully dressed, like when he first met her, her hair pulled back tight in a bun once more and the baby in the sling and zipped up in her jacket. The only thing different was her face, pale and white and thin.

"We got to leave," he managed. But he couldn't get up from the floor.

Amy grabbed towels from the bathroom and wet them and pressed them to his side. Then she pulled out some diapers from her purse and opened them and put them underneath, taping the plastic tabs to his skin. Hawley told her to get the bag with the guns and to fetch the rifle he'd dropped and then he told her to open the toilet and get the jar of licorice out of the tank and put it in the bag, too. She did all he asked and when she came back and kneeled beside him her face held that same strange look from earlier when he'd told her that her name was pretty.

He barely remembered coming down the stairs. Amy maneuvered him into the back of her car and then she put the bag in the trunk and then she opened the other door and took the baby out of the sling and strapped him into the plastic seat next to Hawley. The van was still running, the man with the freckles half in, half out of the driver's seat. Clots of hair and shattered bone littered the pavement, and the windshield was sprayed with blood.

Amy got into the front of the hatchback and slammed the door. She gripped the steering wheel and kept her eyes on the rearview mirror. "Do you think the manager's dead?"

"We should check," said Hawley.

They drove around the front of the building. Amy got out, and this time the motel doors were unlocked. Hawley and the baby stayed in the car, the kid watching the spot his mother had disappeared into, kicking his tiny feet and drooling. Hawley pressed the diapers against his ribs and drifted in and out. When Amy came back she froze for a moment, holding on to the handle of the car, looking like she was going to be sick, and Hawley knew he'd been right and the other men were dead and he wished he'd listened to his guts when he checked in and saw those freckles. He could have been miles away by now or even drinking beers with Jove and not dying in the backseat of some girl's car.

Amy fumbled with her seatbelt. Then she put the car in reverse and backed out of the parking lot. "There's a doctor on the reservation," she said, "about ten miles down."

The seat cushion beneath Hawley was wet with blood. There was blood on the seatbelts, blood on the floor. "He'll report it."

"Not if you pay him," Amy said.

And that's when Hawley knew she'd gone into the jar.

He tried to say something about this but it came out slurred. He focused on the little boy strapped in the carrier next to him and did his best to stay awake. The elephant pajamas had blood on them and the baby was staring at the back of Amy's head and his arms were grabbing for his mother like she was the only thing that mattered in the world.

The sun seemed to be coming up—the sky a multitude of pinks and oranges—and Hawley wondered again what time it was. The bullet was turning now, spinning into a dark place and taking him with it. He touched the diapers taped along the side of his stomach. They smelled of talcum powder and were heavy and warm and felt alive in his hands, just like the baby's diaper had when he'd carried it into the bathroom and put it in the trash.

"We're nearly there," Amy said. Then she said, "I'll go back and get your car for you."

Hawley hoped she would. He hoped that when he woke up and stumbled out of the doctor's house into the blazing desert heat she'd be there with the baby and the money and it wouldn't just be his car dusted on the side of the road with the keys in the ignition and a pile of bloody towels. That he wouldn't have to check the trunk to see if she'd left the guns, and that there'd be at least a grand left for him in the licorice jar. She owed him that, at least, he thought. She owed him something.

They went over a bump in the road. Hawley looked out the rear window. It was roadkill, something with fur and feathers mixed together. A rabbit and an eagle, he thought. A coyote and a vulture. In the seat beside him the baby moaned and whimpered and then the baby began to cry.

"He's hungry again," said Amy, but they couldn't stop so she started singing. "Twinkle, Twinkle, Little Star" and "Rock-a-bye Baby." Hawley closed his eyes and listened. Her voice wasn't pretty but she was trying.

"You're a good mother," Hawley said, or at least he thought he did, and then the bullet pulled him the rest of the way into the dark.

Dogtown

WHEN LOO WAS SIX YEARS OLD SHE GOT LOST AT A COUNTY FAIR. SHE WAS distracted by a sword-swallower, disoriented by the swirl of noise and colored lights, turned around by the crowds, and suddenly found herself separated from Hawley. He'd won a giant teddy bear for her earlier that day, and Loo clutched it tightly, the synthetic fur prickling her skin as she looked for him. Without her father the world turned dangerous, each step she made weighted with magnitude and meaning. Loo did not cry or ask anyone for help. She turned away from the sword-swallower, who was busy clutching and gulping his steel, and focused on the carny games and the smell of cotton candy and caramel apples and popcorn and used them to retrace her steps. By the time she found Hawley he was so frantic he'd started scuffling with the security guards. They were escorting him off the grounds when he saw her standing by the carousel, right where she'd let go of his hand.

She still loved going to carnivals. The biggest one near Olympus happened each October, when the leaves turned color and the air got its first chill—a giant county-wide agricultural fair. Underneath tents and inside barns the 4-H clubs judged livestock and ran pig races. There was a draft-horse show and a pie-eating contest and who could grow the largest pumpkin and a midway with games and rides.

The fair fell near her birthday, and her father let her choose whatever rides she wanted. When she was thirteen, Loo asked for the bumper cars. When she was fourteen, they went up in the Ferris wheel. At fifteen, she wandered with Hawley in and out of the House of Mirrors, and they waved at each other and bumped into walls. The year Loo turned sixteen she was ready for something new. She walked up and down the midway with her father and chose the scariest contraption she could find: the Galaxy Round Up. Hawley took one look at the metal wheel covered in flashing lights that spun faster and faster, lifting on its giant arm at an angle into the sky, the floor dropping out beneath the screaming riders' feet, and told her that this time she was on her own.

"I'll wait for you by the exit," he said, and then he took the box of popcorn she was holding and walked toward the gate.

The line was short and Loo was ushered in with the next batch of customers. She hurried along the wheel, past the drawings of Saturn, Venus, Mercury and Neptune, and chose a spot to stand on her own, pressing her shoulders against the padded back wall, gripping the bars on either side of her cage, and lining up her heels so they were firmly on the metal edge. A teenage carny walked the length of the ride and got it ready to go. He was wearing a T-shirt with some kind of writing.

"What's it say?" Loo asked.

"Song lyrics." He flashed a smile as he locked the safety bar in place. He was not handsome but he had nice dimples. "You look scared."

"I'm not."

"Don't worry." The carny winked. "It makes you feel weightless, like a walk on the moon." Then he smiled again and scurried off the ride and flipped the switch.

The motor started and the planets began to spin, orbiting around the sun painted at the center of the wheel. Riders began to shout and scream. Loo's palms were slick against the metal poles. The ride began to lift, and instead of becoming weightless her body grew heavier and heavier and heavier, until it was crushed into the padded wall behind her. She tried to move, but her head was stuck tight, as if her skull had been sewn through with lead. Then the floor dropped out beneath her feet, and there was nothing between her and the world.

Loo screamed and found that the more she screamed, the less afraid she was of dying. The air whipped through her open mouth and the galaxy tilted upside down and it was like some massive creature had rolled over on top of her life until it was flattened. Loo's mind swirled and her boots turned in the open air above the crowd playing Milk-Bottle Toss and Plinko and her father staring up at her, clutching the box of popcorn.

"What'd I tell you," said the carny afterward as he unlocked her cage. "Like flying, right?"

Loo tried to nod but instead she stumbled, her legs gone weak.

He caught her elbow. "Careful."

She tried to read his T-shirt again. It seemed important that she know what it said. But the writing was in a loopy, cursive scrawl that disappeared up his sleeve. And then her father was there and his arms were around her and he was whisking her through the gate and away from the ride and over to a trash can, where she promptly threw up.

"Happy birthday." Hawley handed her a napkin. "Still want your popcorn?"

Loo shook her head, embarrassed. She wiped her mouth.

Hawley tossed the box. "That asshole was flirting with you."

"He was not." She glanced back at the Galaxy Round Up. The carny was flashing his dimples again and locking a blond woman into one of the cages.

"He was," said Hawley, and then his hand slid behind his back, and Loo knew that he was checking his gun. Reminding them both that it was there. As if any part of him would not remember. As if Loo could ever forget.

· · ·

On Monday she was back in school, still flush from the fair. She didn't care that she'd thrown up or that the carny had so quickly forgotten her. All that mattered was that she'd drawn his attention. It felt like she'd discovered some secret ability within herself that had appeared only because someone else had pointed out where it was hidden.

They had lived in Olympus for more than four years now. It had become their home. Each spring Hawley planted a garden in the backyard, and by summer they had beans and tomatoes and corn to set on the grill. They went to the beach and stretched out on towels in the sun and listened to the surf and dug clams on the weekends. They raked fall leaves into giant piles and burned them, and they bought a real Christmas tree each year and set it up in their living room, and used snowshoes to tromp through the woods. They had a garage that Hawley turned into a workshop, full of wires and shovels and tools, and they had shelves lining their walls that Loo filled with books that did not have to be returned to the library. She had spent her life looking at empty closets, and now all the closets in their house were full.

The only thing that hadn't changed was Loo's reputation. She had been in ninth grade when she smashed Mary Titus's head in the bathtub, and now three years later, in her last year of high school, she still could not outrun her rock-in-a-sock. The widow hadn't pressed charges but she made sure the whole town knew about Samuel Hawley and his crazy daughter. The good news was that the widows stopped coming around. The bad news was that people started avoiding them again, except for Pauly Fisk and Joe Strand, who remained Hawley's drinking buddies, and Principal Gunderson, who continued to slip Loo passes to get her out of detention. Jeremy and Pauly junior did their best to steer away with their bent noses, encouraging others to do the same, and the only person who would talk to her at school was Marshall Hicks.

Mary Titus had a big mouth, but her son didn't. He'd never told anyone about Loo breaking his finger. If he had, the air would have gone out of what had happened between them, and the memory would have faded over the years. Instead, his silence had turned the finger into a secret. A secret that he reminded her of whenever he nodded at her as they passed in the hall, or loaned her a pencil when hers broke during a history test, or chose her for a partner in biology, after the long, uncomfortable moment when the teacher said to pair up and Loo sat alone, biting her lip and trying not to notice everyone moving away from her.

"I think it's going to be worms," Marshall said, as he placed the wax tray and metal pins in front of her. "They always start the semester with worms."

"Sea worms or earthworms?"

"Earth." Marshall pulled out a leather pouch from his backpack, stuffed with colored pens. "I'll do the worksheet if you do the cutting."

Two girls at the table across from them raised their eyebrows. And then one of them pretended to pour maple syrup on the other's chest. Loo picked up the scalpel. "Deal."

They got worms. Big ones. Loo cut the skin and pinned the edges back against the tray. Marshall identified the clitellum and gizzard but had trouble with the reproductive system.

"Those look like ovaries to me," said Loo.

"They have male parts *and* female parts." Marshall poked the worm with a pin. "Receptacles and vesicles. They're hermaphrodites. Like Hermaphroditus. He was the son of Aphrodite and Hermes. A nymph fell in love with him and so they merged. Became two people inside one person."

"That sounds kind of amazing," said Loo. "Like being alone but not being lonely."

"They still need another worm to reproduce."

"How do you know all this stuff?"

"My stepfather's a marine biologist. He read me science textbooks at bedtime."

Loo thought of Hawley tucking her underneath a motel bedspread. The two of them sharing a bag of chips from the vending machine and laughing at Godzilla and Frankenstein on TV. Marshall took a pen from his leather pouch. He flipped over Loo's worksheet and sketched a beautiful woman with flowing hair, standing naked in an open clamshell, surrounded by winged cupids. Then he gave this woman a beard.

Underneath he wrote, *Herm-Aphrodite*, and slid the drawing across the table with his crooked finger.

At the end of class, Loo did not turn in her worksheet. She folded the paper up and took it home instead.

Marshall and Loo spent the next few weeks dissecting frogs together, and then a cricket, and then a fetal pig, and then a starfish. For an hour each day they took turns with the knife and labeled organs on their lab sheets and talked. Loo had no problem with the frog or even the pig, which felt the same as gutting a flounder, but for some reason the giant preserved starfish made her nearly faint as soon as she snipped through its thick skin with a pair of scissors and began scraping out its pyloric cecum. Marshall Hicks took over just as the last bit of color drained from Loo's face. The girls who sat across from them noticed, and one of them puckered her lips while the other pretended to make herself vomit with her own finger. Loo stared back, her mouth tasting like old metal filings. She counted forward from zero to twenty, then backward from twenty to zero, and it was just enough to keep her from taking the scalpel and stabbing the pretend-vomit girl in the eye.

AFTER A LONG, HARD WINTER, the teenagers of Olympus witnessed their first sign of spring: an outdoor kegger. Marshall and his cousin got their hands on a half-barrel of Heineken and rolled it about a mile into the woods to the whale's jaw—a giant natural rock formation in the center of Dogtown that looked like a humpback breaking the surface, far from any roads or houses so no one would hear and with plenty of places to hide if the cops showed up. Word spread at school that everyone was invited to drain the keg in the forest. Even so, when Marshall handed her a flyer for the party, complete with a hand-drawn map, the whale's jaw circled in the middle, Loo checked his face to make sure he wasn't making fun of her. When he smiled she said that she would come.

The night of the party Loo waited at the kitchen table with a book in front of her, pretending to read, while Hawley showered and got ready to meet Fisk down at the Flying Jib. She tilted her head and nod-

ded as he said goodbye, and as soon as his truck pulled out of the driveway she stripped off her clothes and put on the outfit she had spent all
week organizing, a practiced combination of nonchalance—jeans and a
T-shirt with the neck ripped out and the sleeves rolled over her shoulders, a pair of large hoop earrings she had lifted from the drugstore and
her steel-toed boots. Then she went to the bathroom and smeared on
her mother's bright-red lipstick, the texture stale and hard. She pulled
back her hair. She was sixteen but in the mirror she looked nearly
twenty. She thought, *Here I go.*

She put Marshall's map and a flashlight in the pocket of her sweatshirt and then got her bike out of the shed and started across town. It
was dusk when she left their house, and by the time she reached the
edge of the woods the sky had darkened and cars had turned on their
headlights. The side road that led to Dogtown was lined with vehicles
of every size and shape, parked one after the other under the trees. The
cars were cold and empty and quiet; they had been there for hours.

Loo was sweaty from the ride. She leaned her bike against a tree by
the entrance, turned on her flashlight and started down the trail. As
soon as she stepped away from the road, the trees closed in, blocking
the stars and the moon. All she could hear was her own breathing and
the sound of her feet in the leaves. Then her flashlight passed over a
giant boulder on the side of the path. The rock looked out of place and
time, like an abandoned spaceship from another world. Loo came
closer, and saw letters carved into the side. Two words six inches high
and perfectly cut, as if for a statue or a grave.

BE TRUE.

Loo took Marshall's map out of her pocket and held it under the
light. There was a small round dot close to the trailhead with the same
words. Farther along on the path she found other stones, each next to
its own corresponding black dot on the map: BE CLEAN. SAVE. TRUTH.
WORK. LOYALTY. KINDNESS. INTELLIGENCE. IDEALS. IDEAS. INTEGRITY.
SPIRITUAL POWER. And PROSPERITY FOLLOWS SERVICE. They were mark-
ers, and she followed them through the forest, each giving her courage,
until she heard voices and music and came to a clearing and saw the
whale lit up in the dark.

The bonfire was right underneath the jawbone, flickering against the granite. There were nearly a hundred teenagers gathered around different parts of the stone whale, clambering up its side or perched on top of its nose or leaning against the blowhole. Now that she had gotten herself here, Loo wasn't sure what to do. She had never been to a party before.

She expected to see kids from her class, and she did spot a few but didn't know them well enough to go up and say hello. Most were older. Everyone was holding red plastic cups and drinking and some of them were smoking cigarettes and some of them were smoking weed and some were roasting marshmallows. Loo saw a girl catch a marshmallow on fire, turn it until all the sides were blackened, then blow it out, peel the goo off and stuff the whole thing in her mouth before turning to the boy next to her and kissing him, the white insides dripping between them and the rest of the crowd hooting their approval.

Marshall was back in the woods, pumping the keg and serving beer. He was wearing a Greenpeace T-shirt and a pair of faded jeans. Loo stood in line and took a cup from him.

"You came," he said.

"I got lost. But the boulders helped. They're huge."

"I know. My stepdad used to bring me here to hike when I was little. This place is like Stonehenge. These giant rocks got picked up someplace else a million years ago and then dropped here when the glaciers melted. They're called 'erratics.' Some guy named Babson carved slogans into them in the thirties."

Marshall's words came out hurried and slurred and Loo realized he was drunk. His eyes looked straight at her, not ducking away as they usually did in science class.

Loo took a sip of beer. It was warm and flavorless. She wiped her mouth.

"Do you have a favorite?"

"'Never try,'" he said, "'never win.'"

Some kids came forward and asked for drinks. Loo stepped to the side and watched Marshall work the tap, holding the spigot in place with the finger she had broken. If she touched it, she was sure she would be able to feel the split in the bone. Marshall poured her more beer, tipping the cup to keep down the foam, and then he told another kid to take over and walked with Loo to the fire.

"Who are these people?" she asked.

"My cousin's friends," Marshall said. "He graduated last year."

"I thought Jeremy and Pauly junior would be here."

"They don't talk to me anymore. Not since my mom started that petition for the marine sanctuary."

"Want me to beat them up for you?"

Marshall laughed. "No thanks."

They sat down on a log in front of the fire, not touching but close. The heat felt good after the long walk through the forest. Everyone was in silhouette, the flames animating their faces.

"My stepfather showed me how to tap the trees in these woods," said Marshall.

"For maple syrup?"

Marshall nodded. "The sap runs when it's below freezing at night, but above freezing during the day. I'm out here most of February and March. It's a lot of work."

"I can imagine," said Loo, and for a moment she did imagine—the branches dropping their leaves and turning bare, the snow rising up around them, and Marshall passing through the icy drifts in his boots, carrying his buckets and a small mallet to drive the spiles into the bark.

"Do you want to see it?" Marshall asked.

"See what?"

He kept his eyes on the fire and took a long gulp of beer. "'Never try, never win.'"

Loo watched the smoke rising, splitting around the whale's jaw. "Sure," she said.

Marshall led her away from the party, down the path. They passed a few more carvings and read them with their flashlights: USE YOUR HEAD; BE ON TIME; IF WORK STOPS VALUES DECAY.

"Do you think any of these slogans made a difference?"

"Probably not," said Marshall. He finished his beer and threw his cup into the woods and then he took her hand. She could feel the hard bump of his broken finger against her palm. *His finger will be like that the rest of his life*, she thought. But she still didn't feel bad about breaking it.

"If I lived here I would have hated Babson. For trying to tell me what to do."

"Come on," Marshall said, and pulled her into the trees.

The music from the party was softer now and the light faded as they moved away from the bonfire. They walked through the bushes and along a trail until the woods got dark and quiet. Eventually they reached another boulder, half buried in the earth. Marshall ran the beam of his flashlight along the length of it—the words were barely recognizable underneath the moss. NEVER TRY NEVER WIN. "That's it," he said and then he turned off the flashlight. Blackness closed around them. Loo could hear everything. The rustle of the trees and Marshall breathing beside her and then she felt his hands and he pushed Loo against the rock and then he kissed her.

His mouth tasted like beer. His lips pushed hers open, his tongue exploring her teeth. It was strange but not terrible. He touched her hip and this time she took hold of his thumb and held it tight. She could feel his pulse, just underneath the skin—a silent, insistent beating. And at once the familiar rusted flavor was there, flooding Loo's mouth and washing away his beery kisses. She squeezed his thumb. Marshall's body went stiff. He pulled away from her.

"Don't," he said.

Someone shouted in the distance. There were footsteps close by, and then the woods around them were suddenly full of movement. People rushing down the path, flashlights going in all directions, boys calling out and girls screaming.

"Cops!" someone yelled as they hurried past. Loo released Marshall's finger. And then she ran, leaving him behind in the dark. She dug her flashlight out of her pocket and dove into the bushes, crawling on her hands and knees through the thicket until she was far away from the path and the bonfire was nothing but a glimmer through the branches.

The police had driven out on a couple of ATVs, and she could hear one of them taking the names of the kids they had caught while the others loaded the keg onto one of the racks. The cops' flashlights were stronger than anyone else's and cast sharp beams that cut through the forest. She was about a hundred feet away, her knees wet and her nails thick with dirt, when the earth dropped out from underneath her feet and she stumbled into a hole.

Loo thought she'd fallen into a grave but it was the cellar of an old homestead, lined with rocks. The hole was muddy and cold, the stone walls still supporting the base of the foundation, six feet down. There was a pricker bush and the thorns raked her hands. Loo watched the beams of the flashlights pass overhead and listened to the police talking to one another. The men found a few more teenagers and then they went back and put out the bonfire, and everyone was rounded up and the police left, a few riding in the ATVs and the others walking out with the kids. One of the girls was crying and another was begging them not to call her parents, and then their voices grew faint and they were gone, and Loo was left alone in the forest.

She struggled through thickets and over logs, a trail of mosquitoes and moths following her and swooping after the flashlight as she searched for the path. She scrambled over rocks and got a mouth full of cobwebs. It seemed like she was lost for hours. All the while shadows just beyond her flashlight moved, until she was sure that someone was tracking her, watching her from the trees. She turned off the light and hid. She waited. And then she ran right into one of Babson's boulders. It smelled of earth and metal and glass. She clicked on her flashlight and touched the words. USE YOUR HEAD. Loo pulled out Marshall's map and found the trail again. She followed the stones, from IDEAS and KINDNESS to LOYALTY and COURAGE until she returned to BE CLEAN and BE TRUE.

Loo stepped out of the woods, relief easing into her bones. It was late, and all of the cars that had lined the street when she arrived had disappeared. She hoped that her father was still out with Fisk; she needed at least forty minutes to ride back to Olympus. Loo took off her sweatshirt, wiped her face and tied the sleeves through her belt loops. Then she went over to the tree where she had left her bike and saw that it was gone.

She checked the woods, searched up and down the road, rooting in the bushes, even walked back down the path before giving up and sitting on the curb. She could try to thumb a ride out on the highway, but the thought of hitching made her nervous. She would have to walk back across town. It was going to take all night and Hawley would be home by the time she opened the door. She'd have to think of some excuse along the way.

Loo stood up and brushed off her jeans. They were covered with dirt and prickers. Her socks were soaked through. Her boots made a squishing noise with each step down one dark road and then another. There was a broken streetlamp ahead, shards sparkling in pieces across the asphalt, covered with dead moths and bird dung. But just beyond this pile of glass was a house, and that house was glowing. Every window, every switch turned on. The house was flaking paint, the front porch crooked. A rusted-out car was in the driveway. Loo would have thought the place was abandoned if it wasn't for all the lights. Then she recognized the pineapple knocker.

If she'd seen Mabel Ridge's house on the way into Dogtown, there was no way Loo would have stopped. But she was desperate without her bike—as well as tired and shaken and covered with brambles—so she turned and headed straight for her grandmother's door. The stairs creaked. The brass pineapple was heavy in her palm as she lifted it and let it fall. A moment passed and then the door opened and Loo was face-to-face with the old woman. Mabel Ridge was in her seventies now, her hair white, her spine curved, her nose and cheeks spotted with rosacea. She was wearing a cardigan sweater and a long black rubber apron and a pair of plastic goggles were pushed back on her forehead.

"Well?"

Loo tried to smooth her ponytail. She was missing one of her hoop earrings. She thought of the dress her father had made her wear on her last visit. How the blood on Hawley's shirt had taken days to scrub out.

"I'm Loo."

Mabel Ridge put her palm against the doorframe, as if she might slam it shut at any moment. The skin of her hand was dyed blue, all the way to the wrist.

Loo tried again. "Your granddaughter."

There was a change in the air between them then and Mabel sucked in her cheeks. Loo wondered if the woman was going to cry, but Mabel's chin slid out and the moment passed. She checked the girl over. She took in all the mess. "You look like you've been in a fight."

"I got lost in the woods."

"You were at that party." Mabel Ridge pulled a tissue from her sleeve, wiped her nose, then tucked it back up the same sleeve. "Your friends smashed my streetlight."

"I don't have any friends," said Loo.

Mabel Ridge opened the door and took a step onto the porch. She glanced over the girl's shoulder, and when she found no one waiting in the shadows, she scratched her chin with her blue fingers. "Well, I guess you'd better come inside, then."

The house seemed smaller once Loo stepped into the living room. Set in one corner was a spinning wheel on three legs, and set in the other, between an overstuffed couch and an old television set, was a gigantic wooden loom. The loom stretched across the wall, taking up most of the space, a square frame of interlocking pieces of wood, a foot treadle and a small bench in front where the weaver could sit and work. It was an enormous machine, imported from another time, the comb holding the threads apart and grinning like a giant mouth.

Mabel Ridge shut the front door and locked it, then wiped her feet on the hallway rug. "You're a little young to be going out to parties."

Loo didn't answer. She squeezed her flashlight tightly with both hands and tried not to stare. Mabel Ridge had the same green eyes as her mother. The same eyes that Loo saw when she looked into the mirror.

"You want to use the phone?" Mabel asked. "Call your father?"

"No," said Loo.

The old woman snorted, then waved her down the hall. "I've got a sink in there. You can clean up."

She led the girl to the kitchen. The counter was lined with jars stuffed with herbs. Four large pots were set on the stove, boiling and steaming. The room smelled of lavender and old potatoes.

"Careful," Mabel said. "You don't want to breathe this stuff." She put the goggles over her eyes, grabbed a towel from the back of the chair and used it to lift one of the lids. She turned off the heat, checked the temperature with a gauge, then picked up a long wooden spoon and used it to dip a skein of blue wool into the pot. As she pulled the yarn out again, the color began to shift, until it had turned an even deeper shade of indigo. Loo peered inside. She expected the liquid to be dark but it was yellow, with a slight milky tinge.

"Are you washing it?" Loo asked.

"No," said Mabel. "I'm turning it blue." She set the twist of yarn onto a small wooden rack. "Indigo is the hardest color to get right. Yellows, greens, reds—they're more reliable." She uncovered the other pots and revealed boiling vats of primary colors, the yarn floating and turning like some kind of strange soup. "Blue has to be added in layers. You dip it over and over and over again, forty or fifty times, until you get the darkness just right." She turned down the burners to simmer, put the lids back on and pushed the goggles to her forehead. Then she handed Loo a bar of Ivory soap and the towel she'd been using.

"You should clean your face, at least."

Loo took the towel and soap over to the sink and wet them both. There was a small hand mirror nailed to one of the kitchen cabinets. She leaned down and went to work. The red lipstick had rubbed off. There was a deep scratch on her forehead that was bleeding, dark mud smeared across her face and neck and a rash of mosquito bites on her left cheek. Loo cleaned herself as best she could, then wet her hands and ran them through her hair, shaking out burrs and twigs and even a beetle that landed in the sink and began frantically running in circles, flapping its tiny iridescent wings. Loo turned the water on and watched the bug get swallowed down the drain.

"That's better," said Mabel. "You looked like some kind of swamp monster. I thought you were the police—otherwise I wouldn't have answered."

"You called them?" Loo asked.

"Of course I did. That party was getting out of control. I keep track of things around here. People think no one's watching, but I always do."

The old woman said this while folding and refolding the towel, and Loo began to wonder if she was touched. There was something off about the way Mabel Ridge moved, her fingers reaching out like a spider feeling around a corner.

"What's all the yarn for?"

"People order my hand-dyed yarn from all over the country. It's simple, but it pays the bills. Kept me in this house after Gus lost all our money."

"Gus?" Loo asked.

"Lily's father."

My grandfather, Loo thought. "Does he live here, too?"

"He's dead," said Mabel Ridge. "Thank God."

Her blue fingers pushed open a door next to the sink. Behind it was a bathroom about the same size as the one in Loo's own house, but instead of pictures and scraps of memories it was filled with color. Skeins of yarn stretched across sets of wooden racks—green, purple, yellow, orange—dripping and mixing hues onto newspaper spread across the floor. Loo reached out and touched one of the loops, and her fingers came back stained. When she glanced up the old woman smiled.

"Come on. I want to show you something."

Mabel led her back down the hall, then sat on the bench in front of the loom. She motioned for Loo to join her. There were pedals underneath the machine, and Mabel pushed them with her feet. Each pedal lifted a different set of strings, creating a pattern.

"Try it," she said. "It's like a piano."

Loo sat down. She ran her fingers across the beater and shifted it back and forth. It was like the safety bar on the Galaxy Round Up.

"What are you making?"

"A blanket," said Mabel. "This pattern, it's called an overshot. You pass the shuttle like this." She took up an oval-shaped piece of wood, with a bobbin of blue yarn wrapped tightly inside. She pressed one of the pedals, one of the harnesses lifted and a pattern of cords rose through the teeth of the comb. With one quick movement, Mabel eased the shuttle underneath, until it slid out the other side. She took

Loo's hand and placed it on the beater. "Now use this to bring it all together."

Loo slid the beater forward and pressed the yarn into place. It felt both odd and familiar, like everything in this house.

"If you want, I can teach you," said Mabel Ridge.

When Loo didn't answer the old woman's mouth set into a hard line. "I thought you'd want to learn something about your family."

"Do you have anything of my mother's?" Loo asked.

Mabel exhaled loudly, then got up from the bench and opened a closet in the hallway, removed a cardboard box, lifted the lid and took out a pair of black lace gloves. They were cut short at the wrist, in the style of the 1940s. "Here," she said, passing them over.

Loo slid one of her hands inside. The fingers were longer than hers. It was like putting on someone else's skin. "I thought only old ladies wore these kinds of things."

"Lily was artistic. She could have gone to art school."

"Why didn't she?"

"She got into trouble instead. The kind you fell into tonight."

The old woman frowned, and for the first time Loo understood that her mother had once been a teenager who had also lied to her parents, and made out with boys in the woods, and snuck out to parties. Her mother had touched this loom, looked in that mirror nailed above the sink, knocked the pineapple knocker. Every object began to glow with possibility. Starting with the gloves on Loo's own fingers.

"She'd do anything to make herself different. Anything that was dangerous. She was like her father that way. The Coast Guard arrested her once, for jumping off the breakwater and swimming laps in the harbor, cutting back and forth between the boats in the shipping channel. We fought about it. We fought about a lot of things. But she thought it was funny."

"Funny," Loo said.

"She had a wicked sense of humor."

Mabel continued rummaging through the box, pulling out books and tins of drawing pencils. A silver belt buckle in the shape of an arrow.

Postcards from Alaska, North Carolina and Wisconsin. A couple of scrapbooks. Loo opened and closed her fingers, feeling the gloves tighten against her skin, and tried to memorize it all.

"This one is my favorite." Mabel Ridge held out an old photograph, bent on one side, and Loo leaned in to see. There was her mother, around eleven or twelve. She was covered head to toe in seaweed, like something washed up on the beach, the creature from the Black Lagoon. Her eyes were rolled back, her arms clawing at the camera.

"Can I have this?"

"No," said Mabel Ridge.

Loo tightened her grip on the photo. "She was my mother."

"In her will she left me all of her possessions. Her clothes and her notebooks and pictures," said Mabel Ridge. "Why do you think she did that?"

"I don't know," said Loo.

"I was *her mother*. Her family," said Mabel Ridge. "Not *him*."

Loo thought of the scraps on the walls of their bathroom. How carefully Hawley took them down and replaced them each time they moved.

"Is that what you said, that day we came here?" she asked.

Mabel pressed her palms together. "Your father wanted me to see you, but I wasn't ready. I wasn't sure I'd ever be ready."

Loo bent the gloves into fists. "I thought you hated me."

"Oh, my dear," said Mabel Ridge, taking the picture back. "I don't hate you. I've never hated you. I hate your father."

She said it without emotion, like she was reciting a fact of the universe. And that was enough. Loo didn't want to hear any more. She pulled off her mother's gloves and tossed them on the table. She stood up.

"I need a ride home."

The old woman wiped her blue hands on the rubber apron. She adjusted her goggles. "I haven't driven for years. But you can take the Firebird." She slid the picture back inside the box and closed the lid, then turned to bring it to the closet, and as she did Loo snatched the gloves up again and stuffed them into her pocket.

Mabel Ridge did not ask if Loo could drive. She just handed over the keys to the rusted-out Pontiac as if they were nothing, walked Loo out to the driveway, said goodbye and shut the car door. Then she knocked on the window. When Loo rolled it down, she passed her a small photo album with a black leather cover.

"You can have this," she said. "But I want you to bring the Firebird back. Not right away, but sometime soon. And then we'll talk some more."

"Okay," said Loo. She watched the old woman shuffle up the steps of the porch and move inside. The lights still shone in all of the windows.

The Firebird looked like it had spent its life on cement blocks, but to Loo's surprise it turned over quickly. She backed out of the driveway and the pedal lurched under her foot. The bucket seat nearly touched the ground, the engine rattled and the brakes were weak—she had to press to the floor before they caught. Loo gripped the wheel and took a breath. *You can do this*, she thought, and then she shifted to drive and started down the empty street, barely moving twenty miles per hour, her heart thumping like she was on a raceway.

The only time she'd ever driven was with Hawley in an empty parking lot. He'd promised to give her more lessons but she didn't have a permit yet. Luckily, the streets were deserted, and the few cars she passed seemed to be driving just as slowly as she was—drunks hoping not to get pulled over. A few blocks from their house, Loo slid the car to a stop next to the sidewalk and turned off the ignition. Her hands were trembling.

She flipped open the album Mabel Ridge had given her, hoping to see her mother's face again, but instead of pictures there was only Lily's obituary and a few newspaper articles, yellowed with age. One of the articles said that it had taken days to find her mother's body. That the lake had been dragged with a net. At the memorial service, they had played "Bye Bye Blackbird." Apparently it was her mother's favorite song.

When Loo had finished reading she closed the book and slid it underneath the driver's seat. She got out and locked the door. As she walked home she thought of the photo she'd held between her fingers of her mother covered in muck, looking like a monster from an old black-and-white B movie. In the tiny mirror above the sink in Mabel Ridge's kitchen, shaking bugs from her hair, mud on her face, Loo had not looked very different.

When she reached the corner she saw her father's truck parked outside the house. She paused for a moment, considering her chances of sneaking in. Then she climbed the front steps. She slid the key into the lock. Instead of flipping the light switch, she kept her flashlight on and maneuvered past shadowy chairs and tables, then up the stairs. When she passed Hawley's bedroom, she felt him there behind the closed door, waiting.

He was awake. She was sure of it. Hawley never slept much, and when he did Loo could always sense the difference in the house— a thickening quiet. Now the floorboards in his room shifted, which meant he was standing and that he had his boots on. He had been out looking for her. For hours, maybe.

The doorknob turned and a flood of brightness came over the hallway. Loo shaded her eyes against her father's haggard face. It was as if a drain had been opened and all the life had been sucked from his features. He looked worse than he did on the nights when he did not sleep and only sat and stared at her mother's things.

"Are you all right?"

"Yes," Loo answered.

Hawley was shaking, the same way he had that day she went missing at the county fair, throwing off the security guards, unrecognizable in the moment before he saw her waiting at the carousel. Loo turned off her flashlight. She braced for the shouting to begin. But instead all she heard was the familiar clink of a gun being opened, and the sigh of bullets sliding from their chambers and jingling into her father's palm.

"Then good night," he said.

"Good night." Her voice came out in a whisper. She waited for something else to happen, but he only stepped back into his room and closed the door, taking the light with him. Outside there were birds singing and inside it was as dark as Dogtown. Loo traced her fingertips along the wall. And then she was in her own room with her own bed and her own door to close.

She threw herself down on the mattress. Slowly she unlaced her boots, peeled off her wet socks. Her clothes smelled like sweat and smoke and the sharp air of the woods. From her pocket she took out her mother's gloves. She slid them onto both of her hands and pressed her fingers against her eyes. The black lace clouded her vision, as if she'd opened her eyes underwater.

She was nearly asleep when she heard her father come out into the hall again. He paced up and down the rug a few times, and then he stopped outside her door. He talked to the wood, his voice winding through the keyhole.

"You're all right," he said again.

"Yes," Loo said.

"Then I don't care where you've been."

"I'm sorry," she said.

"Don't start saying you're sorry," her father said, "or you'll be saying it for the rest of your life."

"I'm still sorry," she said.

"Don't," he said.

For a few minutes there was nothing but his breath at the door and Loo began to wonder if he'd been drinking. Then she heard him strike a match, and the scent of his cigarette filtered through the cracks. She listened as Hawley made his way downstairs. The door to the bathroom creaked open and shut. He would be in there for the rest of the night. Loo knew this like she knew her own body. And now she knew something else, something more than his old photographs and scraps of paper and haunted words. She knew that her mother dove off of breakwaters. That she was strong enough to swim through a shipping channel. That she wore gloves and rolled around in seaweed and had a father of her own. That she had grown up in a house full of color. And that she had lived a whole life before she'd met Sam Hawley.

Bullet Number Three

Jove and Hawley drove from Portland to Seattle, then took the ferry from Mukilteo out to Whidbey Island. It was Hawley's first time in the Northwest and he was surprised how different the air felt, the mist that clung to his skin, the fir trees and cliffs and mountains looming over the edge of the sound. Jove drove their car right onto the boat, and together they bought a couple of coffees from the canteen and watched the hulking white form of Mount Rainier rising in the distance.

Jove leaned over the rail and pointed. "Watch for the spout."

"A whale?"

"Gray, I think."

"How can you tell?"

"It's got two blowholes."

Jove held the cup with the tips of his fingers and passed it between his hands. Hawley peeled back the plastic lid on his own coffee, took a sip and burned his tongue.

"How big do they get?"

"Around fifty feet."

The men waited in silence. Hawley had never seen a whale before. He kept his eyes on the spot Jove had pointed to and felt a strange thrill in the pit of his stomach. He tried to imagine the whale's body, hidden under the waves. All that weight lifted by fins and tail, the thick, crusted skin and giant gaping mouth beneath, opening and swallowing. Minutes came and went. The creature did not surface, and Hawley realized that the whale was just another thing in life that he was going to miss out on.

"You think this fellow Talbot knows we're coming?" he asked.

Jove shook his head. "Not a chance."

He took out a map and passed it over, showed Hawley the road that would lead them to the north end of the island, where Talbot was supposed to be holed up. Talbot was a hired gun, like them, but he'd taken off with the goods he was supposed to deliver. Now it was their job to get the goods back. As long as they got the drop on Talbot it would be easy. Collect what had been stolen and bring it back to Ed King, Jove's old friend from prison. If things went well, King had promised there would be other jobs. And Hawley and Jove both needed the money.

"How's your hand?"

"It's all right."

"You should use your left more."

Hawley tossed his coffee lid into the ocean, then wrapped his busted knuckles around the warm paper cup. Last night Jove had had too much to drink at the hotel bar and a couple of bikers had pushed him off his stool and tried to take his wallet. They hadn't realized Hawley was with him, even though the two had been sitting next to each other for hours. Hawley had been thinking on this all morning—how good it had felt to throw those punches, the satisfying crunch of bone, the blood on the barroom floor; and also how he'd been so closed off that everyone had thought he was drinking alone.

Before they had finished their coffee, the captain announced they were landing, and the men got back into the Chevy. They'd stolen the

car in Portland and it was on the small side—Hawley had to move the
seat all the way back to fit his legs. The boat hands waved them through
and they drove off the ferry and onto the island. They went past Useless Bay and then got on the road to Freeland and up through the state
park. The house they were looking for was on a reserve, perched high
above an embankment overlooking the water. They pulled onto an un-
marked gravel road and traveled a mile into the woods until they
reached a low wooden gate. Hawley got out and lifted the rope latch
and then looped it over the post again after Jove had driven through.
They parked, blocking the entrance, and went the rest of the way on
foot.

Hawley had brought his father's rifle. He always felt better with a
rifle if he was in the woods. It reminded him of hunting, of listening
close and feeling ready. Jove took a .45 revolver and stuffed the gun
down the back of his pants. They walked another quarter-mile up the
road and then Jove said they should cut through the forest. They passed
a grove of cedars, trunks ribbed and flared where they met the ground,
then came to a shaded ravine that was awash with bright-green ferns.
Hawley stopped for a moment, knee-deep in those ladders of leaves.
The ferns were thick and lush and Hawley was flooded with the same
sense of anticipation he had had on the water, when he was looking for
the whale. Then Jove called his name and he gripped the rifle and continued on through the trees.

Twenty-nine years old and Hawley still carried the feeling he was
not where he was supposed to be. He had spent the last years drinking
and moving from place to place, having one-night stands, working retrievals like this, pulling the occasional robbery, playing cards whenever
he could find a game and losing, losing, losing. The bad luck had gone
on so long now he felt marked, like a smudge had been left on his forehead. He kept expecting something to happen, some outside force to
sweep in and change everything and take him in some new direction,
give him a more normal life. But instead it had been years of loneliness,
and now here he was again with Jove.

Talbot's place was set in a clearing at the top of the ridge, overlooking the water. The view was spectacular compared to the house, which was not much more than an old beach shack. The boards were worn white by the weather and the front steps sagged as if soaked through with water. There was a crumbling chimney releasing a thin cloud of smoke. Parked beside it was a cherry-red monster pickup, high off the ground, with double tires and a cabin big enough for six.

A woman opened the door and stepped out onto the porch. She was in her fifties, with high cheekbones and thick gray hair that curled around her face. She was wearing men's clothes, a flannel shirt over a tank top and a beaded Indian belt holding up a pair of jeans. Right away Hawley saw there was something wrong with her eyes. The left was all milked over and wandering, while the right was the color of violets and stared straight and clear and curious.

"You Talbot's wife?" Jove asked.

The woman nodded. "He's out fishing," she said, and then she noticed their guns. Her mouth had been a little bit open as she spoke and now it closed up tight. She moved into the house and tried to slam the door, but Hawley got there before she did and jammed it back. The edge of the wood bashed her nose and she stumbled and blood ran down across her lips and chin.

"Ed King sent us," Jove said. "You know who Ed King is?"

She stayed bent over, pressing the sleeve of her shirt against her face. She nodded.

"Talbot disappointed him."

"He disappoints me, too," she mumbled.

"I guess he's not a very good husband, then," said Jove, and he stepped past her into the house.

The woman raised her head. Her milky eye twitched nervously over to Hawley, who was still gripping the door. She shuffled out of the way and let him pass.

Inside he felt like a giant in a doll's house. The place was only one floor, the ceilings low and the furniture close to the ground. There was a fireplace with a fire going in it, a pile of wood in a basket, a worn-out sofa and two chairs, a rolltop desk and a card table in the corner.

"You know what we're here for," said Jove. "Why don't you get it for us, and there won't be any more trouble."

Talbot's wife didn't answer. She kept her sleeve pressed to her nose. She walked past both the men and their guns and into the kitchen, which was just off the living room, opened the freezer and took out a bag of peas and leaned her face into it. With her other hand she picked up a teakettle. She filled it with water from the sink and then she set it on the stove and lit the burner. Her nose was already swelling up, blood smeared across her chin. "He'll be home soon. You can ask *him* where it is."

It was Hawley's experience that retrievals like this usually went one of two ways: people put up a fight for the goods they were holding, or they got scared, in which case they went straight to bargaining or fell down crying. But Talbot's wife was taking out a tablecloth and dishes. She spread the cloth over the rickety card table and set knives and forks and spoons, as if the men were expected guests coming over for dinner.

Jove took a chair at the table but Hawley stayed in the doorway. When the woman returned to the kitchen the men exchanged a look and then exchanged their guns. Jove watched the woman with the rifle, and Hawley slipped away with the .45 to start searching the house.

He checked the bathroom first. Inside was a tub with no curtain around it, a toilet and a sink made of pink porcelain, with a stained plastic cup and two toothbrushes on the edge. The towels on the rack were damp. The toilet was running. Hawley pulled out the vanity drawers and emptied them out onto the tile floor. Cotton balls, Band-Aids, razors, a hair dryer. He opened the medicine cabinet and sent the bottles of pills and ointments crashing into the sink.

Next he went through the bedroom. Hawley looked behind the rumpled mattress and then he went for the jewelry box, emptying it onto the blankets. Nothing but some old turquoise necklaces, hollow silver bracelets and painted earrings. He rummaged through the bureau, tossing clothes onto the floor as he searched, knocking a line of paperback mysteries from an old bookcase, turning shoes upside down.

When he'd looked everyplace he could think of, Hawley went

across the hall. There was one more door, shut tight. Next to it was a framed photograph of a skeleton, holding a scythe in one hand and a set of scales in the other. Both the scythe and the scales were made with pieces of bone—vertebrae and scapula. On the mat surrounding the picture was handwritten: *Santa Maria della Concezione dei Cappuccini, Rome.* Hawley waited a moment, listening. He looked at the picture. Then he grabbed the handle of the closet door, pulled it open and threw himself forward. He was met with a tumble of cardboard boxes falling down from above, knocking him to the floor.

"What the hell is going on out there?" Jove shouted from the living room.

"He opened the closet," Hawley heard the woman say.

And that's what it was: a closet so jammed full of stuff that it had collapsed as Hawley stepped inside. Now he was surrounded by mountains of old shoes, rolls of wrapping paper and unopened mail, a rusted tool chest, some kind of ancient vacuum, the broken pieces of a chair, an old dog collar, a pile of Mexican blankets, boxes filled with yellowed photographs and files of papers, overturned. It would take weeks to go through it all.

Hawley glanced over the papers. There were tax forms, a pile of handwritten letters and some pencil-and-ink sketches of nudes that looked like Talbot's wife. In the drawings she was younger, her hair still vibrant, her body trim, her violet eye shyly gazing. The lines followed the curve of her back and shoulders, her arms and breasts. Hawley put the papers down and backed away. He left everything where it had fallen and returned to the living room.

Jove had pulled the card table over to the sofa. Talbot's wife sat opposite, in one of the chairs, her neck stiff. In one hand she held the bag of frozen peas and in the other a wad of bloodied tissues, applying them both in turn to her face. There was an empty mug with a tea bag in front of Jove and another mug in front of the woman. Hawley took the other seat.

"Thought you were wrestling a bear out there," said Jove.

"Felt like it," said Hawley.

"I keep meaning to clean it out," said Talbot's wife, "but there's nowhere else to put anything." She shifted the peas across the bridge of her nose.

Hawley thought of the nudes and wondered if Talbot had drawn them. If maybe that's how they'd met. If she'd been some kind of model, and what happened between them was strong enough and important enough that she'd stuck with Talbot through all the troubles that followed.

Jove looked around the room. "This is quite the hideaway."

"It belonged to my father," said Talbot's wife. Her milky eye strayed to the window. It caught the light and clouded further, as if a shade had been pulled across the iris.

"Feels like the edge of the world," said Jove. "I bet you thought that no one would ever find you."

All three of them sat still for a while, Jove tapping the mug in front of him and Talbot's wife swapping the peas for the bloody tissues. Hawley was thirsty but he didn't want to ask the woman for anything. Then Jove stopped tapping and Hawley knew he was going to give the speech.

"You know what they call us?" said Jove. "The Takers. That's what we do. We take things. And if we don't get what we want we take something else. Anything that matters. Anything that you care about." He wiped his fingers on the tablecloth, then sat back against the couch. "We'll take your husband, if he doesn't give us what we want."

The way Jove said it was final, and the room, which was already charged with their coming, got tighter. Jove was good at this, at squeezing a place so there was hardly any air left.

"He didn't mean to cross anyone," she said.

"But he did," said Jove.

Talbot's wife took the frozen peas off her face. The skin underneath was red, a dark bruise starting from the bridge of her nose to the corner of her clouded eye. Something hit the window, a tiny thud, a small bird or a giant bee. They all turned to look, but there wasn't anything there, just clouds and the rippling water and rows of firs and pines. Talbot's wife put down the peas and the tissues. Her nose was nearly twice the size it had been when she opened the door. She began to unbutton the cuffs of her flannel shirt and roll up the sleeves. She did it slowly, like she was getting ready to clean the house.

The kettle started whistling on the stove. Talbot's wife went into the kitchen and Hawley followed her. He stood in the doorway with the gun and watched her turn off the burner, his mind going to the drawings in the closet. Her beauty was still there, behind the swollen nose, haunting the wrinkles at the corners of her eyes, the sloping of her waist and shoulders.

She looked up at him. "What?"

"Nothing," said Hawley.

Talbot's wife turned away and took down a mug from the cabinet. "You want some tea, too?" Her voice was flat. "There's coffee but it's instant."

Hawley saw a bottle of whiskey on the top shelf. He thought of asking for it. "Tea's fine."

She took a pot holder and lifted the kettle to fill his cup. She added a tea bag from the box on the counter.

"Milk and sugar?"

"Oh, I'm sweet enough," said Hawley.

It was something he always said to waitresses, and it came out automatically now, but the words just hung there between them, out of place. She let out a cough that could have passed for a laugh and handed Hawley the mug. It was white with a photograph printed on the side, the kind you get at the mall. The picture showed her and Talbot, their arms around each other. The man was older, maybe by ten or fifteen years, with thick, gray, hairy sideburns that came to the edge of his chin. He looked like some kind of Amish farmer.

The woman caught Hawley examining the side of the mug. She probably hadn't looked at it closely in years. But she looked now. Then she said, "He gave it to me for Valentine's Day."

"Oh," said Hawley. He felt strange then and didn't want to drink from the cup anymore. He carried it into the living room instead and set it in front of Jove on the table. He pointed at the picture.

Jove leaned close, but didn't get up from the sofa.

"I'm not going to beat on some old guy," said Hawley.

"We're not beating on anyone yet."

"I'm just saying."

The toilet was still ringing in the bathroom. Hawley thought of going to fix it. He wished that Talbot would arrive, so they could be through with this. His palms started getting sweaty, just considering what he might have to do. There was an ache in his stomach and another in his back by his ribs. He put his hand there. He touched the scar. He wished he'd asked for the whiskey.

Talbot's wife came out carrying the kettle, her arm elbow-deep inside a quilted pot holder. "Let me fill your cup."

Jove lifted his mug. The tag of the tea bag was stuck to the side of the porcelain. Talbot's wife began to pour. The water came spilling out and then it was spilling everywhere, on the table, on the mug, on the floor, on the sofa, on Jove's hand and arm and face and hair and he was screaming.

Talbot's wife threw the kettle at Hawley's head. He ducked as she ran for the door, then lunged and caught her around the waist. She clawed at his arms, but he pinned her tightly against him. For a moment all he could feel was her struggling along his side.

"That was stupid," Hawley said. He twisted her arm up behind her back so that her knees buckled. He shoved the card table aside and used his belt to tie her to a chair. Jove wailed the whole time, his hands covering his face. His clothes were soaked through and steaming. Hawley went over and tried to pick him up and his own arms stung from the heat and then he felt Jove's skin slide and come loose under his fingers.

"Fucking fuck! Fuck!"

Jove pressed his hand to the place Hawley had touched him, the skin bubbling into blisters. Hawley supported him into the bathroom. Once they were inside he turned on the cold water full blast and Hawley helped his friend into the tub. Jove fell back against the porcelain with a grunt. The water filled quickly, billowing his pants and shirt around his thin frame.

"I think I'm going to pass out." Jove's face was stretching tight, ridges of boils rising across his cheeks. Hawley grabbed a towel and soaked it in the cold water. He pressed it to Jove's neck.

"I don't know what to do," he said. "Tell me what to do."

Jove's hand came out of the water. He grabbed on to Hawley's sleeve.

"Shhhhhhhhhhhhhhit."

There were footsteps on the front porch. A jingle of keys. The lock on the door turned, followed by a shuffling of boots, the creak of hinges, the sound of something heavy being set on the floor. And then the old man's voice called down the hallway.

"Maureen?"

There'd been no sound of a car. Talbot must have taken a boat, climbed up from the beach. Hawley drew the .45. It was only a few feet from the bathroom to the hall, but before he could move, the woman started shouting.

"They came for it!" she screamed. "Get out of here!"

The door slammed shut and footsteps pounded across the porch. Hawley hurried out of the bathroom, turned the corner and tripped over an enormous plastic cooler, now sitting in the middle of the hallway. By the time he scrambled off the floor and got the door open again and stumbled outside, Talbot was only a few paces from the woods.

Hawley caught sight of a rifle, just as the man disappeared into the trees. Before he could make it across the lawn Talbot had found cover and started firing in earnest. Hawley sprinted back to the house, counting the shots as they rang past, and when they stopped he guessed Talbot was carrying a rifle with a five-round magazine. He slammed the door and drew the bolt behind him. It would be only a minute before Talbot got the rifle loaded again, less if he had extra clips ready. The old man's aim had been off, but there was no telling what he was capable of once he'd had the chance to collect himself.

For a moment Hawley just stood there in the hallway, breathing hard, wondering what else could go wrong. He opened the lid of the plastic cooler. It held two salmon—a Coho, still silver, with dark-blue specks along its back, and a good-size Chinook, at least twenty-five or thirty pounds. The fish stared up at Hawley, their eyes round and flat and unblinking.

He carried the cooler into the living room and put it next to Talbot's wife. She'd been nervous before but now she smiled like she'd won some kind of contest. Hawley felt like slapping her but he didn't. He stepped next to the windows and peered out. The line of trees was closer than he'd like it to be. Talbot's wife wasn't trying to get loose anymore. She just sat there, grinning, blood running down from her swollen nose into her mouth.

"I guess you love him," Hawley said.

"I guess I do."

"And he loves you?"

She turned her face to the window, her cloudy eye catching the light. She nodded.

"You sure?"

"I'm sure."

"Well, we're about to find out," Hawley said, because the rest of the job now depended on it. If Talbot came back for his wife, they'd get what they came for, and if he didn't, all they'd have is some dead salmon. The tap was still running in the bathroom and he could hear Jove groaning. A piece of skin was stuck to Hawley's thumb, thin as a flower petal, and he wiped it off on the curtains.

The fire was nearly out, the logs smoldering. To Hawley the room seemed unbearably warm, the midday sun beating across the carpet. The fish had just been caught but he could smell them. Hawley kept the .45 in his hand and stayed next to the window, watching for Talbot. A shadow moved through the trees at the edge of the forest and then it disappeared.

"Untie me," the woman said.

"I don't think so."

"I could get you a drink," she said. "A real one."

Hawley thought of the whiskey he'd seen in the kitchen. Then he shook it off and glanced at Talbot's wife. She'd guessed this about him just by looking, five minutes with her one good eye.

"My husband made a pledge to give it up," she said, "on our wedding day."

"Then why do you keep a bottle around?" Hawley asked.

"I didn't say he'd stopped."

The belt Hawley had used to tie the woman was cutting into her wrists. He could see the marks. She leaned her head to the side and wiped her nose on her shoulder. Even with the blood on her face she was lovely. In her men's clothes she looked tough and worn-out, but there was a softness, too.

"He wrote me a letter," she said. "It was the most wonderful letter. When I read it, I was so happy I cried. I don't think I've ever been happier."

"But he broke his promise," said Hawley.

She rolled her violet eye at him. "Love isn't about keeping promises. It's about knowing someone better than anyone else. I'm the only one who knows him. I'm the only one who ever will."

The woman seemed convinced but Hawley knew a raw deal when he heard one. He thought of the whiskey in the cabinet, and all it represented—the weakness and the lies. He wondered what would happen if he left now and took Talbot's wife with him, if they walked away from her husband and Jove and all the rest. There was at least twenty years and a world of differences between them, but Talbot's wife held something deep inside of her that Hawley knew he could spend the rest of his life trying to uncover. He took a step toward the chair. He reached down and touched the belt, and that's when the first rifle shot came through the window.

It hit Hawley in the shoulder, the pain searing like a hot poker driven through and turned, the bullet twisting and tearing and then continuing out the other side of him, through the air, and jamming into the frame of the skeleton photograph, hanging next to the closet. A second bullet went wide and hit the wall and then another shattered the glass and tagged Talbot's wife in the neck.

Hawley's left arm was useless, and he dropped the .45, spun away, then fell to a crouch on the floor. If he counted right, Talbot had two more bullets before he'd have to reload. Hawley waited until another windowpane broke and then he yanked a napkin from the kitchen table and pressed it against his shoulder. It hurt like hell but he'd had worse.

The gunshots stopped. The only sound was Talbot's wife, still tied to the chair and wheezing. Hawley slid over and managed to untie the belt. As soon as she was free her fingers dug at her throat like she was trying to strangle herself. Hawley pulled her hand away—there was a lot of blood. He gathered the .45 and together they crawled into the kitchen. By the time they reached the linoleum, her face was pale, her shirt dark red. She pressed her back against the cupboards. Hawley pointed the gun.

"You give him some kind of signal?" he asked.

"No," she managed.

Hawley pulled a pot holder from the counter and ran it under the sink and pressed it to the side of her throat. "You're going to tell him to quit. You're going to get him to come inside here and talk."

"He's not one for talking."

"Well, then, you talk," said Hawley.

They both heard someone outside the front door, shaking the handle against the lock, and then the old man's voice came through. "Maureen?"

"She's here," Hawley called out. "She's hit."

"Fuck," said Talbot.

"Don't come through that door," said Hawley.

"If you hurt my wife I'll kill you," said Talbot.

"You're the one who shot her," said Hawley.

"Maureen!" Talbot was shouting now.

"Doug," Talbot's wife said. "I'm all right. Stop yelling."

"She's bleeding, though," said Hawley. "She's bleeding a lot." And she was. The pot holder was soaked through and turning the same rusted color as her shirt.

"We just want what we came for," said Hawley. "We don't want to hurt anybody. Just tell me where it is and you can take her to the hospital."

They were all quiet. The only noise was the running toilet, still chiming through the door to the bathroom. Hawley started to worry that Talbot had left and was coming in another way. Then he heard a thud against the wood, like someone had punched it.

"It's in the closet," said Talbot.

"Fine," said Hawley. "That's just fine. She's coming with me to check, so don't try anything. Okay?"

Talbot didn't answer.

"Doug," the woman said.

"Okay," said Talbot. "Okay."

"Can you walk?" Hawley asked. Talbot's wife nodded, then winced. Her cloudy eye was spinning up, down, left, while her violet eye stayed on Hawley. "We're going to the hallway," he called to Talbot, and then they did, moving slowly, her pressing the pot holder to her throat and Hawley right behind with the gun, leaving two trails of blood behind them.

When they reached the closet, Talbot's wife slid down against the wall. The floor was still littered with all the junk that had collapsed on top of Hawley earlier, mountains of clothes and boxes and all the drawings.

"Where is it?" Hawley asked.

Talbot's wife shook her head.

"Tell me where," Hawley yelled. "Now."

"The dress." Talbot's voice came from behind the door. "Her wedding dress."

Hawley turned to the wife.

"It's in the back." She closed her eyes. "Behind everything else."

Hawley moved the gun to his bad hand. The tendons in his arm burned with the weight of it. His palm was covered with blood and the metal was slippery. With his right he started throwing things out of the closet, a life's worth of memories. Overcoats and photo albums and dishes, a set of old 78 records, silk flowers, a moth-eaten batting for a quilt, fire tongs and lightbulbs and stiff leather jackets. Hawley's shoulder ached with hurt as he tossed everything, groping in the dark as he went deeper, dragging the boxes and kicking them behind, the smell of mothballs permeating it all, until at last his fingers grazed a soft shape covered in plastic, then the crush of crinoline against the back wall of the closet. Hawley felt for the hanger and pulled the garment bag out. It was awkward and heavy as a body, the plastic yellowed and torn at the seams.

He hung it on the hall light and pulled down the zipper. The dress looked like something out of the fifties, with lace sleeves and a tulle skirt. The shape was stuffed with tissue paper and cardboard, so that it held the form of a woman. A headless ghost bride.

"I was skinnier then," Talbot's wife said.

Hawley didn't know the first place to start. He'd already bled on the dress, a streak of red across the bodice. "Where'd he put it?"

"Try the purse," she said.

There was a pale silk drawstring bag attached to the neck of the hanger. Hawley yanked it free and stuffed his hand inside. He pulled out a piece of lace. There were a few bobby pins in the bottom, but nothing else.

Talbot's wife held out her hand and Hawley passed her the veil. She didn't put it on, just pulled the lace across her lap and fingered the edges. Hawley listened for Talbot. He listened for Jove. But all he could hear was the toilet running. "Where else?"

"There's a pocket," she said. "He put the letter there, the one I was telling you about. I carried it with me down the aisle."

Hawley groped the skirt, pushed the tulle aside, and then he felt the pocket, hidden on the left, just where the bride's hip curved out from the waist. He pushed his fingers inside and found what they'd been searching for, there beneath the folds, cold and hard and waiting.

The watch was not nearly as large as he had expected it to be, but it was heavy, resting in the center of his palm, a precious thing from another century. He ran his thumb over the winding key and the intricate carving of a deer on the cover before he pushed on the knob and the clamshell flipped open, revealing a face set with luminous numbers and four smaller dials, including a flyback chronograph, a calendar indicating the day and month and a window displaying the phases of the moon. Hawley pressed the crown for a second time and the gold lid split in two. This was the feature he'd been told to look for—the rotating sky chart hidden within the lid, set with hundreds of tiny stars and constellations—yellow diamonds and sapphires of the brightest, darkest blue. Hawley wound the key and lifted the watch to his ear. The gears connected. The heart of the machine began to whir.

"Was it there?" the woman asked.

"Yes." Hawley closed the shell. He slipped the piece into his front pocket. "Here's what's going to happen," he said. "I'm going to get my friend and we're going to leave. Then your husband's going to take you to the hospital."

"All right," she said. But Hawley could tell she didn't believe him.

"I'm sorry about your dress," he said.

"I just want to lie down."

"I don't think that's a good idea." Hawley was afraid she'd bleed out. "Talbot," he shouted. "You still there?"

"Yeah," the old man answered.

"Here comes your wife."

The woman tried to stand, then fell back on the floor.

Hawley bent next to her. "Hold on to me," he said, and together they got off the ground, his good arm at her waist, his bad arm holding the gun. They stood on the drawings. She clutched the veil in one hand and with the other hand she kept the pot holder pressed to her throat. Hawley half-carried her down the hall, his shoulder streaming with pain, the wood slippery under their feet.

She began to mumble, her breath close to his ear.

"You want something?" Hawley asked.

"The letter," she said. Her voice was so soft it could have been a secret, it could have been the name of someone she loved.

"Maureen?" Talbot called, but she was too weak to say anything else, too weak to walk, too weak, Hawley could see, to make it to the hospital.

"I'm going to open the door now," said Hawley, "and you're going to take her and put her in the car and then you're going to drive her to the doctor." He put his hand on the doorknob. "Deal?"

"Deal." Talbot's voice sounded like it was coming from the other side of the keyhole. Close enough to shoot point-blank. Hawley positioned himself behind the woman. He switched the revolver back to his good arm, then he unlocked the door.

Talbot looked the same as he did on the coffee mug: like he was from another time; like that watch could have belonged to him when it was brand-new. He was wearing a fisherman's vest, with all of the extra pockets and zippers. But his hair was wild and gray and thick with curls, the sideburns stretching along the edge of his chin and nearly touching. He was as tall as Hawley and strong, despite his age. One of those tough guys who thickened with muscle as he got older.

Talbot's eyes grew wide as he caught sight of his bloodied wife. Hawley was afraid the old man was having a stroke—but Talbot rushed forward and took the woman in his arms and started shaking her instead. Shaking her like she was choking and he was trying to dislodge a bone that had caught, until the pot holder fell to the porch and exposed the gaping wound, and a stream of blood splattered across the floor. The old man still had his rifle. His hands clutched the barrel as tightly as they clutched his wife.

"Give me the gun."

"If my wife dies I'm going to kill you," said Talbot. "I'm going to hunt you out of your fucking hole and rip your guts out."

Hawley bent down slowly and picked up the pot holder with his bad hand, keeping the .45 pointed at Talbot. It hurt to use his fingers but he lifted the cloth and passed it over. Talbot exchanged his rifle for the pot holder without another word, pressing the thick quilted square against his wife's neck. The woman looked worse than ever; with each passing moment her violet eye became more like the clouded eye, unfocused and turning. And then she coughed out a stream of blood all over Talbot's fishing vest.

Together they managed the woman across the lawn and over to the pickup truck. Talbot cranked open the giant red doors. Hawley lifted her and Talbot climbed in and laid her across the backseat, then he hurried around and started scrambling into the front. Hawley held the door open a moment longer and took in the wife's swollen nose, her milky eye searching the sky behind him. She was still holding the veil.

"She wants that letter you wrote," said Hawley. "The one in the dress."

"It's gone," said Talbot. "I threw it out."

"Then tell her what it said. Tell her while you're driving," said Hawley, and he slammed the door shut on them both. Talbot revved the engine and tore down the road, spitting gravel and dust, and it was only then that Hawley thought of the stolen car they'd left blocking the road. He waited. He waited some more. Then he heard the crash and crunch of metal and the sound of the Talbots' monstrous truck pushing past the gate.

Back inside the house the carpet was soaked with water. Hawley made his way down the hall, then opened the door to the bathroom. Jove was right where he'd left him, the bathtub full to the brim and overflowing across the tile floor. It looked like Jove was sleeping. His head was tilted back against the lip of the porcelain and his face was covered with tiny white blisters.

Hawley closed the tub faucet. Then he walked over to the toilet, lifted the back lid, reached into the rusted water and stopped it from running. The high-pitched squeal of the pipes eased off and then there was silence. Hawley went to the kitchen, his boots squishing along the carpet, took down the whiskey and drank straight from the bottle, until his nerves started to settle again. Then he went back to the bathroom, checked his shoulder, cleaned out the wound with some hydrogen peroxide and packed it with bandages and tape. He found a bottle of expired Percocet and took two and washed them down with the whiskey. Then he shook Jove.

The man opened his eyes. He took the pills from Hawley's hand and tossed them down his throat. "You got it?"

"Yeah," said Hawley.

"Let me see it."

Hawley reached into his pocket and took out the watch. He pushed the key and showed him the hidden star chart. Jove blinked and leaned in close. He lifted one of his arms out of the cold water and stroked the diamonds with his burnt red finger.

"Hard to believe it's worth so much."

They took Talbot's rifle and their own guns and the whiskey and the cooler of salmon between them and started down the driveway. Jove limped along in some dry clothes taken from the closet, while Hawley tried not to move his shoulder, wrapped up in a wool coat to hide the blood.

When they reached the gate it was just as Hawley had suspected— Talbot had driven right through, ramming their tiny car into a gulley with his truck. The side was crushed in, the axle twisted.

"I think I'm going to need another Percocet," said Jove.

Hawley handed the bottle over. Then he opened one of the broken doors and rummaged for the map they'd used to get there. When he shut the door again, what was left of the window spiderwebbed and shattered onto the ground.

"Now what?" Jove asked.

"The boat," said Hawley.

They hustled back to the house, then cut through the trees and down into the ravine, traveling through another carpet of bright-green ferns. Hawley's legs were heavy. It was getting hard to catch his breath. He found a path and they followed it to the water. There was a ladder and then an old aluminum ramp leading to the beach. The ramp was steep and rattled as they climbed down. Jove went first, sending the plastic cooler of salmon sliding ahead like a giant block of ice. It shot along the ramp and tumbled over the edge to the beach, tossing the fish onto the sand. Hawley felt dizzy and nearly fell, too, catching himself with the rail. His shoulder pulled and it was like knives shooting across his back.

Down on the beach the whole shoreline was full of wreckage— piled with branches and driftwood and enormous, twisted roots that had spent years in salted water. Fallen pine trees lined the base of the cliffs, jumbled together like the giant whitewashed bones of mythical beasts. Hawley climbed over the trunks until he found Talbot's boat, a dinghy with an outboard motor. It was barely big enough for two people, but it would have to do.

Jove picked up the fish from where they'd fallen in the sand, washed them in the water and lovingly placed them back in the cooler while Hawley finished the last of the whiskey. Between that and the Percocet, the pain in his shoulder was manageable, as long as he didn't move too much. Hawley glanced up at the cliffs and told Jove to hurry. If Talbot's wife was dead it wouldn't take long for Talbot to return, and the old man could pick them off from the top of the cliff if he had a rifle with the proper range.

Hawley reached into his pocket. The watch was warm from his body and heavy against his palm. He looked closer at the etching of the deer. The animal was running. There was an arrow in its side, and one of its horns was broken. Hawley brought the watch to his ear. It was still ticking from when he'd wound it earlier. A beating pulse in an ancient tomb. He heard a gear click into place and then the watch began to chime.

It was more than a simple marking of the hour. The watch was playing a song. Sweet and melancholy, with the tone of a windup music box, as if a miniature orchestra made of tiny bells had been waiting for this exact moment to perform for him. It made Hawley remember something Jove had been saying at the bar, before the bikers knocked him off his stool and tried to take his wallet. *Complications*. That's what they were called. Features of these one-of-a-kind pocket watches that went beyond the telling of time—playing music or charting the stars or marking the tide or the weather. The higher the number of complications, the higher the price of the watch. The one in his hand was supposed to be worth eleven million.

"Debussy," said Jove.

"What?" said Hawley.

"That's the music that it plays."

Hawley ran his thumb over the deer again.

"Don't get any ideas."

"I'm not," said Hawley.

"Good," said Jove. "Because King would send somebody even worse after us."

He limped over and put the cooler into the boat.

"Just so you know," he said, "I can't swim."

"I thought you grew up on the Hudson."

"No one swims there. It's polluted."

"Well," said Hawley, "I can't swim, either."

Together they slid the dinghy across the crush of dark stones toward the water. It made a terrible noise, like the bottom was being torn out. The men set the guns in the bow and then Jove climbed in and Hawley pushed them out into the open water with his good arm. When they were deep enough he climbed over the stern and lowered the motor. Then he grabbed the starter and pulled and pulled, each movement a shot of fire down his side, until the engine turned, the rumbling noise of metal and gas connecting and echoing off the cliff. The blades began to spin and then they were moving forward, away from the beach. Hawley tried to clear some distance from shore, then steered them to the right, wondering how far the property ran, imagining Talbot chasing alongside.

A series of waves came in from the channel, hit starboard and set them rocking. Jove gripped the sides of the boat with his blistered hands. "I thought your father was a fisherman."

"He was," said Hawley.

"Then why the hell didn't he teach you to swim?"

"He didn't know how, either."

"Jesus, doesn't anybody do their jobs right anymore?"

Hawley didn't tell Jove the reason his father had never learned to swim. It was so he would drown quickly if his boat went down in a storm. So he wouldn't flail and suffer for hours alone in the sea.

The dinghy hit the rolling wake of a container ship, the bow rising and falling hard. Hawley kept his eye on Mount Rainier. The snow held the shape of the mountain like a blanket covering a body. Hawley pointed the boat directly into the waves. He felt dizzy again, and couldn't tell if it was from the whiskey or the drugs or the bullet that had passed through him.

In the distance there were ferryboats crossing, frothing up a giant trail of white through the harbor, and at last the weight of the job began to lift from Hawley's shoulders. He glanced behind them at the cliff. It seemed far away. Far enough that Talbot couldn't hit them, even if he was up there with a rifle. Even if his wife was dead. There was no way the old man could make the shot.

As soon as he thought this, a spray blasted, hissing not thirty feet away. Hawley immediately ducked down, thinking it was Talbot after all. Then the boat began to pitch and Jove started making a noise in the back of his throat, like he was going to be sick. Hawley checked for blood but Jove wasn't hit. He was staring over the port side, at a widening plane of flatness among the waves. And from this open place, the whale appeared—rising like a dark and crusted slice of doom, only ten feet away from the boat. The creature slid along the hull, five times the length of their dinghy from bow to stern, its snout covered in barnacles and parasites.

It was a gray whale, the kind Jove had spotted from the ferry that morning. Fifty feet of blubber and muscle and skin the color of storm clouds. With all his might Hawley leaned into the tiller, spinning the boat away. But the whale turned and followed, its giant mouth opening wider, like a black hole sucking in all of the ocean.

Hawley reached for the cooler. Jove shouted and grabbed the handle with his ruined fingers but Hawley shook him off and threw the salmon overboard as an offering, their silvery skins landing with a smack before sinking under their own dead weight.

The creature was not distracted. It ignored the fish and passed underneath the dinghy, then bumped into the hull. Both men were sent sprawling. The motor choked, flooded with water, sputtered for a moment and died. Hawley gripped the rail, trying to steady the balance. He crawled to the stern and yanked the starter, but the engine refused to catch. Without power the tiny boat floundered. Waves crashed over the bow.

The tide around them swelled in broad circles, then slid sideways as if it were being pulled down a drain. A low rumbling began, a subterraneous hum, and the whale emerged once more, blasting air and raining a flood of brackish wash down on the men like a fountain. The creature hovered on the surface beside the boat, an expanse of scarred and unforgiving rock, its snout like the head of a sunken galleon. And then the whale bashed the dinghy again, nearly upending it, and another rush of cold water poured across Hawley's legs.

Jove got to his knees and started bailing. Everywhere there was water, and Hawley lunged for the handgun. Then he got to his feet, aimed as best he could and pulled the trigger. The shots echoed off the cliffs, loud as fireworks. For a moment Hawley could sense each bullet as it left the chamber, as it traveled through the air, as it penetrated the whale's dark skin and tunneled through flesh, slowed and then came to a stop, nestled in some hidden corner of the leviathan's body, a token to be carried until the end of days.

He squeezed the trigger over and over, until all the bullets were gone and there was nothing but the sound of the ocean and the click of an empty barrel. Blood colored the water. Another spray rose high over their heads and rained down upon them with a roar. Hawley watched the spouts on the animal's back, swelling with air. They sealed tight, like two lids over a single eye, and the whale sank beneath the waves.

Jove clutched the bailer, breathing hard. "Where'd it go?"

"I can't tell," said Hawley.

The men waited. The boat rocked.

A distant tone came from the cliffs overhead. A burst of air, a hiss. Hawley turned, trying to place the sound, then saw the cut of the whale's back in the distance. He said nothing, only pointed, and the men watched as the whale dove, the long, dark slick of its back sliding along the waves and then the bend of its spine and then the scarred tail rising high in the air like a pair of beckoning hands before vanishing beneath the surface.

Hawley's shoulder was raw, his clothes soaked to the bone. He thought of the holes in the whale's back, the way they opened and closed together, and it was like he could feel the same opening and closing in his own chest, and then the plug, and the sinking. He dropped the gun. He sat down in the flooded boat.

"Hell of a thing," said Jove. His face was streaked with salt water, the burns like shadows carved into skin. He picked up the bailer again and began to scoop and pour, scoop and pour, returning ocean to ocean.

"I'm finished," Hawley said, "with all of this."

It felt good to say it, even if it wasn't true. Hawley peeled back his coat and checked the hole in his shoulder. The bandages he'd used were wet and covered with blood but they had not fallen apart. Not yet. He turned to the engine. He tried to get it started again. He checked the vents, switched to neutral, opened the choke, looked for a sign. Hawley wrapped his fingers around the starter and pulled. He listened for the catch. He pulled again. And the motor roared to life.

Firebird

Principal Gunderson's office smelled like fish and watermelon. The brine wafted up from his old gray desk, as if it had been made from pieces of driftwood dragged in from the beach and the drawers filled with day-old scrod, while the candy he was eating produced a synthetic, fruity cloud that hovered in the center of the room. He rolled this candy in his mouth, from one cheek to the other. He offered the bowl of candy to Loo.

"We're here to talk about your future," he said.

Loo plucked one of the cellophane-wrapped squares but she did not open it. She pressed it in the palm of her hand until she felt the sugar begin to melt and soften at the edges. She tried to breathe through her mouth instead of her nose.

"What about it."

"College." Principal Gunderson cleared his throat. "Or maybe a trade school?"

"I haven't graduated yet."

Principal Gunderson set the bowl of candy back on the desk. "Your best grades are in science. But you've missed the last four classes, and if you don't make up the work, you *won't* graduate."

"I've been sick." Loo had no intention of returning to biology. Whenever she approached the lab door her hands would start to sweat and she would end up hiding in the library. She'd felt powerful when she broke Marshall Hicks's finger, but kissing him had made her insides shaky and vulnerable. Avoiding embarrassment now seemed more important than getting an A.

Principal Gunderson shuffled some papers to show that he did not believe her. "Your teacher wants to fail you. But I convinced her to let you write a paper instead. On condition."

"Of what?" Loo asked.

"Of you working. For me. At the Sawtooth. As long as you control your temper," Principal Gunderson said, "you'll be starting this Saturday at four."

Loo could think of a hundred things she would rather do.

"I'll have to ask my father."

Gunderson released a soft bubble of air. "He already knows."

"What?"

"It was his idea, actually."

Loo squeezed the candy in her hand harder. She knew Hawley was mad at her for sneaking out and going to Dogtown. But she had not been expecting anything like this.

Principal Gunderson opened a drawer and took out a clean, folded apron. He slid the apron across the desk, and at once it revealed itself to be the source of the fishy odor. Even then Loo knew that nothing would ever wash out the scent of scales and guts. Its stink seemed to be woven directly into the cloth.

"Your mother was always reckless with her life. I hope you won't be."

Loo stared at the balding, middle-aged man sitting behind the desk. It was hard to believe that Lily and Principal Gunderson had ever breathed the same air.

When she got home Loo did her best to change her father's mind.

She tried arguing and promises and even slammed the door to her room but Hawley would not budge.

"If you're old enough to go out partying you're old enough to have a job," he said. "And I still want you there on the mudflats every weekend, helping me bring in the clams."

Loo shoved her hands into her front pockets. She wondered what Hawley would think if he knew that she had her mother's gloves hidden there.

She felt fierce, holding this secret that her father did not know. Loo found herself savoring the details, sliding the lace over her fingers, and poring over the album that Mabel Ridge had given her late at night. The pages were pasted with clippings about Lily's death. A short notice from a police blotter about a missing woman. A few articles about the Forest Service helping search the lake for her body. Others about her being found. A prayer card with an excerpt from the Book of Wisdom. Then Lily's obituary from the local paper in Olympus. An accident, they all said. A terrible, tragic accident. At night Loo read the pages over and over, until the phrases floated through her mind like lyrics from a song. *Young mother, morning swim, dragnet, search and rescue, loving husband and infant daughter left behind.*

Hawley had become more agitated since the night Loo went missing. He paced the house, checking the locks, then got into his truck and disappeared for hours. He even smelled different, his sweat taking on a more acrid tone, the stench of it filling up the laundry basket. He drove Loo to school. He drove her home. And he cleaned his guns more furiously than ever. He seemed to sense that something had changed, but she didn't want to tell him about Mabel Ridge yet, so she kept the book hidden from him, just like the gloves she was fingering now in her pocket.

"I get it," Loo said. "You're teaching me a lesson."

"Supporting yourself isn't a lesson. It's reality."

"You don't work for anyone. You don't have a real job."

Hawley grabbed the stinking apron off the table and threw it at her.

"You," he said. "You're my job."

. . .

AT THE SAWTOOTH LOO SPENT her time cleaning and setting the tables, answering every *ding-ding* of the chefs, holding plates with the side of her hand, the crook of her arm, the edge of her shoulder, filling and refilling glasses of water, washing dishes in a body-length rubber apron, hauling ice from the cellar and helping drunken captains tie their motorboats at the dock outside. She learned to wipe the corners of plates before picking them up, and to carry them by the edges; she learned to wash wineglasses with burning-hot water, not soap; she learned to never ask the chef if he could do a special order unless he had smoked a joint within the past hour; she learned to carry bouillabaisse by itself, or risk spilling it all over the customers; she learned to sidestep "accidental" butt grabs and boob brushes, ignore lustful, drunken stares and smile away propositions by men old enough to be her grandfather; and she learned to curb the hate that flushed through her veins and made her want to slam plates of food into customers' faces, slam the waitresses into the walls, slam the hand of the sous-chef who had tweaked her nipple—*a joke, a joke*—over and over in the freezer door until his fingers were cut in two.

The Sawtooth was owned by the entire Gunderson family, including Principal Gunderson, whose father had passed down the establishment to his six sons. Hawley provided the clams and mussels, but the fish and lobsters and crabs served were all caught by the Gunderson brothers—who would drag their catch in the back door still alive and take turns bashing it with a club. Then they would go home to their families. But Principal Gunderson had no family. His wife had left him for an Outward Bound instructor, and so he acted as general manager for the Sawtooth, opening the restaurant each morning and then returning after school for the night shift. On weekends he sat in a corner booth and drank coffee and did the books.

Food runners and bar-backs got tipped out by the waitstaff. At the end of the night, when the final customers were persuaded to leave, and Principal Gunderson rang through credit cards, and everyone from the back of the house and the front of the house was sitting exhausted at the bar, covered with food and the smell of food, fingernails thick with oil and grease, smoking and drinking too much to be driving, Loo waited for the waitresses to count their money and decide how much they would give her. It was supposed to be ten percent. More, if she'd helped them out especially. Usually Loo got tipped her proper share. Unless Mary Titus was working.

The fishing widow looked the same as she had bleeding in Loo's bathtub, small and childlike but her face lined with middle age, her body slick with patchouli oil and covered in beaded jewelry, a hippie skirt around her waist and a tank top with no bra and the same dark tufts of hair poking from beneath her armpits. On the day Loo started as a food runner, Mary Titus went straight to Principal Gunderson, then returned carrying a fistful of forks. She said, "You've got him fooled, but not me." Then she walked over to the coffee station, where the other waitresses were gathered, and showed off the stitches in the back of her head.

"Mary says you tried to kill her," said Agnes, the tallest of the waitresses, after Loo had refilled her breadbasket. The hair on top of her head was dyed pink and the sides were orange. A metal stud pierced her lower lip.

"It was an accident," said Loo.

Agnes ate one of the shrimp on her surf and turf. She smelled of Vaseline and paint thinner. "That's what my boyfriend said. Now I'm pregnant again."

"Boy or girl?" Loo asked.

Agnes clicked the metal stud in her lip against her teeth.

"Neither," she said.

Loo went back to folding napkins. She kept her head down and did her work while Agnes ate half the food she served and Mary Titus swooped in like a magpie, snatching any tips left behind on the tables. At the end of the night Principal Gunderson cashed everyone out and Loo left the Sawtooth with a roll of bills in her pocket. Her own money. It almost made her forget the smell of the apron, the frying oil she couldn't get out of her hair and how bone-tired she felt at the end of her shift. It almost made her forget that the job had been her father's idea.

When Loo got home she emptied her winnings onto her bed, a sea of fives and tens and ones, and then she counted and stacked, counted and stacked, and hid the money in a manila envelope in her underwear drawer, until the next morning at breakfast, when Hawley tossed the envelope onto her lap.

"You need to get better at hiding things. Top drawers are the first place that anyone would look."

"You think someone's going to rob us?"

Hawley pulled on the rubber boots he wore to go clamming. Then he took the .45 out of the breadbox and tucked it into the back of his pants. "Not today."

Loo snatched up the envelope, and when she hid it again, she sealed the money in a plastic baggie and slipped it behind the insulation in the attic. Later, after Hawley had picked up his tools and driven off to dig some soft shells in Ipswich, she removed a twenty from the envelope for gas, put on her sneakers and jogged fifteen blocks to where she'd parked the Firebird.

Loo had not returned Mabel Ridge's car, though the first few times she got into the Firebird it was her intention to do so. The day after the party she had traveled to Dogtown, then went right past Mabel Ridge's house and down Route 127, a twisty road that hugged the rocky shore from Olympus all the way to Beverly, going faster and faster until her hair caught in her mouth, the danger of being caught filling her chest as she sat behind the wheel.

Now she unlocked the car with the key and turned the ignition. She needed time to think. After filling the tank, she took a left and went to the farthest point of Olympus, where the road turned from asphalt to dirt and then to sand and rocks until it simply stopped in a maze of thorns and blackberry bushes.

Loo parked and climbed out onto the beach. The waves roared and crashed against the shore and sent torrents of white spray in the air that landed with a loud clap into the tidal pools. She rolled her pants up to her thighs and scaled a sloping boulder slippery with lichen. The farther she went out, the wilder the ocean became. She could see the currents and whirlpools and the waves fighting against the undertow. She picked up a stone, flat and porous with flecks of mica that shimmered in the sunlight, hooked it with her thumb and sent it skipping along the surface, then watched as it was sucked down into the ocean.

Hiding an envelope of cash was one thing. Hiding a car was something else. If she couldn't come up with a safe place to stash the Firebird, she'd have to return it to Mabel Ridge. But the thought of losing the freedom that flooded her body each time she slid behind the wheel made her want to run someone over with the car instead.

Loo covered her face with her hands. Made a mask like her father had taught her, blocked out the world and listened. Over and over the waves hit with a boom and then receded, sucking and pulling at the shore. It sounded like trees caught in a storm. Like an animal being slowly ripped apart. Loo spread her fingers, expecting her vision to focus. A direction to become clear. But instead she saw a splash. Something tossing in the water, thirty or forty feet from shore.

At first Loo thought it was a bit of wreckage. Then a head rose to the surface. Through the tunnel of her fingers Loo recognized the face, the one she knew only from the bathroom and the newspaper clippings she pored over each night. So many times she'd imagined Lily's death, and now here it was before her. Black hair spread in the water. Eyes as green as the sea. A hand rose from the depths and waved at her.

Loo dropped the mask but the figure in the water remained. A tumbling in the eddy. The tide yanked the body under, and with a roar of foam, spit a tangle of legs and arms into the shallows. Only now it was no longer her mother.

It was Marshall Hicks.

"Are you all right?" Loo called down to him.

Marshall coughed and choked and sputtered, clothes plastered to skin, salt leaking from his nose, shoes digging ruts as he clawed away from the water. The boy shook his head in response before collapsing onto a mountain of kelp. He pressed his face into the rubbery leaves.

Loo scanned the horizon, then climbed down to where the boy was struggling. "Did you fall off a boat?" she asked, though Marshall was not wearing the right clothes for fishing. He was dressed as if he were going to church. His shirt buttoned to the collar. His leather shoes tied tight. A tie caught around his neck like a piece of rope. He turned and looked up at her. He touched her foot.

He said, "Your knees are dirty."

Her knees *were* dirty, but it was only sand, stuck to her skin from kneeling on the wet beach. Marshall's eyes traveled above the two dark circles to the pale skin of her thighs. For a moment he looked like he was still underwater, still being tossed in the roar of foam and salt water. Then Loo's hands came down and brushed her knees, and the sand sprinkled across his face like sugar.

As she helped him over the beach, she remembered the beery taste of his lips, the sensation of him pressed against her in the dark of Dogtown. She had not spoken to him since the party in the woods. But she had seen him across the cafeteria, and once in the stairwell, and a few times when she'd peered through the window of the biology lab, wondering how this boy had managed to make her afraid again. Now she settled him into the Firebird, wondering if he remembered their kiss, too, but the only thing that Marshall seemed concerned about was his mother's petition. He'd been sitting on the jetty, drawing in his notebook, when a rogue wave came and washed the clipboard into the sea.

"You went in after it?"

"The water didn't look that deep, but when I got in I couldn't get out." There was a piece of brown seaweed caught around Marshall's belt. His button-down shirt was so soaked it had become translucent, the color of his skin pressing through where the cloth touched his elbows.

Loo wrapped her fingers around the steering wheel. It was the first time she had driven with a passenger in the Firebird, and it changed things: the adventure suddenly magnified, the feel of the clutch, the grip of the wheels.

Loo glanced at the boy's wing tips. "You didn't even take off your shoes."

"It was the only copy," Marshall said. "All the names we've collected so far. I was supposed to be out knocking on doors." He looked down at his pants. "I'm getting your seat all wet." There was something pinched about Marshall's face. His eyes were bloodshot and bleary, and there were lines fanning out between his eyebrows, as if he'd spent the past two months getting ten years older.

"Don't take me home," he said.

"All right," said Loo, but she didn't know where else to take him. So she brought him to her house instead.

Loo BOILED WATER FOR COFFEE and gave Marshall a towel and some of her father's clothes. They were ill-fitting, and when he stepped out of the bathroom, clutching his bundle of soggy belongings, he looked like a kid, the sleeves too long, his clavicle bare. On his feet were a pair of Loo's own socks. They were orange and blue; she could see a hole in one of the toes.

"Who's the woman on the walls?" he asked.

"That's my mother," said Loo, and instantly regretted it. She'd felt concern for Marshall down on the beach, but now it seemed wrong to have him walking around in her father's clothes. She wasn't sure why she'd let him into the house. He was looking too closely at everything, stripping her life to the bone. His eyes rested on each object with an eager curiosity—the chair, the bookcase, the picture hanging on the wall—noticing everything in the room but Loo's uneasiness.

"Nice rug."

"We've had it forever."

Marshall bent down and stroked the head of the bear. "He looks pissed."

"My dad calls it our guard dog." When they had lived on the road, sleeping in the truck, Hawley would wrap the skin around her like a blanket, and she'd wake up to the bear's glass eyes staring into her own.

The boy took a step back, as if Hawley's name might bring the bear to life again. Then he seemed to collect himself, and walked into the kitchen and sat at the small wooden table in Loo's regular spot, like a customer ready to be served. And Loo was used to serving, and so she poured some coffee, then took Marshall's clothes and threw them in the dryer. She sat down in Hawley's chair. She could feel the boy's eyes watching her, and a prickly sensation started along the back of her neck, as if her body had been dug up from the cold, wet sand and turned out into the glare of the sun.

"You look like your mother."

"Only when I'm being good."

It took a moment for Marshall to realize she was not joking. Then he said, "You must always be good."

Loo spun her mug on the table, round and round her father's watermark.

"Do you want me to leave?" Marshall asked.

"No," Loo said. "Just don't talk about her."

"All right," said Marshall. But Loo could tell now that was all he could think of, the woman with the dark hair and green eyes and the bathroom with its bits of paper and photographs and old buttons and dried flowers. She looked over at Marshall's shoes, which she had set on the windowsill to dry.

"You always wear wing tips when you go to the beach?"

"My mom makes me wear a tie when we go canvassing. I knock on the Republican doors, she knocks on the Democrats'." There was a bowl of shells in the middle of the kitchen table. Mussels and lady's slippers and a few small conch that Loo had collected over the years. Marshall chose a lady's slipper and began to turn it over in his fingers, the shell lined with purple, the inside thick as cream.

"You don't know what it's like," said Marshall. "People don't even try to be polite. They just slam the door in your face."

"Like me."

"Like you," said Marshall. "Like everybody. I'd rather be drawing, or out on the water, but it's important to my mom."

Loo pressed her fingers around the mug. Although she didn't like Mary Titus, she was still curious about her, in the way that she was curious about all mothers. On the street, at the beach or in the supermarket she watched them change diapers, wipe mouths, fix hair, tie shoes, apply suntan lotion, break up fights and endure tantrums, sometimes fussing with kisses and hugs and sometimes cursing at or hitting their children or ignoring them completely. Even in their neglect, these women seemed powerful.

"What will she do? When she finds out you lost the signatures?"

"I don't know." Marshall put the shell back in the bowl. "When I was little we'd go around protesting with my stepfather. But after he left, my mom stopped caring. She got really depressed. For a while she even checked herself into an institution. I had to go live with my aunt. Then *Whale Heroes* happened and my stepfather was on TV, and my mom got so mad that she snapped out of it. She started working on the petition. She said she wanted to make her own mark on the world."

"What about your real dad?"

"What about him?"

"She told me he was a fisherman."

"He died when I was little," said Marshall.

"Do you remember him?"

"Sure," said Marshall, glancing over at the bathroom. "But knowing them doesn't always make it better."

"What do you mean?"

"I don't think he wanted a family. I mean, he loved my mom. But mostly I just remember him making excuses to leave us."

Marshall's eyes floated down to Loo's star chart, set underneath the sugar bowl as a coaster. "Is that a planisphere?"

Loo nodded.

The boy picked up the wheel, and Loo watched him spin the dial to the correct day and month. She still remembered the first time she'd used it, watching a meteor shower from the balcony of a roadside motel. The chart in her hands. The desert an orchestra of light over her head. Some of the meteors were thin white lines shooting through the blackness, others were giant, shimmering blazes that flashed straight down to the horizon. She remembered feeling an overwhelming sense of alignment. As if holding something that had belonged to her mother allowed Loo to reach through time. *Something is making this happen*, she'd thought. *The whole world is alive and moving and I was meant to be here doing exactly this.*

Marshall lifted the planisphere to the window. Small pinpricks of sun shone through the plastic and onto the kitchen table. Loo touched his arm, her hand resting for a moment on the fabric of her father's shirt, a navy-blue plaid she had washed without thinking for years but now noticed was the same color as Marshall's eyes. A loose thread was hanging from the end of the sleeve, and she reached for it, thinking, *This is right, this is right*, pulling until the string came loose in her hand, separating from the shirt.

Marshall leaned closer. Loo felt his breath on her cheek. Saw his lips open. Then his eyes fixed on something behind her shoulder and he stopped. He lifted the arm she'd been tugging at, and pointed at the kitchen counter, where a .357 Magnum was resting between the bread-box and a bowl full of fruit.

He said, "Is that real?"

"Oh," said Loo. "Yes. You want to see it?" She went over to the counter and picked up the revolver. She checked to see if it was loaded, then set it in front of Marshall. The boy stared at the .357 for a moment, then picked it up, weighing the metal in his hands.

"Heavy."

"They always are."

Marshall turned and stared at her. "This is yours?"

Loo shook her head. "I use a rifle." She crossed the living room and opened the chest in the corner and took out the M14. She kept the gun pointed down as she went back to Marshall, then laid it gingerly on the table. The wood glowed from years of polish, the trigger hung loose. Loo ran her fingers down the side. "That's my grandfather's name, on the barrel. He used this in the war. These marks on the side—that's how many men he killed."

She pointed to the fifteen notches carved near the handle. Loo had grown up with guns in the kitchen, guns in the bathroom, guns in the car, but this one was special. When her father picked it up, the rifle was practically an extension of himself. It was the oldest gun in his collection, the one he had carried through the past he would not speak of. The rifle was the most impressive thing in the house, the best she had to offer.

"You want to try it out?"

"I've never shot a gun before," said Marshall. "The only weapons I've ever used were on my stepfather's boat, trying to slow down a whaler. And those were just stink bombs and prop foulers."

The rifle stretched across the table between them. Loo watched the boy watching the gun.

"I could teach you," she said.

Marshall ran his fingers over the kill marks the same way he had touched the lady's slipper. Then he pulled his hand away.

"I don't know."

"Come on." Loo returned to the chest, slipped a few magazines and a box of ammo into the pocket of her shorts and headed for the door. Marshall stayed at the table. But when she turned at the entryway and looked back at him, he left the table and followed, as if she were a magnet drawing him away from his better judgment.

She gave Marshall a pair of her father's boots and they headed into the ravine behind the house. The light was filtering through the leaves, creating layers upon layers of green. Once they were fifty yards in, it got darker, and the temperature dropped. Loo led Marshall down a steep slope toward the sound of moving water until they reached the gully that Hawley used for target practice.

"Here." Loo handed Marshall the rifle. Then she took the box of ammo from her pocket and started loading one of the magazines. Marshall held the rifle as if he were waiting for it to go off, even though the safety was on and it was not loaded.

"What's wrong?"

His neck flushed.

"Are you scared?"

"No," he said.

Loo paused over the mag, a bullet in the palm of her hand. She did not say anything in return, only motioned for him to give the rifle back. Marshall passed it over, his face anxious. Loo wondered if she had made a mistake by bringing him here, but the clip was already loaded. The safety flipped. The handle of the rifle pressed high and tight to her shoulder. The sight was there to guide her as she tilted her head slightly, lifted the barrel a fraction of an inch, took in a breath and let half of it out. She squeezed the trigger.

And there was the boom.

The sound was so loud it pushed everything out of Loo's mind— like an eraser wiping all her thoughts clean. For a brief moment she was nothing but a person in a place and there was no past and there was no future, only this single moment where her life flashed open—and she was awake and she was alive and she was real. Then the boom began to fade until it was only an echo, and she was her old self again, the memory of the previous moment nothing but a powdery smell in the air, like a match lit and quickly blown out.

Loo pointed at the mark she'd made in the distance, the bark exploded from the mossy base of a tree and scattered across the forest floor. She passed over the rifle. "The trick is to hit the same spot." She put her hands on Marshall's shoulders and stood behind him, positioning his body like a marionette's—legs, hips, shoulders, fingers. She pushed until the wood was nestled into the crook of his arm.

"That's going to kick," she said. "Most of the power's going out with the bullet, but some of it gets sent back into your body."

"Kinetic energy," said Marshall.

"See?" Loo said. "You're going to do fine."

Marshall kept perfectly still while she leaned her head toward him, until her cheek nearly touched the length of the barrel. "Look," she said, and he bent his head so that it was next to hers. She could smell his hair, damp and earthy, like long grass after the rain.

"The bullet won't travel in a straight line," said Loo. "It gets pulled down. So you should always aim a tiny bit higher. You're shaking," she said. "Stop shaking."

"Sorry."

"It's instinct. You're afraid of what's coming. But that's the best part." She wrapped her arms around him. "Take a breath," she said. She heard Marshall inhale deeply, and she opened her lungs and took the air with him. Between the raised metal sights, there was the mark she had already made. She slid her hand through the trigger guard, then pressed down on top of his broken finger. The whole world was waiting.

"Now," she said.

Bullet Number Four

THE DINER WAS RIGHT OFF THE HIGHWAY, JUST LIKE JOVE HAD PROMISED. In the parking lot there was a sign with the name in lights and a cartoon drawing of a giant hairy pig with tusks, munching on a slice of blueberry pie. The place was old-fashioned—a railroad diner, booths along one side and a long counter edged with chrome, a door with a bell and a big neon clock set near the ceiling. There was one waitress on duty and a cook behind the kitchen window, frying some bacon and sometimes stepping out to work the cash register. It was between the breakfast shift and the lunch shift and the place was nearly empty, just Hawley and a couple of old truckers drinking coffee in one of the corner booths, taking their time before getting back on the road.

Hawley took a seat at the counter and ordered some eggs. He'd just finished a string of jobs in Florida—two that went well and one in Gainesville that went bad—and now he was making his way back up the Eastern Seaboard in a stolen car. He'd made it as far as North Carolina, but the southern heat still had him sweating. Once this favor for Jove was finished Hawley didn't have a plan, but his gut told him to keep going north, maybe all the way to Nova Scotia. He'd never been there before but he'd seen pictures. He'd started having dreams of cold water and rocky shores.

At long last he was going to meet Ed King, Jove's old friend from prison. Since King got out he'd been handling security for a few high-end gangsters and running deals, collecting lost merchandise. As cover he owned a boxing gym and occasionally fixed fights on the side, banking on the gloves he'd worn himself back in the day. King had had a reputation for punching opponents so hard in the head that it sheared the nerves from one side of the brain to the other. The men who'd fought King would have to relearn things—how to walk, how to talk, who their wives were. Finally he had killed a guy in a bar and had been sent to jail for manslaughter. That's where he'd met Jove. Hawley had never been to prison but he knew that men who did their time together were like soldiers who served in the army—bound for life, even if they didn't like each other that much.

Jove was in jail again now, doing two years for possession of a stolen firearm. He'd been picked up right after delivering Talbot's watch, running through a red light in downtown Seattle. It was Jove's fault for not being careful but Hawley still felt bad about it. So when he got the message through Jove's lawyer, telling him where to find the key to a safe-deposit box and asking him to make the drop at the diner, Hawley wrote back a postcard saying he'd take care of it. This was a big bet, nearly all the savings Jove had, on a fight Ed King was calling. Enough to finally get that sailboat on the Hudson if it came through, and it would come through—it was a sure thing. Jove encouraged Hawley to put money in, too, but Hawley bet only on games where he was holding the cards.

The cook put the eggs and toast in the kitchen window. The waitress picked up the food and slid the plate in front of Hawley. She gave him silverware and a napkin and brought a mug and filled it with coffee.

"You want milk and sugar?" she asked.

"I'm sweet . . ."

Hawley remembered saying the same words to Talbot's wife, and before he knew it, he was thinking about her milky eye. He still felt sorry about her, and he still worried sometimes about Talbot tracking him down. But nearly a year had passed and he'd stopped looking over his shoulder.

He'd meant for things to be different after the job on Whidbey, after the whale had left them and they got the engine started and made it back to Seattle. But once they tied the dinghy up at the dock and delivered the watch and got their payment and parted ways at the train station, Hawley bought his ticket as planned and went on to Oklahoma for the next job. It was easier to fall back on what he knew than try to change, even though he understood things weren't right anymore. At night he had strange dreams, and Maureen Talbot snuck into his thoughts, holding a metal pitcher suspended over his cup of coffee and asking him if he needed milk or sugar.

". . . I'll take it black."

The waitress put the pitcher down and went back to wiping the tables and Hawley started in on the eggs. He hoped King would show up soon. He wanted to get on the road again and it was nearly 11 A.M. The neon clock shone like a beacon, the second hand running smoothly from one number to the next.

The door opened, chiming the bell, and a girl walked into the diner. She was in her twenties, with dark hair and a narrow waist and a pair of hips that she nearly had to turn sideways to fit through the entryway. She was wearing a black dress and heels and gloves that came to her wrist and a small hat with a sprig of black veil that fell across her eyes. She walked through the diner, swinging one hip and then the other, and then she slid those same hips over the edge of a stool by the counter, right next to Hawley.

The girl took off her gloves and unpinned her hat and set it beside her purse. Her hair was a mess of tangles; it made her look like she'd just gotten out of bed. Hawley had to force his eyes back to his plate so he'd stop imagining it: her long hair tossed over a pillow and her naked back and that pair of beautiful peach hips slung sideways underneath a clean white sheet.

The waitress was outside smoking. The cook stuck his head through the kitchen window and asked the girl what she'd like to eat. She ordered a hamburger and a glass of water and the cook said it would be right up. While she waited, the girl read the menu and then she kicked off her high heels and started spinning around and around on the stool. Hawley tried not to watch but he couldn't help it. Each time she turned, her knees nearly touched him and then he shifted a little and they hit.

"I'm sorry," she said. But she didn't look sorry at all. And she didn't stop spinning.

"You're going to lose your lunch."

"Haven't had it yet," said the girl, and started turning in the opposite direction. She pushed off with her toes and spun in a circle, smooth as a carousel.

"I love these seats," she said. "I love that no one can move them."

He'd never really thought about it before, but Hawley had to admit there was something nice about the bright-red stools, all bolted in place and lining the chrome edge of the counter.

"Where you headed?" he asked.

"Oh," said the girl, "I'm not going anywhere."

"You live here, then?"

"Nope," she said. "Guess again."

"I'm not so good at guessing." Hawley moved the duffel bag with all of his things and the smaller satchel with Jove's money in it, shoving it between his stool and the counter. He took a sip of coffee and another bite of eggs. There were mirrors angled in the corners of the diner, one over the kitchen window and another at each end, so the waitress could keep an eye on the tables and the door when her back was turned. Most diners were set up this way. It's why he liked eating in them. That and he could sit alone at the counter and no one would think it was strange.

The cook brought out the girl's hamburger and the water and she stopped spinning. The cook was an old guy, wrinkles all the way up his forehead. He wore an apron and a hairnet, even though he didn't have any hair. He set out some mustard and ketchup and then he went back to the kitchen. After a minute he stuck his head through the window and asked the girl if the food was okay and the girl said it was more than okay, it was great. She was a careful eater, cutting the burger into fourths and picking up a corner at a time to chew, taking slow sips of water in between.

"There's supposed to be a meteor shower tonight," she said.

"That so?" Hawley said. He picked up his coffee, but didn't drink it. "I saw one out in Wyoming one time."

"Was it a Geminid?"

"I don't know what you'd call it. They were just shooting stars."

"Showers are named after their radiants. That's the constellation they fall from. But they're not really stars, just debris left over from comets going around the sun. Space garbage." She poured some salt onto one of her French fries and ate it. Then she poured some salt onto another and ate that, too. She kept the shaker in her hand, going through the whole plate, one fry at a time. "Tonight's called the Perseids, because the meteors look like they're coming from Perseus. He's the one who killed the Gorgon. The hero."

"How do you know all that?"

"I heard it on the radio," said the girl. "Plus, I have this." She held out her foot and showed him a spray of tiny stars tattooed around her ankle.

Conversations like this usually made Hawley feel backed into a corner, but the girl had him curious. He thought about the stars getting needled into the skin of her leg. He thought about lifting that same leg and resting it on his shoulder and kissing those stars. And he thought about the meteors he'd seen out West. For bits of garbage, they'd shone awful bright.

The waitress came in from her smoke break and took the coffeepot and brought it over to the truckers and filled their mugs. Then she started cleaning the counter.

"You got milkshakes?" the girl asked her.

"Sure," said the waitress.

The girl gave a big smile. "I'd like one, if it's not too much trouble."

"Harry," the waitress called. "Milkshake."

The old cook's face popped up in the window. "What kind?"

"Chocolate," the girl said.

"Sure," said the cook and he disappeared again.

"You finished?" the waitress asked Hawley.

He was but he wanted to watch the girl drink her milkshake. "I'll have some more coffee."

The waitress took away his plate and filled his mug to the brim. They all listened to the blender going and then the cook set up a tall metal canister and a small glass in the kitchen window and the waitress put them in front of the girl, along with a straw with the paper still on. Then the waitress moved to the other end of the diner and started wiping down a pile of plastic menus.

The girl poured some of the shake into the glass. She opened the straw and stuck it into the metal canister, started drinking and pushed the glass over to Hawley.

"No thanks," he said.

"Shakes have to be shared," she said. "It's a rule."

"All right," said Hawley. He couldn't remember the last time he'd had ice cream. The milkshake was cold and slid down the back of his throat, a great creamy dollop.

"You've got one more chance," the girl said.

"I said I'm no good at guessing."

"Then I'll tell you." She took a long sip, her cheeks sucked in, her lips tight around the straw. Then she slid her hand off the icy metal cup, leaned close and touched the tip of his elbow with her frosty fingers. "I'm going to rob this place."

Hawley checked the mirrors first, the corners, then over the kitchen window. The waitress was still cleaning the menus, the truckers still talking loudly in the corner, the cook nowhere to be seen. He glanced down at the duffel bag and Jove's satchel, safely tucked between his stool and the counter. Then he turned and caught the tail end of the girl's breath, coated with milk and ice cream.

"You're kidding," he said.

The girl laughed and let go of his arm and Hawley took another drink from the glass, tasting the chocolate syrup. He wiped his mouth with the back of his hand.

"You believed me," she said.

"Nope."

"You did."

The truckers all got up at once then and moved over to the cash register to pay their bills. They'd asked for separate checks, so it took the waitress a while to ring them up. She counted out the change while the men tipped her. Then the truckers straightened their hats and said their goodbyes and hit the bathroom and strolled out of the diner and climbed up into their cabs and started their semis and eighteen-wheelers and drove them out of the parking lot. All the while Hawley blushed and the girl kept smiling.

"That was the best milkshake I've ever had," she said. "I think I'd like another."

"We've got strawberry," said the waitress.

"Fantastic," said the girl.

The cook fired up the blender again. The waitress looked the girl over. "You coming from a party or something?" she asked.

"No," said the girl. "A funeral."

"I'm sorry," said the waitress.

"It's all right," said the girl. "I didn't really know him."

The cook finished the shake and rang the bell. The waitress collected the glass and the metal canister from the window and put both in front of the girl with two straws this time. Then she gathered the sugar dispensers from the tables and started refilling them in the corner.

The girl opened both straws. She put one in the canister, one in the glass. She poured part of the milkshake and slid it over to Hawley.

"That's okay," he said. "I'm full."

"I told you, it's a rule." She took a sip. "Real strawberries. I wasn't expecting real strawberries." Then she put her head down on the counter and closed her eyes. She was wearing lipstick and it had worn away in the middle from eating her hamburger and sucking on the straw, but the edges were still bright.

"Who was it that died?" Hawley asked.

"My father." She kept her head on the counter, her eyes closed. "I didn't know where to go after the funeral. It was either this or a bar."

"Need a drink?"

"Yes," the girl said. "And no. I've been sober for a year. So it's only milkshakes for me."

Hawley kicked his bag aside, so there was more room between them. He could feel the bottle of whiskey he had there roll underneath his foot. "You never met your father?"

"He left when I was a kid. But he used to send me singing telegrams for my birthday each year. He never forgot. It made my mom so mad. I used to think I'd get along better with him. I even ran away a few times, trying to find him. And now I have his truck. A giant snow truck, with a plow and emergency lights and everything."

Hawley didn't know what to say. His own father had died of a stroke when he was fifteen. Since then Hawley had been on his own, and now he was the same age his father had been when he was born. Thirty. It didn't seem young and it didn't seem old, exactly, but it was half a life gone, at least.

Hawley took a long sip from the glass. The girl was right—the cook had used real strawberries. The seeds were there, at the back of his tongue, tangy and fresh and full of flavor. It was as if he'd stepped into a garden, brushed aside the spiders and found a perfect berry, unspoiled and ripened by the sun.

"A snowplow could make a good getaway car," he said, "if you still wanted to rob the place."

The girl opened her eyes. For a moment Hawley thought she was going to start crying, but instead she laughed. It sounded like a baby laughing. She lifted her head from the counter and wiped her eyes and then she put her hand on his elbow again. Her fingers were warm this time. "Thanks," she said.

And Hawley knew that he had said just the right thing. It was a good feeling, to know that he had. Soon they would get off these stools and never see each other again but for now they sat in a quiet that held just the two of them and sipped their milkshakes. Then the bell over the door rang and Ed King walked into the diner.

He was wearing a shiny, oversize dark-brown suit. His hair was shaved close to his head and he had a nose that hung from his face like a door off its hinges. The man was older than Hawley, close to Jove's age. But he still carried himself like a boxer.

"You Sam Hawley?"

"That's right."

King came and stood next to him at the counter. They shook hands and Hawley could feel the strength in the man's arm. All the time King was staring at the girl, the corner of his eyelid twitching. "Looks like you already ate."

Hawley realized that if he introduced them he might find out the girl's name. But he didn't want her to know Ed King. He didn't want her to see the kind of people he ran with, or to find out any of the rotten things he'd done. Hawley picked up the duffel bag and Jove's satchel and motioned to the waitress that he was moving to one of the booths.

"Nice talking with you," the girl said.

"Sure," said Hawley.

They took one of the booths in the corner. Hawley sat with his back to the girl so he wouldn't be tempted to look at her. He focused on King's broken nose. He checked the mirrors, nudged the money with his foot, took a swig of water to clear the sweetness out of his throat. The waitress came over and brought a menu.

"Got any specials?" King asked.

"The pork. We roast our own every day out back. And the pie. We've got eight different kinds." Ed King ordered a pulled-pork stew and a cup of coffee and a slice of pie.

"What kind of pie you want?" the waitress asked.

"Bring me what's fresh."

"All our pies are fresh."

"Then bring them all."

After the waitress left them, Ed King took the satchel from Hawley and placed it on the seat next to him in the booth. He opened the top and slipped his hand inside and moved it back and forth like he was testing bathwater. "Everything here?"

"What he told me."

King closed the bag. The waitress returned with the bowl of stewed pork and the coffee. She brought over a napkin and a teaspoon and a soup spoon and some milk and sugar and left it all on the table. King turned the sugar upside down over his coffee. The canister was glass with a metal spout in the middle and the sugar fell from it in a rush.

"How's Jove?"

"He's okay," said Hawley. "Can't wait to get out."

King put down the sugar and took a gulp of coffee. It made Hawley's teeth ache just to watch. "Wish he could watch the fight."

"Maybe he can," said Hawley.

"Dayroom at that prison's only open until six. And lights out at ten. I did eighteen months there myself, back in the day." King started in on the pork stew. Every few bites, he'd glance over Hawley's shoulder. Hawley could tell King was looking at the girl. He wished now that he had taken the other seat.

The men discussed Jove's chances for parole and then King started talking about the fight, how he'd trained one of the boxers and how the other owed him money. Hawley nodded but all the while the rest of him was listening for the girl. He heard the slurp of the straw as she reached the bottom of the milkshake. The click of her purse opening. The sound of paper as the waitress slid the check across the counter. The cash register ringing and shooting out its drawer. A scuffling as the girl slipped her feet back into her high heels. And then a small *ting* of a pin falling, and Hawley knew she was clipping the small black hat onto her head again and after that she would be gone.

The waitress came over to the booth carrying a giant plate with eight slices of pie. There was blueberry, cherry, pineapple, peach, key lime, pecan, chocolate pudding and banana cream. Each piece had a dollop of whipped cream on top. "There you go," she said as she put down a fork and another napkin. But Ed King wasn't looking at the pie. He was staring across the diner and his eye was twitching like crazy.

"Hey," he called out. "Didn't I just see you at Gus's funeral?"

Hawley spun around. The girl was about to leave, the door already open, the black hat perched on top of her head like a little animal. Hawley felt his guts stir, a thrill mixed with dread as she let go of the handle and the glass door softly closed. She blinked twice before answering. "I'm Gus's daughter."

"I knew it," said King. "All this time I've been trying to place you. But the hat was missing."

The girl walked over to their table. "That's a lot of pie," she said.

"Have some with us," said King.

The girl stood there for a moment, making up her mind. She glanced at Hawley and smiled. "All right."

Hawley slid over and she sat down next to him in the booth, holding the purse in her lap. She was close, her hips spreading across the seat. King called for more forks and the waitress brought two. Then she went outside for another cigarette. Hawley was already full from the milkshakes but the girl picked up a fork and took the point off the banana cream.

"I'm sorry about Gus," said King.

"It's all right," said the girl. She glanced at Hawley. "How do you two know each other?"

"This lug works for me sometimes."

"Really." The girl licked the edge of her fork. "Are you from around here or did you know my dad from Phoenix?"

"I know him from New York," said King. "It's a funny story, but I don't think you'll want to hear it."

"You can tell me," she said.

"All right, I will. But I wish I had a drink. I'm usually drinking when I tell this story and it comes out better that way." He scratched his nose. "I met Gus placing a trifecta at Aqueduct. After that he helped me with a couple of jobs. He was a real little guy and he was nearly always short on cash, because he spent all his time at the track. I liked him because he drank harder than anyone I ever saw and he was never sorry about it. It's funny he didn't say anything about having a daughter. And you're pretty. You'd think he would have been proud to have a daughter like you.

"When he was drunk it was like he was a different person, and he used to do crazy things for money. If someone said, 'I bet you won't punch that guy,' he'd go up to a bouncer and punch him. Or if we said, 'I bet you won't toss your wallet,' he'd give his credit cards away to strangers. He'd pitch all his clothes off a balcony, or throw his keys down a sewer grate. Everyone would be laughing and he'd say, 'Sober Gus is going to love this!' Then I'd see him the next day, his face all busted up, trying to cancel the cards, or on his hands and knees in front of a sewer grate by the side of the road, with a hook at the end of a string and he'd say, 'Drunk Gus did this to me.'

"A few months back when he was Sober Gus he asked me for a loan, to help him cover a debt. So I gave it to him, but Drunk Gus put the money on a horse instead and lost. When I went to collect, Sober Gus cried, and I kept thinking of him crouched over that sewer grate, all pathetic, fishing for his keys, so I told him I'd give him more time. And you know what Drunk Gus did? He went to my gym that same night and busted the safe and stole my deposit for the week. He drove to Atlantic City and spent every bit of the dough, and then he up and died there, owing me, owing everybody. So that's how I know him."

The girl put down her fork.

"You didn't have to tell her that," said Hawley.

"I did," said King. "Now she knows all about her old man."

The pie fillings were starting to run together, the colors mixing on the plate. Hawley could feel heat coming off the girl beside him.

"Why did you go to the funeral?" she asked.

"Because he owed me five thousand dollars."

"It's not so much," said Hawley. But he knew that it wasn't about the money. What bothered King was that the guy had turned on him.

"It's plenty."

The girl wrinkled her nose. "I haven't got that kind of money. I don't know if any of this is true."

King stabbed a piece of pie with his fork. He put it in his mouth. "Believe it."

The bullet hole in Hawley's back began to ache, the first one he got in the Adirondacks, and as soon as it did, his mind started taking inventory—his father's M14 rifle and extra ammunition in the duffel by his feet, a loaded Smith & Wesson revolver tucked into his belt. Hawley's body was ready, every muscle tight.

The girl slid out of the booth. She had taken her gloves out of her purse, and she held them crushed between her fingers. She was shaken but she still thought she could just leave. "Thank you for the pie."

Fast as lightning, King threw out one of his boxer's arms and caught her around the wrist. It made Hawley jump to see him do it.

"Let go of me." The girl struggled against him. She was looking for the waitress.

"Sit down," said King.

The girl opened her fingers and the gloves floated to the table. She stopped fighting and King relaxed his grip, but he didn't let go. The little black hat had come unpinned; Hawley saw her eyes flashing underneath the veil. The girl acted like she was going to sit down again, but instead she bent forward and sank her teeth into King's wrist.

The man screamed and his fingers released. As soon as they did, the girl snatched her gloves and ran for the door. King scrambled out of the booth to go after her but Hawley got up and blocked the way.

"Just let her go," he said.

"Fucking hellcat!" The girl's teeth had gone right through the skin, and now King was bleeding on his baggy suit. Hawley listened to her heels running away and then the bell rang over the door.

"You don't need that money," said Hawley.

"This doesn't have anything to do with you."

"It does." He hadn't meant for the words to come out like that, but they did. And as they did, Hawley knew they were true. This knowing was different from before, when his body had sensed the bullets coming for him. It was more like the meteor shower he'd told the girl about, a trail of cold rock suddenly burning to life. He'd unlocked something, a possibility, and the entrance was here, in this thin aisle of space before him, between the booths and the counter and a row of spinning stools.

Ed King's eye was twitching, the nostrils of his broken nose wide open. He leaned back and then his fist flashed forward, as fast as when he grabbed the girl's arm. But Hawley had been waiting for it, and he dodged just enough for King to miss and topple over onto the table. The dishes went smashing onto the floor, pie tossed in every direction.

The cook stuck his head through the kitchen window. "What the hell is going on out there?"

It distracted Hawley just enough so that King's next punch connected, a strong blow to the chest and then another quick to the jaw, and before he knew it he was on the floor of the diner. King had the satchel and he was crossing over him and Hawley reached up and took hold of the man's legs and threw him to the ground and scrambled on top of him and then he started beating him with all of his might.

It was what he was meant for.

Hawley's body recognized every turn, like a well-worn path—the adrenaline, the heat of his shoulders working, the shifting of weight, the tumble of skin and hair, the blows to the ribs, the ache of breathing, the familiar sensation of his knuckles crunching, and it felt wonderful, the flood of it like some smooth, dark air flowing from a deep cavern. He grabbed the Smith & Wesson from the back of his pants and stuffed it into King's mouth.

The cook stepped out from the kitchen carrying a shotgun. He still had his hairnet on. "That's enough!" he shouted. "Drop it."

Hawley slowly removed the revolver from between King's teeth. He had been so close to killing that his fingers shook. It wasn't the way he'd meant to go and now he backed away from the edge, his heart beating and the blood roaring through his hands, even as he lifted them over his head. The cook walked around the counter, keeping the shotgun level, and backed over to the entrance. He cracked it open.

"Barbara! Get in here!"

The waitress came in, smelling of cigarettes. Her eyes went wide as she took in the mess. "Jesus Christ!" she said.

"Call the police," said the cook.

"You don't have to do that," said Hawley. "Nobody's hurt."

"You were going to murder that guy," said the cook. He made Hawley give him the revolver. Then he sent the waitress over to the pay phone by the bathrooms to call the police. She didn't have any change and had to take it out of the cash register.

Hawley stood up, slivers of pain shooting from his knuckles to his wrists. At his feet King groaned and rolled to his side. There was pie all over the floor. Peaches and pineapple and blueberries and whipped cream were smeared across King's suit. His hanging door-nose now swung in the opposite direction. Hawley kept his eyes on the cook. His nerves ached. He took a step closer to the duffel bag.

The waitress hung up the phone. "They're coming," she said, and went to stand behind the counter. The cook remained in the aisle between the counter and the tables, the shotgun poised.

"I don't want any trouble," said Hawley, "but I'm going to leave now. I'm going to walk out real slow. I won't bother anybody."

"You'll stay and talk to the police," said the cook.

"Sorry," said Hawley. "I can't do that." He checked the mirrors, gave one quick glance at the parking lot. Then he reached down and picked up the duffel bag and the satchel with Jove's money and took a step toward the old man.

"Stay where you are," said the cook.

"I'm going to walk past you," said Hawley, "and then I'll be gone. You'll never see me again. All I want is to go through that door." He moved down the aisle. He could smell something burning on the stove. The neon clock was flickering overhead, the light bouncing off the edges of the chrome. It was so quiet he could hear the buzzing current that moved the hands of the clock, sweeping the thin black line past the numbers.

The cook did not lower the gun, but he backed into one of the booths and let Hawley pass. And as soon as he did, it was as if Hawley had entered a dream. Like he'd done all of this already in another life, and knew the cook was going to let him go because he had already let him go, long before. Hawley had never felt so certain, so clear of what would happen next. He reached for the handle. The bell rang as he pulled the door open. He could feel the sun warming the pavement outside, smell the gasoline, taste the exhaust of the highway, and beneath all of this he could hear a whirring. There was a grove of pine trees behind the diner, the entrance to a clutch of woods that traveled up a rocky ridge and then spread out across the hills into the distance. He had not noticed the trees on his way in but now they seemed to be hissing directly for him, the needles combing the wind. And then he heard something else. Hawley turned a fraction of an inch, just enough to see Ed King's fist coming toward him.

The blow was the kind the boxer was known for, the kind that split men's minds in two. Hawley could feel parts of himself pulling away from each other. Dividing the man he was from what he might be. *I was almost there*, he thought. *I almost made it.* And then there was an explosion of shimmering noise, and the world closed in like he was falling backward into water, the light far above the surface moving out of reach, and then darkness swept forth and extinguished the rest.

When Hawley came to, he was just inside the entrance to the diner. The glass door was smashed where he'd fallen against it. He shifted and felt all the tiny glimmering pieces roll off his chest. There was a pounding in his head and blood dripping from his ear. Somewhere behind him King was shouting at the cook. Hawley didn't know how long he'd been out. He looked up through the broken door at the bright-blue sky. The wind had picked up and the clouds were passing quickly.

Hawley tried to stand. His vision spun, so he concentrated on the line of seats by the counter—red seats fixed in place and still. Over by the cash register, King and the cook were wrestling over the shotgun. The old man tried to keep the boxer off but King bent quickly and jabbed him in the guts. The shotgun went off and blasted a hole through one of the windows, sending more glass across the diner tables and a spray of shot that hit Hawley in the thigh as he turned away.

The waitress screamed and dropped behind the counter. With one hand King wrenched the gun from the old man, spun it around and cracked him on the side of the head with the barrel. Hawley's leg burned. He pressed his fingers against the wound. It was birdshot but it was bleeding badly. He could hear the waitress sobbing. The old man groaned on the floor. The hairnet had slipped off. King leaned against the counter, breathing heavily, his suit covered in blood and eight different kinds of pie, his tongue moving inside his mouth like he'd tasted something sour. He turned the gun back around and pumped the handle. The empty shell flipped out of the chamber, hit the floor and rolled across the diner toward Hawley.

Flashing lights—red and blue—flooded the windows. Then a siren started up outside. King cursed and lowered the gun and crouched behind a booth. Hawley got to his hands and knees, his head still spinning, the glass crackling beneath his palms. The car he'd stolen in South Carolina was parked on the far side of the lot—there was no way he was going to make it past the police. Still he tried to crawl out the door, dragging the duffel bag and the satchel behind him.

A truck pulled up in front of the entrance, emergency lights spinning, siren blaring, and a giant snowplow attached to the grille. The driver's side opened and the girl jumped out. Her feet were bare but she was wearing the same black dress and she still had the little hat pinned at the top of her head. She raced to Hawley and caught him under the arms and lifted him.

"Get up, asshole!" she said.

Hawley had to lean on her to get to the cab. She pressed her big hip against him. They moved quickly together across the lot and scrambled into the truck. Hawley glanced at the diner and saw King sighting the wheels from the window.

"He'll get your tires."

"They've got chains," said the girl.

The shot blasted the cab but didn't penetrate the metal. The girl threw the snow truck into gear and peeled out of the parking lot. Hawley turned to see King running after them. Then he tripped, the shotgun clattering out of his hands and into the street. The diner and its giant pig fell away into the distance. The girl turned off the siren. In three turns she had them on the highway and dropped the speed down. Two police cars sped by in the opposite direction, their lights going.

"I thought you'd left," said Hawley.

"I was waiting for you to come out. Then I saw that guy clock you. You looked like you were dead."

"I thought I was." Hawley's face was already starting to swell, his eye growing bigger by the minute. He watched her hands twist on the steering wheel, her bare foot circled by stars and pumping the clutch. "Why'd you wait for me?"

"I don't know." Her eyes checked the rearview, then the side mirrors, before glancing over at him. "You're bleeding."

"He shot me," said Hawley.

"Does it hurt?"

"Sure."

She put on her blinker and got in the right lane and took the next exit. They drove off the highway and entered a suburban neighborhood, with schools and churches and supermarkets, normal streets and normal houses and families. The girl took a right and then pulled over under a maple tree and parked.

"Let me see."

Hawley lifted his hand and a stream of blood washed over his jeans.

"You need to go to a hospital."

"I can't."

"Don't be ridiculous." She reached for his belt. She tugged hard on the buckle, shifting his hips. She yanked the leather free from his belt loops, then wrapped the belt around his leg and tightened it above the wound. The girl was half his size but she had a grip like iron and he was in a daze just from the feel of her fingers on his thigh. He looked down at the back of her head as she worked on him, the way her hair came to a point at the nape of her neck. He could still smell the hint of strawberries on her breath.

When she was finished her hands were covered in his blood. She wiped them on her skirt, leaving streaks across the black dress. Then she leaned back in her seat and looked at him hard.

"What's in those bags?" she asked.

Hawley felt like he was going to be sick. "Don't," he said.

Before he knew it, she had the duffel bag open and her hands were going through his life. She took out some of his clothes, his toothbrush and the newspaper he'd been reading. Then she found his father's rifle and the ammunition.

"I've got a license for that."

"Sure." She reached inside the bag again and wrapped her fingers around a jar of black licorice. She unscrewed the lid and pulled out a roll of bills. Hundreds layered together and held tight with rubber bands. She opened another jar and found the same. All the while her face stayed impassive, as if she saw that kind of money every day. Then she put the cash back and sealed the jars tight and returned them to the bag. She let out a sigh as she pulled the zipper closed. She'd kept a piece of candy, and now she slipped it into her mouth like a piece of black spaghetti.

"I've always liked licorice."

Hawley felt all his strength go out of him. Something must have shown on his face because she reached over and touched him underneath his jaw, searching for his pulse. She stroked his neck and then pressed down, and the new start he'd been looking for opened up before him. The girl had found it with the very tips of her fingers, a thread of life hidden all this time underneath Hawley's skin.

He watched her lips counting softly.

She let go.

Outside there were trees and sidewalks and picket fences. Inside the engine ticked. The girl reached over Hawley's shoulder, pulled the seatbelt across and buckled him in. She buckled herself in, too. She turned on the ignition. The truck rumbled and shook. "I'm going to take you to the hospital now. Okay?"

"Okay," said Hawley. Her eyes were green with flecks of gold. He tried to concentrate so he wouldn't forget.

She flipped the switch that started the lights. Flashes of color streaked down the length of the windows. She checked the mirrors and then she pulled onto the road.

"So let's decide now," she said.

"Decide what?" Hawley asked.

"What kind of accident this is. For the hospital. They might be looking for you, so we should cross the state line." Her hand went to the gearshift and she shifted, then shifted again. They drove for a few blocks in silence.

"What's your name?" Hawley asked.

"I don't know if I should tell you that. You're probably a criminal."

"Well," said Hawley, "now you're one, too."

"All right." She cleared her throat. "It's Lily."

"Lily," Hawley said, rolling the word in his mouth. "Lily."

"That's me," Lily said. Then she turned on the siren and all of the cars pulled over, and even the red lights turned green.

Weathervanes

Every Sunday Loo would pick Marshall up in the Firebird. She enjoyed waiting, parked down the street, knowing that he was just inside the white house on the corner, combing his hair, tying his shoes, brushing his teeth. It was like the world was holding on to something enormous, something secret and amazing, all while she sipped at her paper cup of Dunkin' Donuts coffee.

After graduation, they'd both convinced their parents they needed a year off before starting college. Marshall because he was planning on volunteering for Greenpeace, and Loo because she'd skipped a grade and was still only sixteen. Hawley was more than grateful for the delay, and was so proud when Loo walked across the stage in her cap and gown that he'd taken her picture and added it to the bathroom wall, taping it next to the photographs of her mother. With the help of Principal Gunderson, Loo had applied for an internship at the Museum of Science in Boston that would start the following January. In the meantime she was waitressing, and Marshall was collecting signatures for his mother's petition, and the rest of the summer months stretched before them with all kinds of possibility.

The front door opened and Marshall stepped out in his shirt and tie. Behind him was his mother, wrapped in a Sawtooth apron. Loo had asked Principal Gunderson to schedule them on opposite days. This week Mary Titus was on the lunch shift and Loo had worked until midnight, hefting trays and buckets of ice. Agnes was six months along now, and needed more help. She had started wearing thrift-shop muumuus and resting her feet in the walk-in cooler, so Loo had taken on some of her tables. In exchange, Agnes showed Loo how to apply liquid eyeliner, standing side by side in the Sawtooth's bathroom mirror, elbows braced to steady their hands. It was the same way that Loo's father had taught her to hold a gun.

"You look beautiful," said Agnes, flashing the stud in her lip.

The black lines made Loo's eyes seem different, although she was not sure they were beautiful. It was more like she was meeting a stranger who had stolen her face. This stranger talked back to the chefs, joked with the customers more easily and worked harder than Loo had ever worked before, the frenzy of the weekend crowd swirling like fireflies that she danced around and slid between and guided through to the end of the night. In the morning she felt tired down to her very bones, and only coffee and the prospect of seeing Marshall kept her awake.

From the car she watched Mary Titus hand over a stack of pamphlets and say something to her son, an urgent look on her face, then kiss Marshall's cheek and close the door. The boy hurried down the stairs, his wing tips slapping the sidewalk, his sketchbook hidden beneath the clipboard, his face breaking into a smile, bit by bit, as he got closer to the Firebird. Once he reached Loo he glanced back, to make sure his mother wasn't watching from the house, and then the car door opened and the car door shut and they were sealed inside together.

Loo handed Marshall the coffee she had bought for him. "Got the map?"

The boy dug into his coat pocket and shook the folded paper. "Phone book?"

She nodded at the backseat. Marshall grabbed the directory and flipped through the thin white pages. They had checked off each name as they added it, printing the addresses that were closest to each other, street by street. It had been Loo's idea to re-create the petition that had been lost. Marshall had figured the details, estimating the hours, the miles he would have walked, the doors opened, the possible names. Together they forged the signatures. Now it was like a project from biology lab, each of them contributing their part.

They drove to Dogtown, carefully taking side roads so they wouldn't pass by Mabel Ridge's house. Loo still wasn't ready to go back yet. She'd told Marshall about her grandmother, but had left out some of the details about the car (borrowed) and the lace gloves (stolen). Marshall had called the gloves sexy when she'd tugged them over her fingers to drive, and she didn't want to say they had belonged to her mother.

The woods had become their regular spot. A place where they were least likely to run into anyone they knew from school; a place where they could be alone together without feeling they were doing so on purpose; a place where there was always something to see and point to—bird nests or giant mushrooms, beaver dams or wild batches of ferns; a place that filled empty spaces with the sounds of the forest; a place with just enough dangerous history that they felt they were taking a risk each time they walked down the path and the trees closed in behind them.

They hiked Babson's boulders, from TRUTH to COURAGE to LOYALTY, all the way to Peter's Pulpit, which was one of the biggest erratics—with a wide, flat top and sheer sides—a giant, imperfect, sloping piece of glacial rock. There was only one way to climb up, a thin crack along the side, and a tiny ledge they had to scramble and boost each other over. Once they reached the top they were hidden from the trail. An island of stone floating above the leaves. Loo spread out a blanket and they ate the lunch she had packed: cheese sandwiches, a bag of pretzels, some Cokes, a sleeve of Oreo cookies and an apple that she cleaned on her jeans and cut into sections with her knife.

After lunch they took out the map and the phone book and started adding to the petition. Marshall called out street names and Loo ran her fingers down the pages until she found a match.

"Thank you, Mrs. Paula Hayden, for your support."

"The codfish thank you, too, John Pane."

"Can you hear them, Robert L. Kendrick?"

"Blub, blub, Miss Beam. Blub, blub."

Marshall wrote out the addresses in his slanted print, and then they took turns making signatures, first with their left hands, then with their right—loopy scrawls, single lines and careful curves—until their fingers began to cramp.

"Let's take a break," Marshall said. "Here. I brought you something."

He reached into his coat and pulled out a book, thick with photographs and charts of the solar system. A quote from Carl Sagan was on the back cover: *Somewhere, something incredible is waiting to be known.*

"Wow," said Loo. "Thanks."

"I thought it could go with your planisphere." He leaned over and turned the pages until they reached Neptune, a blue swirl of hydrogen, helium and ice. "Look at this." He traced his finger around the circle, showing the planet's orbit. "One year on Neptune is a hundred and sixty-five years here."

"It's hard to think about," said Loo. "Time moving so differently."

Marshall flipped the page. "This is called the perihelion. It's the point at which an orbiting body comes closest to the sun. For Neptune, it's two point seven-six billion miles."

Loo touched a point on the planet's trajectory. "It looks like it crosses paths with Pluto."

"Every two hundred and forty-eight years," said Marshall. "Then Pluto is actually closer to the sun. But they're on different orbital planes, so they'll never actually meet."

"How romantic."

"Yeah," said Marshall. "Anyway, I thought you might like it."

"I do," she said. And she did. There were chapters on black holes and the big bang and asteroids and comets and satellites and centaurs and moons. In the back there was a chart with each planet's mass and gravitational constant, with an equation to determine your own weight across the universe. Loo borrowed a sheet of paper and did the math while Marshall took out his sketchbook.

On Jupiter, Loo would weigh 283.6 pounds, while on Pluto she would weigh only 8. On Mercury she'd pull a respectable 45.3 but if she ventured to a white dwarf star, her body would balloon to 156 million pounds. Changing where you were could change how much you mattered. Loo stretched out her legs. Her muscles ached from waiting tables. The stone was hard beneath her body but also warm from the sun. She leaned back. She closed her eyes. It could have been a minute. It could have been an hour.

When she woke up, her body was stiff, her cheek pressing into the spine of her book. She could hear the fluttering of pamphlets, the scratch of pen against paper. Marshall was still drawing, but one of his hands was resting on her lower back. She turned her head toward him and his palm slid away.

"I was afraid you might roll off," he said.

"What are you drawing?"

He turned the notebook. Across the page was a spaceship. There were round hovercraft holes along the bottom releasing steam, two rusted-looking engines with flame propulsion attached to the side with metal bolts, a bubble windshield and a weathervane marking north, west, south and east.

"I wish I could draw like that," said Loo.

"My mom thinks I'm wasting my time." Marshall held the pen tightly between his thumb and forefinger, ink smudging his skin. Loo watched his hands connect straight line to straight line, a simple back-and-forth movement until the formula changed, his knuckles bending, fluid and sinuous.

"She's been trying to get me a spot on *Whale Heroes*. They're following the humpback migration now, and just filmed an episode out on Stellwagen Bank. It hasn't aired yet, but they brought in a bunch of local environmentalists and did a phone interview with my mom about the petition. She thinks if my stepfather puts me on the program, she'll get more publicity."

"You want to be on TV?"

"Not really," said Marshall. "My stepfather is kind of an asshole."

"Why'd she marry him, then?"

"She said she didn't want to be alone anymore." Marshall wiped his nose. "Didn't your dad ever have any girlfriends?"

"Nope."

"Maybe he did and you just didn't know about it."

Loo thought back to all the women who'd approached her father over the years—waitresses and teachers and librarians and checkout girls—and how Hawley always seemed to be backing away. "I don't think so."

Marshall looked at her, then back at his notebook. He took his eraser and rubbed at the page. "Maybe that's why he has so many guns."

"What's that supposed to mean?"

"He's making up for something."

"You don't know what you're talking about."

"My father did the same thing. Except it was fish instead of guns. He was always off on his boat. Then he drowned at the Banks, because he went out in a storm when he shouldn't have. My mom says it was because of the fish. But the guy just did whatever the hell he wanted. We got evicted from our apartment, and my mom was on tranquilizers for over a year. He never thought about what it would do to us."

The wind blew harder, and the pamphlets Marshall was supposed to be handing out began to fall over the edge. Loo and Marshall watched them go, the paper spiraling to the ground, then Marshall snatched the rest and stood. He wound up like he was throwing a baseball and pitched the whole bunch of them off the boulder. The pamphlets unfolded in the air, taking flight in the breeze. Some dropped onto the grass, some got caught in the branches of a maple tree and some blew across Dogtown and were eventually shredded by birds and chipmunks and squirrels and groundhogs and used to line burrows and nests.

Marshall was breathing hard, his body blocking the sun.

"Finish the picture," Loo said.

"I'm out of paper."

Loo put her head back down on her folded arms. She pulled her T-shirt up so that her lower back was uncovered. The space just above the belt of her jeans. The place Marshall had his hand before. "You can draw on me," she said and then she closed her eyes. She did not want to see his face if it was saying no.

A flock of geese passed overhead. She could hear them honking.

"What should I draw?" he asked.

"How about Neptune," she said. Every muscle in her body was now on alert. A chill spread across her skin. Loo realized this was what she had been thinking of since she woke up and felt his hand slip away. She'd been looking for a reason to make him touch her again.

The pen was like a needle being traced along her skin. Marshall started in the middle of her spine, hesitant but soon pressing harder, sliding carefully over each vertebra. The lines went up her back and then began to spread out, first in one direction and then in the other. He drew Neptune and Saturn and then the rest of the planets. He pushed up her sleeve for a cluster of stars, then pulled open the neck of her shirt to draw an asteroid. He crawled over, the weight of him brief against her legs, and then the pen began tracing the side of her ribs.

"Try not to breathe for a second," he said.

Loo pressed her forehead against the stone. There were flecks of mica and quartz embedded in the rock, catching the sun. She stared directly at these tiny points of light, until she felt her body start to come loose beneath his pen. An unsettling sense of vertigo flooded her mind, just as it did whenever she stretched out on her roof at night and stared at the stars for too long, her body spinning upward into the depths of a velvet sky, until up was no longer up and down was no longer down and she wasn't a single, tiny, insignificant being anymore but the entire earth, hurtling through space, tilting past comets and meteors and blocks of ice that fractured into crystals and left streaks behind in the darkness. Then this understanding began to slip away from her, and she fell back into herself, until she was nothing but a girl stretched out on a hunk of rock with a pen pushing against her ribs.

And then even the pen was gone.

Marshall shifted back onto his knees. He put a hand on either side of her waist, his fingertips below her shirt, his palms along the edge of her jeans. He bent down and started blowing, drying the ink. His breath came out in a stream, cool and direct, following her spine and then circling her skin, until the lines were set. She felt his lips hovering, and then they came together and kissed the base of her spine.

"I'm finished," Marshall said. Then he pulled her shirt down over the drawing.

By THE TIME THEY LEFT the woods the sky was turning dark. Loo eased the Firebird out of the parking lot and drove slowly past the edge of Dogtown. Her lips were swollen and her cheeks were scratched from the stubble on Marshall's face. She'd thought she'd known everything about him, so it was surprising that he even had stubble, or that his body could find so many ways to cover hers. All she had done on the rock was turn over, his kiss still warm on her back, and everything else had followed. Now they sat beside each other in the car grinning, as if they'd been caught for something they were not sorry for and would gladly do again.

Marshall had not taken his hands off her. As they climbed down from the rock, as they made their way through the forest, he kept touching her arm, her wrist, her neck, her waist, and then apologizing, and then touching her again. His hand was tucked underneath her leg now, his thumb pressing the outer seam of her jeans.

"I don't even know your name," said Marshall. "I mean your real name."

"It's Louise."

"Really?" he said.

"My dad was the one who started calling me Loo. I think he wanted me to be a boy."

"Come on. Loo is nice."

"You're just saying that."

Marshall rolled down the passenger side window, and in an instant he had pulled his body halfway through, his feet on the seat, his butt on the sill, his upper body wrapped around the metal frame of the car. He knocked on the windshield. The car sped along and he started screaming her name.

"*Loooooooooooooooooooo!*"

He flattened his nose against the glass, his shirt flapping behind him like a flag. Then he crawled inside again, his hair wild, his face flushed red, and pressed the back of his cold fingers against her neck.

"You're crazy."

"You're pretty."

"I'm not," said Loo, though it thrilled her to hear someone say so.

Marshall tucked his shirt back into his pants. He tied his tie and pulled the knot close to his throat. And then his hand was sneaking back across the seat, tapping her belt, slipping around her waist. Loo had never felt so happy. And then she looked in the rearview mirror and saw the lights.

The police car had been following them for a block, maybe two. The siren wasn't on but the red-and-blues were flashing. Loo slowed and pulled to the right, hoping that the driver would go around, but instead the squad car stayed close, and when she came to a stop at the side of the road, it parked right behind the Firebird, high beams flooding the interior.

Loo rolled down the driver's side window, then slid her hands to the top of the wheel to 10 and 2. In the side mirror, she watched the policeman get out and slowly move alongside the Firebird, checking the backseat with a flashlight, a hand on his gun holster. He was close to her father's age, his hair cropped short and his uniform tight.

"License and registration." He was at the window now, peering in at them both. Loo leaned over and opened the glove compartment, hoping there would be something inside and there was, stained and torn and zipped inside a plastic baggie.

"I left my license at home," she said and handed the papers over. The cop looked at them, then turned the flashlight into Loo's eyes.

"You been drinking?"

"No, sir," said Loo.

"We were just fooling around," said Marshall.

"I wasn't talking to you," said the man.

Maybe I can cry, Loo thought. He might let us go if I cry.

The policeman told them to stay put and walked back to the squad car. Loo bit hard into the side of her cheek but instead of tears her mouth flooded with the taste of rust.

"Do you even have a license?" Marshall asked.

"No."

"Maybe it won't matter. Maybe he'll just give us a warning."

They sat together in silence, all the closeness that had wound between them seeping away. Marshall was no longer touching Loo. Instead he was pressed against the passenger side door, his fingers on the handle. Loo kept her eyes on the rearview mirror. After a few minutes she saw the cop come back along the car, stopping for a moment to double-check the license plate. He lifted his radio and said something into it. Then he took his gun out of the holster and pointed it at her.

"Step out of the vehicle."

In all of her years—with all of the weapons Hawley carried and hid around the house, the derringers and .48's and .35's and rifles— Loo had never had a gun pointed at her before. Bile rose in her throat. It was as if she'd been locked down into place on an amusement park ride that wouldn't stop spinning. The policeman's Glock was loaded. She imagined the boom it would make when he squeezed the trigger. The velocity of the bullets. She opened the door and stepped out of the car.

"You," the policeman said to Marshall. "Put your hands on the dashboard and keep them there. And you," he said to Loo. "Put your hands on the hood."

She turned her back and pressed her palms against the car. It was like watching a movie, like this was all happening to someone else, until the policeman put his gun back in its holster and began to run his hands along the length of her body, touching her back, the sides of her breasts, and each of her legs. Then he took hold of one of her arms and twisted it behind her and she felt the snap of the handcuff pulling tight around her wrist.

"I'm not drunk," she said, her voice shaking.

"Maybe not," the man said. "But this car is stolen." He took hold of her other arm and there she was, a criminal, and he was leading her back to the squad car. He put Loo in the backseat and slammed the door. She watched through the metal grate as he took Marshall out of the Firebird and went through the same process, patting the boy down and handcuffing him. Marshall was pushed in the back beside her and the policeman got into the driver's seat. He turned off the lights and then they were pulling away, leaving the Firebird behind on the side of the road.

"You've made a mistake," said Loo. "That's my grandmother's car. She knows I've got it."

"Then why'd she report it stolen?"

"I don't know."

"What's your grandmother's name?"

"Mabel Ridge."

"The registration says the car belongs to Lily Ridge."

Loo swallowed hard. "That's my mother."

"Then she can sort it out."

"My mother's dead."

"Sure she is." The policeman got on the radio and gave his location. When the reply came through it was loud and garbled with static, like someone moaning into a fan.

"It'll be all right," said Marshall. "I've been arrested before."

"You have?" Loo asked.

"For protesting. With my mom. We snuck on board a commercial trawler and slashed the nets."

The policeman rolled his eyes.

"My mother is *dead*," said Loo.

The policeman turned up the radio.

• • •

AT THE STATION THE LIEUTENANT on desk duty tried calling Mabel Ridge, but the phone just rang and rang. In the meantime the officers separated the teenagers, made Loo take a Breathalyzer, then put her in a small, tight room with no windows that smelled of greasy Italian sandwiches, with a bench and a chipped plastic folding table and wire mesh over a slot in the door. The walls were covered with water stains, and there was a metal air vent in the ceiling with a wad of old chewing gum pressed into the corner. Loo knew the police were trying to scare her. She knew that, and yet the room was so depressing, and no matter how hard she tried, she found that she *was* scared, just like they wanted her to be.

When Hawley arrived he was out of breath, as if he'd run all the way from their house. She expected him to yell but he wouldn't even look at her. He sat down on the bench and put some papers on the table. He asked for a pen, and the desk clerk who had brought him in handed over a ballpoint and Hawley thanked him. Then the clerk stepped into the hall for a moment and they were alone.

"Dad," Loo said.

"Don't say anything," said Hawley.

The policeman who had arrested her came into the room and propped the door open with a wedge. He sat on the table, the polished leather of his holster creaking, the Glock he had pointed at Loo snug beneath its strap.

"I'm Officer Temple." He shook Hawley's hand. "Have we met before?"

"I don't think so," said Hawley.

"Her boyfriend says he didn't know the car was stolen."

"She doesn't have a boyfriend," said Hawley.

"Whatever you say," said the man. "The boy's got a record. But your daughter was the one driving. It might be time for you to get a lawyer down here."

"All right," said Hawley.

But it wasn't right at all. It was never going to be all right.

Loo put her hand on her father's arm.

"Could we have a minute?"

The officer nodded, then kicked the wedge so it was set firmly under the door. "This locks from the outside. Just knock if it slides shut."

As soon as Officer Temple was down the hall, Hawley got up and snatched the wedge from the floor and put it in his pocket. The door closed slowly. The lock clicked. Hawley took the cap off of the pen. He was sweating, dark patches underneath both arms and a strip in the center of his T-shirt.

"After all I've taught you," he said.

"I'm sorry."

"You're supposed to think things through before you do them. You're supposed to be smart." He spread his fingers across the paper on the table and filled in their address, his phone, her name. "Maybe this is my fault. Maybe I've sheltered you too much," he said. "The world is a rotten place and you've got to find a way to be rotten if you're going to live in it. But you also have to be smart."

"I didn't steal that car," she said.

Hawley kept writing. "I told you not to open your goddamn mouth."

And so she didn't. She said nothing as her father filled out the rest of the form and then showed the police his license. She said nothing as they went through her bag—dumping her wallet and loose change, tissues and tampons onto the chipped plastic table. And she said nothing when Officer Temple came back into the room and said that he'd finally gotten through to Mabel Ridge, and that the old lady wasn't going to press any charges, that she only wanted the car back, and that they were free to go, once they paid a fine for Loo's joyride and promised to get her enrolled in driver's ed.

Hawley jumped up and shook the officer's hand. He thanked him for his help. He apologized for the trouble. He made Loo apologize, too, and she hated him, and she hated the policeman, who stood there with his dull smile as the words came out of her mouth.

She looked for Marshall as they left. The boy was nowhere in sight, but in the lobby she saw his mother. Mary Titus glanced up from her chair as they passed. The first expression that crossed her face was surprise, and in that moment Loo saw a flicker of the woman she had once been, before her first husband had died and her second husband had left her. Before she'd been evicted or institutionalized. Before she had even been Mary Titus. When she had just been a girl like Loo, doing the wrong thing at the wrong time, ashamed and sorry but also glowing from the thrill. And then the woman's eyes narrowed, and Loo was nothing but another nail struck into the coffin of her life.

"Hey!" she called.

The Sawtooth apron was still wrapped around her waist. She must have come straight from the restaurant, which meant that Principal Gunderson knew about Loo getting arrested, and so did Agnes, and all of the chefs and probably the busboys, too. Loo's cheeks flushed. She tried to walk around Mary Titus, but Hawley stopped.

"I want an apology," the widow said. "And a check for two hundred dollars."

"The charges got dropped," Hawley said. "They're both free to go."

"The apology is for involving my son in a felony. And the money is for my sanctuary." Mary Titus smelled the same way Loo did at the end of a shift—like a greasy order of fish and chips. She reached into her purse and pulled out one of her pamphlets. She handed it to Hawley. He looked it over and gave it back to her.

"People don't care about the future," said Hawley. "And fishermen need to earn a living today. You should leave this thing alone. You're only making enemies."

"Somebody has to save the world instead of just destroying it." Mary Titus squeezed up her tiny face. "One day, when all of the fish are gone in the North Atlantic, and you're eating expired tuna out of a can, you're going to remember this conversation."

Loo tried to pretend that nothing was wrong, stretching her mouth into a tight grin for the people waiting in the lobby, a vagrant handcuffed to a chair in the corner, and the desk sergeant eyeing them from behind the bulletproof glass. It was only a matter of time before Hawley lost his temper.

"Dad," she said. "Let's get out of here."

Then she turned and made for the exit. But before she got away Mary Titus grabbed hold of the back of Loo's shirt. The widow was fast and sure as she lifted the cloth in her tiny fist, revealing the solar system drawn across Loo's skin, her ribs lined with asteroids, the base of her spine circled by Mercury and Venus.

"Looks like my son's been doodling on your daughter. Maybe you'll care about *that*, Sam Hawley."

Hawley stared at the spray of stars on her skin. The comet that disappeared in a trail beneath her belt buckle. And the ripple that Loo had been waiting for shuddered along the length of his face. Loo yanked her shirt back down. She shoved the widow away from her. Mary Titus stumbled and fell against the vending machine.

And that's when Marshall came out of the bathroom.

"What are you doing?" he asked.

They all looked at one another. Then Hawley picked the boy up and threw him against the wall. Marshall came down hard on the edge of the water fountain and collapsed to the floor in a heap. Mary Titus screamed, and the policemen came scurrying out from behind their desks and everyone was separated again and eventually more sets of forms were produced that they all had to fill out. It was another forty minutes before they were finally released, and by then Hawley had cooled down and stepped back inside his shell, apologized for losing his temper, paid a fine for disturbing the peace and even paid Mary Titus the two hundred dollars. He took Loo's arm as they left, brought her to the truck, opened the passenger door and pushed her inside the same way Officer Temple had done only a few hours before.

"Can I talk now?" Loo asked.

Hawley did not answer her until he had walked around and climbed into the driver's side. He closed the door and gripped the wheel. "I can't believe that piece of shit had his hands on you."

"He's not a piece of shit."

"He told the police you stole the car. He would have walked for this and you would have gone to jail."

Loo did not care. She worried only that her father had scared Marshall away and that now he would never shout her name again or draw another universe across her back.

"I didn't—" she began. But Hawley cut her off.

"You're still a minor, but grand larceny means you'd go away for at least two years. And you weren't even careful. I mean, for God's sake, of all the people in the world, you had to rip off Mabel Ridge?"

"I didn't steal the car!" Loo shouted. "Besides, it's not even hers. It's Mom's."

The lights of the police station filtered through the windshield of the truck, casting Hawley's face in a bluish glow. For the first time, he looked at her.

"Are you sure?"

"The registration's in her name."

The muscles in her father's shoulders tightened. He turned his head and began scanning the building, the other cars, the fence. "Is it here?"

"No," said Loo. "We left it on 127."

Hawley gunned the engine. He stepped on the clutch and shifted. He said, "Show me where."

Loo directed him along the back routes. Her father flicked on the high beams, the truck springing forward along the twisted road. Oncoming traffic honked, but Hawley kept the brights full force as he slid to the edge of the driver's seat.

"We should have passed the car by now," she said.

"What kind was it?"

"A Firebird."

"Firebird." For a moment Hawley's gaze drifted. He shook his head.

"What is it?"

"Nothing. I just never thought your mother would own a Pontiac."

When they hit Beverly Farms, Hawley pulled off to the side of the road. In the glow of the hazard lights she could see him working his lip.

A moth fluttered through the open window and began throwing itself against the dashboard, the roof, the glimmer of the clock radio.

"It's gone," said Loo.

Hawley watched the moth, then threw out his fist and smashed it against the windshield. He wiped the wings off on his jeans. Then he signaled and spun the truck around. He shifted gears and leaned on the gas.

"It's not gone," he said.

It was after midnight and they were the only car on the road. All of the traffic lights had switched from red to a constant, blinking yellow. Hawley turned down a side street. They passed a self-locking storage unit, a garage with several tow trucks parked in front, a tire shop and a back lot full of vehicles, surrounded by a chain-link fence and topped with swirls of barbed wire. Hawley drove onto the shoulder, into the dark shadows and away from the streetlight that flooded the road. He turned off the truck. The engine ticked and then quieted.

"Where are we?" Loo asked.

"The impound lot."

Hawley got out of the truck and started rummaging through the back. He took a long thin metal rod, a screwdriver and a set of wire cutters from his tool chest. Then he unlocked the side compartment and grabbed his long-range rifle, a suppressor and a scope. He closed and locked the compartment and then he walked into the woods. Loo sat for a minute in the passenger seat, watching the place where he had disappeared.

"Shit," she said. "Shit. Shit. Shit." She spread her fingers across the dashboard and gripped it tightly, as if she had the power to rip the whole thing off. Then she got out of the truck.

Her father was only a few yards in, thirty feet from the outer edge of the fence. He had his rifle on his shoulder. He'd added the suppressor. He lowered the gun and handed it to Loo.

"Is it there?"

She set her eye against the scope. Through the crosshairs she could see maybe thirty cars behind the fence. Most were in some state of disrepair, windshields smashed in or back ends crumpled. An old Chevy was missing its hood entirely, the engine exposed. But at the far edge of the lot was a shiny black BMW, a truck with new rims, a small sports car with a custom cover pulled tight across its small body, and behind that—her mother's Firebird.

"In the corner."

Hawley took the rifle back and peered through the scope. "What do you know," he said. And then he just stayed there, watching the car, his mouth twitching.

"Okay," said Loo. "You've seen it."

Slowly, her father began to sweep the barrel of the gun toward the left, like he was tracking something.

"What are you looking for?" Loo said.

"Cameras."

"Cameras?"

"There," said Hawley, and he shot out the first one. A small black security box by the front gate. It was hanging in place and then it was shattered to pieces, nothing but wires and a bit of loose plastic. Hawley shifted, lined up the rifle close to his shoulder and pulled the trigger again. The gun shook in his arms and another camera, set on the roof of the garage, went down. Then another, mounted near the back door. Each shot left behind a muffled huff of displaced air from the suppressor that Loo could feel in her chest, like an underwater explosion.

"What you *doing*?"

"It's a Guard Rail system," said Hawley. "They come in sets of four." The rifle shuddered again and Loo saw a spark as the final camera, mounted on the fence, went down right over the tiny sports car. The black box bounced off the hood and crashed onto the asphalt.

Hawley lowered the rifle. He flicked the safety, then loosened the canvas strap and slung the gun over his shoulder. He picked up the shell casings from the ground and slipped them into his pocket, then grabbed the wire cutters and moved quickly toward the fence. Loo followed, pushing past bushes and stumbling through vines. By the time she reached the fence he had already started clipping through.

"Let's go," she said. "Let's go before somebody comes."

"Do you think I'd cut this fence if anyone was here?" said Hawley. Then he was rolling back the chain link as if it were the entrance to a teepee. When he was on the other side, he held the wire for her, and Loo got to her hands and knees and crawled through.

They crossed the parking lot, exposed under the floodlights. Loo kept her eyes on the darkened windows of the auto-body shop, waiting for a lamp to flick on, an alarm to go off, but everything remained quiet.

Hawley walked straight over to the Firebird, then circled the frame, examining the dings and scratches, slipping his finger into a dent by the left wheel well. When he got around to the driver's side, he stood for a moment, his hand on the roof. Then he put down the rifle, and took out the long metal rod he'd brought from the car, and the wedge he'd lifted from the police station out of his pocket. He jammed the wedge into the edge of the door, slid the rod into the space he'd made, and in less than a minute he had the car open. With the screwdriver he loosened the access cover under the steering wheel. He put the car in neutral, took out his pliers and started stripping a set of wires. He bound two red ones together. And then he used a black wire to hit where the copper was exposed. There was a spark, and then another, and then the engine came to life and started rumbling.

"Wouldn't it be easier to find the keys?"

"There's an alarm on the building. Besides," Hawley said, looking back over his shoulder, "this is half the fun."

Loo turned toward the garage. A home security sticker was on the corner of one of the windows. Inside there was a tiny red light, blinking steadily. By the time she turned back to Hawley he was examining the gate that enclosed the property. He pumped his rifle and aimed at the center of the lock. The zip of the suppressor pierced the night air, followed by the thump of the lock coming loose. He pulled what was left off the fence. Then he bent down and picked up the bullet casing from the dirt.

He was already looking beyond the chain-link fence, beyond where the trees covered the road, and beyond the road to the rotary and then the bridge. For a moment it all seemed connected—Hawley's shadow stretching from the gate to the highway, past the borders of Olympus and to another place in time, when Loo was seven or eight, and Hawley was waking her up in the middle of the night. He'd wrapped her in the bearskin rug and carried her out of their motel room and into a brand-new station wagon, with wood paneling on the sides. She remembered the station wagon because it looked just like the family car on one of her favorite television shows. *It's ours now,* her father had said. And she'd felt so excited, and wanted people to see them driving in it, her teachers from the school she'd just left, and the kids who'd teased her on the playground, which made it even more upsetting when they stopped at a salvage yard a few days later and Hawley swapped the car for a pickup truck. The only thing that raised her spirits was watching the station wagon being put into the crusher, the windows bursting into the air like glitter, the metal compressing down into folds until it was the size of a suitcase.

Hawley opened the gates of the impound lot. Then he went back to the Firebird and slid his hand along the roof. "We need to steal the rest."

"What do you mean?"

"If only the Firebird is missing, the police will suspect you. But if more cars are gone, they'll think someone came to rob the place. A professional," Hawley added.

Loo watched him shoulder the rifle and understood, in a flickering moment, that her father was exactly that—a professional. All the guns in their house. All the scars on his body. All the ways that he was careful. It was because of this.

He slipped the metal casing he'd been holding into his pocket with the others. Loo could hear them clinking against one another. His eyes scanned the lot. Then he walked toward the covered sports car. He pulled the canvas loose from the bumper and the wheels, then tugged the whole sheet free. Underneath was a sky-blue coupe. The body was all curves, the hubcaps gleaming. Hawley used the wedge to prop the door and the metal rod to turn the lock. Then he took his screwdriver and pliers and held them out to Loo.

"Your turn," he said.

As Loo worked, Hawley gave her directions. *More pressure. Turn there. Only strip the ends.* He opened the glove compartment, pulled out an envelope and threw it onto the passenger seat. "Registration," he said. "It's the easiest thing to alter. You can do it on a computer, or even a Xerox machine. Just get them matched and lined with whatever license you're carrying. Cops only check the names and numbers. And you should always carry extra plates. After that it's the ID numbers, on the engine and to the left of the steering wheel, but you only need to worry about those if you're holding on to a car for a day or two. And you should never hold one for long. Pick and drop. That's how you work it."

"Why are you telling me this?" Loo asked.

"So that next time you'll know how to do it right."

Loo twisted the copper filaments together. She held the black wire and the red wires in her hands. She glanced over at Hawley.

"Go on," he said.

Loo struck the wires together. There was a small spark that jolted her fingers.

"Again," said Hawley.

Loo hit the wires hard, like she was striking a match. The engine sparked and turned and the dashboard lit and the radio turned on. It was set to an oldies station, the volume up loud. Some fifties crooner singing about love. Loo snapped the tuner off.

"Now what?"

Hawley tossed his guns and tools in the trunk of the Firebird. He climbed inside and moved the driver's seat until it was pressed against the rear bench. The engine was humming. Hawley touched the steering wheel, touched the gears, touched the radio dial. Then he seemed to remember himself. He glanced over at Loo and cranked the window open.

He said, "Follow me."

The headlights rose from the tip of the Pontiac like a creature waking from a deep sleep. Then the wheels reversed out of the parking spot and Hawley shifted and drove toward the gates. The Firebird slipped out from the floodlight and onto the dark road. The tires squealed as the car took the turn.

Loo pulled the door shut on the coupe and sat there for a moment, breathing in the leather seats. The steering wheel was glossy and smooth, a piece of polished mahogany. The rearview mirror was the same amber color, and so was the compass on top of the dashboard, the needle dangling and still. Loo clutched the wheel until her knuckles hurt. Her mother's Firebird was a piece of junk, but this car smelled like money. Would she go to jail for longer if the coupe was worth sixty grand? Seventy? Her foot slipped off the clutch. The engine stalled and died. Loo hit the brakes.

It had been only a few hours since she was stretched on a glacial rock, the universe being drawn on her skin. She could still feel the planets beneath her clothes. The comets on her back that had lifted her out of her own body and toward some new and different way of being in the world. And here was another. Half a mile up the road were two flashes of red. The Firebird's hazards, beating off and on. Like a pulse. Like a set of eyes blinking.

And so she did what she had been taught. She reached under the dashboard. She struck the wires. Later there would be time to worry, time to be afraid. Now there was only her foot on the pedal. The motor kicking. The wheel in her hands. The compass spinning from one direction to another. And her body, covered with stars.

Bullet Number Five

MABEL RIDGE WAS SUPPOSED TO BE ON THE TEN O'CLOCK TRAIN. BUT THE ten o'clock train had come and gone, and also the eleven-fifteen, so Hawley and Lily ate lunch across the street and came back for the twelve-thirty. Lily got out of the car and stood rocking back and forth on her toes in the parking lot as people hurried past, dragging their suitcases. Hawley leaned on the steering wheel and watched her wait. Every once in a while he would check the clock on the dashboard. *12:40. 12:45. 12:51.* The minutes passed and it started to rain but Lily stayed outside, her hair getting darker and darker. When the platform finally emptied and the train pulled out of the station, she climbed back into the truck and slammed the door.

"We can wait for the next one," said Hawley. "I'll get us some more coffee."

"No," said Lily. "Let's go back to the woods."

Hawley felt relieved as they pulled out of the parking lot. It meant something, to meet Lily's mother, but he could tell from the start that the woman wouldn't be easy. Whenever Lily talked to her mother on the phone she'd get anxious, and when a letter arrived from Mabel Ridge, it would sit unopened for days. Hawley signaled and shifted onto the highway, then took exit nineteen and headed toward the forest. The rain came down harder. Even with the wipers going full tilt, he had to slow down to see the road.

Lily pulled out her tobacco and rolled a cigarette, licking the paper and then pinching and twisting the ends. She snapped the wheel of her Zippo, then put her boots up on the dash and opened the window a crack. She tapped ashes into the small sliver of air as rain splattered both sides of the glass. The ember at the end of her cigarette burned and faded with each sucking pause. Hawley had never liked the smell of smoke before but now the smoke was Lily and every time she lit up he inhaled.

"You're killing yourself with those things," he said.

"Yes," Lily said, "but it's slow."

They'd spent the morning shooting rifles off at a range Hawley had set up deep in the forest. Lily had been quiet, drinking hot coffee from a thermos as he shot off his .387, handling a gun only when he put one in her hands. He'd hoped a round or two would help her blow off some steam, but Lily shot wide and soon gave up trying. She could load and reload now as fast as he could, but her aim hadn't improved any, no matter how many hours he'd spent trying to teach her. She'd get caught up in the details instead of feeling her way through, and Hawley wasn't sure how to fix this.

For the past week she had been cleaning their apartment, preparing for her mother's arrival. Every surface had been scoured, the windows washed, flowers planted in the window boxes, curtains bought and hung. Hawley got up one night at three in the morning and found Lily kneeling in the bathtub, scrubbing the tile with a toothbrush.

"What do you think she's going to see?" he'd asked.

"Everything," Lily answered.

. . .

THEY DROVE DOWN A SIDE street, then into a small lot that marked the entrance to the trailhead. The place was empty and littered with gravel and potholes. Hawley parked under a cluster of pine trees. The sound of the rain eased as they pulled under the canopy. He turned off the engine. The dashboard went dark.

"Right now," said Lily, "I'm glad you don't have any parents."

"Me, too," said Hawley. But he was lying. There'd been plenty of times over the past six months when he'd wished he had someone to show Lily off to.

It was too wet to shoot, so they sat together in the car, listening to the storm. Every once in a while the branches of a tree would bend and hit the windshield. Hawley reached over and took Lily's hand. He was always taking her hand. He felt better about things, just by holding her fingers.

"Your mother can't be that terrible," he said.

"She isn't. But when I'm around her, I don't feel like Me anymore. I feel like Old Me."

"One of these days I'd like to meet Old You."

"Trust me. You don't."

Lily's Old Me was a lot like her father's Drunk Gus. She hadn't told Hawley too many details but it was enough. Alcohol poisoning. DWIs. Bridges burned with friends. She couldn't make it through college. She got fired from work. Growing up, she'd thought she was better than everyone else in her hometown, but when it came down to it, Lily said, they didn't want to be around her, either. At least not when she was Old Me.

Mabel Ridge had done her best to help. She'd brought Lily to the hospital and had her stomach pumped. She'd paid for her daughter to dry out at a fancy rehab clinic. When that didn't work she tried to have her committed to a mental hospital. And when that didn't work she had her daughter arrested. Eventually she dropped the charges, and Lily started going to AA. But things were never the same between them.

It was hard, at first, being with someone who was sober. Especially when Hawley had used whiskey to keep himself warm for so many years. But once he'd let it go, he found that drinking was a habit more than a need, a habit he was willing to break for Lily. She was better company than any bottle. And he wanted so much not to disappoint her.

"I might have to go to a meeting tonight," Lily said.

"I'll go with you," said Hawley. "If you want."

Instead of answering him Lily sneezed. And sneezed again. And again. She'd warned Hawley about these attacks when they first got together. Like hiccups, she said, but with her nose. Sometimes she'd sneeze twenty or thirty times in a row before it stopped. The whole thing embarrassed her, but Hawley didn't mind. When she was finished her face was blotchy and her eyes were wet. It was the closest he'd ever seen her come to crying.

Hawley turned the key in the ignition and the dashboard lit. Heat radiated from the vents. The air blasted their faces. Lily pulled a tissue from her pocket and blew her nose.

"When's the next train?" she asked.

"Three o'clock."

Lily unzipped her coat, shrugged it off her shoulders and climbed onto his lap. She smelled smoky and tart and cold. Her skin was damp and her hair fell in clumps around her ears. Hawley unbuttoned his jacket and wrapped it around them both, pulling her against him. He could feel her thin arms thread up the length of his back. Hawley hoped that Mabel Ridge would never come. They could spend all afternoon in the car like this, tangled up in each other and listening to the rain.

"Sometimes I feel like I could kill her."

"You'd probably miss the shot."

Lily rested her face against his neck. He could feel her eyelashes against his chin. "Tell me the worst thing you've ever done."

"Marrying you," said Hawley.

"Very funny."

IT HAD BEEN LIKE STUMBLING into someone else's life.

After Lily had dragged Hawley into the snowplow, after they'd crossed state lines, after she'd lied to the clinic in South Carolina about accidentally dropping her father's favorite shotgun at his funeral, waving Gus's prayer card and crossing herself and shouting *Our Father*s and *Hail Mary*s at the small-town doctor until he agreed not to report it to the police, and after Hawley had gotten patched up, they had stopped at another diner, one that sold cake instead of pie, and had split another milkshake and fallen in love. It was that easy. They talked until the diner closed. They paid their bill and tipped the waitress. Then they got a room at the motel across the street.

She'd taken his hand in the parking lot. He would remember that moment more than the sex they had that night. How he'd stared down at Lily's fingers latched together with his, hardly believing the change in his luck.

They spent a week together in that motel. Reading the paper in the morning, ordering takeout for meals, sharing stories, playing cards and making love until they were tired enough to sleep. Lily changed the bandages and kept the wound in his leg clean, and once the sun set Hawley hobbled out to the pool and watched her swimming through the blue lights in her underwear. Her legs were long and powerful, her back flexing with muscle, her face a blur as she snatched a breath between each stroke.

When she was through swimming, Lily pulled herself from the water in one fluid motion, then walked dripping toward him across the cement. He held out a towel and wrapped her in it and felt the chill of her body through the fabric.

"What're you doing here with me?" he asked.

She pressed her cold lips against his skin.

She said, "Warming up."

At the end of the week they drove north until they hit Maryland, got a license and went to city hall. Hawley in a new shirt and Lily in her dress from the funeral, with daisies picked from the side of the road threaded through the veil of her little black hat.

Now here they were, newlyweds, their hands in each other's pants. The rain battering the roof of the truck. The trees swaying in the wind. Their bodies pressed close enough to be a single person. She had a way of kissing that took the air out of Hawley and then pushed it back, down to his lungs, as if she'd taken over his breathing. With each inhalation, he felt stronger. Smarter. All the things he'd ever wished to be and knew he wasn't.

The knock on the window startled them both. Lily scrambled back into her seat and buttoned up her shirt. Hawley pulled his jacket across his lap. The glass was steamed and they couldn't see out. Hawley used his fingers to clear the condensation. Outside in the rain there was a teenage boy, maybe fifteen. Hawley rolled down the window a crack and the boy leaned in, curling his fingers around the edge, dribbling water inside the car.

"Have you guys seen a dog?"

"What kind?" Hawley asked.

"A mutt," said the boy. "But she looks like a Lab."

"We haven't seen her," said Lily.

"My dad's going to kill me," said the boy. "I took her for a walk and she slipped out of her collar."

In a locked metal box bolted in the rear of Hawley's truck, there were two long-range rifles with scopes, a SIG Sauer pistol, a set of derringers he'd been saving as a surprise for Lily, his father's M14, ammunition for all of the guns and a set of targets. Hawley checked the kid's eyes, but he didn't seem like he was on anything. The rain came down steadily and the boy kept his fingers on the window.

"Do you need some help?" Lily asked.

"Sure," said the kid, and his face brightened.

Hawley didn't want to leave the car. But Lily had already pulled her jacket on and tied up her boots. Before he knew it, the door was open and she was outside. Hawley reached under the seat, where he kept his Colt. He put the gun into his pocket and then stepped out of the truck into the rain.

"What's your name?" he asked the kid.

"Charlie."

"And what's the dog's name?"

"Her name is Charley, too. But with a *y*," said the boy.

"Is the dog named after you or are you named after the dog?" Hawley asked.

"She had that name when we got her."

"Funny."

"Yeah," Charlie said. He was a skinny kid. He had on torn-up jeans, purple sneakers, a leather coat that was too big for him and a sweatshirt underneath, the hood pulled up against the rain, the fabric shiny and wet. The dog leash was wrapped tightly around his palm several times, the empty leather collar dangling from his wrist like an oversize bracelet.

Lily opened the door to the truck again and pulled out an umbrella from under the passenger seat. The umbrella was from a bank where Hawley kept one of his safe-deposit boxes. Lily pressed the button on the handle and the umbrella sprang to life, extending twice its length, then spreading its mechanical arms. The web of nylon stretched into place with a pop, and Lily stood under the bright-yellow dome, circled with the logo of the bank—a beehive made of dollar bills. YOUR MONEY IS SAFE WITH US HONEY.

"Which way did the dog go?" Lily asked.

"That way," said Charlie, and he pointed into the trees.

"You should follow the trail," Hawley said. "We'll flank the sides."

The kid hesitated.

"You want to find this mutt or not?"

"Yes," said Charlie. Then he started calling for the dog and hurried into the trees.

"I think you scared him," said Lily.

Hawley ducked under the umbrella. Inside the dome the rain sounded like static. "What are we doing out here?"

"We're helping," said Lily. "What if that was our dog?"

"Do you want a dog?"

"No," said Lily. "But I'd want someone to help if our dog was missing."

Hawley took the umbrella from her and lifted it so he could stand without crouching. All around them the rain poured down, and her green eyes looked greener than ever.

"Give me the gun," Lily said.

He hadn't pulled a job since they'd been married. They were living off some money he had stashed away. It was enough to keep Hawley out of the game for at least a year. Even so, he kept a weapon close. For the first time he had something to lose, and it was funny how that changed things, how it made Hawley imagine himself living past the next day, into the next week, the next year. He'd started wearing his seatbelt. He brushed his teeth. Sometimes he fell so deeply inside his new life that the edges of himself felt like they were coming loose. Then Lily would catch him in one of his old habits—checking and rechecking the locks, or doubling back on streets when he thought they were being followed— and the years he'd spent alone would rise up solidly around him, reso- nating in the dark like blood pushed out of a pinprick.

He took the Colt from his inside pocket and handed it over. Lily checked the barrel and then put the gun in her coat.

"Let's go find that dog."

They went in different directions, each taking a branching path from the one where the boy had disappeared. Hawley was glad Lily had the umbrella. It let him keep an eye on the yellow dome bobbing through the branches. Then the woods got thick and he lost sight of her.

The air smelled of moss and mushrooms, things that spring to life from the muck. All around him the branches shook and spattered and spilled. The rain was still coming down hard and Hawley was soaked up past his knees. He could hear Lily's voice calling, *Charley, Charley.* Prickers stung his hand. Water ran down the neck of his coat.

If the dog was smart, Hawley decided, she'd be looking for shelter, not off wandering in the woods. There wasn't any solid cover here— not for miles. Except for the truck. That's where Hawley would go, if he were a dog.

For a moment he scanned the bushes ahead for movement. Then he turned around and started walking back toward the parking lot. He hoped he was right—that the dog was huddled underneath the engine. Hawley pictured a chocolate Lab, overweight and panting in the mud. With some coaxing the dog would crawl out and lick his hand, and he'd carry it down the path and show Lily that he was the kind of man who could find things.

When he got back to the parking lot, he saw the kid, Charlie, crouched beside the truck instead. At first he thought the boy had had the same idea, and was checking beneath the undercarriage for the dog. But then he saw that one of the backseat windows was smashed and the driver's side door was propped open. Charlie didn't look up. All around them, water was pelting down, hitting the trees and covering the sound of Hawley's footsteps as he left the woods and stood behind him.

"You should have gotten inside and closed the door before you pulled the wires," he said. "Now you'll never get it to start."

The boy looked so frightened that Hawley almost didn't hit him. But then he did. A few heavy punches to the gut and a couple more to the face for good measure. He could feel the boy's jaw bust out under his knuckles. He saw a tooth flung onto the mud. The kid was sobbing. He tried to crawl away and Hawley dragged him back and then kicked him twice in the ribs.

It was one thing to jack a car, and another to lure them out with a sob story about a missing dog. It was the dog that got him, and it was the dog that he thought about as he beat the boy—Charley the dog wandering around out there alone in the rain, scared and lost and feeling ready to curl up and die, and with no one even looking for her, because she didn't exist.

Hawley was swinging his leg back for another kick when he heard the shot. The bullet grazed his lower leg, dug out a chunk of flesh and then kept on going, right into the front tire. Hawley stumbled and fell, and when he hit the ground he saw the air streaming out of the wheel, the black rubber slowly collapsing around the hole and then slumping onto itself, the truck tilting over onto its axle and into the mud.

Lily stepped out of the woods, the Colt held just as Hawley had taught her, arms braced and fingers locked, pushing and pulling to steady her hand. She stood ten feet away but didn't lower the weapon.

"Are you okay?" she asked.

"You shot me."

"I'm sorry," she said. "I'm so sorry."

Hawley lifted his pant leg. The bullet had gone through the back of his calf, a slice of flesh carved off in a straight line.

"I'm all right," he said. "But I think you killed the tire."

Lily lowered the gun. She wiped her face with the sleeve of her coat. When she was through, she looked relieved and washed out. The rain tore down from the sky between them and Hawley began to feel the flush of pain, a burn like his leg was being held against a fire. He bent over and pressed the wound to stop the bleeding, while Lily hurried to the back of the truck and opened the cap and got the first-aid kit. She fell to her knees in the mud, rolled up his pants, wiped Hawley's leg with alcohol and started wrapping it with gauze.

"This looks bad."

"It was an accident."

"I dropped the umbrella."

"We'll get it later."

Lily tied off the bandage and stood. Then she turned away from him and leaned against the car. For a moment Hawley was reminded of the diner. He'd said the right thing then but right now he didn't have any words. And when she lifted her face he knew something else was wrong.

"What happened to Charlie?"

Hawley spun around, checking the edges of the forest. There was no sign of the boy. The only thing he'd left behind was his tooth, a gleaming bit of white in the mud. Hawley crouched down on his good leg. Then he saw a flicker of something, and he glanced underneath the car, and found Charlie the boy where Charley the dog should have been, curled up in a ball with his purple sneakers, just beyond the rear axle.

"Come on out of there," said Hawley.

"Get away from me!" screamed the boy.

"My wife just wanted us to stop fighting," said Hawley. "She didn't mean to hurt anybody. And she's sorry now. Aren't you sorry, honey?"

"Yes," said Lily, her voice tight.

"Are you hit?" Hawley asked.

"What?" the boy said.

"Did you catch a bullet."

"I don't think so."

Lily kneeled down and stuck her head under the transom. "Is your name really Charlie?"

"Yeah," said the boy.

"Listen, Charlie," said Lily. "I promise nothing is going to happen. He's not going to hurt you, and I'm not going to shoot you, and no one's going to call the police. Okay?"

Charlie thought this over for a few moments, then slunk out on his stomach, just as Hawley had imagined the dog doing. But once he was in front of them he did not look grateful. He didn't even look that scared—only thin and hungry and tired. His jeans were sopping wet, his leather coat covered in gunk. There was blood leaking from his nose and mouth, the skin around his eye was cut and his lower lip had started to swell. He kept his palm against his jaw, as if he were holding it together with his fingers.

"Let me see." Lily examined his face. When she touched his chin, he cried out, and she made a shushing sound, as if she were soothing away a bad dream. "We need to take you to a hospital." She pulled a tissue from her pocket and handed it to the boy. "Do you know how to change a tire, Charlie?"

The boy pressed the tissue to his nose and shook his head.

"Well, you're going to learn now." Lily walked around to the back of the truck and started to unlock the spare.

Hawley stepped up next to the tailgate. Lily's body was trembling, but when he touched her she pushed him away.

"What are you doing?"

"You just beat up a kid, Hawley." She pulled out the tire iron.

"He was stealing our car."

"He knows what we look like. He's got our license plate number."

"He doesn't know what he's doing. When I was his age I was robbing gas stations and sleeping in a different car every night."

Hawley took the tire iron out of her hands. The wind picked up and a gust of rain blasted them both. Lily covered her eyes. When she lowered her fingers her face was pale and dripping. She shook her head at Hawley and rolled herself a cigarette. She flicked the wheel on her lighter but the paper was too damp to catch. Lily tossed the cigarette into the mud.

"I need a minute," she said. And then she stepped away from him and into the woods.

Hawley watched her go. Then he pulled the spare out and carried it to the boy.

Charlie backed away.

"I promised her I wouldn't hit you again," he said. "But I'd like to. So you better do what I say."

"It hurts to talk," Charlie mumbled.

"Then don't." Hawley threw the tire iron on the ground next to the spare. "Go get some rocks. Big ones. Stick the rocks behind the wheels. It'll keep the car from rolling off the jack."

The boy limped to the edge of the forest. He clutched his side. "It hurts to breathe."

"Then don't do that, either."

Charlie pried two big stones from the mud and kicked them beneath the back tires. Hawley took off the hubcap, then used the tire iron on the first four lugs and slipped them into his pocket. He put the jack under the frame rail and started cranking the lift.

"I thought you were supposed to lift the car first," Charlie said.

"Pulling the nuts off in the air can throw the car off. But you should leave one screw on so the wheel doesn't pop out. It goes faster that way."

"You a mechanic or something?"

"Something." Hawley pushed his weight against the wrench until the truck dangled in the air. He screwed off the last lug and wiggled the dead tire loose. He could hear the bullet rolling around inside as he set the wheel under the car, behind the jack.

The boy looked at the tire, then back at Hawley.

"In case the car falls off. This'll keep the car high enough so you can get the jack under the frame again."

"Right."

This kid had no business stealing a car, Hawley thought. A Ford should be easy. Hawley still remembered the model and make of his first—a Buick Skylark sedan—he was only fifteen when he hot-wired it, and he'd driven that clunky boat with the sticky gearshift all the way to Tennessee.

"Where'd you get that leash?" he asked. It still bothered him about the dog.

"Oh," said the boy. "My dad ran Charley over in the driveway last year."

"That sob story ever work?"

"Mostly," said Charlie. "On girls."

The storm was slowing, the rain turning into mist. Hawley tried to wipe the grease off his fingers. "Give me the spare." The boy rolled the tire over. Hawley centered the wheel on the hub, fished the lugs out of his pocket and tightened them with his fingers.

"Sorry about the car," said Charlie. "I just wanted to get out of here."

Hawley leaned back on his heels. He picked up the flat and pressed a finger against the bullet hole. The rubber was soft where it was torn but hard everywhere else. One of his nails had ripped from working the screws. He stuck it in his mouth and tasted grease and blood and dirt.

"Well," said Hawley. "I guess I know about that."

Through the trees there was a flash of yellow, then Lily stepped out of the forest carrying the umbrella. Her face was resigned, the same way it got before she snapped on her rubber gloves and pulled out the bleach.

"Is she mad at you or something?" the boy asked.

"Just don't tell her about the dog," said Hawley.

Lily crossed the lot, the umbrella floating bright over her head like an idea. By the time she reached the truck the rain had stopped. She held her hand out, testing the air, then she pushed the button on the handle and the arms of the umbrella retracted, folding back.

"Finished?"

"Almost," said Hawley.

"I need to talk to Charlie."

The boy seemed more scared of Lily than of Hawley. He got off the ground reluctantly, wincing a bit. Together they walked a few paces away from the truck, until Hawley couldn't hear them. Lily spoke and the kid nodded. Then she slipped something into his hand.

Hawley lowered the jack and the truck settled onto the spare with a sigh. With the tire iron he tightened the lug nuts. By the time he was finished, Lily and Charlie were done talking. They loaded the equipment in the back and everyone got into the truck. It took Hawley a couple of minutes to reattach the wires the kid had pulled. "These are for the radio, not the starter," he said.

The boy sat in the backseat, beside a pile of broken glass. He still clutched his jaw, and with the other hand he cradled his ribs. He peered over the seat at the wires. "Which ones should I use?"

"The red is the battery," said Hawley, "and this yellow one is the starter. Then you need the ignition wire."

"You shouldn't teach him that," said Lily.

"He's going to do it anyway. He might as well do it right."

"Can we stop at McDonald's?" Charlie asked. "I'm starving."

Hawley turned the key and the engine caught. The clock on the dashboard had reset, blinking like a bomb about to go off. *12:00*, *12:00*, *12:00*.

"Anyone know what time it is?"

"Three-thirty," said the kid.

"Your mother," said Hawley.

Lily took the Colt out of her pocket. She opened the cylinder and removed the bullets. She put the ammunition in the glove compartment and closed it and put the Colt back under the seat.

"No McDonald's," she said.

WHEN THEY PULLED INTO THE train station Mabel Ridge was waiting, sitting on a bench next to a giant suitcase on wheels that was adorned with a name tag and a bright purple ribbon. Her hair was loose and wild. There were a number of sewing needles, of different sizes and lengths, woven into the collar of her sweater, like stripes on a soldier's uniform.

"My little girl," said Mabel.

"Mom," said Lily. They put their arms around each other.

"This is Samuel Hawley," said Lily. "This is my husband."

Mabel Ridge took his hand. She had long fingers and a heavy grip. As he hefted her bag into the back of the truck, she pulled down the glasses that were propped on her forehead, and her eyes went straight to Hawley's injured leg. He turned it behind him and the woman lifted her chin, fast. She had green eyes, just like her daughter. Beneath her gaze Hawley felt pulled open, straight to his bones.

"And who is this?" Mabel peered through the window.

Lily opened the door. She brushed some of the broken glass off the seat. "This is Charlie. We're bringing him to the hospital."

Lily's mother considered the boy and his swollen face. "What happened to Charlie?"

"He lost his dog," said Hawley.

The boy sighed and slid closer to the broken window. Mabel Ridge got in back next to him. Hawley took off his coat and tied it low around his waist, covering the blood on his pants.

"Why weren't you here when I arrived?" Mabel asked as they pulled out of the parking lot.

"You said you were coming in at ten," said Lily.

"I was always going to arrive at three o'clock," said Mabel. "You probably didn't write it down."

"I did write it down."

They rode in silence for a few minutes, then got onto the highway. The wind whipped through the car as they increased speed. The wheels hit a puddle on the far shoulder and a wave splashed the side of the car.

"Why don't you shut the window?" Mabel Ridge said.

"It's broken," Lily said.

Their voices were similar. A musicality beneath the words that Hawley had always considered unique about Lily. As the women argued he watched and listened to them both. His wife seemed changed by her mother's presence. Diminished, somehow. It made him wonder what kind of memories she was fighting off. And it made him feel protective, even though he knew Mabel Ridge had saved Lily from spinning down the drain.

He took the next exit. The wind in the car died as they slowed and stopped at a light. They were maybe twenty minutes out from the hospital. He kept glancing over at the clock on the dashboard, wishing the time to pass, but the numbers flashed *12:00, 12:00*, like a record skipping, extending the moment, until Hawley felt as if the four of them had been trapped in the car forever.

"So." Mabel Ridge took off her glasses and wiped them on her scarf. "I haven't heard that much about you, Samuel Hawley."

"I've heard about you," said Hawley.

"I'm sure." Mabel set an elbow on each of their headrests. "How did you two meet, again?"

"At a coffee shop," said Lily.

"Really."

"I told you before."

"I must have forgotten," said Mabel Ridge. "Like you forgot to invite me to your wedding."

Hawley had met some tough broads over the years, but they were honed that way from rough living. Mabel was something else. Her hardness was built into her very foundation, and she rammed that hardness into others, like an oil tanker barreling through a fleet of rowboats. It made Hawley wonder about Lily's father. From what he knew Gus was a real bum, but he must have had some balls to make love to a woman like Mabel Ridge.

"Mom," said Lily.

"I deserved to be there. I deserve to know about your life. Don't you think I deserve that?"

"What would you like to know?" Hawley asked, trying to be friendly.

Mabel Ridge leaned in. "Lily never told me where you're from."

"I grew up near Galveston Bay." When she blinked at him he added, "Texas."

"And what is it you do for work?"

"He's a mechanic," said Charlie.

Hawley gave the boy a look in the rearview. "I'm in between jobs."

"That's too bad." Mabel wrapped her fingers around the headrest of the driver's seat, close to Hawley's face. "Well," she said. "You must be good at something."

"He's good at beating people up," Charlie said, then wiped his bloody nose with the sleeve of his leather coat.

This kept Mabel Ridge quiet for a while. Hawley watched her stew and slowly add up the details. Meanwhile, in the passenger seat, Lily seemed to be shrinking, sliding down bit by bit as her mother hovered between them. Before long she'd end up in the wheel well. Hawley knew they were in trouble but he wasn't sure what to do next. They'd barely made it fifteen minutes, and Mabel Ridge was supposed to be staying for a week.

By the time they reached the hospital, the silence in the car had taken on its own weight and substance. Hawley pulled next to the emergency entrance and parked. All he wanted was to get out of the car. "I better take him in," he said.

Lily touched his good leg and gave a squeeze that said not to take long.

"Goodbye, Charlie. Remember what I said."

Charlie nodded, then wrinkled his brow like he was already trying to remember Lily's words, his fingers pressed against his swollen jaw. He struggled with the handle and slid out, dragging along some pieces of the broken window that rang like tiny bells as they hit the asphalt.

"It was nice to meet you," said Mabel Ridge, but her smile wasn't nice at all.

The hospital was a low brick building with wheelchair ramps coming out both sides. As they passed through the sliding doors, Hawley saw half a dozen people waiting on metal chairs and a TV on in the corner with the sound off, playing the news. The room smelled of moldy carpets even though the floor was covered in tile. Clustered together on one side was a middle-aged lady with her arm in a sling; an old man clutching a crying toddler; and a Chinese woman patting the back of her son, who was getting sick in a bucket on his lap. Sitting away from everyone was a homeless guy, his stuff piled in garbage bags around him, holding a plastic burger container on his lap. Behind a glass booth, a nurse shuffled papers.

"What do I say?" said Charlie.

"Just tell them you got in a fight at school," said Hawley.

The boy went up to the counter and talked to the nurse. Hawley considered ducking out but then remembered that Mabel Ridge was in the car, probably pumping his wife for information, and decided he should wait until the kid was admitted. He dropped into one of the empty seats near the homeless guy and held his breath against the man's stale, dank smell. Inside the burger container was an ear, resting on a paper napkin.

"What happened?" Hawley asked.

"Oh," said the homeless man, "it's not my ear. It belongs to a friend of mine. I'm just holding it for him."

"Is he in the hospital?"

"Not yet," said the man.

The ear was only half an ear—the lobe and a bit of the outer cartilage. The knife must have been sharp. It was a clean cut. There was hardly any blood.

The nurse gave Charlie an ice pack and a clipboard and a pen. He carried the stuff all back over to Hawley and touched the ice pack gingerly against his lower jaw.

"I need you to sign this."

"What is it?" Hawley asked.

"A parental permission form."

"No way."

"You have to," said the boy, "or they'll call my dad."

"That's probably a good idea."

"Trust me," said Charlie. "It isn't."

Hawley glanced up and caught the eye of the homeless man. He thought about the missing ear resting inside the plastic container, and the other guy out there wandering around without it, and this man waiting here for his friend, just on the chance he'd show.

"What did my wife say to you?"

"She gave me a hundred bucks," said Charlie. "And she told me to keep my mouth shut."

"What else?" Hawley asked. He knew there was something.

The boy shuffled the papers. He clipped them back onto the clipboard. "She said to stop stealing cars, and doing other bad stuff. Otherwise I'd end up like you."

There it was.

Hawley signed the paper.

After a while the nurse called Charlie's name and he followed her behind the glass partition. Hawley stepped into the bathroom and got some paper towels and washed out his leg again. It looked more like a knife wound than a bullet wound, the skin sliced off clean, but the blood had completely soaked through the bandage and run down over his boots and changed the color of his laces. He needed stitches. And antibiotics. When he got home he'd sew it up, or use Super Glue to bind the skin together (a trick that Jove had taught him). For now he took off his belt and wrapped some paper towels around the cut and then tied it off tight with the belt and rolled his pants back down.

When he came out of the bathroom, Lily was there talking to the nurse. "Where've you been?" she asked.

"It won't be that much longer," said Hawley.

"We're out there waiting." Whatever Mabel Ridge had said in the truck, Hawley could tell it had done its job. Lily was blinking at him with tight, tired eyes, and then they widened.

"There's blood all over your boots."

She was going to leave him, Hawley thought. Maybe not today but someday. Hawley couldn't hide his Old Me, or detox from it or talk it away at meetings. He untied his jacket from around his waist and held it open. He gave his wife a good look.

"Why didn't you say anything?" Lily cried, and then she sneezed. It was a great big honking sneeze, exploding over the waiting room in a spray. Lily's hands came up and covered her face, and then she sneezed again, and again and again. She swayed and Hawley caught her arm. Her face blossomed into splotches, her eyes became glassy as she sneezed and sneezed and sneezed, until everyone, even the homeless guy holding the ear, was staring at Hawley like it was his fault. And he guessed it was.

He walked his wife outside, back into the rain. The automatic doors opened wide and then shut the hospital away behind them. "It doesn't even hurt," he said.

"You looked like you were going to kill him," said Lily.

"I wasn't," said Hawley.

"You looked like you were." She sneezed again.

Hawley thought back to the way Lily had stepped out of the trees, holding the gun just right. Her arms braced and steady. Her eye trained on her target. All those hours spent practicing together in the woods. It had been for something, after all.

"You *meant* to shoot me?"

"Of course I did," she said.

Her nose was running in two clear streams, one from each nostril, over her lips and down her chin, and yet she still looked beautiful. He stared into her torn-up face. She was scared, just as much as he was. Not about Charlie or her mother or even if Hawley would end up in jail, but whether or not they'd make it.

"It was a perfect shot."

"Except for the tire," said Lily.

"Yes," said Hawley. "The tire." His wife leaned into him, clutching the back of his shirt. Her cheek was warm against his chest, her hair frizzy from the rain. He pressed his lips to her neck and inhaled her skin.

He felt as if he could face a thousand Mabel Ridges.

They turned and went back inside the hospital. Hawley told the nurse he'd cut his leg open on a lawn mower. Before long he was stretched on one of the padded benches, holding his wife's hand as the doctor stitched him up and gave him a tetanus shot. When they were finished, Lily bent down and kissed the black thread holding his skin together.

"That scar will always be mine," she said.

"They're all yours," said Hawley. "Every last one of them."

. . .

It was after seven when they finally stepped back into the hospital parking lot. Hawley could tell right away which car was his. The truck was lit up like a bar. Mabel Ridge had all the lights on, the overhead and the headlamps, too. The radio was playing full tilt and the windows were steamed. He could see the outline of Mabel Ridge and her hunched shoulders, perched in the driver's seat.

"What's *he* doing here?" she said when Hawley opened the door.

Lily got into the passenger seat. "He needed a ride."

Charlie's ribs were taped up, the left side of his jaw was wired and he had a metal splint across his nose. He was heavily doped, carrying a bag full of prescriptions, and slid into the backseat without a word. He'd been released the same time Hawley had, and when they offered him a lift, he just nodded.

"I've been out here for *hours*," said Mabel.

Lily reached over and turned off the radio. She did not apologize.

"Why don't you get in the back," said Hawley.

"I nearly drove off." Mabel Ridge wrapped her fingers around the steering wheel and slid out of the car. She got in next to Charlie and slammed the door behind her. Hawley turned on the air to clear the windows.

"Rear re ro ragain," said Charlie.

"What did he say?" Mabel Ridge asked. "I can't understand a word."

They left the parking lot. Before long they were on the highway and the wind was whipping through the broken window. Hawley kept thinking how much faster they seemed to be going. He glanced at the clock but it was still frozen at 12:00. Hospitals always did this to him. Days became nights and nights became days.

"I want to know who this boy is," Mabel Ridge shouted over the wind.

Lily turned her head. "He's a friend."

"Where are you taking him?"

"Rome," yelled Charlie.

"He means home." The kid had given them an address, not far

from the woods. But now, as he glanced in the rearview, Hawley caught sight of the empty dog leash sticking out of the kid's pocket and wondered if they should be bringing him home after all. More trouble was probably waiting for him there. Trouble enough to make him try to steal a car in the rain when he didn't know the first thing.

Hawley turned toward the backseat. "We could drop you someplace else, if you want. Or if you're still looking for a way out of town, I'll buy you a ticket."

"Don't be ridiculous." Mabel Ridge raised her voice. "This boy is hurt. He needs to be with his family."

"He can make up his own mind."

Charlie removed the ice pack from the side of his face. He looked out of the window for a while, watching the exits pass. Then he straightened up and caught Hawley's eye in the mirror. "Rain!"

"What's that?" Mabel was yelling now.

"Train!" Hawley put on his blinker and crossed two lanes and barely made the exit. The wind died down as the truck slowed and turned off the exit ramp, their hair and clothes settling and finally going still.

Mabel Ridge leaned forward. She took hold of her daughter's sleeve. "Lily," she said. "I'm not going to allow this."

Lily cracked the front window. "It's none of your business."

"Yes it is," said Mabel Ridge, tightening her grip. "There are guns in this car. I found one under the seat and bullets in the glove compartment. I don't know what you've gotten yourself into. But I'm getting you out."

"I've got a license," said Hawley.

At this point Mabel had nearly climbed into the front seat. In another move, she would be sitting between them. "I'm not going to watch you wreck your life again. We'll get this marriage annulled. You'll move back home, where it's safe."

"She's safe with me."

The older woman ignored him. "If he won't let us go, I'll call the police."

"Ron't," said Charlie.

Lily unbuckled her seatbelt. She turned onto her knees and put a hand on Mabel Ridge's shoulder. Then she pushed her mother back into place, until the woman was sitting next to Charlie again. "You're not calling anyone."

The light turned green. Hawley waited to see if Lily would let go of her mother, and when she didn't, he wrapped an arm around his wife's waist, then hooked a sharp left and pulled into the train station. Lily eased back into her seat, but she kept her eyes locked on Mabel Ridge, daring her to move. As soon as the truck stopped, Charlie hopped out and started running.

"Hang on," Hawley called. He opened the door.

Charlie was already two cars away but when he saw Hawley coming after him he stopped. "Ron't runch re."

"I'm not going to punch you." Hawley took out his wallet. "I promised to pay for a ticket. You can use it or you can save the money for later." He gave the kid some more cash, on top of what Lily had already paid him. Enough to get out of the state.

Once he'd pocketed the money Charlie put his hand out. He shrugged and Hawley realized he was saying goodbye. The boy's hand was bony and thin. As he shook it Hawley wondered how long he would last out in the world.

"Ranks," said Charlie.

"Your jaw will feel better in a couple of weeks. Don't go through the pain meds too fast. Cut the pills if you need to. And find some straws. They help a lot. You can steal a bunch from the concession stands, where they keep the napkins and the ketchup."

Charlie nodded and clutched the bag full of drugs to his chest. It started raining again and he took another step away in his purple sneakers. In the distance a train blew its horn. They could both hear it making the approach. The boy seemed nervous. He glanced at the platform, then back at Hawley.

"You'll be okay. You can get a job changing tires."

"Ra," said Charlie. Then he limped away toward the station.

When Hawley got back to the truck Lily was sitting on the hood.

Mabel Ridge had taken the keys and locked herself inside the cab. Hawley thought back to the morning, when he'd watched his wife waiting on the platform.

"I don't know why I asked her to come," said Lily.

"You're going to get all wet," said Hawley.

"I'm already soaked."

Hawley walked around the truck and stuck his head inside the broken window.

"Look," he said. "Maybe you should just leave."

Mabel Ridge pressed farther into her seat. "I came to visit my daughter."

"You came to meet me, and we've met." Hawley reached through and unlocked the door and opened it. Then he opened the back of the truck and slid the giant suitcase out and set it on the asphalt.

For a moment they both remained fixed in place, staring each other down. The woman's eyes were furious. Ramming speed. But Hawley had seen much worse than Mabel Ridge. He took hold of her arm.

"Don't you dare touch me!" she shouted. She threw his hand off, but Hawley knew fear when he saw it. Mabel climbed down from the truck. Then she wrapped her long fingers around the handle of the suitcase.

"You don't know anything about my daughter," she said.

"I know enough," said Hawley. "I know not to lose her."

Mabel Ridge threw the keys at his feet, then rolled her suitcase around to the front of the car and stood in front of Lily.

"You could have married that nice Gunderson boy. He would have treated you right. And you would have stayed at home, where you belong."

"I don't belong there," said Lily. "I never did."

"You're wrong."

Mabel Ridge said this with so much conviction that Hawley almost believed it was true. He looked over at his wife but her face was unreadable. Lily climbed down from the hood. She put her arms around her mother and held her close. Mabel's fingers came off the suitcase and pressed against her daughter's back, stroking her hair. Then Lily put her hands on her mother's shoulders, just as she had in the car, and pushed the woman away.

"There's a northbound train leaving at nine o'clock."

Mabel Ridge snatched up her suitcase again. "You're going to be sorry."

"I know," said Lily.

Hawley got the yellow umbrella out from under the seat. Then he came around with the keys, and this seemed to spur Lily's mother into action. In one swift movement she turned and hurried off toward the train station, dragging the wheeled suitcase behind her.

The umbrella unfolded just as it did before, the beehive made of dollar bills opening for business, the metal arms snapping the logo into place. Hawley brought it over to Lily, who was sitting on the bumper, watching her mother's retreat.

"I checked the schedule before we left this morning," she said. "I must have known this would happen."

"I can go after her," said Hawley. "Give her the umbrella, at least."

"No," said Lily. "This is our umbrella."

They sat together under the yellow dome as Mabel Ridge marched into the gloom. At one point her suitcase got caught between two closely parked cars, but she managed to wrest it free. She used the station's handicapped entrance, zigzagging up the ramp, the wheels of the bag rumbling against the concrete. Once she'd made it to the overhang, she stopped and shook her jacket free of water. There was a spotlight at the entrance and they could see her clearly as she turned to glare back at them.

Hawley felt his wife flinch. He put his arm around her and pulled her close. Then he lowered the umbrella, until Mabel Ridge was out of sight, and it was just the two of them again. The fabric shuddered against the raindrops, but inside their small shelter Lily's face was radiant. He kissed her. After a moment, she kissed him back, pulling at his hair. Hungry.

"I promise," she said, "I'll never shoot you again."

The Net

Marshall Hicks came in for Loo's breakfast shift at the Saw-tooth at eight in the morning and ordered hash browns and the meat lover's special without meat: cornbread and stuffing and mashed potatoes. He also ordered a banana split.

"I've been waiting for you," he said when Loo brought him his cornbread.

"Waiting for what?"

"For whatever it takes."

It had been two weeks since they were arrested in the Firebird. She had thought of Marshall every day but she had not called him, even after she'd found his mother's petition in the back of the car, the pages wrinkled and smudged with dirt. Now the clipboard was underneath Loo's mattress—hundreds of signatures making no difference in the world at all.

"I need to talk to you," said Marshall. "Can you take a break or something?"

The boy looked like he hadn't slept in days. He was wearing his shirt and tie but the legs of his pants were splashed with mud. He reached for her hand and Loo wanted to take it but instead she shoved both fists into her apron pocket. She felt the bills there, all of her tips, folded over, and in her head she heard Hawley's voice. *He would have walked and you would have gone to jail.* The cook hit the bell for pickup. A group of fishing widows called for refills. Joe Strand and Pauly Fisk were eating breakfast with their sons, and now they waved Loo down for their check. She turned her back on Marshall and his meal. She was grateful for a reason to walk away. Folks at the counter were already whispering, and the rest were glaring at him over newspaper headlines: NOAA SETS NEW CATCH LIMITS and CAPTAIN TITUS STRIKES AGAIN.

The New England episode of *Whale Heroes* had finally aired. Loo had tuned in, hoping to see Marshall on television, but all she got was his stepfather, the wiry, ex-hippie captain of the *Athena*, who cursed a salty mean streak that was bleeped for audiences, and maintained a beard that reached the middle of his chest. Flanked by a crew of large-chested coeds, Captain Titus discussed the decline of the codfish next to the carcass of a beached whale. He then conducted a dissection of the whale, pulling out the contents of the stomach and matching them to a chart demonstrating the collapse of the local ecosystem. A marine sanctuary, he said, would not only reinvigorate the North Atlantic cod population. It would also provide a vital feeding ground for migrating humpback whales. He called three senators on a satellite phone to demand an investigation into overfishing near the Bitter Banks, then he chased down a trawler that was dragging for cod and dove into the water to cut their net with a bowie knife, sending a mountain of skates and flounder and seaweed and crabs spilling back into the ocean. The episode ended with the captain and his team being pelted with water cannons by a flotilla of local fishermen. Loo had recognized many of the same ruddy faces that morning at the Sawtooth, eating bacon and eggs.

Agnes waved Loo down at the coffee station. Her stomach pushed against her muumuu. Her body had swollen so much she'd had to remove her piercings. Without the stud in her lip she looked much older, even with the pink hair and eyeliner. She gestured with a packet of Sweet'N Low.

"That boy looks hungry."

"I'm trying to get rid of him."

"He's here for you?" Agnes tore the paper in half. "You better hope his mother doesn't find out."

"She already knows," said Loo.

Agnes raised her painted eyebrows. "Mary said you got him arrested. And then your father beat him up."

"It was a misunderstanding."

"You seem to have a lot of those." She rubbed her belly with the palm of her hand. "You know Gunderson's brothers want to fire her."

"Because of us?"

"Because of that," said Agnes, pointing across the restaurant.

Over in Loo's section, Jeremy Strand and Pauly Fisk, Jr. were standing at Marshall's table. Jeremy still smelled of sauerkraut, and Pauly junior still thought he was going to be a rock star. Since graduation they'd been working as fishermen, but now, with the catch limits, they had been laid off and were living in their fathers' basements. The boys were talking low and Marshall shook his head. Then Jeremy knocked the meat lover's special into the boy's lap. Two old-timers sitting at the counter glanced up from their plates. Another set down his newspaper and coffee. The rest of the customers stared at Marshall Hicks while Jeremy and Pauly junior walked out the door and got into their fathers' cars and drove away.

Agnes snatched Marshall's ticket out of Loo's hands.

"I'll drop the check," she said. "I know how to make men disappear."

But Marshall didn't leave, despite the food in his lap and despite Agnes's lousy service. He cleaned up in the bathroom and returned to his seat. He waited out all of the dirty looks from the fishermen. He ordered French toast. He ate every last bite. And when the breakfast rush subsided and Loo's shift was over, he followed her outside.

"What do you *want*?" Loo asked.

"I want you to invite me over," he said.

She spun the dial on her bike chain. "I'm too tired to talk."

Marshall scanned the parking lot, as if he expected someone to come charging out from behind one of the cars. "I'm sorry I got you into trouble."

"I'm not in trouble," said Loo.

"You're not?"

"My dad is actually kind of happy about it."

"God," Marshall said. "I thought he was going to kill me."

"Oh," said Loo. "No. He's not happy about *that*. He's not happy about you at all."

Marshall brushed cornbread crumbs off his tie. "I'll add him to the list."

"What did Pauly and Jeremy say?"

"They wanted to make sure I knew they were assholes."

Loo pulled her bike free of the rack. For a moment she thought of the old yellow bicycle that Hawley had bought her, that had been stolen outside of Dogtown. This one was black and more rugged, with tires thick enough for mountain trails. She'd bought it with her own money. She knew that she should climb on and ride away but she didn't.

"I saw *Whale Heroes*. Your mom must be happy."

"They cut the scene she was in."

"But it got everyone's attention."

"My stepfather took all the credit for her work. But she's trying to make the most of the publicity before the show moves back to Antarctica."

"So you still need the petition."

"I need you," said Marshall.

The August sun was beating down, the heat reflecting off the roofs of the cars. It was like staring through the bubbled edge of a camera lens, a circle of emptiness coming into focus. Nothing—and then something. Marshall's pants were covered in stains, his tie askew, his hair as shaggy as ever. He smelled like maple sugar candy.

"My dad's out fishing," Loo said.

Marshall took hold of the handlebars. "That's all I needed to know."

They rode together. Loo sat on the bicycle seat and Marshall stood, pumping the pedals, the frame bobbling whenever they slowed. She wrapped her arms around his waist. Kept the tips of her toes on the axle. She hoped no one would see them. She hoped that everyone would.

As soon as they got inside her house he started kissing her. His hands clutched at her shoulders, her hair, the sides of her face.

"I smell like food," she said.

"So do I."

It was different, being indoors. There were sheets, and she felt less self-conscious twisting underneath them in her darkened room. More willing to try. She pushed off her sneakers. She undid his belt. There was sweat and dirt on Marshall's neck, and he tore at her clothing like he was searching for something she had stolen from him. He felt the same. He felt like a stranger. She pulled his shirt up and the collar got stuck on his chin and for a moment he was headless and flopping like a fish in a net and she had his arms caught tight and then the shirt fell loose in her hands and there was nothing left to take from him—there was only skin and there was so much of it.

When they were finished, every pillow and blanket was on the floor. The fitted sheet had pulled up from the corners, exposing the hidden buttons of her mattress and the plastic tag's wrinkled warning. All that was left was their slick and salted bodies and a thread of a blanket that Loo pulled from their ankles and drew across her chest. Marshall had gone so still that she was certain he was asleep. At least she hoped he was, because she was afraid that if she opened her mouth now the truth might spill out: that she missed him, even though he was right there in the room.

When his voice came, it was muffled by the pillow. "Your planets are gone."

"I had to scrub for days."

Marshall sat up and looked around Loo's room, his eyes resting on each piece of furniture and item on her bureau. A bowl of shells, a strip of Skee-Ball tickets from the county fair, a pile of comic books, novels and astronomy guides, some half-melted candles from a power outage, a wad of balled-up tissues from her last cold, a small batch of cormorant feathers that she'd found and kept, because she liked their iridescent black color. Loo watched him puzzle over each object. It was as if he was measuring her life.

"My mom thinks you're crazy. You and your dad."

Loo clutched the blanket. She wished she could stuff the words back inside his mouth. Together they had been flying along the edge of something, but Marshall was making the world ordinary again. And so she kissed him, and for a moment they connected. He touched her shoulder. He ran his fingers over her back. All the places where he'd touched her with his pen. A part of her thrilled to this. A part of her wanted to pull away.

He took hold of her hands and pressed them over her head. He kissed her neck. Then he stopped and rested his forehead against hers and they waited like that, breathing into each other. He was there, with her, in the room. And then he wasn't. He slid his palms away. He crawled back to the edge of the bed and started pushing through the blankets, looking for his clothes.

"I can't lie anymore."

"About me or the petition?"

Marshall grabbed his boxers and slipped his legs through. Then he picked up his pants. Coins fell out of the pockets and scattered across the floor, rolling into the corners.

"Both," he said.

"Then tell your mom the truth."

"I don't think I can," said Marshall. "Things got weird at the police station. She already made me promise not to see you anymore."

"My dad was just being protective."

"It wasn't your dad. It was you," said Marshall. "You shoved her into a vending machine."

"She lifted my shirt."

"It doesn't matter what happened. You can't hit my mom. She's my mom."

Loo stared up at the ceiling. There was a crack in the plaster, directly over the bed. When she tilted her head to the right it looked like a monster and when she tilted her head to the left it looked like an alien. The more Marshall talked, the more alone she felt, and the more she tried to avoid looking at the spot, the more it drew her attention. She edged her chin back and forth. Alien. Monster. Monster. Alien. The image refused to hold form one way or the other. Her memories of her own mother were the same way. Sometimes she didn't know if they were real or Hawley's, a fabrication made from old photographs and snippets of stories or facts she'd read in Mabel Ridge's scrapbook.

"I need you to promise," said Marshall. "Not to hurt her again."

It would be so easy to say yes. But Loo was already curling around the soft places inside her that had been exposed. She thought of the whale dissected on TV by Marshall's stepfather, the giant liver and intestines, lungs and heart strewn across the beach. He had opened the creature and spilled all that was inside her into the world.

Marshall made Loo feel the same way. Ripped open. At times, she could barely stand it. The boy wanted to kiss her, even though she had broken his bones. Even though she had smashed Mary Titus's head open until it bled across her bathroom floor.

"You should be glad you even have a mother."

Marshall sat back down on the bed. "You know my dad drowned, too," he said. "A dead parent doesn't make you special. It just makes you sad."

She wanted to agree but no part of her did. Loo pulled the sheet from under him. "They eat the eyes first," she said. "Fish. And eels. But your dad was in the ocean, so it could have been a shark that got him. It would have been fast, if it was a shark."

The boy looked so startled that Loo did not tell him the rest of what was on her mind, all the facts she'd been collecting, all the bits and pieces she had learned from Mabel Ridge's newspaper clippings—that it had taken them a week to find her mother, that the police had to drag the lake with a net. She did not say, *Think of that. Think of your mother at the bottom of a lake.* She did not tell him how deep the lake was: more than half a mile. She did not tell him about the list she had made, of the different kinds of fish that swam in that particular lake, so that she would know what kind of fish had eaten her mother.

"I'm sorry I said anything." Marshall reached for his watch. He'd taken it off earlier, when the winding pin got caught in her hair. Now he pulled the strap tightly around his wrist.

Loo stayed beneath the covers. She wondered how to put her clothes on without revealing herself to him, even though, only a half hour earlier, Marshall had explored every inch of her with his tongue.

"I think . . ." said Marshall, and then he stopped. He stood and yanked his pants on quickly, with his back turned to the bed. His belt came next. And then he was searching around on the floor, picking up the coins that had fallen out of his pockets.

Across his back was a heavy, dark bruise, just starting to yellow at the edges, where Hawley had thrown him into the wall at the police station. And now, as he slipped the quarters and nickels back into his front pocket, Loo noticed marks across Marshall's forearm, the size and shape of her father's hand.

"I wish you'd never stolen my shoes," she said.

"I had a crush on you."

The back of her throat tasted like salt water. "That wasn't a crush."

"It hurt, didn't it?" Marshall lifted his crooked finger. "I know, because you gave me this."

Loo's face flushed, remembering the way his bone gave way beneath the skin. The pleasure she'd felt while it was breaking. She wanted to be a good person but she wasn't sure she would ever be good. "You don't know what you're talking about."

"Fine." Marshall put on his shirt. He walked to the door. "For the record, I didn't come here to break up with you."

She turned away. She stared up at the monster hidden in the ceiling.

"Loo."

He said her name like it was something he'd already left behind. She could feel her heart twisting inside the walls of her chest.

"Wait," she said. "Just wait a minute."

She pulled the sheet around her like a towel. She went into the living room and opened the trunk. She took out the Beretta with the slide lock, one of the handguns they'd used to practice in the woods. She dropped the magazine and filled it. She made sure the safety was on.

"Take this."

"I don't need a gun."

"Just in case. It will keep those guys from screwing with you," she said. Then she stepped away so he couldn't give anything back. And when he continued to hesitate, staring down at the machine in his hands, she added, "Never try, never win."

AFTER HE'D LEFT, LOO DREW water, poured salts and took a bath, trying to wash Marshall off her skin. She ducked her head under the surface and ran her fingers through her hair. On the ledge around the lip of the tub were bottles of her mother's shampoo and conditioner, the labels so curled and blurry that it was impossible to determine the brand.

When she was younger and they were on the road, living in temporary apartments, the first thing Hawley would do was unpack the shampoo and conditioner and put them on the edge of the bathtub. Then he'd wipe the bottles down with a towel and pack them again when they were ready to leave. The sticky gel inside was a pinkish color, and smelled of berries. Loo would stare at the bottles from underneath the water, to see how long she could hold her breath. She'd gotten better over the years. Now she could stay under for nearly two minutes before her lungs began to burn.

Loo heard Hawley coming up the front steps. She lifted her head, batting drops off her eyelashes. He set down something heavy on the porch. Then she heard him come inside and open the trunk and start putting away his guns. He'd taken the Colt and the long-range rifle, but it wasn't until Loo heard the familiar chink of the Remington and the Winchester, too, that she wondered why he needed so many guns to go fishing.

"Loo?"

"I'm in the tub," she called.

Her father stepped to the bathroom door. Loo thought of the night she'd locked herself inside with Mary Titus. The blood on the tiles. The bite mark on her palm.

"You all right in there?"

Loo squeezed her mother's shampoo. "I'm fine."

"Don't fall down the drain."

She heard him cross the floor and close the lid of the trunk. Then he went outside and she heard the sound of the new padlock unlocking and a rumble as the garage door opened and closed.

It had taken Hawley and Loo hours to make space for the Firebird in the garage. Now the car was nestled inside, between the lawnmower and a cord of stacked firewood. The time Hawley used to spend in the bathroom shut up with her mother's things had shifted to the Pontiac, which he tinkered on for hours, even though it was never going to see the light of day again. As he dug around beneath the hood, Loo would stay inside the house, feeling jealous. For months the car had been hers alone, and she hadn't realized how much she had needed it—a way to be close to Lily that did not involve Hawley and his endless grief.

The rest of the cars from the impound lot—the coupe, the BMW, the SUV and the hatchback—had been driven to Ipswich and abandoned on a dirt road near the bird sanctuary. It had been a long night, commuting back and forth. By the time they were finished, dawn was breaking and the robins and cardinals were chattering in the trees. Hawley had made a phone call, and an hour later, when they drove past again after eating breakfast, the stolen cars had vanished.

"Somebody owed me a favor," was all her father said.

Since then there had been a shift in Hawley's mood. He wasn't happy, exactly—but he was content, as if the job had settled something. Once they emptied the garage and slid the Firebird inside, he'd carried the sniper rifle he'd used to the kitchen table, and showed her how to remove the serial number, just as he'd shown her which cables to pull and hit to spark a motor to life.

. . .

ON THE OTHER SIDE OF the bathroom door the phone was ringing. Loo waited to see if Hawley would answer. She wondered if it might be Marshall—and then she *knew* it must be Marshall—and she grabbed a towel off the rack and scrambled out of the bathroom and hurried, dripping, across the living room floor. She snatched the receiver and pressed it to her ear.

"Hello?" she said.

"Your mother's car was stolen again. I thought you should know."

Mabel Ridge's tone was so cavalier, so unconcerned with all the trouble she'd caused, that Loo wasn't sure how to respond. Ever since the arrest two weeks ago, she'd wanted to curse the old woman out. But now the words wouldn't come.

"You gave me those keys," she managed at last. "You told me I could take the car."

"Not forever. Not to keep."

Loo went to the front door and opened it, but there were no police cars, or any signs of anything unusual. Only Hawley's plastic cooler set on the welcome mat. She dragged it inside and lifted the lid. On a bed of ice were two large fish, their eyes wild, their speckled brown-and-yellow coats gleaming.

"Well," Mabel said with a sigh. "In any case, Lily's car is gone now. The police say it's probably gone for good. Chopped up into pieces and sold for parts. If you had come back to visit me, none of this would have happened."

"I didn't want to see you," said Loo.

Mabel cleared her throat. "I suppose you think I'm a bitter old woman. I suppose you think I'm hateful. But I've got reasons for the things I do."

"Like getting me arrested?"

"Like telling the truth," said Mabel Ridge.

The fish inside the cooler had wide-open gills. Single stripes cut through their speckled skin, and beneath each pair of fleshy lips, a single barbel dangled like a lure. Atlantic codfish. Loo recognized them from the pamphlets that were now scattered all over Dogtown. She shut the lid and sat down on top of the cooler.

"Did you read the scrapbook I gave you?" her grandmother asked.

"There weren't any pictures. You could have given me one, at least."

Mabel Ridge sighed a great big bellowing sigh. "Your mother was a good swimmer. She could swim through open ocean, from the Point all the way through the harbor. That's nearly five miles."

"You said that before."

"The day it happened, at the lake—the newspapers all wrote that it was perfect weather. No waves on the water. Like a mirror, one of them said. And the lake was only half a mile wide. Your mother never would have drowned in a *lake*."

It could have been Loo's own voice talking. Not now but twenty, thirty years in the future. She felt the towel brush up against the back of her knees. There was a puddle on the living room floor. She didn't know if it was from her or the cooler of fish but she was standing in the middle of it.

"He killed her," said Mabel Ridge. "Your father. I know it. And now you know it, too."

Loo slammed the receiver back into the cradle. The phone slid away and let out an echo of a ring, as if someone had tried to call and then hung up before connecting. Loo's hair was trailing rivulets of water, running like open faucets down her back. Her hand reached for the phone and drew it toward her. She picked up the receiver and slowly brought it to her ear again, listening to the steady hum of the open line, wanting and not wanting to know what came next.

When she glanced up, Hawley was standing in the doorway to the kitchen. He was so still he looked like a ghost.

"Who was that?" he asked.

"No one," said Loo.

Hawley's hands were covered in grease. She pictured the hood of the Pontiac propped open, her father feeling around all that cold metal, touching her mother's car the same careful way he took his guns apart and cleaned them. He watched Loo now with the same kind of carefulness as she set the phone back down in the cradle.

"I've got some fish for dinner. Just need to gut them."

"I saw," Loo said. "They look good."

Hawley walked toward her. It seemed like he was going to say something else. But instead he picked up the cooler, smearing grease across the plastic handle. "Twenty minutes," he said. Then he walked out the door.

Loo pulled her towel closer and padded across the living room, leaving a trail of footprints behind on the hardwood. She closed and locked the door to the bathroom. It had been open long enough for all the steam to leave. The mirror was clear again. She stared into her own face.

Outside in the yard, she knew that Hawley was cutting open the codfish. He was sliding the knife underneath their ribs, just as Captain Titus had done to the whale on the beach. Her father was clearing out the intestines and stomach and liver—gray and pink all mixed and spilling onto the grass. Next he would cut off the head of the fish and then he'd start scraping the scales. The seagulls always came and carried away the insides, but the scales would remain, flickering on the driveway, tiny chips of iridescent bone, until they began to rot and smell and Loo washed them away with the hose.

The bath had cooled but Loo climbed back in. She stayed there, shivering and thinking until the tips of her fingers became raised and swollen. Then she slid underneath the water and opened her eyes. Her mother's shampoo and conditioner peered down at her from the ledge, two worn-out sentinels. Loo focused on the bottles, the shapes distant and blurred. She started counting.

As she counted, she pictured her mother at the bottom of the lake, the flesh lifting off her bones. It would be peaceful there, and dark, and quiet, with all the weight of the water above. There would be no room for air—only pressure, pushing through her ears and up into her nose, squeezing her lungs and then ironing them flat. Loo held herself down for another minute, feeling more alive than ever, pressing hard against the porcelain, until she heard Hawley's fist pounding on the door, and her spine bucked, and she broke the surface, sputtering, choking, gasping—drawing the deepest part of the water back with her and turning it out onto the bathroom floor.

Bullet Number Six

THE WHITE NIGHTS IN ALASKA BEGAN IN LATE SPRING. EACH DAY GREW longer, until the sun set for only five hours, then four, then three, leaving the sky a troubling, otherworldly gray. As the days stretched and lengthened, Hawley found he could not sleep. Nothing seemed to help—warm milk, hot baths, pills, even the blackout shades Lily had bought. He tossed and turned, and then he paced the house, and then he put on his boots and went for a walk.

The roads were unnaturally silent and deserted. Hawley considered walking to Cook Inlet but instead he went past the elementary school and along Old Sterling Highway. It was their first summer in Anchor Point, and for the most part, they liked it. The beaches reminded Lily of Olympus, and Hawley fished and gathered oysters, which he hadn't done since his father was alive. Living in Alaska they didn't need much, and Hawley had been able to stretch out the last of his money, but now the safe-deposit box was nearly empty and they had a baby on the way.

Hawley's father had a set of rules for living in the wilderness. It was all about the number three. A man could go three minutes without air. Three hours without shelter. Three days without water. Three weeks without food. And three months without seeing another person before he'd start to go crazy. Hawley had gone longer than that, once or twice before he met Lily, hiding out in the woods after a job, and he still remembered the shock of returning to town, sitting in a diner drinking coffee while folks chattered around him. Maybe he had gone a little off, being alone that much. It always took a few days before he was able to speak to anyone properly. And even longer to shake what haunted him in the woods—that the world had been emptied of everyone and left him behind in that emptiness. It was the same feeling he got walking the streets during midnight sun.

Eventually he came to the bridge that crossed Anchor River. He stood there with his hands in his pockets, watching the current and his own breath cloud the air, thinking about his call with Jove the day before. Hawley had reached out looking for a job, and Jove knew of one in Cordova. The trick was it was working for Ed King.

The original hire had been a bush pilot, but the pilot had skimmed off the payment he was supposed to deliver, and King had him taken down one fine morning while the pilot's girlfriend was making pancakes. The girlfriend was killed, too. Hawley had read about the murder in the papers. It was a real mess, the breakfast burning on the stove and the girl collapsed in front of the refrigerator, her blood mixed up with the milk. But it was also lucky because now another man was needed, and that other man was Hawley.

"This can't get screwed up again," said Jove. "I need someone I can trust."

"King won't want me anywhere near this." Hawley could still picture the old boxer running after Lily's truck, pie smeared across his suit.

"He told me to find someone who could handle it," said Jove. "We just won't tell him that it's you."

The plan was a simple exchange, cash for carry. Hawley would be gone for only a few days. He hadn't told Lily yet. He didn't want her to worry. He hadn't worked anything like this since before they got married. But he was feeling restless, and they needed the money. At least this is what he told himself as he turned away from the river. And what he said when he told Jove he'd take the job.

Their front door didn't make a sound as he slipped back inside the cabin. He took off his boots, hung up his coat and went to the bedroom. Lily was still sleeping, her black hair piled on the pillow, the comforter pulled up under her rounded stomach. The perpetual daylight did not bother her. Ever since they'd found out she was pregnant, she'd developed a knack for falling asleep anywhere, day or night, in a car or on a couch or even when they were eating, dropping her head onto one of her arms and quietly disappearing for a few minutes, her mouth open.

Hawley sat on the end of their bed. He smoothed her hair and kissed the back of her neck. Lily opened her eyes, rubbed her face and began to pick the crust off her lips with the edge of her fingernail. She was a drooler.

"Get my notebook," she said.

Hawley opened the closet and rummaged around until he found Lily's purse. Inside were her wallet and keys, a package of tissues, some shells from the beach and a small black notebook, with an elastic strap across the cover and a small pen that fit inside. He grabbed the notebook and brought it back to the bed. Lily yawned as she took it from him, then opened the pages and began to draw. In the old days she used to roll a cigarette when she woke up but she'd quit as soon as she'd found out about the baby. Without the nicotine she was irritable, especially in the mornings. She'd started a dream journal to keep her mind off lighting up.

"What was it this time?" he asked.

"A flock of birds. There were so many of them I couldn't see the sky."

She took his hand and put it on her swollen stomach. Recently, the baby had started to move. Whenever Hawley felt the fluttering deep inside his wife, it made him want to get in his car and drive.

"I think it's asleep."

"Wait for it." Lily flipped the page of her notebook. She drew feathers and wings. "I always wake up too soon," she said.

Too soon for what, Hawley wanted to ask, but he already felt like a fool for being jealous of the baby who had brought these vivid dreams, along with everything else that was upsetting their lives: the visits to the doctor, the boxes of diapers, the tiny clothes, the stretch marks on Lily's skin. He still remembered that day in March when she got home from the doctor's office. Hawley had been eating scrambled eggs in the kitchen when she told him the news. He'd held her, but the only thought he'd had was that his eggs were getting cold.

"There," said Lily. "Did you feel that?"

Something rumbled beneath Hawley's fingers. Like a clam tunneling deeply through tightly packed sand. He shook his head. "I must have missed it."

Eventually the midnight sun turned into a true morning, and as soon as it did, Hawley closed his eyes and started to fall asleep. As he drifted, he was aware of his wife getting up and getting dressed, pulling up her maternity pants, sliding her breasts into a bra meant for nursing. When she tried to wake him, he turned over and groaned.

Lily shook the car keys. "It's the ultrasound," she said.

"Do I have to go?"

Her hand fell and began stroking her stomach, as if she were working out a muscle that had just been pulled. "I guess not."

She turned away from him and walked out of the room, and he could hear her in the kitchen, washing the dishes. Then he heard her gather her things and get in the car and leave. As soon as she did, he opened his eyes and picked up her notebook from the bed. The birds had necks like swans, twisted at odd angles, their beaks drawn to sharp points, their talons spread wide.

Since she got pregnant Lily's mind had been full of monsters, and yet she never seemed bothered by her dreams—the three-headed dogs, the bulls with red eyes, the packs of man-eating horses. She drew them in her notebook and then they were gone from her life. But each time Hawley snuck a look at those pages, he felt like he was reading his future.

I'll tell her the truth, he thought. *As soon as she gets home.*

. . .

HAWLEY SAID HE WAS GOING hunting. He told her that he'd be gone overnight, maybe longer. Lily tugged on her braid and didn't say a word in return. She went into the kitchen and packed him a lunch with sandwiches and sodas and a thermos of coffee. While she did this Hawley got his duffel and went through his stash in the basement. He took the Colt and his father's long gun and a SIG Sauer pistol. Then he packed bullets. Hornady InterLocks, A-Square Dead-Toughs and Winchester Silvertips. When he came back upstairs Lily was sitting on the front steps, the lunch bag resting on her knees.

"You're not happy," she said.

"I'm happy," said Hawley.

Lily grabbed the collar of his shirt and pulled him close. He bent his head and inhaled the scent of her. For a moment he considered staying. She slid her hands into the back pockets of his jeans, squeezed his ass and then let go. She handed him his coat.

"Promise that you'll call me tonight."

"I promise."

"You mean it?"

"I said I will."

Lily watched Hawley as he loaded a sleeping bag, his mess kit, the food and his ammunition inside the cab of the truck. Then she picked up a rock and threw it at him. Hawley ducked but the rock still hit him hard—right in the soft spot underneath his ribs. He pulled up his shirt and touched the mark she'd made, bright red and smarting.

"You better be happy when you get back," Lily said. And then she went inside and closed the door.

WHEN HE GOT TO ANCHORAGE Hawley walked into the bank and was led by the manager down to the locked rooms where the safe-deposit boxes were. The drop was there waiting for him. It was a small aluminum suitcase, with a handle and wheels. He zipped the sides open and looked at the money. The bills smelled of fresh ink and all the excitement of his old life. For a moment he thought of taking the case, going home for Lily and heading to Mexico. Then he remembered the pilot and his girlfriend, and he closed the lid, locked the handle and wheeled the suitcase out of the bank.

At Whittier he took the ferry to Cordova. By then it was early evening, but the sun was still bright. The boat was full of oil rig workers, drinking and playing cards. Hawley sat at a booth and opened up the lunch bag Lily had packed for him. Inside were two cans of ginger ale, a roast beef sandwich on white bread, a ham-and-cheese sandwich on marbled rye, some pickles wrapped in tinfoil and a note that said: *It's a girl.*

The paper had been torn from Lily's dream book and was folded in two, so that *It's* was on one side of the crease and *a girl* was on the other. Hawley opened and closed the note several times, as if the content might change if he did this enough, but the handwriting remained solid, an indelible mark. He put the sandwiches and the pickles and the ginger ale back into the bag. Then he went to the canteen and ordered a beer. The ferry pitched into the wake of a crossing tanker, and all around him men held on to their seats and groaned.

It was the first alcohol he'd had in more than a year. Lily had never asked him to stop but it didn't feel right to drink without her. Now whenever they walked past a bar, she'd say, "I just added another year to your life." And for a long time the thought of all those extra years with Lily, stacked up in some vault of the future, had been enough to make him keep walking.

By the time they'd arrived in Cordova Hawley had nursed his way through four beers and half a bottle of whiskey he'd traded with one of the oil riggers for Lily's pickles. He bought a coffee from the canteen before it closed and then made his way unsteadily down the stairs and waited in his truck for the deck hands to wave off the cars. Once he was over the ramp he drove straight through town and got on the Copper River Highway. After he passed Eyak Lake and the military base, the paved road turned into gravel and wove through a swampy forest, lined with spruce and hemlock. His truck swerved back and forth, kicking up dust. It was close to nine o'clock at night but still looked like the middle of the afternoon.

He passed a moose and a calf, munching weeds in a pond. Then up ahead he saw something dead in the road. Antelope or deer, maybe. It was too torn up to recognize. There was a young eagle ripping into the belly, spilling intestines onto the road. Hawley swerved around, and as he did, the eagle took flight. Hawley watched in the rearview as the bird circled, its wings spread like fingers, then the eagle landed and continued its meal.

He drove for an hour and never passed another car. Twice he dozed, waking up just as the truck was veering off into the brush. He drank more of the coffee and ate one of Lily's sandwiches, and then he came to the bridge where the highway ended. Before he crossed, Hawley saw the sign for Childs Glacier. He took a left and followed a narrow dirt road along the south side of the river to a parking lot. There was only one car parked there under the trees, an old Chevy Silverado. Hawley slowed the truck and idled a few spaces away. There was no one in the Silverado, but the back was covered with bumper stickers. IT'S CALLED TOURIST SEASON: WHY CAN'T WE SHOOT THEM?; JESUS IS COMING—LOOK BUSY; and WHAT IF THE HOKEY POKEY *IS* WHAT IT'S ALL ABOUT?

Hawley parked the truck. He found the bottle of whiskey under the seat and took a few more pulls. He read the bumper stickers again. If things went wrong and he had to kill the man who owned the Silverado, he could deliver the package, get his payment from Jove and still keep the aluminum case. With each sip of whiskey the idea took stronger shape in his mind, until he'd imagined every detail, from the grizzled lowlife no one would miss, to the moment when Lily laughed as Hawley dumped the money across their bed.

Hawley made sure his guns were loaded. Then he opened the lunch bag and took out the note. He'd folded and refolded it so many times on the ferry that the crease had grown soft, and now the paper came apart in two pieces, the one that said *It's* and the other that said *a girl*. Hawley thought about Lily writing the words. He put the half that said *It's* back in the bag. He took the half that said *a girl* and slipped it into his front pocket. Then he got out of the car.

The parking lot was deserted, so he made his way toward the marked trail. There were several signs about grizzly bears, and another that warned people about tidal waves. Hawley stepped from the tree line and down a deep slope. From there he could see the glacier, looming on the opposite shore.

He'd seen icebergs since moving to Alaska, but this was something completely different. This was where icebergs were *born*. The glacier was a giant, rippling wall of blue ice, over three hundred feet high and three miles long, with the Copper River churning at the base—a marvel of gravity, pressure and time. The shelf moved each day, bit by bit across the mountains, and eventually broke off—calved—into the water below, creating instant tsunamis. Hawley had read about a few lunatics who'd tried to ride the giant waves on surfboards. Two had been crushed beneath a chunk of ice. The Forest Service had cordoned off the river downstream but they never found the bodies.

There were two women waiting along the shore of the beach, dressed like hikers. They had boots and packs, a tent and walking poles—the kind people used to climb mountains. One of the women had a camera set up with a zoom lens on a tripod, and the other was standing and watching the glacier with a pair of binoculars, her hair in pigtails. She was a little old to be wearing pigtails, Hawley thought. It made her look like a teenager from a distance, but as he got closer he could tell she was somewhere between forty and fifty. She was built, though. Thick shoulders and muscled, ropey arms. Skin weathered and toned. She looked like she'd lived her whole life outdoors. The other woman was young, maybe twenty, and had a military buzz cut and a tattoo of a crow on the back of her neck.

"Here for the view?" the woman with pigtails said.

"Nope," said Hawley.

"I guess you're meeting us, then."

They were both carrying. Hawley could see the bulge underneath the tattooed girl's shirt where the handgun was tucked into her jeans. There was a rifle next to the tripod, and the older woman with the pigtails picked it up and set the gun into the crook of her arm like it had been made to live there.

Behind them came the sound of thunder. A cracking and splitting of air. Hawley could feel the boom in his chest, the rumble of an approaching storm. He glanced up but the sky was clear. Not a cloud overhead or in the distance.

"We've been here for an hour," said the tattooed girl. "There's been some avalanching, but the glacier hasn't calved yet."

"It'll break soon," said the woman.

"I want to get a picture," said the girl.

"You will," said the woman.

She put her hand on the crow tattoo and rubbed the girl's neck. The way she did this made Hawley realize they were lovers. Then the girl shrugged off the woman's touch. She did it like she was trying not to, the same way that Hawley had pulled away from Lily when they'd said goodbye.

He felt for the Magnum in his pocket. He said, "Steller?"

"That's right," said the older woman.

"I've got your money."

"That's what I like to hear."

Hawley went back to the truck and retrieved the suitcase. He rolled it across the gravel. It made a lot of noise, so he grabbed the handle and carried it the rest of the way onto the beach. He flipped the case onto the rocks. "You can count it if you want," he said.

"Don't mind if I do."

Steller put her rifle down, then came forward and unzipped the case. The girl hung by the tent and kept her eyes on Hawley and a loose hand on her gun. She had a pretty face, but her body was too thin. She had another tattoo of a bird, between her thumb and forefinger. She scratched her chin and the bird looked like it was flying.

Every once in a while there'd be another popping sound, like distant gunfire, and Steller would stop counting the money and glance over at the massive shelf of ice. Whenever she did, Hawley found himself looking, too.

"The Tlingit call it 'white thunder,'" said Steller.

"The glacier?" Hawley asked.

"No," said Steller, "the sound the glacier makes when it breaks."

She was crouched at Hawley's feet, rifling through the suitcase. He looked down at the part in her hair. There was a small area at the back of her head that was starting to go bald. The skin there was red from the sun and covered with brown spots. Hawley imagined putting the barrel of his gun there. He tried to shake the thought, but the idea haunted him the whole time she was counting the money.

Steller zipped the suitcase back together. Then she extended the handle and tried to wheel the bag across the beach. The aluminum banged against the rocks and wedged itself between two large boulders. It made Hawley think of Mabel Ridge, her giant roller-bag stuck between cars at the train station.

Hawley helped the woman get the case loose. "What kind of name is Steller?"

"My father was a scientist. He named me after Georg Steller. You know, the sea cow?"

Hawley shook his head.

"First white man to step foot in Alaska. But the sea cow is why he's famous. Discovered the last ones, right before they went extinct."

"He doesn't give a shit about Steller," said the girl.

The older woman shot the girl a look. She tugged at one of her pigtails.

Hawley said, "Maybe I do."

The girl was still scratching at her chin, the skin there growing red, the bird tattoo fluttering its wings open and closed. "Can't we get this over with? I just want to get this over with."

Steller moved close and touched the back of the girl's neck again. Hawley waited for the girl to shrug it off. He wished the girl wouldn't. But she did. And this time something crossed Steller's face, like skin tightening up over a scar.

"Behave yourself," Steller said. Then she ducked down and crawled inside the tent. When she came back out, she was holding a square wooden crate, about the size of a small television set. She set it down on the beach, pried the top off with the back of a hammer and started pulling out handfuls of straw.

Inside was an old ceramic bowl, the color of sand. The sides were covered with engravings. Figures of people and some sort of writing.

There were also bands of rings, circling all the way down to the base, chips along the edges and a hole pierced through the bottom. It looked like a crusty old flowerpot.

"What the fuck is this?" Hawley asked.

"It's a clepsydra," said Steller.

"It's supposed to be a clock."

"It is a clock." She ran her finger along the rings. "You fill this with water, and as the level goes down, you know a certain amount of time has passed. Like an hourglass," she said.

Hawley picked the clepsydra up and turned it in his hands. He thought of all the money stashed in the aluminum suitcase. "A bowl," he said.

"A clepsydra," said Steller.

He set the piece back down. "How do I know it's not a fake?"

"There's only seven of these left," said Steller. "The rest are in museums. This one should be, too."

"How'd you get your hands on it?" Hawley asked.

"You don't want to know," said the girl.

The gashes and shapes along the sides of the bowl seemed to hold meaning by the way they repeated. There was a wedge that looked like a double cross, another that resembled a mountain turned on its side. Hawley peered into the bowl, ran his finger along the rings. He wondered what this clock had measured. Hours. Weeks. Years. Maybe entire lifetimes.

The women flanked Hawley on either side. As they stood there he imagined two bowls full of water. One for Steller, another for the girl. The time they had left streaming through. He touched the hardened clay around the base of the pot, then slid his finger through the hole in the bottom. The channel felt cool and smooth, deep as an exit wound. When he removed his hand, his knuckles were covered with a thin powdering of dust.

"Next time," Steller said, "they should send someone who can read cuneiform." She reached and fixed one of her pigtails again, and as she did Hawley realized that all this time, as they'd been standing there on the beach and talking, she'd known that he was thinking of ways to kill her.

"It's breaking!" shouted the girl.

They all turned. A spray of ice slid down the side of the glacial shelf and fell into the river. It looked like a waterfall of snow. For a moment the white powder seemed to be gathering in force, and then it trickled away. Some one hundred feet above, inside a dark furrow of blue ice, another waterfall began, arcing in a shimmering line. Then that, too, stopped.

Hawley felt the air get thin.

The girl had gone back to her camera, crouching before the viewfinder. She twisted the lens back and forth with her hand, scanning the glacier. One last plume of snow spattered into the river, underneath a giant overhanging block of ice the size of a three-story building. The shower of flakes slowed, then stopped, and the river evened out and became calm.

Hawley waited with the women. They waited some more.

"Ah, man," said the girl.

And then the air cracked and split and roared. The front of the glacier was breaking apart. Chunks of ice, one after the other, and then the giant block came loose. All three of them froze, rooted in place, as if they'd been cast under a spell. Time slowed as the hunk of ice traveled, and when it finally smashed into the river, a ripple went back up the side of the glacier, and then the whole face of the shelf came loose and started sliding down.

It was as if the earth were collapsing. A skyscraper thrown over a cliff. The sight made Hawley ill, like some part of himself was falling with the ice. Everything that ancient, frozen water had seen, the passing of millennia, the formation of the continents, and now, here it was—the end of the road. When the slab finally hit, the river exploded in a spray of brown and white, shooting columns of ice and water so high into the air they transformed into clouds of smoke and sparkled like glass, splintering and shimmering and shooting directly for the beach.

Hawley stumbled backward and fell over the wooden crate, scraping his ribs. All along the shoreline the river sank and pulled away, like a drain had been pulled. Chunks of floating ice were sucked under as the river displaced and began to crest. Steller and the girl were already making a run for it, the camera slung over the girl's back and the aluminum case banging between them. Hawley snatched the clepsydra and followed. The women were yelling something but the roar of the water covered it all. Together they scrambled over the rocks, up the incline toward their car. Hawley caught his ankle and fell again. Up ahead, the girl had reached the parking lot. She turned and threw her arm back. Steller dropped the suitcase and the women grabbed hold of each other and then the wave was upon them.

The force of the water caught Hawley up from behind. The shock so arctic-freezing-cold it knocked the wind out of him. As he struggled for air, he had the sensation of being carried along, pushed toward some higher plane, and then his feet lost hold and he was tumbling in the froth of white, his body flipped and the weight of the water crushing him down against the rock bed, then dragging him backward by the ankles. He was inhaling water. Sand and dirt and salt. The clepsydra was filling, filling, filling, an anchor pinning him in place, and then the river tore it loose from his hands.

His only thought was that he could not breathe. He fought the current but he could not find the surface. His father had always been afraid of drowning, so he'd kept Hawley from going in over his head. He'd wanted to protect his son, but as another wave of ice crashed into Hawley he understood that by doing this, his father had failed him. And that he did not want to be a father who failed.

His hand passed over something solid, a tree fallen over into the river, and he grabbed the branches and held on long enough to pull his face out of the water. Hawley forced a breath. Everything around him was movement. A heaviness caught around his legs, dragging him under again. He pulled and kicked until he saw a flash of purple nylon. It was Steller's tent.

He was maybe two hundred yards downstream. The wave had

picked him up, pushed him forward and then hauled him along the edge of the river. The current was still choppy and rolling, chunks of blue slush bobbing along the surface. Hawley clung to the tree and used it to pull himself toward shore, his limbs aching from the cold. The entire beach was still flooded, but he could see the current pulling back through the boulders, receding to its original shape. Hawley reached the base of the roots where the tree had been forced over, the wet bark scraping his nails, and in one final push dragged himself free of the river.

The beach was swamped, pools left behind cloudy with rust-colored water. Hawley touched his ribs. They were tender. The side of his cheek was torn open where he'd hit the rocks. He'd lost his gun and his wallet. His body was shivering, his clothes drenched. He turned to look at the glacier's altered face, the empty hole where the ice had sheared away.

His coat was so heavy with water that it felt like the weight of another person across his back. Hawley shrugged out of the sleeves and threw it to the ground. He pulled his shirt over his head and wrung it out, his muscles shaking, his skin awash with goosebumps. When he put the shirt on again, he felt colder than before. He slid his hand into his front pocket. Lily's note was still there, but the ink had blossomed and bled, so that each letter was now three times the size. *A GIRL.* Hawley held the paper between his fingers. Then he folded it carefully and put it back into his pocket.

His boots squished as he staggered toward the parking lot. When he climbed over the embankment he saw the women, soaked and slick as rats. They still had the aluminum case. They were standing by their Silverado with the hood open, pulling out blankets from the trunk. Hawley glanced at his pickup truck. The bed was full of water.

"You made it," said the girl.

"I guess so," said Hawley.

"The engines are flooded." Steller was holding a flashlight. She let it slide down the length of her hand. But the girl gave him one of the blankets.

"You get your picture?" He wondered if they had even tried to look for him.

"Nope," said the girl.

"I've never seen a piece that big fall before," said Steller.

"I thought we were dead," said the girl, and she started to laugh. Steller laughed, too. The women were giddy, their voices pitched high. They had held on to each other and it had been enough to keep them on land. It was something they'd talk about in years to come. And later—when their lives were full and they no longer loved each other—forget.

But Hawley would never forget.

"Where's the clepsydra?" Steller asked.

Hawley looked down at his hands. He could still feel the bowl's weight pulling him to the bottom of the river. "Gone."

"You lost it?" said the girl.

"I think it broke," said Hawley. He remembered the pot being wrenched away from him, the sound of something fracturing beneath the waves.

Steller hurried back toward the beach, but stopped just short of climbing down. She stayed on the upper banks of the river and scanned the shore. Hawley and the girl followed her, blankets wrapped around their shoulders, and all three went back and forth along the edge of the parking lot. The beach was covered with debris, branches and piles of fish tossed up from the wave. A massive swarm of birds—hawks and gulls and crows and starlings—were eagerly devouring the salmon, picking out chunks of flesh and carrying away pieces in their claws, as the fish flopped and twisted on the rocks. Hawley saw the ragged remains of the purple tent in the distance, floating downstream. But no sign of the clepsydra, or the crate.

"Maybe it will wash up," said the girl.

"You know what I went through to get my hands on that thing?" Steller said. "It was more than three thousand years old, for fuck's sake!"

Hawley would have to return the money to the bank in Anchorage. Then he'd call Jove and tell him the deal had been a bust. There'd be no extra cash, no happy reunion with Lily, just a long ride home with his tail between his legs. His hand slid to his belt. It wasn't until he felt the gap there that he remembered his gun had been washed away.

He said, "I'm going to need that case back."

Steller took a step closer to the girl. "We delivered the clock as agreed," she said. "We did our part."

"It's your fault it got lost," said the girl.

"The only thing that matters is that I didn't get what I came here for."

"You think we're going to just give you the money back?" the girl asked.

They didn't know he'd lost his gun. But then again, maybe they did. The adrenaline and icy water had cleared his head completely. Even with the blanket the girl had given him, he was in danger of hypothermia. His body was starting to shut down, his shoulders trembling, his teeth chattering. But he couldn't go back with nothing. It was either the clock or the money.

"I'm sorry," he said.

"I'm sorry, too," said Steller, and from underneath her shirt she produced a snub-nosed Ruger. It was the kind of gun an old man might own. Someone who didn't care anymore about how things looked, only if they felt right. Hawley had always thought Rugers looked like toys, the handles longer than the nose, but they were tough guns. He'd seen Rugers run over by trucks and still fire without any problems.

"I'm going to give you five seconds," said Steller, "to get in your car and get out of here."

"You're not going to shoot me," said Hawley.

"That's one," said Steller. She cocked the hammer, and the cylinder spun into place. Hawley saw there were at least three slugs inside. "Just stop," he said. "Wait a minute."

"That's two," said Steller.

Hawley stood there in his wet clothes, trying to figure if the woman was serious. She looked serious enough. He glanced around, trying to gauge the distance for cover. He didn't have much to work with. The Silverado, his truck. And the girl. She was twitching like mad, holding on to the hood of the car. In a few steps he could have his hands around her neck.

The sky rumbled and they all felt the glacier shift. Steller kept her eyes straight, but Hawley turned to the river. There was no waterfall of snow, no signs of cracks on the surface. But he could feel the change, an internal compaction coming loose, deep within the ice shelf, a place so used to pressure, the molecules had shrunk and now there was a stirring, a cave full of secrets about to yawn and spill open.

"Three," said Steller.

"All right." He raised his hands. The blanket fell from his shoulders. He started walking backward, toward his car. "I'm leaving."

Steller backed off from the Silverado and followed him. "Check it first," she said to the girl. "He's probably got a rifle in there."

Hawley waited while the girl hurried over and opened the driver's side door. He watched her rummaging and calculated how many hours he had left before he had to make the drop. Once the window was missed, King would contact Jove. And Jove wouldn't have a choice—it was too much money—he'd have to tell him it was Hawley who had failed to deliver. Then someone would be on their way to Anchor Point.

The girl took his long gun from the dashboard. She checked under the seat and found the Colt. "I think that's it," she said.

"Four," said Steller.

Hawley climbed up. He sat there like a fool with the door open. The sun was just above the horizon, the sky beginning to gray. In another hour, the sun would rise again to a full and bright morning. Back in Anchor Point, Lily was probably still sleeping. But soon she'd be awake. She'd put on her slippers and head to the kitchen and see what there was for breakfast. She'd open their fridge. The light would illuminate her face. And then there would be blood mixed with milk. Pancakes burning on the stove.

He couldn't leave without the money. He couldn't take the chance. He got out of the truck and faced the women. "My wife," said Hawley. "She's having a baby."

"Shit," said the girl.

"Five," said Steller. And then she shot him.

• • •

IN THE END IT WAS his father who came. Hawley saw the old man walking toward him across the parking lot in the old brown waders he used to wear surf casting. The waders came up to his chest and had a pair of green suspenders. Whenever he got home from the beach Hawley's father would shed the rubber like a second skin and hose the waders off in the yard—the legs smelling of mold and fish guts, no matter how often they were rinsed out. Afterward the waders were tied to the clothesline, and whenever a breeze came up and filled the legs with air, it looked like a ghost dancing in the wind.

"Are you all right?" Hawley's father asked.

"I've been shot." Hawley's voice came out soft and quiet. He wondered if the man could hear him.

"Shit," said his father. "How long have you been out here?"

Hawley wasn't sure. He remembered waking up facedown in the gravel. The way the small rocks stuck to his eyelids when he raised his head. A few of the pebbles were still there, clustered on his cheek like barnacles. He could feel them but he could not lift his arm to brush them off.

His father set down the cooler and the fishing rod he was carrying and pressed a set of fingers against Hawley's neck. "Who shot you?"

"A woman." He couldn't get any air. It felt like he was mouthing the words.

"Isn't that always the way." The man was lifting Hawley's shirt. "You packed the wound pretty good."

And then Hawley remembered. The women screaming at each other and tossing his guns, the Silverado peeling out of the parking lot. How he'd crawled back to his truck, found a towel and jammed it up inside of himself and even started to tape the mess to his side. But then he couldn't breathe and got dizzy.

"All right," said his father. "Hang on. I'll be right back."

As he waited Hawley looked at the fishing rod his father had been carrying. It wasn't the old fifteen-foot Kilwell he'd always used. This rod was more delicate, only nine or ten feet. And it had a fly reel, not a spinning reel. The line was the wrong weight, too. It got Hawley thinking that maybe this man wasn't his father. But it had been more than fifteen years since Hawley had seen him, and he guessed a fellow could change what kind of fishing tackle he used. And then his father was back, carrying a first-aid kit, and Hawley decided it didn't matter if the man was his father or not.

"Was that towel clean?"

Hawley nodded.

"Let's leave that part for now, then," said his father. He was pulling rolls of bandages and heavy dressing out of a bright-orange box with a red cross on the lid. "I think the bullet might have punctured your lung. That's why you're having trouble breathing." He used some scissors to cut up the back of Hawley's shirt. He snipped a plastic bag in two, and then he rolled Hawley over, removed some of the packing, cleaned the exit wound, dried it with some bandages and started taping the plastic to his back. He taped three sides and left one side open. Hawley took another breath and suddenly his lungs caught and filled.

"God," he said.

"Better?" his father asked.

"Yes." Hawley exhaled and felt the plastic flutter a little.

"What'd she shoot you with?"

"A Ruger."

"Ah," Hawley's father said. "I've been thinking about getting one of those." He reached inside the kit and took out a jar of cayenne pepper. He unscrewed the top. "This is going to sting a little," he said. And then he lifted the edge of the towel and poured the whole jar into Hawley's wound. Right away he put the towel back on and pressed down hard. Hawley could feel the pepper burning through the hole inside him. He could taste it in his lungs. Every movement felt like a refrigerator thrown down on top of him.

"Fuck," Hawley said.

"Nearly there," said his father. He ripped a couple more bandages open and pressed them on top of the towel. Then he got some cold packs out of his cooler and placed them around Hawley's midsection. "Hold this," he said. And as Hawley did, he took some duct tape and wrapped it around everything a few times, looping over Hawley's chest, keeping it tight.

"Now you should last another forty minutes or so, until we get into town. Unless there's internal hemorrhaging."

"I need some water," said Hawley.

"No water," said his father. "You've lost too much blood. Come on, get under my arm, here. I've got to get you back to my car."

There were so many things Hawley wanted to ask him. But right now he could only lean on the old man and try not to throw up from the pain. His father smelled of chewing tobacco and the rubber of the wading boots and something else, underneath his breath—a faint hint of Ring Dings, the synthetic chocolate cakes wrapped in cellophane and sold in gas stations, which Hawley had secretly loved as a boy. On his eighth birthday, his father had surprised him with a plateful, eight matches stuck in for candles. He'd never forgotten it. The appearance of those individually sealed snack cakes had Hawley believing for at least a month that his father could read his mind.

"My guns," Hawley said, and gestured to the bushes. He hoped that was enough, and it seemed to be. Once his father managed to get him across the parking lot and leaned him against the Jeep parked there, he went back and poked through the bushes, and it took him only a minute to find Hawley's shotgun and the Colt. He returned with both and admired the Colt for a moment and then he opened the back of the Jeep and locked the pieces inside the metal gun box that was bolted to the floor.

"Not that I don't trust you," he said. "But I don't."

Once he had Hawley settled into the passenger seat, he went through the first-aid kit again. Hawley could see now that the kit was actually a toolbox made of heavy-duty orange plastic. The red cross had been hand-painted on the cover, along with the words THESE THINGS WE DO THAT OTHERS MAY LIVE. Hawley's father took out a sealed plastic bag full of lollipops. He unwrapped a pink one and gave it to Hawley. "It's laced with fentanyl. Should help with the pain."

Hawley slid the lollipop into his mouth. It tasted like cherries.

The car was an old Jeep Wrangler with a hole the size of a dinner plate in the floor. As they drove, Hawley watched the road passing beneath them. The shifting blur gave him a strange feeling, like time was speeding up and slowing down all at once. When they passed through a dense patch of gravel, stones would clatter against the metal undercarriage of the Jeep, and rocks would be tossed up through the hole and roll around in the well near Hawley's feet.

He could already feel the fentanyl going to work—the refrigerator slowly lifting from his chest. His body started to glow, as if he were falling into an illuminated pool of light, becoming warmer and brighter with each lick. Hawley pulled the lollipop out of his mouth.

"Where'd you get this thing?" he asked.

"I used to do air evacs during Vietnam. Those pops are great for gunshot wounds."

"I thought you were in the marines."

"Nope. Air force. Fifty-sixth Squadron."

"How come you never told me before?" said Hawley.

"Son," said his father, "I don't even know you."

And Hawley supposed he was right. His father had died so young that Hawley never got the chance to know what kind of man he was. There were probably lots of secrets that had died with him. Things he'd never told anyone. But he'd been a good father. He'd taught Hawley how to fish and how to shuck oysters. And he had a quiet way of noticing things, like how much his son had wanted those Ring Dings, even without him saying a word.

"You've been dead so long," said Hawley. "I guess I forgot."

For a moment he thought his father might throw him out of the car. But the old man set his mouth and stared through the windshield instead. They drove over another patch of gravel, and a handful of rocks came up through the hole in the floor and hit Hawley in the legs.

"Good thing I still fish," his father said, "or I wouldn't have found you."

When the lollipop was finished Hawley eased back into his seat, feeling dazed, as if he might float right through the hardtop of the Jeep.

He'd been fifteen when his father died. What he remembered most was being scared—scared to be on his own, scared to talk to anyone. He ran away from social services and went back to their old house and broke a window and crawled through and packed a bag and took his father's rifle and some ammunition. He started off with an idea of finding his mother but he ran out of money before he even got out of Texas. He thought of trying to sell the rifle but it was all he had left and so he used the gun to hold up a liquor store instead. Made $752. His very first job. All on his own.

Now his father was back. It wasn't something he'd ever thought to count on. The old man was leaning over the steering wheel, like the Jeep was a horse he could press to go faster. Hawley saw the way his father's face had tightened up, and realized he'd probably said something wrong again.

"I'm sorry," he said. And it felt like all the other times he'd said those words—for things he both was and was not sorry for, for all the things he had not done.

Hawley's father didn't answer him. But after they crossed over the next bridge he cleared his throat. "The woman who shot you, was she your wife?"

"I'd never met her before."

"Then why's she trying to kill you?"

Hawley thought of the clepsydra, the glacier sliding into the river. His body was still glowing but his hands had started to shake, his teeth aching like they'd been drilled.

"You don't look so good." Hawley's father reached into the backseat, keeping the other hand on the wheel. The Jeep swayed and nearly veered off the road. He produced an old Mexican blanket covered in dog hair and threw it at Hawley. "I think you're going into shock. Wrap yourself up. But don't fall asleep."

The blanket itched. Hawley's heart was beating like crazy. He wanted to pull off the ice packs, but whenever he touched the dressing, the cayenne pepper worked deeper inside his wound. He did his best to pull the blanket around himself. Every movement sent a wave tingling down his side—not pain, but an echo of pain, like he was hearing it from far away. He took a deep breath and then exhaled and felt the flutter of the plastic strip taped to his back.

"You don't have to tell me how this happened," said his father, "but you're going to have to tell me something."

"I'm married," said Hawley.

"You still love her?"

"Sure."

"Think that woman will go after her?"

Hawley realized he meant Steller. "No," he said. "But someone else might."

As soon as the words left his mouth Hawley felt their truth sink into the very center of his bones, like a crack filling with ice water. No money, no goods—even if he found some way to make it square with King, they'd have to be careful. They'd have to run.

"She's pregnant."

"You better not die, then," said his father.

Up ahead was the same roadkill he'd driven past on his way out to the glacier. The eagle was still there tearing pieces out of the belly. Hovering nearby, waiting for the eagle to move off, were some seagulls and a couple of terns. As the Jeep drew closer, the birds dispersed and flew away screaming at one another. Then the Jeep rattled over the dead creature and Hawley caught a flash of fur through the hole in the bottom of the floor.

It made Hawley think about traveling through the desert in Arizona, the girl driving—what was her name?—and the baby strapped next to him in the car seat. There'd been roadkill then, too. It had felt like he was driving past his own mangled body. And here he was, shot in the chest, bleeding out again. Only the landscape had changed. It was like he was skipping on some kind of record of his life. But he wasn't the same man he had been out in the desert. Now there was somebody waiting on him and it mattered whether he died or not.

It felt like three hundred years since Hawley had been swept into the river.

"I need a phone," he said.

"There's one under the seat," said his father.

Hawley leaned down, his side burning, his skin clammy with sweat. He felt a canvas strap and pulled out a satchel. Inside was a military field phone, rigged with a headset. "Does this thing work?"

"Just crank the handle. The signal's encrypted. I rigged it for WROL."

"What's WROL?"

"Without Rule of Law."

"You mean the end of the world?"

"No," said Hawley's father. "Just the government."

Hawley lifted the receiver and put it on his lap. With his better hand he cranked the generator and started punching in numbers. The line was full of static but it seemed to be working. Hawley waited for the connection. Below his ribs, standing out in the middle of all the duct tape and bandages, was the mark Lily had made when she threw the rock at him yesterday. A tiny blue spot. He pressed his finger against the bruise and held it there but he couldn't feel a thing.

"Where are you? Are you hurt?" Lily wasn't yelling but she sounded like she had been yelling for a long time, the edge of each word torn and ragged. Hawley was so glad to hear her voice that he didn't say anything. He just leaned his face against the receiver. The plastic smelled like it had been dipped in oil, as if it could catch fire at any moment.

"I'm all right."

"You were supposed to call. But you didn't call."

"I'm all right, I said."

Lily sneezed. She sneezed and sneezed and sneezed.

"Listen," said Hawley. "I want you to pack a bag and drive to Anchorage and get a room near the airport. I want you to wait for me there." The line was breaking up already, his wife's voice thinning out to a crackling line. "Lily," he said. "Lily."

"I'm here," she said.

"We're here," said Hawley's father.

Through the cloud of dust before them Eyak Lake came into view, and beyond that Hawley could see the outskirts of Cordova. The Jeep shifted gears as the gravel road turned into pavement, the wheels catching for a moment and then gliding over the suddenly smooth surface. Instead of sucking up rocks, the hole in the car floor now seemed intent on expelling them. Hawley watched as one stone after another left the safety of the wheel well and was lost to the road below. And then Hawley found himself drawn toward the hole, his legs gone heavy, his body sliding out of the seat. His father was saying something. Hawley tried to listen but he knew it wouldn't do much good.

"Tell her you're coming home," said his father. "Tell her you love her."

Hawley clung to the receiver that held his wife's voice. He thought of all the things his child would never know about him. Future memories shot through with blank spaces. He took a breath and felt the plastic catch and plug the opening in his back. His lungs filled. The air tasted of pepper and blood.

"Lily," he said. "I'm happy. I'm happy it's a girl."

Fireworks

TRY AS SHE MIGHT, LOO COULD NOT GET THE THOUGHT OF MARSHALL Hicks off her skin. Each morning she woke and stretched her arms over her head and imagined his hands threaded in hers. She remembered the small white scars on his knuckles, the bump of the finger she had broken. She closed her eyes, and for a moment she could still feel the weight of him, the hovering of his mouth, his fingers pulling her hair. She could hear his voice, the whisper of a groan under his breath. She did this over and over in her mind until the entire length of her body was shaking. And then she heard her father in the hallway, and she waited one moment longer, and then she opened her eyes and got out of the bed.

Hawley knocked on the door.

"Time to go."

Loo got dressed, then went downstairs and gathered the buckets and wire baskets and spade and rake from the garage. Her father filled a cooler with ice. On the porch they pulled on their boots, Hawley his waders and Loo a pair of old rubber Wellingtons. They walked quietly through the woods to the open shoreline. The tide was all the way out, the beach wet and rippled from the waves and covered with tiny air holes.

Hawley put down the buckets. Then he walked out onto the hard-packed sand and jumped in the air. He landed hard with both feet, and small sprouts of water squirted up all around him like fountains. He turned to Loo, a look of expectation on his face, but she pretended not to notice. She picked up her spade and started digging. She could barely stand to look at him.

It had been a week since Mabel Ridge's phone call and she was still processing her grandmother's words. At night, after Hawley had gone to bed, she perused the scrapbook of her mother's death, looking for answers. Trying to find some link. Loo had added more to the pages, pasting in a few things of her own that she'd researched at the library and photocopied. A map of Wisconsin, a sketch of hiking trails at the state forest nearby, addresses of the closest houses and details about the lake—the length of its shoreline, its maximum depth, the size of its watershed, its longitude and latitude. The different species of fish and their eating habits. None of these facts convinced her of what her grandmother had said. All they did was make her feel more lonely.

Hawley dug into the sand beside her. "Are you going to the Labor Day fireworks tonight?"

"I don't think so," said Loo.

"We could watch them together. Bring a picnic out to the beach."

There was a piece of seaweed caught in her father's beard. She stared at the tiny bit of green.

Your mother never would have drowned in a lake.

Hawley pressed his boot down on the back of the rake. "You used to be so scared of fireworks, especially the finale. You'd hide under the bearskin."

"I don't remember that."

But she did remember. The smell of the animal's hide. Holding on to the claws for comfort. The feeling of each explosion deep inside her chest, as if her heart were about to burst open.

"You know," Hawley said as he dumped sand into the wire basket, "it's all right if you'd rather go with that boy."

Loo turned away and coughed so that he would not see her face. Her father always seemed to know what she was thinking. Lately, he'd started eating his meals at the Sawtooth whenever Loo was there. Even when he was asleep she could feel his presence. It was like there was a string tied between them. Sometimes it went loose and then, like this, the line would snap tight again.

"We broke up."

Hawley put down the rake, picked up the basket and began to sift, shaking it back and forth, revealing a cluster of small white cherrystone clams, each one the size of a silver dollar.

"So that's why you've been sulking." Hawley walked the basket into the ocean, until the water was up to his knees. Then he bent down and rinsed the clams off. He opened the cooler and began transferring the shells.

"His father's causing a lot of trouble in town."

"Stepfather," Loo said.

"Either way. It's not going to end well."

"That's not Marshall's fault."

"No," said Hawley, "but it's his family. And he's stuck with them. Just like you're stuck with me."

WHEN THEY GOT BACK TO the house there was a large cardboard box on the porch. Hawley put down the cooler and went up the stairs. He checked the label. He took his knife out of his pocket and handed it to Loo.

The package was addressed to her. For a brief moment, she thought it was from Marshall, and her heart rose with excitement. Then she saw the look on her father's face.

"My birthday's not until next month."

"Just open the box."

Inside was a telescope. The same kind her science teacher had used for demonstrations. A Schmidt-Cassegrain, with an Equatorial mount. The telescope must have cost at least two thousand dollars. Loo suspected Principal Gunderson had helped her father pick it out.

"What am I supposed to do with this?"

"Learn something I don't know," said Hawley.

And so she did.

While her father took their catch to the fish market, Loo spent the afternoon assembling her new telescope, setting it up on the roof outside her bedroom window. She knew the gift was a bribe, meant to change her sour mood, but she didn't care. For hours her mind was distracted. She read the instructions on how to align with the Earth's axis, dialing the setting circles to the correct month and day. Then she dug out her planisphere and the book on the solar system that Marshall had given her. In the back there was a chart listing the coordinates of the planets. She peered through the viewfinder, blinking against the sun. There were still hours to go before it would be dark enough to see anything.

Loo climbed back into her bedroom. From the closet, she took out her only dress. She'd worn it once, on graduation, and then put it right back into the plastic bag. Loo unknotted the bag now, then reached her hand up the skirt, past the zipper, and unclipped the envelope she'd pinned to the cloth there—her new hiding place, after Hawley found her stash of money in the attic. Inside the envelope was everything she didn't want her father to see: the black lace gloves, the scrapbook of her mother's death and the clipboard with Marshall's petition.

She removed the clipboard, then gathered the local map and the phone book they'd been using, brought everything down to the kitchen table and started copying out names. She used every kind of pen—ballpoint, gel, fountain, fine, ultra-fine, bold, blue, black, red, purple, even green—so the signatures would all look different, each loop and turn unique. She was no longer just replacing names that had been lost. She was building an environmental movement. At the library Loo had researched what she needed to complete the petition. The description of the marine sanctuary, the maps, the criteria and, most important, the support of five thousand members of the community. As she copied each signature she thought of Marshall Hicks. Every Harry, every Jane, every Archibald and Rocco was keeping him tied to her. And after a night of hot-wiring cars, forgery was a crime that seemed small enough to fit in her pocket.

She wrote until her shoulders ached. She wrote until her hands burned. She wrote until the tendons in each finger were so stiff she had to take breaks to stretch them, splaying her palms across the table. She was copying out the address for 756 East Main Street, Apartment #5—with 3,678 signatures forged and 1,322 signatures to go—when there was a knock at the door.

The man on their porch had gray hair that swept his shoulders and thickset hazel eyes. A week's worth of stubble scrabbled across his chin. He was wearing a brown leather jacket and jeans and cowboy boots. The toes were very pointy and made his feet seem very small.

"I'm looking for Samuel Hawley." He was carrying a worn-out army-green duffel bag. It was just like her father's. The one he kept locked in his closet, full of guns and ammunition. The stranger set the duffel on the porch. Loo heard the clink of metal on metal.

"He's not here." She took a step back.

"You the daughter?" The man looked her up and down and shook his head. "My God."

There was something wrong with his face. All along one side of his cheek were tiny twists of scars, and patches of skin that were redder than the rest, like he'd been born with a stain of juice running down his cheek and neck. His hands had the same kind of blotches, on the wrists and knuckles.

"My name's Jove." He raised one of his scarred hands. "I'm an old friend of your dad's."

"Loo."

Jove took her hand and pressed his other hand on top of it, so that she was caught for a moment between his palms. His fingers were rough but warm.

"You're lovely, Loo," he said. "But your father is one son of a bitch." The man let out a snort like this was some kind of joke.

She pulled her hand away.

"He'll be home soon," said Loo. "Any minute, actually," she added.

"Guess I'll wait for him, then," Jove said and walked past her into the house.

There was something in the man's ruined face that reminded her of the fishing widows that used to come knocking. A need that seemed both desperate and dangerous. He hauled the duffel bag with him into the living room. Then he released a small, joyous shout and dropped to his knees and wrapped his arms around the bearskin rug.

"I can't believe he still has this thing." Jove tapped the bear on the snout. "The last time I saw this guy I was pulling a slug out of your father's back."

Loo said, "What are you talking about?"

"We were just kids screwing around," said Jove. "Trespassing, you know, and some old coot ran us off. Took forever to dig that bullet out of his ribs. And the whole time Hawley was calling for some girl like it was the end of the world."

"What girl?"

"Hell if I remember."

"Lily?"

Jove stroked the bear again. "No, he didn't know her yet."

Loo knew which scar this was—the crater beneath Hawley's right shoulder blade, which bloomed out like the head of a jellyfish. Hearing the details of how it had been carved into her father's skin made her crouch down and touch the bear. She had walked over this rug her entire life. She'd never thought of where it had come from. She'd never thought to ask.

"I probably shouldn't have told you about him getting shot." Jove picked up his duffel bag and began to walk toward the kitchen. "I've always talked too much. That's why we got along so well, because Hawley never says a damn thing." He went to the fridge and opened it. He took out an apple, then lifted a small paring knife from the dish rack and began to cut slices, one by one, and put them into his mouth with the edge of the blade.

"Hey," said Loo. "This isn't your house."

"I settle in quick." Jove's eyes went to the table. The phone book and Loo's pile of pens. He snatched one of the scraps of paper she'd been practicing signatures on.

"Not bad," he said. He held the paper up to the light. "Forging checks?"

"It's for a petition."

Jove picked up the clipboard. He read the statement at the top. He flipped through the papers. "So you're some kind of environmentalist?"

"My boyfriend is."

"Boyfriend!" said Jove. "Ha! Poor Hawley—has he beat the crap out of him yet?"

Loo took the clipboard away from him. She stuffed it into one of the cupboards, along with the phone book, map and pens.

"I'll take that as a yes," said Jove.

Loo watched him eat his apple. "How do you know my dad again?"

"We used to work together."

"He's never mentioned you." Loo glanced down at the duffel bag. He'd kept it right by his side the whole time he was in the house.

Jove followed her line of sight. He bent down and unzipped the front. "Come take a look. I've got some great stuff in here." He pulled the sides apart like he was opening a person, spreading the ribs with his hands.

The duffel was full of watches. The heavy kind, with powerful leather straps, that told the month and the day and marked the time zones of Paris, New York, Rome and Tokyo—waterproof, with glass thick enough to go scuba diving, gold and silver and platinum faces that were meant to be passed down from generation to generation.

"Beautiful, aren't they?" Jove jammed his fingers into the pile and pulled one out by the clasp. "Just listen."

Loo looked down at the open bag. So many numbers jumbled together, and all she could think of was Marshall's watch, catching in her hair, and the way he'd wrapped it so tightly on his wrist as he was leaving.

"Are you some kind of traveling salesman?"

"You could say that. I deal with antiques, mostly. I'm a bit of a specialist," said Jove. "Now the Egyptians, they didn't think about time the way we do. They thought night and day were two separate worlds. Twelve hours of light, twelve hours of darkness. They used sundials during the day, and then kept track of the stars, starting at twilight and ending at dawn. They didn't count seconds like we do, either. Time was more"—he waved his fingers at her—"flexible. Sometimes an hour would be sixty minutes. And sometimes an hour would be forty. Do you wear a wristwatch?"

"No," said Loo.

Jove let out a disapproving puff of air. He reached into the bag again. "Watches used to be important. When you got your first, it was special. A reminder of the days you had left, ticking away right there on your arm."

He pulled out a man's wristwatch, held the face between two fingers and let the band dangle in the air. "This one is an automatic. It doesn't have a battery—you don't even need to wind it. The movement of the arm, just swinging back and forth—it keeps the gears going. All you have to do is put this on someone living, and it'll come to life."

He took hold of Loo and slid the watch around her wrist. The strap was too wide, her arm too thin. She lifted her hand and the face slid away.

"It doesn't work if you're standing still."

Loo got up from the table and walked into the living room. She turned down the hall, past the bathroom, and then she came back to the kitchen. Jove was still sitting in the same chair. He snatched up her hand as she entered the room and pressed the watch to his ear. He frowned.

"Did you swing your arm?"

"Yes."

Jove shook her wrist back and forth, then he listened again. "Goddammit."

Loo lifted the watch to her own ear. There was no heartbeat. But outside the window came another noise. A car pulling into the driveway. The truck door slamming, and then Hawley's boots climbing the stairs. Loo glanced from Jove to the bearskin and back. She listened as her father dumped his gear, then fit his key into the lock.

Jove put a finger to his lips. He hid in the shadow of the bookcase.

"I'm home," said Hawley.

Across the living room Loo saw her father pause. His eyes locked on hers where she stood in the kitchen, and then slid down to the giant watch on her wrist.

Jove jumped out, laughing, but he didn't even get the chance to say a word before Hawley was across the room and on top of him. They threw each other into the walls, two giants wrestling inside a dollhouse. Together the men tumbled into the bookcase and it all came toppling over as they struggled and the books fell, crashing across the floor. Loo hurried over and pulled the frame of the bookcase back. Underneath Hawley had Jove pinned and the knife Jove had been using to eat his apple was sunk deep into Hawley's arm.

"It's me, you fuck!" Jove shouted. "It's me!"

Hawley was breathing heavily. "Jove."

"Did you gain a hundred pounds? Get off. I can't breathe." Jove shoved at Hawley's chest. Loo watched her father crawl off the man and slump against the wall. He swallowed hard and closed his eyes.

"I pull you a favor and this is the thanks I get." Jove sat up and pressed his fingers to his nose. There was blood streaming from his left nostril. "See what you made me do?"

Hawley opened his eyes and glanced down at the knife in his arm. He sucked air through his teeth. Then he took hold of the handle and pulled it out. Blood bubbled up behind, quick and fast, spreading over his shirt. He pressed his palm against the cut and turned to his daughter.

"Get the kit."

Loo ran into the bathroom and threw open the cupboard underneath the sink. Inside was the orange toolbox with the red cross. Loo grabbed the handle and nearly slammed into Jove in the doorway. He was pinching his nostrils and had his head tilted back.

"Got anything I can fix this with?"

"Check the medicine cabinet."

She hurried past him and got down on the floor beside her father. "Dad," she said. But her voice stopped there. She wished she'd smiled for him at the beach.

Hawley opened the toolbox. It was jammed full of gauze pads, tape, scissors, plastic gloves, rubbing alcohol, bottles of drugs, vials of liquid and needles. There was a set of surgical tools and a stapler. There was also a bottle of styptic powder. Her father reached for it and tipped a stream of yellow dust onto his arm.

"How long has he been here?"

"About half an hour," said Loo. "Does it hurt?"

"This?" Hawley shrugged the wound away like it was nothing. He brushed the extra powder off his arm, then handed Loo the bottle.

"Is that guy really a friend of yours?"

"He used to be."

Jove came back from the bathroom, his nostrils full of toilet paper, a Band-Aid across the bridge of his nose. He had a bottle of hydrogen peroxide tucked into his elbow like a bottle of wine. "Well," he said, "I've never seen a bathroom quite like that before."

Loo waited for Hawley to pick up Jove and toss him out onto the porch. But her father ignored the man's comments and pressed a bandage to his arm. Jove set the hydrogen peroxide down on the floor. He put on a pair of rubber gloves from the kit and inspected Hawley's wound. To Loo's surprise, Hawley let him do this, holding out his arm and grunting. Jove poked through the medical supplies and took out the stapler and some gauze. He poured peroxide over Hawley's arm and they all watched it bubble and burn. He winked at Loo.

"Don't worry," he said. "I'm a doctor."

Once Hawley had been patched up, Jove helped Loo set the bookcase right and put the volumes back in place. He took his time, perusing the spines and opening the covers. "I could write better crap than this."

Hawley wiped blood off the floor. "What the hell are you doing here, Jove."

"Can't a man come visit his friend?"

Hawley's eyes went to the duffel bag.

"He's selling watches," said Loo.

"I thought you were retired."

"I'm retiring my retirement." Jove put the last book on the shelf. Then he clapped his hands, and, like magic, turned himself from an intruder into a guest. "Well, what's for dinner?"

In the kitchen, Loo cleaned and debearded some of the mussels they'd collected that morning, while Jove washed the salad and chopped carrots and celery in a blur, tissue paper still wadded in two tiny spirals up his busted nose. Hawley leaned against the counter, touching the staples in his arm and drinking a beer. Through it all Jove kept talking, his voice booming in the small room, listing name after name that Loo had never heard of. There was something about him that was *like* her father—and she'd never met anyone who was like Hawley before.

"Rodriguez, he's still inside, but Thompson got out about a year ago, I saw him in Detroit. Eaton is flying helicopters in South America. Stein moved to Memphis. Blago quit and became a farmer. Vermont, I think. Something with goats. And Frederick Nunn—remember Nunn?"

"How could I forget."

"Well, he's dead."

Hawley took a sip of beer.

"Parker told me. He's working for Miller."

Steam began to leak out of the pot on the stove. Loo's father checked to make sure all of the mussels had cracked open. Then he turned off the heat. "I don't know how you keep in touch with all those guys."

Jove used the butcher knife to slide the carrots into the salad bowl. "Christmas cards," he said, and chopped the head off a bunch of broccoli.

Everything Hawley did slowly, Jove did fast, even the drinking. For every empty of Hawley's there were two for Jove. By the time Loo served the mussels, the men were through a six-pack. And by the time the meal was finished, another six-pack was gone. Jove reached into his bag and pulled out a bundle of papers. He slid them across the table to Hawley.

"You know how long I've been looking. Well, I found her. And she's perfect."

"What's her name?" Hawley asked.

"Pandora," said Jove.

"I thought it was going to be Cassandra."

"That was before I dated a girl named Cassandra, and she slept with another guy when I was out of town. I don't want her thinking I named my boat after her."

"How's she going to know?"

"Believe me," said Jove. "That bitch will know."

The boat Jove was buying was a forty-foot sloop with a decent-size galley, refrigeration and a head. The design was based on old cargo sailboats that originally brought supplies up and down the Hudson. It was built with those changing currents in mind, the need for quick tacks to navigate narrow channels.

"Can't believe it's finally happening," said Hawley.

"Only took me thirty years," said Jove. "All that's left is to finish off some old business. Don't want to leave any outstanding debts."

Hawley took out his pouch of tobacco and started rolling a cigarette. He tucked in the filter and licked the ends, then flipped the Zippo against his palm.

"Those things will kill you," Jove said.

"Yes," said Hawley.

Loo stood and started gathering the plates, but her father stopped her. "We'll do the dishes," he said. "Why don't you go get some sheets for the couch."

There'd been no invitation extended, but Hawley and Jove already seemed to be talking in a shorthand that wove around Loo's presence. She wondered what that intimacy was built on. How the man who'd just stabbed her father was now piling dishes in their sink.

She climbed the stairs, pulled a blanket and an extra pillow from the closet in her bedroom. Outside her window, the telescope Hawley had bought her was standing alone, pointed at the heavens. Loo slid open the sash and stepped onto the roof. She set her eye against the lens.

Overhead the stars and planets were going about their business. The moon hovered in the shape of a crescent, only two hundred and thirty-eight thousand miles from the earth. Listening in the dark, she felt closer to that hunk of ice and rock than to the men talking below, their voices soft beneath the running water.

"I thought you said Pax would take care of the cars."

"He did. I told you. Pax is great. Always clean. But then he called me back afterward with a job up here. A big exchange with some merchandise we've dealt with before. The buyer's willing to pay half now and a bonus if we can go verify the goods."

"I'm not interested."

"It's a lot, Hawley. These wristwatches will cover the cost of the boat. But Pax's job will be enough to really retire. Get out of the business and never look back. The request had both our names on it, though. So I had to ask. Half of it's yours if you want it."

Loo held her breath and leaned over the edge of the roof. Down below in the kitchen the men had stopped doing the dishes but the water ran and ran and ran.

"Suit yourself. I've cleared my conscience. And I've got your cut for the cars."

"I told you I didn't want it."

"You doing that good?"

"I'm okay."

"That tragic fucking mess in the bathroom doesn't say okay."

Loo could hear steel wool scrubbing around and around inside an iron skillet.

"It's how I remember."

"That's not remembering. That's burying yourself alive."

The dishes clattered. They sounded like they were breaking.

"I've been buried before."

A flash of light streaked overhead, followed by an explosion that shook the roof of the house. Loo could feel the echo of it in her lungs. She crawled back through the window and hurried down the stairs.

Hawley was wiping down the counter, and Jove was standing over the sink, pulling off the rubber gloves he'd worn earlier to staple her father's arm.

"That sounded like thunder."

"Fireworks," said Loo. "We can see them from the beach, if you want."

The men blinked at her.

"Where's the blanket?" Hawley asked.

Loo went back upstairs and the men grabbed a bottle of whiskey and some glasses. As they made their way through the woods, they could hear the crackling of the rockets. Then the path opened onto the shore and they stepped against a sky sparkling with gold and silver, long trails of smoke left hanging in the air.

Loo spread the blanket. They took off their shoes. Jove carefully wiped off his cowboy boots and set them side by side on a pile of seaweed. Then he poured out the whiskey. Loo watched her father lean his head back and drink.

"Jesus, Hawley, what happened to your foot?"

"I stepped on something."

"What, a pitchfork?"

Her father wiggled his toes. The big one and the pinky moved, but the ones in between didn't. On the sole of his foot the skin spiderwebbed in pink lines where it had been split and sewn back together.

"Still works. That's all that matters."

Jove poured himself another glass and raised it at Loo. "Here's to keeping your dad out of trouble."

A burst of white stars shot across the harbor and they all lifted their faces to the sky. A moment later, when Loo looked back, her father had buried his twisted foot in the cold, dark sand.

"Never thought you'd settle down like this."

"Things change," said Hawley.

"Sure do," Jove said. "I even joined the YMCA."

"I don't believe it," Hawley said.

"Scout's honor. I'll prove it." Jove saluted and started to unbutton his shirt. And then he was running toward the ocean. He went full-tilt and then he hooted and hollered as he jumped into the waves and dove under. After a minute he rose to the surface, his toes up, floating.

"Who *is* this guy?" Loo asked her father.

"He's a taker," said Hawley. "He takes things."

"And you used to work with him?"

"A long time ago."

"Come on in," Jove yelled at them. "Water's fine!"

"He's an idiot," said Loo.

Hawley stood up. He pulled his T-shirt over his head. Even in the shadows she could see his scars. The skin was different there. Puckered and ghostly. And now she knew the story behind one of those ghosts. She imagined Jove's hands searching her father's back, finding the bullet, digging it out—with what? His fingers? A knife? A spoon? None of the instruments she thought of seemed possible.

They walked to the shoreline. A wave came and splashed them both to their knees.

"It's cold," said Loo.

"A little," said Hawley.

"You have to keep moving," said Jove.

"You know, there's sharks out there," Loo called.

Jove stopped paddling.

"She's kidding," said Hawley. And then he walked into the water. He walked all the way up to his waist, not stopping but not rushing, either, and then he sank under the black surface of the ocean and disappeared.

"I can't believe it!" said Jove, after Hawley surfaced next to him. He splashed his friend in the face. "Since when do you swim?"

"I took classes with Loo when she was little."

"He was the only adult," said Loo.

Jove hooted. "I would have paid to see that."

Another flare went up from the staging area across the harbor. Blue bursts, then a set of screaming meemies popped and spun out across the sky, curling in bright spirals, illuminating the rippling water and the faces of the men. Loo went back and sat on the blanket. She rubbed her feet together. There were sand fleas and her legs were getting bitten.

She remembered Hawley tucking her hair into a tight rubber cap, the smell of chlorine on their skin from the heated pool. Before class, they'd sit with just their legs in the water. They'd kick up a storm, Hawley's ruined foot flashing through the waves next to her own. They'd learned how to blow bubbles together. He'd talked her into walking the long length of the diving board. And she'd been there the very first time he'd dog-paddled across the pool without a float. She remembered that all the kids had cheered for him. And she remembered that when her father looked back from the other side, gripping the concrete ledge, breathing hard, there was no joy in his face.

She still had the watch on her wrist, but it was too dark to read the numbers. The fireworks were supposed to end at ten o'clock. A grand finale and then the folding of lawn chairs and a traffic jam as everyone went home. She waited for the next burst to hit. It seemed to take forever. She watched the men swimming and thought of the scrapbook hidden in her closet. All those details and numbers. She had believed the facts would change things. But her father was still her father.

She could hear the crowd hooting and blasting their air horns in anticipation across the harbor. A flare went up. And then another. And then another and another and another. She saw the smoke trails intertwining, and then the burst of rockets and pinwheels and dragons and hydras that ignited and extinguished in a barrage of cannons. Jove shouted and clapped. It seemed like the explosions would never end. Loo fought every impulse to cover her ears. To dive under the blanket. She leaned into the surge of maddening noise, and watched the light expanding and reflecting off her father's wet skin, until his body was dappled in red and orange, and his whole back looked as though it had caught fire.

Seven, Eight, Nine

WHEN LOO WAS FIRST PUT IN HAWLEY'S HANDS AT THE HOSPITAL, HE felt nothing at all. Just a fear of dropping the baby or hurting her somehow or tipping her head wrong. It was such a soft head, the neck loose, the black, downy hair brushing against his callused fingers. Her skin was red and blotchy and her limbs out of proportion. He touched her arm and he could feel the bones underneath her pudgy flesh. Bones so new they felt like plastic—pliable and easily broken. Hawley had the urge to bend the baby's arm to see how far it would go. As soon as he could, he gave her back to Lily. Then he took out the camera and flashed the flash. He held the Polaroid between his fingers and together they watched it develop, the chemicals mixing into the shape of his wife and daughter.

"Look at that," said Lily. "It's your family."

After Alaska they had moved to Wisconsin—away from both coasts—and settled near the Chequamegon-Nicolet National Forest, in a small cabin with a trail leading through a grove of balsam firs to the shore of a private lake. Every inch of their home was covered with things for the baby—blankets and toys and cribs and formula and diapers and a special bathtub and tiny socks and tiny clothes, mobiles of sheep that hung from the ceiling, side sleepers and Snuglis and carriages and multicolored blocks and board books and the smell of cream meant for rashes and talcum powder and warm, piss-soaked Pampers that were deposited into a Diaper Genie that lived in the bathroom next to the toilet.

At first Lily was too tired, too focused on the baby, too busy sleeping and feeding and flowing with hormones to notice Hawley's indifference toward their daughter, but as the months passed and the baby grew larger and learned to roll over on her own, and then cut her first tooth, and then swallowed her first bite of rice cereal, Lily began to sigh whenever he made an excuse to leave the house—sighed when he went for a walk, sighed when a diaper needed to be changed and he slipped out of the room, sighed when he feigned sleep at the baby's 2 A.M. feeding. These sighs grew in length and volume and pitch, until the day of their daughter's baptism, when Lily spooned pea puree into the baby's mouth, and then bathed her and wrapped her in a white gown and bonnet, and then squeezed herself into an old sundress, and brushed her hair, and put on lipstick, and stood by the door, expectant and waiting, and Hawley said he was going fishing.

Lily shifted Louise from one hip to the other. Then she inhaled the biggest sigh yet, a sigh that sucked in with the roar and power of a vacuum, and pushed out a torrent of air. "You are not going to catch any goddamn fish today," she said. "You will go upstairs. You will put on a goddamn shirt. And then you will drive us to the goddamn church and get our daughter baptized."

Hawley didn't know why she cared. Lily wasn't religious. But she said she had memories of attending mass as a child, and those memories were good memories and therefore important. Kneeling down, lighting candles, saying prayers—all of it had made Lily feel safe and connected to the universe somehow, and they needed to do the same for their daughter. It didn't matter if they believed in God or not.

"We're parents now, and baptism is part of the job," Lily said. "It's an insurance policy."

"For what?"

"In case there's heaven and hell. I don't want our baby stuck in purgatory. It's like a waiting room where your name never gets called."

The ceremony was just the three of them and the priest, who spoke English with a French-Canadian accent. They didn't bring any godparents, but the man knew Lily from the meetings she went to down in the church basement, so he just wrote their names twice on the baptismal certificate. Then he slipped a purple robe over his shoulders and cinched it around his waist with a gold rope. He lit some incense and said some prayers and had Lily hold the baby over a bowl. He poured water on the baby's forehead and then he poured oil.

The church smelled like the cold underside of a rock. On every wall there were stained-glass windows that obscured rather than filtered the light. In the shaded colored panes Hawley could make out figures and symbols. Crucifixes and lambs, a severed head on a plate, a heart with seven swords jammed through the middle and a man stepping out of a cave, over a pile of skeletons.

"Father," the priest said, "at the very dawn of creation Your Spirit breathed on the waters, making them the wellspring of all holiness. By the power of the Spirit give to the water of this font the grace of Your Son. You created man in Your own likeness. Cleanse him from sin in a new birth to innocence by water and the Spirit. May all who are buried with Christ in the death of baptism rise also with Him to newness of life."

The priest asked Hawley to hold the baby and Lily passed their daughter into his arms. Red and orange light from the windows fell across them both. It made him think of the emergency hazards on Lily's truck, flickering over his body as he crawled along the floor of the diner, the crunch of broken glass cutting into his palms. The baby shivered as the priest poured more water onto her face. Then she threw up pea puree all over Hawley's clean shirt.

He waited out the rest of the ceremony in the back of the church, stretched out in a pew in his undershirt, the button-down Lily had asked him to wear balled up in the trash. The priest said his goodbyes and slipped behind the altar, and then Lily made her way up the aisle, dragging the car seat, her dress askew, the baby's bonnet tied around her wrist.

"You could have helped."

"Sorry," Hawley said, though the truth was he'd been relieved to have an excuse to step away, to sit and watch the colors paint the ceiling. He pointed at the man climbing over the skeletons. "What's that one supposed to be about?"

Lily shifted the baby onto her other hip. She turned and peered up at the window behind them. "Lazarus. Or maybe the resurrection. It looks like Jesus rising from the dead."

"And now our kid gets to rise along with him, to the newness of life." Hawley snorted. "You really believe that crap?"

His wife's lips pressed tightly together. She snatched the keys from him and marched to the parking lot and took the driver's seat. She didn't say another word the whole ride home. He spent the trip trying to come up with ways to make it up to her, but the baby was crying and he could barely think. When they arrived at the cabin Lily pulled over but kept the truck running.

"Take Louise," she said. "Take her and get out."

"Where are you going?" Hawley asked.

"I need to drive. I need to drive until I don't feel like driving anymore," said Lily. "I'm sick of being a mother. And I'm sick of being a wife."

Hawley unstrapped the car seat. He took the baby and slammed the door. Her cries were pulsating now, one after the next, enough to make his hands shake. "What am I supposed to do with her?"

"Figure it out," said Lily. And then she pulled away.

The baby didn't look wet. Hungry, Hawley decided, and carried her in the car seat into the kitchen. He searched the diaper bag and found an empty bottle as well as the baptismal certificate, folded in half and slipped into the side zippered pocket. He threw the certificate into the living room, then dug up a container of powdered formula and mixed it with water. He shook the bottle until the liquid inside was frothy. Then he put the bottle in a pan of water and lit the stove. Louise continued to howl in the car seat. Hawley walked back and forth from the pan of water to the carrier. Whenever the baby saw him getting closer she would start kicking her legs.

"You're not the only one who feels bad," said Hawley.

The bottle took forever to get warm. He'd seen Lily test the milk on her wrist, but Hawley had scars there, so instead he stretched out his tongue and squeezed a few drops. The formula didn't taste like much. He expected it to be sweet but it was more like unflavored yogurt. Tangy, with a scent of wheat.

When the milk was warm enough he turned off the stove and took the bottle to his daughter. He leaned over and tried to put the nipple into her mouth but it was too big. The baby kept screaming, her face red, her lips pulled down. She mouthed the rubber a bit but the tears kept coming, and then some of the milk dribbled down her throat and she gagged. The baby coughed and her eyes went wide. Then she started crying again, louder this time.

Hawley put the bottle down and went to the door and opened it and stood out in the yard, looking for Lily. He half-expected her to be parked down the block, waiting. But she wasn't anywhere he could see.

He went back inside and unbuckled his daughter from the carrier. Once his fingers were cradling her skull, he lifted her out of the bassinet. He pulled her close to his chest. She was squirming and screeching and her body was hot. Hawley sat down on the couch and laid the baby across his knees. He tried putting the bottle in her mouth again but she wouldn't take it. He got some baby food out of the fridge and tried spooning it into her mouth but she spit it onto the floor. He leaned over and sniffed the diaper, but it seemed clean enough. She reached up and grabbed hold of his ear. She had sharp fingernails. A lock of his hair tangled in her small fingers and she yanked it out and then held the strands like a wilted bouquet.

"You think you're tough?"

He turned the baby onto her stomach. Then he turned her back. He jostled his legs up and down like a carnival ride. He put her on his shoulder, then he tried the other shoulder. He walked the room. He lay down on the floor with her. He rocked her in the crook of his arm. He tried sticking his finger in her mouth. It didn't do any good or stop the screaming.

At this point Hawley was desperate. He went back to the front door, holding the baby this time, and opened it again. It was getting dark outside, and he stared into the darkness, as if he could conjure Lily out of the night sky, out of the stars and the gathering moon. But there was no sign of her.

Hawley closed the door and went down into the basement, the baby still crying. He brought down a metal box from the shelf above his workbench, got the key from where it was hidden behind the boiler, unlocked it, reached inside and took out a flask.

At night Hawley still dreamed of the clepsydra, the feel of it filling with water and being ripped from his hands. He woke up sweating with the same dread he'd felt when the glacier cracked and the blue ice fell. The only thing that settled his mind was a drink. So he'd started to keep bottles stashed around the house, in places he hoped that Lily would never find. After the mess he'd made in Alaska, Jove had done his best to cover for him, but in the end King had sussed it out. Now both he and Jove were on the line for all of that lost money.

Hawley brought the flask upstairs and poured himself a glass. He threw the whiskey back in one shot and exhaled loudly. The baby's sobs grew softer, and her eyes seemed to focus for a moment. Hawley examined her blotchy face. Then he poured another shot, dipped his pinky into the glass and stuck his finger into his daughter's gaping mouth. She stopped crying instantly. She sucked on his finger and her eyes locked on to his face. Her tiny hand came up and wrapped around the side of his hand and she watched him and she sucked the whiskey off his skin.

The room vibrated with the silence she had left behind. Hawley took a breath. He took another. Then he collapsed onto one of the kitchen chairs. He kept the shot of whiskey nearby. When the baby fussed he dipped his pinky into the glass again. As soon as the finger was in her mouth she went to work, her tongue pressing against his nail. The pull was wildly strong. A dark, animal need.

When he heard Lily come in the front door, he grabbed the shot he'd poured and threw what was left down his own throat, then quickly tossed the flask into the garbage can. His daughter was sound asleep, heavy in his arms. He'd kept his finger in her mouth for over an hour, not wanting her to wake and start crying again. The baby's face was peaceful, and Hawley felt as if he'd earned that peacefulness, as if he'd made all that haunted them both disappear.

He wiped the inside of the glass with his pinky and slid it back inside the baby's mouth. The baby breathed for a moment, then her reflexes kicked in and her lips closed around his finger. It was the first secret between them.

Lily came around the corner of the living room, carrying her shoes. Her face was tired, her makeup worn off, her hair loose around her shoulders. She lingered in the doorway, watching Hawley and the baby.

"You smell like cigarettes," he said.

"I bought some. But they don't taste as good as I remember."

"Where'd you go?"

"To a meeting, down at the church. Then I drove some more and then I had some ice cream."

"Did you bring me any?"

"Nope."

"She's been screaming all night," he said. "The least you could have done was bring me some ice cream."

Lily walked up to the table, picked up the glass and lifted it to her nose.

Hawley said, "It's not what you think."

"Tell me, then."

He didn't know how to answer. He knew only that the whiskey had worked. And now the pride he'd felt at getting things right with their daughter was draining away.

"You need to step it up if you're going to be a parent. You can't keep living like a criminal."

"Is that what the folks at your meeting told you?"

"This group is full of midwesterners from the Wisconsin Dells. A priest and a librarian and a ballet teacher and a guy who does commercials on the radio. I couldn't tell them the truth about why we moved here. I can't talk about our real life, about you disappearing and getting shot somewhere out in the wilderness and almost dying. I know it was hard but I took care of you afterward—don't you remember? And now I take care of her. And I'm so tired I forget who I am sometimes."

She sat down at the table. She bent over and smelled Loo's head.

"That's what *I* do when *I* want a drink."

Lily picked up the shot glass and walked over to the counter. She turned on the water, washed the glass with a sponge and set it on the dish rack.

"You regret this," said Hawley. "Coming back for me at the diner. Getting married."

Lily turned off the faucet.

"You like being the bad guy. But our story—it isn't only about you, Hawley."

She dried her hands on a towel, then came and sat down next to him again.

"I'm going to tell you what I shared tonight at the meeting. What I could share," she said, wiping her lips. "When you went away on that job in Alaska, and you didn't call and you didn't come home, I thought you'd left me. I thought you didn't want a baby and weren't ever coming back. So I went to a bar. I went to two bars. But nobody would serve me because I was pregnant. I was waiting for the liquor store to open when you rang from that guy's truck." She reached over and took his hand. "You think you're alone. You think you're the worst. But you're not."

Hawley shook his head. There weren't any words he could say and not start choking.

"Go on," said Lily.

He leaned over the baby. He pressed his face into her soft, black hair. She smelled of orange blossoms and sweet, freshly churned butter.

"I thought she'd never stop crying."

"Well, she did."

"You can't ever leave like that again."

He tried to hand the baby over. Lily wouldn't take her.

"You're just scared," she said. "I am, too."

They watched their daughter sleeping. Then Lily leaned on his shoulder and closed her eyes. Hawley could feel himself dozing, too. He slipped his finger out of the baby's mouth and then he carefully lifted her and carried her into the living room and set her down in the bassinet. She startled for a moment and he froze, terrified. Then she threw her arms over her head and turned her face toward the wall. He covered her with a blanket. Then he picked up the baptismal certificate that he'd tossed on the floor earlier that night.

" 'Louise' makes her seem old," he said.

"You got another idea?"

Hawley peered down at their daughter. The baby was still asleep, her mouth open in a perfect pout, her tiny hands clenched in tight little fists.

"Lou."

"That's a man's name."

"Then we'll make it prettier," said Hawley. "Switch the *u* with an *o*."

"Loo," Lily said. "I like it."

Hawley sat down on the couch and took Lily's hand. Just above her wedding band there was a tiny callus, a bit of skin worn tough from the pressure of the ring. It seemed like this hardened part of her had always been there, though Hawley knew there was a time when it wasn't.

"You still want to be a mother?"

"I don't think I've got a choice."

"What about a wife?"

Lily ran her fingers through his hair. She sighed, but the sigh was light, with hardly any anger left. Hawley lay down and pulled her down beside him. They pressed against each other on the couch. Lily tucked her head underneath his chin, and Hawley stroked the back of her neck, feeling the bones there, thinking of the rounded pieces of spine, linked and holding his wife together.

"You're not mad," Lily asked, "about the ice cream?"

Hawley took her face into his hands and kissed her forehead, her eyes and then her lips, slow and grateful and brimming with the hundreds of ways he wanted to touch her.

In the morning Hawley woke to the baby fussing. Not crying yet but getting fixed to start. One of his legs was off the couch, tangled in the mess of clothes on the floor. Lily was curled naked beside him, her skin on his skin, her breath warming his chest, her arms tight around his waist, a thin blanket over them both. Hawley closed his eyes and waited. Then the cries began again. He peeled away from his wife. He slipped into his jeans and leaned over the bassinet. The baby was wearing different pajamas. Lily must have already been up with her in the night. Changed her and fed her and put her down again while he'd been sleeping.

"Troublemaker."

The baby looked at him and waved her arms.

"Yeah, you."

He picked her up and brought her into the kitchen. He found the bottle from before and warmed it up again on the stove. This time Loo latched on as soon as he placed the nipple near her mouth. With one tiny hand she touched the side of the plastic, bending and releasing her fingers. When the milk was half gone she started to go heavy in his arms again, her eyes fluttering.

Lily came into the kitchen with only the blanket wrapped around her. If she was surprised at Hawley feeding Loo, she didn't show it.

"What time is it?"

"Around six."

"Let's go to the beach."

"Now?"

"Right now," she said. "Memorial Day isn't until next weekend, and most of the summer cabins should still be closed up. I like going when nobody else is around. It makes me feel like the whole lake belongs to us."

They got some towels and their suits from where they were drying in the bathroom. Lily packed the diaper bag with everything they needed and Hawley put together a cooler of drinks and some sandwiches and chips and some apples and two slices from a peach pie Lily had made the day before. It was nice out, so they decided to walk. They strapped the baby into the stroller and Lily pushed her and Hawley carried the cooler down the road and through the woods to the shore of the lake.

It was still early and the beach was empty. The sand was warm and the air unusually muggy, more like August than the end of May. The dock that ran out into the water had an aluminum canoe tied up but no paddles. Someone had made a bonfire the night before near the woods. There were charred logs piled up, blackened in the middle of a ring of stones. A lawn chair had been left behind, with a webbed fabric seat. Lily sat down right away. She dug her feet into the sand and leaned back and closed her eyes.

"This chair is my chair," she said.

Hawley unbuckled Loo from the stroller. He helped Lily put sunblock on the baby's skin and then Lily put a sunhat on top of Loo's tiny head and carried her out into the water. The baby was wearing a tiny polka-dot bathing suit. She liked to bend down and slap at the surface, at the places where the sun caught and flashed. Lily had on a green one-piece with straps that tied around her neck. She was shy about wearing the suit in public, shy about the way her body had changed since she had the baby, but Hawley thought she looked great.

"Is it cold?" he asked.

Lily shook her head but he could see goosebumps running across her back. She never admitted if the water was cold, even if it was freezing. She'd been taking the baby into the lake for over a month already. Loo had fussed at first but now she'd grown used to the chill. Hawley stretched out on their blanket and put his hands behind his head. He listened to the breeze coming through the leaves. He felt the early-morning sun warming his skin. He turned his head and watched Lily bending into the water, dipping the baby. They were making a game of it. Lily whistled low and then high as they dropped deeper. The baby squealed, then clung tighter to Lily's neck.

Hawley got up from the blanket and walked over to the dock. He stood for a while looking out at the wooden planks leading into the lake, at the canoe drifting from the end of its rope and at the water, which stretched out smoothly before him like a piece of glass. Lily turned to watch him from the shallows, ripples going out in circles from her waist, the baby still in her arms. Hawley saluted her. Two fingers straight from his brow. Then he went to the end of the dock and sat on the edge and dipped his feet in.

The water was ice-cold. He looked down through the surface, past schools of fish and minnows toward the bottom of the lake, where shadows lurked among dark tendrils of old vegetation. Hawley held on to the edge of the dock and slid the rest of his body into the shallows, next to the metal canoe. He clung to the float at the bottom of the dock and kicked his legs out behind him, practicing the different leg movements Lily had started to show him.

"You're getting better," she said.

"You think so?"

"Yes," she said. "Now watch this." And she let go of the baby.

Loo sank under the water. Lily took a step back and the baby swam toward her. Then Lily picked their daughter back up again. Loo didn't look bothered at all. She pumped her legs, her eyelashes dripping, and rolled her tongue around in her mouth.

"I can't believe you just did that," said Hawley.

"Everyone is born knowing how to swim," she said. "You just forgot."

She had been giving him lessons since they moved to the lake. The first few times he'd been so nervous all she could get him to do was dip his feet in. But eventually she got him to go chest-high, explaining that the more air he got into his lungs, the higher he'd float. Then she stood beside him in the shallow water and stretched her arms out and told him to lean back. He was twice her size but she held him like he was a child, just like she held the baby now. Hawley hadn't made much progress, but he could hold his breath underwater and he was starting to float on his own.

Lily let the baby swim a few more times, and then she got out. She wrapped a towel around Loo and one around herself and then she changed the baby's diaper and Hawley watched her putting more sunscreen on the baby's legs and arms. She sat in the lawn chair and fed the baby a bottle. Then she walked up and down with her on the beach and finally she put the baby into the stroller and pulled down the shade to keep off the sun and Hawley could see that the baby was asleep. Lily stretched out next to the stroller on the blanket and soon she was asleep, too.

Hawley watched them from the end of the dock. When Lily put her head on the blanket, he turned over and tried to float, keeping one hand grounded on the edge. Overhead there was light coming through the hemlocks and dappling the water. Hawley took a deep breath and felt his body lift higher on the surface. Then he exhaled and he began to sink, just enough for the water to rise around his face and slide inside both ears. He couldn't hear the trees anymore. The only sound came from inside him—his own heartbeat, and his lungs taking air, and the tiny splashes of his hands and feet, magnified as the waves rolled over them and the movement of the current broke and slid around his body and then came together on the other side of him and continued on, just as it passed through everything else, gently but surely in the same direction, past the dock and the fish and the stones below.

And then Hawley heard someone calling his name. Through the echo of the water. A voice was saying his name over and over and it was Lily.

Hawley righted himself. He felt for the floor of the lake but he'd drifted too far out. Some water got up his nose and he coughed and tasted the warmth of algae and rust. His hand grasped for the dock. He got hold and steadied himself. He looked toward the shore.

There was a man sitting on the lawn chair. Resting on one of his knees was a pistol with a suppressor attached to the barrel. On the other knee, nestled into the crook of his arm, was Loo. The man was wearing dark jeans tucked into boots, a flannel shirt and a fishing vest. The pockets of the fishing vest were stuffed with ammunition. At least fifteen loaded magazines. He looked like an old biker, bristly gray hair and sideburns down to his chin. His body had become thin beneath his fishing vest. His skin pulled sharply over the bones of his face, but Hawley knew him at once.

Talbot said, "Sure took me awhile to find you."

All Hawley could think was that he didn't have a gun. How could he not have brought a gun? He watched the old man slide the pistol back and forth against his leg. Overhead, the leaves stirred and shadows played across the lawn chair and across the face of the sleeping baby. Just a few feet away, Lily was kneeling Japanese-style on the blanket in her green bathing suit. Her shoulders were twitching and her hands were palm down on the sand in front of her like they'd been nailed in place and her eyes never left Loo.

"I'm just going to enjoy this for a minute," said Talbot. "I'm going to sit here and take in the scene." He rocked back and forth in the chair, and each rock drove him a bit farther into the sand, until there were two furrows around the aluminum legs. The baby slept on in his arms.

"What do you want?" Hawley asked, but he already knew.

Talbot scratched his knee with the back of the pistol and Hawley inched forward, staying low in the water, feeling for the bottom of the lake. It was there, soft and rotten beneath his toes. He planted both feet deep in the muck and stood. He tried to catch Lily's eye but she only stared at Loo. He could see her lips moving, stringing one word after another: *Please, please, please, please, please, please, please.*

"Let them go. And we'll settle things. However you want."

Talbot shifted his boots in the sand. He seemed intent on this for a moment, his jaw set. Then he stopped and squinted up at the sun. He wiped his brow with the back of his arm, the one not holding the baby. "You got any sodas in there?" He pointed at the cooler. He was talking to Lily but she didn't answer.

"I'll get you one," said Hawley.

Talbot lifted the gun. He kept the pistol on Hawley but his head turned toward Lily on her knees, her arms still spread across the sand.

"I've been watching you for weeks. I've been watching you live your life. I've been sleeping in my car and watching you and it made me miss having a wife to serve me a cold drink when I wanted," Talbot said. "You can move those hands now."

Lily clawed her fingers into the sand and leaned slowly back on her heels, drawing her palms to her knees. She blinked her eyes like she'd been released from a trance. The cooler was sitting between the blanket and Talbot's lawn chair. She shifted on her knees, then lifted the lid, and took out an orange soda, opened it and handed it across to Talbot.

Talbot took a long sip. "It's been years since I had an orange soda." He took another drink and some of it spilled on the baby's face. Loo woke up, pushed against the elephant blanket wrapped around her and started to fuss.

There had to be a second gun. That was what Hawley was hoping for. That Talbot had brought a second gun or even a third. He watched the old man drink his soda. He took a step forward. And then another. His toes sinking into the silt of the lake. He could tell Loo's crying was screwing up Talbot's nerves. It was the cry she did when she was hungry.

"She's only a baby," said Hawley. "She never hurt anyone."

"You think Maureen ever hurt anybody?" Talbot blew air out of his cheeks. "And look how she went. Over a fucking watch."

"You're the one who shot her."

Talbot kept his eyes on Hawley, but he moved the pistol so that the muzzle was now pointing at the baby. Lily started to get up from her knees, as if the gun had a rope that was pulling her toward it.

"Stop," said Hawley. He raised his hands out of the water. He took another step closer to shore. "You're right. And it's your right to come. I won't give you any trouble. But you need to let them go." He waited to see what Talbot would do next. He didn't want to move again until the old man was ready. But Talbot just leaned back in the lawn chair and took another sip from the orange soda.

"Her name is Louise," Lily said. "She just got baptized yesterday. We call her Loo."

Talbot said nothing in response, but Hawley could tell he was listening. He put down the can and pressed his palm against his knee, wiping the condensation onto his jeans.

"She swam for the first time today, just before you came here." As she spoke, Lily lifted her hands and inched toward Talbot and the baby. "She sleeps through the night, and she's started eating real food. Rice cereal. Mashed bananas. She cut her first tooth last week. And she laughs. If you kiss her hand, she laughs." Lily leaned over and smiled at the baby. Loo's crying slowed, and then stopped at the sight of her mother. Talbot was watching, out of the corner of his eye, not really looking at them but looking. Lily took the baby's hand and bent down, her face so close to the gun Hawley's stomach ached, and pressed her lips against Loo's tiny knuckles, making a big, exaggerated *mwah*.

The baby's eyes went wide, and all at once her mouth opened and a small noise came out, so perfect and clear it was like a made-up sound of a baby laughing. Then Loo lifted her hand all on her own, like a queen, so that her mother would kiss it again.

Talbot looked embarrassed. He shifted the baby onto his other knee, as if Lily were a stranger, bothering them in a supermarket line. "Get out of the water," he said to Hawley. "Keep your hands where I can see them."

Hawley made his way slowly out of the lake, thinking of ways to wrestle the gun away from Talbot, and dismissing them all. Either the baby or Lily was bound to get shot. He calculated distance, tracking escape routes. It was too far to the tree line. Even if he could snatch Loo away from Talbot, the old man would have time to shoot all three of them before they reached the woods. Hawley's eyes went down the length of the dock and rested on the metal canoe. And then he remembered there weren't any paddles. He stood dripping in front of the blanket. A breeze swept down and his skin turned cold.

The trees shifted overhead.

"You can pick one," said Talbot. "One gets to live."

Talbot's words joined them all tightly together. Hawley could sense every tremor and thought of Lily, frozen in fear on the blanket, every breath of their child, warming Talbot's lap, every shift of the old man's finger on the gun.

But Hawley was made for decisions like this. And he didn't hesitate.

"My wife," he said. "I pick my wife."

For the first time Lily's eyes left the baby. She stared at Hawley like he'd just pulled off a mask. "No," she said. "No."

But Talbot seemed satisfied. He slid to the edge of the lawn chair. He bounced Loo on his knee, then waved the gun at Lily.

"Tell her not to call the cops."

Hawley said, "Don't call the cops."

"If she does I'll come after her, too."

"You're a terrible person," said Lily.

"Tell her to go now," said Talbot. "Or that's it for chances."

There was no time to waste. No time to let the old man change his mind. Hawley grabbed his wife by the arm and yanked her from the blanket. When she struggled to get away, he slapped her in the face and shoved her toward the path. And when Lily spun and came back pushing at him, he hit her harder. Hit her with his whole fist. She stumbled and fell to the sand. She stared up at him.

"Get the fuck out of here," said Hawley.

Only then did she seem to get it. Hawley did not have to hit her again. She was up and hurrying across the beach and barreling into the forest, toward their house and Hawley's guns. If Lily ran the whole way she could make it home and back in fifteen minutes. When she reached the top of the hill she paused and glanced over her shoulder. He tried to think of a way to say he was sorry, but all he could do was touch his forehead, like he was tipping a hat that wasn't there. His wife stood looking ill for a moment and then she wrinkled her nose and turned away, and she was gone.

Hawley returned to the blanket and stood in front of Talbot.

"Now what?"

The old man gestured at the cooler.

"You got any food in there?"

"Sandwiches and pie."

"Ham and cheese?"

"Baloney."

Talbot grunted his approval. He made Hawley pull the cooler over to him and open it. He transferred the baby from the crook of his arm onto his lap so he could keep the gun pressed against Loo's stomach while rummaging inside. He pulled out some sandwiches wrapped in tinfoil and cellophane and the small plastic container that held the pie. He never took his eyes off Hawley, feeling blindly and throwing the food out onto the blanket. He told Hawley to unwrap the cellophane from one of the sandwiches and Hawley did and gave it over. Some mustard slipped out from the bread as the old man took a bite and landed on his fishing vest. He didn't seem to notice.

"I brought Maureen to the clinic in Oak Harbor," said Talbot. "The bullet was from my gun so they thought it was some sort of domestic dispute. The police locked me up so I wasn't with her when she died. Then they found your car, and some of your blood in the house. They let me go after that. But once they did, I wished they hadn't." Talbot took another slurp of his soda. "Hand me some of that pie."

Hawley opened the plastic container. He found one of the forks they'd packed. He imagined sticking the tines in Talbot's neck. The old man took the fork from him and ate the crust and peaches with a slow and exhausted look, like it was the last course of a giant meal he'd been making his way through for days. Like the pie was something sweet he didn't need or have any desire for but felt he had to finish.

"We'd been together a long time," said Talbot. "And I didn't know how to breathe without her. Everyplace I looked there was a part of her and I just about lost my mind with thinking about her and going over everything in my head of what I'd done wrong. And that dress. That fucking wedding dress. I dragged it out to the cliffs one night and threw it over the edge. Almost threw myself over, too."

Talbot dropped the fork into the container. He put the container on the ground. "You're still a young man and you don't know anything," he said, "but one day God is going to remember all the things you've done and then He's going to bring down His judgment and teach you more than you ever wanted to learn."

"It was just a job," said Hawley. But already he was remembering Talbot's wife, and the way her violet eye turned cloudy as she clutched her veil.

Talbot took a sip of orange soda.

"You know I'm not the only one looking for you."

At the end of the dock, the canoe stretched the length of its rope and then swung back, bumping against the worn-out wood.

"I heard you bungled things in Alaska."

"Something like that."

"You're lucky I found you first," he said. "King wouldn't have given you a choice."

Hawley wasn't sure what to say about that. In his mind he tried to count the minutes, each second bringing Lily closer to the guns. He tried shifting, bit by bit, hoping Talbot was so caught up in talking that he wouldn't notice. The old man poured the rest of the soda out onto the beach. The liquid sizzled and fizzed, darkening the color of the sand. He stared at the spot.

"Know where we went on our honeymoon?"

"No," said Hawley.

"Rome," Talbot said. "But Maureen didn't want to visit any of the normal tourist places, like the Vatican or the Colosseum. She wanted to go to a chapel made out of human bones. It was the creepiest thing I ever saw. But Maureen loved it. Some of the bones were broken apart and made into patterns. Maureen said it was the patterns that made the place beautiful. Showed how everything in life is connected and repeated and reflected in each other. That a hip bone or a piece of vertebra can look the same as a flower. She said that it made her believe in God."

Talbot was running his fingers through his sideburns, over and over, like he was searching for something caught between his chin and the frazzled gray hair. The old man's face was drawn, his shoulders hunched around the baby in his lap. But he still carried the same dark edge of violence he had on Whidbey, and his time spent searching for Hawley had only sharpened those corners of himself. There was a pinned hardness to his eyes, like he was taking in all the smells and sounds of the world and also walling himself against them. Loo began twisting around and kicking her legs. She reached out and touched the muzzle of the suppressor. Talbot looked down at the baby but did nothing to stop her. And that's when Hawley realized that the old man planned to kill himself, once he'd finished with them. All along, that's what he'd been working himself up to. That's why he was stalling.

"You broke her nose," said Talbot. "She had such a beautiful nose."

Hawley slid his hand the rest of the way across the blanket. He gripped the fork tight in his fist. He couldn't wait any longer. There was no more time. Hawley took in a breath. He held half of it back. And then he swung out long and hard and jammed the fork into Talbot's leg with all his might. The old man screamed and sprang up from the lawn chair. He dropped the baby but not the gun.

Hawley snatched Loo just as she hit the sand. And then he was running down the length of the dock. The baby felt light in his arms, like nothing at all. Loo's mouth was open but she wasn't crying. Her breath was wet against his cheek, smelling of formula, and her fingers clutched the skin of his neck. He set her in the bottom of the canoe, and yanked the rope free and shoved the boat adrift with all his might. The canoe shot out some thirty feet, then caught the current and started floating across the lake. He could see Loo's chubby legs kicking underneath the elephant blanket. He'd done it all without thinking. Without even looking back. Then he heard the sound of Talbot coming up behind him.

Because of the suppressor there was no bang or boom—just a huff of air and the shots whizzing past him. Hawley crouched to protect his head and gripped the dock. Even with a gun trained on him, he was afraid to get into the water. Then Talbot tagged him with two bullets. Snip. Snip. Right in the ass.

Hawley would have thought it was funny if it didn't hurt so much—the pain bursting out of his flesh and flying up the base of his spine. His knees buckled, and he sensed his body falling, falling, falling, falling until he was ready to scream for the water to come. His shoulder hit with a crash, and everywhere was white froth and bubbles. Hawley tried to push himself deeper, tried to remember the lessons Lily had given him, to keep his fingers together as he scooped his hands, to let out tiny bits of air instead of blowing it all at once.

He stayed under as long as he could. Then his lungs began to fail and he surfaced beneath the dock, gasping. The pain threaded around his thighs whenever he moved his legs. With one hand he gripped the underside of the dock and with the other he pressed the wounds, trying to stop the blood. Overhead Talbot was dragging his injured leg along the boards.

"I know you're under there."

Hawley tried not to move. Not to make a sound. It was too dark to see and so he just stared at the slits of light. The floats under the dock were covered with slime and smelled of rotted foam and cobwebs and the hollow casings of dead bugs and spiders and the years that had passed since the boards had been placed there and all the waves that had run through. It smelled of being caught and being left behind and it smelled of being forgotten.

Hawley couldn't get his footing—the reeds were tangled around his knees and the sand was full of silt and washed up bits of life and then the dragging noise stopped and he heard Talbot slide another magazine into the pistol. The first shot went long and broke through a board five feet ahead of him. The second and third were two feet away, and left holes that immediately shone circles of light on his skin. Hawley took a deep breath and pushed against the dock and sank as far as he could, hoping that if he kept moving and if he went deep enough Talbot would keep missing, until the gun was ready for the next magazine and that by then he might figure what to do next.

But Talbot didn't miss—the fourth shot went past Hawley's face and took off the bottom of his left ear, and the ear bled so much that it became hard to see through the clouded water. As he kicked, the bullets in his ass seemed to dig farther into his tailbone, until he could barely move his legs for the pain. Soon his lungs were pushing for air again. Hawley knew he'd have to surface and when he did Talbot would kill him.

The current churned gold and red, and Hawley's chest twisted hard with the desire to open—to air, to water. The reeds at the bottom of the lake were waving in the gloom, and Hawley pushed down and grabbed for them. The tendrils wrapped around his wrists, slimy and seemingly sentient, until it was hard to say if he was anchoring himself or if the reeds were pulling him down into the shadows.

His hands sifted stones and algae and trash, beer bottles and what felt like a piece of a grill, and then the dead bodies of creatures, fish and birds, half broken down and making their way back into the earth. Hawley plunged his fingers into the icy murk and thought of Loo. He hoped that he had saved her. He hoped that he had done enough.

The clump of reeds broke free and came loose in his hand. Hawley clutched another patch and another, but none would support his weight. He could feel his body coming adrift, drawn back toward the surface. The cold faded as he rose. A pattern of thuds radiated through the depths, footsteps along the dock, and then came a much louder boom— like a sudden crack of lightning from a storm, followed by an explosion overhead that Hawley felt more than heard, the water displaced by a torrent of bubbles. He turned his head toward the surface, and through the gloom saw the body of a man coming toward him.

For a moment it seemed like Hawley himself, or perhaps Hawley as he might have been, if he had lived to be an older man. Thick shoulders and gray hair, a flannel shirt and work boots. Hawley floated up into the lake and the man floated down into the lake and the two of them met in the middle. And then Hawley saw there was a hole in the center of the man, blasted through his chest. He could see right through the hole. He could see the gleam of sunlight coming down from the surface through the bloody water. He could see the edge of the dock, the flannel shirt blooming and the man's guts trailing behind like the tail of a kite.

Talbot's eyes were open and staring past Hawley, past the reeds and past the floor of the lake. He looked more surprised than angry about the hole, his mouth open and taking in water, the remains of his fishing vest torn to pieces. Hawley pushed at Talbot's shoulders, and for a moment they were tangled in each other, arms and legs heavy, Talbot's sideburns brushing Hawley's cheek, the fishing vest casting hooks into them both, tying the men together, metal to skin. Then Talbot dropped down into the dark of the reeds and Hawley continued to rise.

His first breath was half water, half air. His lungs vibrated deep in his chest from the effort. His head knocked against the side of the dock and he was sputtering and thrashing, bile rich and deep snaking its way up his throat. He tried again and the next breath was easier, less pressure against his ribs, but his vision blurred and then he was under again.

The bullets burned. He could barely move his legs. He threw out his arm once more, groping for the float, and a set of thin, strong fingers snatched hold of him. Lily's fingers. Hawley would know them anywhere.

She couldn't heft him onto the dock and so she towed Hawley to shore, dragging him along the edge of the wooden floats until he felt the lake bed beneath his back, his whole body clenched around the pain. Lily pulled him onto the sand. She put her mouth on his but she didn't kiss him. She squeezed his nose and blew down into his lungs. Hawley coughed. He turned to the side and retched.

"I'm okay," he wheezed, the air ripping his throat. "I'm all right."

And then Lily was hitting him, smacking his shoulders and his face. She was kneeling in the sand. There was blood spattered across her green bathing suit, across her face and shoulders and legs. Hawley couldn't tell if she was screaming or crying. His right ear was blocked and the left was still ringing from where the bullet had torn through.

"Louise!" she shouted. "Where's Louise?"

Hawley rolled up onto his elbows, an agonizing hurt threading along his spine. He peered across the lake. The canoe was nowhere to be seen.

"She's in the boat," he said.

Lily pushed to her feet and started limping back down the length of the dock, holding on to her right side. She scanned the horizon. Hawley crawled after her, the pain too much to stand, his mind whirling. They swayed together like drunks. Lily's whole body was shaking. Her hands covered with blood as she lifted them to block the sun from her eyes. Hawley's twelve-gauge shotgun was at her feet.

"You're hurt."

She looked at her own trembling fingers. Then at the dark stain spreading across the fabric of her bathing suit. "His gun went off when I pulled the trigger. I don't think he meant to shoot me. It was some kind of reflex," said Lily. "I don't feel anything."

"That's the adrenaline." Hawley reached up and put pressure on the hole with his fingers. There wasn't an exit wound. He worried about the caliber and what it might have done to her insides. If the bullet had torn through her kidneys or liver. If it had ruptured her stomach. If it had nicked an artery or major vessel, she would bleed out right here on the beach. He pressed harder. Lily screamed.

"Stop it," she said.

"You're in shock. We need to get you to a hospital."

Lily's eyes darted left, then right.

"I pushed the barrel against his chest. He let me walk right up and do it."

"You had to."

"No. I wanted to kill him," she said. "The shotgun made a hole so big—I could have put my hand right through his body."

Every movement she made seemed both frantic and slow. Beneath their feet, the dock was splattered with guts and fragments of bone. While overhead the sky was filled with the sound of a sputtering engine. A Cessna was chugging somewhere above the clouds, the pilot probably looking down on this very patch of blue water.

"What if she drowned? What if the boat sank?"

"It's a good boat. A steady boat."

Hawley kept his hand tight against her waist. Lily's breath was coming in short, small bursts.

"You could have saved her. Instead of me you could have saved her. But you didn't."

"I was trying to save all of us," said Hawley.

The sun emerged from behind a cloud and the lake began to shimmer. Hawley could still hear the airplane. He imagined it falling, wings askew, the propellers churning empty air. And then he was certain the crash was going to happen, as if he'd dreamed fragmented pieces of this lake and this plane and this exact sky all before, and was only now understanding how they fit together. He grabbed Lily's arm and waited for a plume of smoke, the smell of gasoline. He cast his eyes on the horizon, and the flash of aluminum came like a sign.

"There," he said, and pointed across the lake.

The canoe was nestled in a grove of trees on the opposite shore. A large branch covered the nose of the boat. Hanging over the edge, soaking up lake water, was a corner of the elephant blanket.

Lily ripped away from him and then she was stumbling along the length of the dock. She ran past the shotgun, past Talbot's blood soaking through the boards. She leapt from the edge, pushing the splintered wood away with her feet, and dove headfirst into the waves. She stayed under for a long time but then surfaced, some twenty feet away, and as soon as she did she started working a fast crawl, until there were only her arms churning, elbows bending in and out of the waves and the occasional flash of her face dipping to the side to snatch a breath. The silver canoe that held their daughter floated in the distance, and his wife swam toward it, met by her own reflection, moving away from Hawley and the dock with such speed that she left a wake behind her, a V of flattened water that spread from her body like a formation of birds flying south for the winter.

And then, about halfway across the lake, her pace began to slow. Her face tilted more often for air. Her arms lowered and then barely lifted. She switched to a breaststroke, and then a sidestroke and then she stopped to rest. Her head tilted back. Her mouth open.

Hawley jumped off the dock. He tried to make his way to her.

He thrashed.

He sank.

He choked.

He tried.

He sank.

He choked.

He grabbed the dock. He looked out across the lake. She was still treading water.

"Lily!" he shouted. "Come back!"

But she only started moving away again. The wake around her was widening into a rippling circle, with her at the center. Then she slowed once more, her neck craning, her mouth at the edge. Her hands moved in place like she was climbing an invisible ladder. She looked up at the sky. And then her head dipped under the surface.

"Lily!" Hawley pushed away from the dock. He let go of everything. He coughed and sputtered and willed his arms and legs forward. But he could not get himself closer to her. His body was lead. It dragged him under the current. His lungs filled with water. The waves churned with his own blood. His chest twisted tighter and tighter until he felt he would split in two. When he broke through the surface again, the spot where Lily had been was empty and the lake was as flat as a mirror.

Hawley's mind raced back to when he'd opened his eyes that morning, Lily's skin sealed to his own—no—back to when she pushed him out of the car and kept driving, if only she'd kept driving—no—back to the church, Lily at the baptismal fountain and the baby in his hands under the colored lights and the priest saying a blessing. A prayer, Hawley thought. If only he could remember the words. That's what he needed now. Some way of sending a flare to the heavens. Like bones broken apart and made to look like flowers. A pattern of some hidden meaning that Hawley carried inside his own body, but had no way of tearing open to read, and no witness but the Cessna, circling in the sky like some kind of mechanical bird, and between the choking sputters of its engine Hawley heard no answers and no reasons for living except the cries of his daughter, echoing inside the metal canoe.

Pandora

"I'VE BEEN WAITING FOR YOU TO SHOW UP," SAID MABEL RIDGE WHEN SHE answered the door. Her hands were still tinged slightly blue, but this time there were no goggles strapped to her head, no heavy apron around her waist. She was wearing a cardigan sweater and a turtleneck, her gray hair pulled back neatly in a bun. She did not seem surprised to see Loo. She did not seem surprised to see the Firebird in the driveway, either.

Mabel's porch was covered with pumpkins that had been carved too soon. It was only the beginning of October, and already one of the angry jack-o'-lanterns had its teeth caving in, and one of the happy jack-o'-lanterns was leaking a sticky substance across the steps. Loo wiped her sneakers on the mat. The screwdriver she'd used to crack open the panel beneath the dashboard was inside the pocket of her sweatshirt, and she turned it over and over with her fingers. "I brought your car back."

Mabel patted the railing. They stood facing each other on the dull gray porch. Then the old woman turned around and left the door open. "I'm making some tea," she said. "Why don't you join me, Louise."

Loo stood on the threshold for a moment longer, then stepped inside. Mabel Ridge's living room looked the same as before. The corners of the end table baby-proofed for some long-ago child. The arms of the sofa showing pulls from some long-forgotten cat. The rug threadbare from shuffles along one side. The loom in the corner, looming.

She followed the old woman down the hall into the kitchen, which was small and cramped as ever, the giant pots used to dye her yarn still on the stove. Mabel Ridge dragged one off and set it on the floor. Then she filled a kettle with water from the sink and lit the empty burner.

On the table was a copy of the local newspaper. Loo picked it up and read the headlines. PETITION PUTS PRESSURE ON POLS. LOCAL FISHER-MEN ARRESTED. COAST GUARD DOUBLES PATROLS NEAR BITTER BANKS.

"Which side are you on?"

"No one's," said Loo.

"I thought your father was friends with those fishermen."

"He is."

"Well," said Mabel Ridge, "the TV show was one thing, but if the Banks really gets turned into a marine sanctuary, it would mean big changes around here."

Loo set down the paper. "You're probably right."

It had taken her nearly a month to finish the signatures. She had added Mabel Ridge's name, along with thousands of others, and mailed the petition to the National Oceanic and Atmospheric Admin-istration, the EPA, city hall, the governor, state representatives and state senators, as well as the newspapers and local TV stations. She'd brought all of the packages to the post office, put them in manila envelopes and mailed them off like bombs she'd cooked up in her base-ment. Now they were starting to go off. But she still hadn't heard from Marshall.

Loo sat down in one of the creaky kitchen chairs, the screwdriver tight against her palm.

"Don't you want to know how I got the car back?"

"I think it's better that I don't." Mabel opened the cabinet and took down two teacups and saucers. She set the cups on the table.

"Are you going to call the police?"

"Not unless you want me to."

Mabel reached into the cabinet again and removed a teapot, then started rummaging around for tea bags. The china cups were thin and white with gold around the edges. The suggestion of rose petals was traced into the sides, the saucer a perfect single leaf, the handle a ring of porcelain thorns. Loo slid her fingers inside the ring and lifted. The cup was light and delicate, the edges strangely comforting in her hand. Loo pressed her thumb against one of the thorns.

The kettle began to whistle. Mabel used an oven mitt to lift it off the stove.

"I want to know whatever it is you think you know," said Loo.

"Seems to me you've already figured it out," said Mabel, "or you wouldn't be here." She poured the hot water into the teapot, steam rising around her shoulders. "Your father's been lying to you."

The kettle went back on the stove, the lid set in place.

"That doesn't make him a killer."

Mabel Ridge sighed. "Your mother used to look at me like that. Like she knew all the answers. But she didn't know anything. And neither do you."

Loo shifted in her seat. She pressed her nails against the screwdriver.

"He's your father but he's not a good person. You should know that by now." The old woman took out a carton of milk and filled the small white creamer on the counter. "I was married to a man just like him. Gus was all caught up in the same world. I took Lily and I got out." Her hands twitched at her sides. She brought the creamer over to the table and set it on a placemat. "A year from now you'll be eighteen. Old enough to choose your own life," she said. "You can get out, too."

"Get out of what?"

"Trouble." Mabel Ridge poured out the tea. "Your father acts like he's got nothing to hide but that trouble is a part of him and he's a part of it and as long as you're with him you're in danger." She added milk and a spoonful of sugar to both cups.

"I don't take sugar," said Loo.

The old woman smiled a tired old smile. "Try it anyway."

Loo wrapped her fingers around the porcelain. She brought it to her lips and took a sip. The tea was the color of toffee, the sweetness of the sugar and milk coating her tongue. The cup warm against her hand. She took another drink. She ran her thumb along the side of the handle, and then she felt it: a small rough spot, where a thorn had been broken off.

And then: she remembered breaking it.

Loo held the cup tightly in her hands, but in her mind she could see the china hitting the black-and-white tile at her feet. The single thorn snapping off and sliding into a crevice near the wall. She saw herself crawling underneath the table, and trying to fish the broken thorn out with her finger. Loo put down the teacup. She glanced under the table-cloth. There, in a crooked gap against the baseboard, was a fleck of white, no bigger than a grain of rice. It was as if she'd placed it there for herself to find.

Suddenly the tea in Loo's mouth was too sweet, so sweet as it went down her throat that she nearly gagged. She stood up and dumped the rest into the sink.

"It's the only way I could get you to drink tea when you were little," said Mabel Ridge. "Lots of milk and sugar." She reached for the pot. "Here. I'll pour you another."

Loo's legs felt weak. She watched Mabel refill the cup. The tea was hot and steaming, tiny dark specks swirling against the porcelain and then coming to rest.

"I've been here before."

"I thought you remembered that night when I gave you the car. And then I realized you didn't. That your father had never told you."

Mabel took a drink, slurping a bit, and then let out a small sigh of satisfaction. She set the teacup back down on the saucer. "I didn't want to scare you off, so I decided to wait. But that's why I wanted you to come back. So I could tell you the truth."

"I don't understand," said Loo.

"Your father abandoned you. After Lily died. He left you here with me. You spoke your first words in this house. You took your first steps on this floor."

Loo stared at the baseboard, the tiny white speck. Everything Mabel Ridge had said was impossible. And yet—she could feel the past tugging at the corners of her mind. It was like trying to remember a dream while dreaming another.

Mabel's eyes narrowed. She was watching carefully, and as Loo grew more confused, a look of pleasure spread across her weathered face. "You're remembering."

"No. You're lying to me."

"I have proof." The old woman pushed herself up from the table. "Wait here. I'll show you."

As soon as she shuffled out of the room, Loo took the screwdriver from her pocket, climbed under the table and slipped the flat edge into the crevice. In one short movement, she flicked the bit of white out onto the floor. She pressed her finger against it. The thorn was real. It did not give.

"What are you doing down there?" Mabel Ridge's legs hobbled into the kitchen. She slid something heavy onto the table.

"Nothing," said Loo. She put the thorn and screwdriver into her pocket and crawled out. The old woman was fondling the edges of a leather photo album. She opened the cover and quickly turned the laminated pages, each crinkling like a layer of skin peeled away. Loo caught glimpses of faces. She could smell the dust and glue.

"Wait," she said. "Is that Principal Gunderson?"

Sealed under the plastic was a glossy photograph of two teenagers dressed for prom. One was a thin boy wearing an oversize tuxedo, his face beaming and his white-blond hair like a beacon against the fake backdrop and balloons. The other was Lily as a young girl, with braces and heavy black eyeliner, wearing a short dress with matching lace gloves.

"He told me they were just friends."

"They were—but he kept trying." Mabel Ridge shook her head. She lifted the photograph from the album, rubbed the edge of Principal Gunderson's ruffled shirt with her finger. "I always thought they would have made a lovely couple."

Loo looked closely at the picture. She thought of all the times Principal Gunderson had tried to help her. And then she saw the reason on his pimpled teenage face, in the brightness of his smile. He had loved Lily. And she hadn't loved him back.

Mabel Ridge set aside the picture of Principal Gunderson and continued flipping through the album. Then she stopped and turned the book toward Loo. She pointed to another picture.

Lily was in a hospital bed, her face flushed, her dark hair askew. She was wearing a green kimono the same color as her eyes—the same robe that Hawley kept hanging on the back of their bathroom door—and she was looking down at a baby in her arms and smiling the biggest smile Loo had ever seen.

"You." Mabel Ridge pressed a wrinkled blue finger against the photograph. Then she pulled the plastic and removed the picture. "She sent this to me when you were born."

It was an instant photograph, with a thick white border, a Polaroid—like the one of Lily in front of Niagara Falls in their bathroom—the coloring thick and slightly blurred. Which meant, Loo realized, that her mother must have held this picture in her hands right after it was taken, just as Loo was holding it now.

Slowly, Mabel turned another page. And then another. They were all full of snapshots of the same baby, taken in this very house. The baby was sleeping on a blanket. The baby had chocolate pudding all over her face. The baby was at the beach, her fists full of sand. The baby was getting older. The baby was walking now. The baby was wearing shoes. The baby was turning into a little girl. The little girl was getting her hair cut, a towel wrapped around her shoulders, her eyes full of tears. The little girl was sitting on a swing. The little girl was wearing some kind of Halloween costume made of silver cardboard.

"What was I dressed up as?"

"An electric toothbrush," the old woman said. "You couldn't get enough of them, for some reason. I don't know why."

Loo and Hawley had always used the free toothbrushes given out by the dentist. When she was little, they had even brushed their teeth together. She remembered the sound of her father gargling Listerine. She remembered contests to see who had the longest drool. But she did not remember this costume. Or the child who wore it, holding out an empty pillowcase for trick or treat.

"How long did I live here?" Loo asked.

"Until you were four years old," said Mabel Ridge.

Inside the palm of Loo's hand was the thorn. She squeezed her fingers around it. The tiny bit of porcelain was the only thing that seemed real. The only thing connecting her to this story.

"I raised you like my own daughter. And then he came one night and stole you away." Mabel Ridge turned her cup in the saucer but didn't pick it up. "I told him that if he took you he couldn't bring you back. But he took you all the same. And then he showed up here years later, without even a phone call or a letter to let me know you were coming, and expected me to roll over." She shook her head and closed the album. "I'm an old lady now. And I wasn't going to let him ruin my life again."

Loo thought of that first day they had driven to Dogtown and knocked on Mabel's door. Hawley breaking the radio with his fist. The blood on his sleeves.

"But then you found me. All on your own. And you looked so much like your mother." The old woman touched Loo's arm, gently this time. Her fingers were thick, the skin chapped. "You're grown up now, Louise. And you can make your own choices. You can be free of him."

Loo's tongue tasted of metal—as if she had bitten through a piece of aluminum foil with her teeth. She pulled her arm away from Mabel

Ridge, swept the cup and saucer off the table and sent them smashing to the floor. Tea splattered across the wall. The cup flung itself apart in white pieces. Now all the thorns were gone.

"That's not my name," she said.

WHEN SHE GOT BACK HOME to Olympus, Loo started with the guns that she knew about. The derringers in the bottom drawer of Hawley's dresser. The high-powered rifles he kept in the back of the closet. The snub-nosed revolver wrapped in a towel beneath the bed. The Beretta, the Smith & Wesson, the .38, the Ruger, each in its own special box inside the trunk in their living room.

The Colt was missing, which meant he had it with him.

Loo had handled these weapons hundreds of times. She knew them each by name. Laid out together, she hoped Hawley's guns would create a map that she could make sense of and follow. Prove whether he was a criminal or a fisherman. A father or a murderer. She gathered the pistols and the automatics, the handguns and rifles, on the bedspread. Hawley had erased the past, both his own and his daughter's. But there had to be some trace, some way for her to pull those lost stories into the present. Loo touched the cold metal. She closed her eyes and listened. But they would not give up their secrets.

Loo tied her hair back. And then she began to dig deeper. She searched underneath his mattress. She went through his sock and underwear drawer. She turned out the pockets of his jeans. She checked inside his boots. She put all the things she found on the bed next to the guns: six different kinds of hunting knives; brass knuckles; a box full of C rations; a spring-loaded pistol; a duffel bag stuffed with a change of clothes; ammunition stashed behind the laundry basket; a crank radio; a police scanner; a shillelagh. There was nothing surprising, not even a dirty magazine. If Hawley indulged in such things, he kept them out of the house.

Loo checked the back of the closet, then pushed aside Hawley's shoes and tested for a loose board in the floor. She groped inside his pillows. She fanned the pages of his crime novels, looking for loose paper, and when she didn't find anything she went into the living room and started searching through everything Jove had brought.

Jove was supposed to stay for only one night, but he had been with them for more than three weeks. His socks and T-shirts spread across the living room from the couch where he slept, along with piles of newspapers; a collection of half-full water glasses; the smell of after-shave, which he splashed beneath his arms instead of deodorant; and a dusting of small, white, downy feathers from a hole in his camouflage sleeping bag, patched on the outside with electrical tape, and quilted on the inside with images of ducks.

Each morning Loo would wake to the men talking and joking in the kitchen and cooking up enormous breakfasts—lobsters and steak and fried ham and even, one morning, a turkey, which Jove must have started sometime in the middle of the night. She caught him bent over the oven with a baster, sucking up the juice from the pan and spitting it out over the skin of the bird. "It's like a baby in there," he said with a sigh. "A little baby we're going to eat."

After breakfast the men worked outside on the new boat. Jove's bag full of watches had been replaced by a wooden hull with a keel full of lead, resting on an immense trailer in front of the garage. There in the driveway the men scraped, sanded and recaulked. They worked until it was too dark to see, and then after dinner they turned on floodlights and worked some more.

After finishing a shift at the Sawtooth, Loo crawled out onto the roof outside her window and pretended to use her telescope, hoping to catch her father and Jove talking secrets again downstairs. But the men spoke only of Jove's plans, unfolding maps and charting his trip, which now went from Olympus to the Hudson and all the way to the Caroli-nas, the Florida Keys and then to Cuba. Over the next few weeks, the men filled the garage with gear for the boat: a set of sails from the ma-rine supply store; a fifteen horsepower motor that Hawley thought would be too slow but Jove insisted on keeping, to minimize drag; cans of gasoline; boat hooks; an anchor; life jackets; bailers; hurricane lamps; a flare gun and a navigation system.

That morning the hull had been dry and ready to go. The men hooked up the trailer to Hawley's truck and drove off to the marina to get the boat into the water. It was the first time Loo had been alone in the house since Jove had arrived. She'd promised Hawley she'd meet them for the launch, waved goodbye from the porch, then opened the garage and jammed a screwdriver into the Firebird.

Now in the living room she shuffled through Jove's meager belongings. Two packs of canceled playing cards from a Colorado casino; a pair of sneakers that smelled; some changes of clothes; a washcloth and a bar of soap in a baggie; a leather pouch full of receipts; two overdue library books—*Great Expectations* and *David Copperfield*—their plastic covers flaking at the spine, their pages stained with other people's dinners; and a catalog for specialty clothes made just for boating, waterproof pants and scratch-proof sunglasses and captain's hats with gold braid trim.

She took a closer look at the receipts. They were from gas stations and diners and motels, from bars and fast-food drive-throughs. Organized and filed by date, as if Jove were a businessman getting ready to file an expense report. She found a handwritten list of watch manufacturers, itemized like a grocery shopping list. She found a nautical map of the North Shore. And she found a ripped page from a motel Bible. Across the text in black marker was the name of the street where Hawley and Loo had left all of the stolen cars.

Loo tore the Bible page into pieces, carried it into the bathroom, dumped the shreds into the toilet and flushed, the ink swelling and bleeding and then spinning down the hole and out of her life. Loo washed her hands at the sink, and then, when she turned off the faucet, she heard the toilet start to ring. The bowl had flushed fine but there was a vibration in the water. Loo jiggled the handle. The ringing continued. She jiggled some more. The ringing would not stop, steady and high-pitched and irritatingly insistent. She eased down the toilet seat, and then lifted the heavy porcelain lid off the tank.

There was something in the water. A row of containers set along the bottom, underneath the float. Loo reached down into the cold wet and pulled out a jar and set it dripping on the counter next to the sink.

The glass was clouded, the metal top beginning to rust along the edges. She pulled out three more jars. Then she opened one. The metal ring left traces of red dust on her fingertips, and the scent of licorice filled the room.

The candy was long and thin as black shoelaces. Loo threaded her fingers into the sticky nest and felt something hidden underneath. She dumped the licorice into the sink and behind it came fat rolls of hundred-dollar bills, held tightly together with rubber bands. Loo pulled one loose and counted ten thousand dollars. The money was crisp and stiff, like it had never been used, and the bottom of each bill was stained a brownish red, the same color that had been left on Loo's fingers when she'd turned the lid. She opened the other jars and dumped out the same candy and rolls of money. She counted it all. She counted it again. There was more than $450,000 in the sink.

Loo sat down on the edge of the tub. She tried to remember the last time she'd opened the back of the toilet. Was it two months ago? Three? There had never been anything inside but murky water. She picked up one of the billfolds and examined it closely, running her finger along the edge. The stain was not powder or rust. It was blood that had soaked through the bills to the center of Hawley's money. All she could think about as she replaced the bandaged rolls, covered them with candy and set the jars back inside the tank was who that blood had belonged to. Then she reached into the water and adjusted the float and stopped the pipes from ringing.

She found Hawley at the marina, surrounded by motorboats and catamarans and day sailors and cruisers of every shape and size—in dry dock or hitched up to moorings in the harbor. The crane operator was in the cabin overhead and calling down instructions and Hawley was securing chains and canvas straps around the hull of Jove's sailboat, which was still perched on top of its trailer. They were using the basin's stiff-leg crane, which was normally busy this time of year hoisting fishing trawlers and luxury yachts out of the ocean and onto their winter storage cradles. Loo locked her bike to the fence, then started across the parking lot, running into Jove as he came out of the harbormaster's office.

"Good—you're here!" he said, shoving his wallet into the front of his pants. "Now you can do the christening, and my send-off will be properly blessed. I'm sure you're sick of having me hanging around the house."

"I'm not a priest," said Loo.

"You're a woman," said Jove. "That's close enough."

He was wearing clothes from the catalog Loo had found at their house—fancy leather boating shoes and a windbreaker covered in reflective decals that was supposed to double as a tent in bad weather. He even had the captain's cap, with the gold braid. He tipped the hat now at Loo, then hurried off to talk to the crane operator.

Across the dock, Hawley lifted his head when he heard her voice. He tied off the ropes he was handling underneath the boat and waved her over.

"What's the matter?" he asked.

"I've got something for you." Loo held out the Polaroid of Lily in the hospital, smiling and holding her newborn baby.

Hawley wiped his fingers on his T-shirt and grabbed the picture. It took a moment for his eyes to focus on the image and then—*was it joy? Was that what she was seeing?* It was as if the sun had shifted to brighten every inch of his skin.

"I brought the Firebird back to Mabel Ridge," Loo said.

Just as quickly as it had come, the happiness drained out of Hawley's face. His hand tightened around the photograph. "What did she tell you?"

"She said you left me after Mom died."

Loo could tell this was not what her father had expected to hear. His gaze faltered and drifted back to the picture, so that when he finally spoke, it was as if he were talking to Lily and the baby instead of her. "I never wanted you to think I didn't care," he said. "That's why I never said anything."

"So it's true."

"Yes," said Hawley. "But I came back."

"After four years?" Loo said. "What the hell were you doing?"

Hawley would not look at her. He stared at the photo instead. Then he tucked the picture under his palm and slid it into his pocket. Loo realized, as she watched him steal it away, that he had probably been the one behind the camera, framing the image, adjusting the flash, taking the shot.

"Did you kill her?"

"What?"

"Did you kill my mother."

Hawley took a step back, as if she'd just hit him with her rock-in-a-sock. She nearly felt sorry for him, even though she was so angry at him for abandoning her, even though she'd had to dig the truth about who he was from the back of the toilet with her own hands. Her father's jaw went tight. She knew he was making up his mind how to answer. And then his face smoothed out, the way it did right before he was about to throw someone off a pier.

"She'd be alive if she hadn't met me," said Hawley. "So yes. It's my fault she's gone."

Loo felt sick. Her father would not meet her eyes. He stuffed his hands in his pockets, but his voice remained steady and cold and hard as he told Loo the rest of the story she'd been waiting to hear. About a young family enjoying a day at the lake, about a shadow stepping in between them, about a baby and a gun and a father and a mother and a body slipping beneath the surface. As he spoke Hawley's voice became more hollow, as if he'd created some distant version of himself, a shell that was standing in for his own body.

"Talbot came after us because of something I'd done. I'd hurt some-body he loved and he wanted to hurt me back. But your mother pro-tected me. She protected us both."

"So he killed her."

"Yes."

"And I was there, too?" It had never occurred to Loo that she had been a part of this story. That the blue dot on the map that fit beneath her finger had contained her as well as her parents. Somewhere, hidden deep inside her consciousness, were her own memories of what had happened. A thorn from a teacup fallen into a crack on the floor. If she could find the right tool to slip it loose, that day would no longer belong just to Hawley, and she would finally know what her mother's breath had felt like on her cheek.

"Yes," said Hawley. "But we made you safe. We made you safe together."

The crane rose and the chains clanked into place. There was a groan as the sailboat lifted off its trailer.

"There she goes!" Jove cried.

Hawley put his hand on Loo's shoulder. "I'm sorry you had to find out this way," he said.

"You told me never to say I'm sorry."

"You shouldn't," he said. "Those words aren't for you."

The hull rose until it was suspended over their heads, and then the sailboat began to move in the air as if it were flying. Hawley left Loo's side and went down to the dock. He helped Jove catch the boat and guide it into place. Dangling over the wharf the sailboat looked beautiful, fresh paint gleaming in the afternoon sun, the mast high and proud, and then the hull sank into the water, and the weighted keel disappeared.

The men hurried around, connecting the electric pumps. The wood needed to swell for a day or two. Until then, the sea soaked into the caulking and filled the bottom of the boat, so that the hull rested low against the dock. Jove tossed the hoses overboard. Hawley pulled the cord on the motor. The pumps started up, sucking in and spewing out.

Jove stood on the bow and waved to Loo. He dug into his rucksack and pulled out a bottle of Champagne. "Get your ass down here."

Loo crossed the aluminum boat ramp, feeling light-headed. The tide was coming in. She could hear waves hitting the pilings down below. The boat bobbed against the floating dock, so full it looked like it was sinking.

"It's bad luck if the bottle doesn't break," said Jove. He handed the Champagne to Loo. He pointed to a large brass cleat screwed down on the tip of the bow.

Loo swallowed hard. "Should I say something?" she asked.

"How about a prayer," said Jove.

Loo tightened her grip on the neck of the bottle. The foil was starting to come loose.

"Bless this boat," she said. It felt strange to say even that much. She'd never been in a church. She didn't know the right words. She looked to Jove, who had pulled off his captain's cap.

"Say something about new beginnings."

"Okay," said Loo.

"And no sharks. And no leaks. And no bad storms."

"All right," said Loo. "Yes. All those things, too."

"No pirates. And no ex-wives, either."

"Is there anything you *do* want?" Loo asked.

Jove shook his head. "This is the only thing I've ever wanted."

A wave came in from an oil tanker. Loo bent her knees to keep her balance on the dock, the bottle heavy in her fist. It was as if she'd lost her sense of gravity and was spinning into empty space, circling away from Earth and past the other planets, to a distant, solitary orbit. Pluto. She was Pluto. Loo tried to remember the chart from the back of the Carl Sagan book. The numbers that told her how much she mattered. She could sense Hawley beside her. She looked only at his hands.

The sinking boat rose and fell.

"Somewhere," Loo said, *"something incredible is waiting to be known."*

They all stood quietly on the dock, listening to the sound of the pumps sucking and spitting. Loo lifted the bottle by the neck, so that it was over her shoulder.

"What's the name again?"

"Pandora," said Jove.

"What if the bottle doesn't break?"

"Everything breaks if you hit it hard enough."

Her father crouched down on the dock. He steadied the boat for the blow. Loo looked at the back of his head. For the first time in her life, it was Hawley she wanted to hurt. Smash the bottle against him instead of the boat. He'd built a shrine in their bathroom, mourned and worshipped the scraps of her mother's memory, and all the while there was $450,000 hidden in their toilet, covered with blood, from the same criminal life that had taken Lily from them. Loo didn't even want to know whose blood it was anymore. She'd uncovered enough secrets.

It was time to make her own choices. Create her own lies. Loo aimed at the metal cleat on the bow, the one meant for securing the anchor. And then she swung the bottle with all her might.

Bullet Number Ten

Hawley got as far as Denver, then took a prop plane over into Wyoming and landed in Sheridan. There were only eight seats on the plane and Hawley's was right on the wing. He had to fold himself to fit. His knees jammed, his shoulder pressed against the aluminum shell as they banked steep over the Rocky Mountains. He watched the blades spinning and churning the air through the stained plastic of the window. The noise blocked everything, inside and out.

Once they landed, Hawley gathered his bag, which carried a change of clothes and the orange toolbox full of medical supplies he still had from the prepper in Alaska. He stole a car and then after one hundred miles he stole another. He found a pawnshop and picked up a .357 with a six-inch barrel. He drove to another pawnshop and got a decent shotgun and a rifle and ammunition for both. He stopped at a feed store in town and wandered the aisles with the cowboys and cattle ranchers and bought some basic camping gear, some Sterno and two blue tarps and some extra socks and a new pair of boots and some rolls of heavy plastic and tape and rope and trash bags and a fence clipper and a knife and a hammer and a metal file, and paid in cash.

He dumped the car and got a motel room and spent the afternoon taking the serial numbers off the guns. There was a baby crying in the room next door. Hawley had almost forgotten the sound. Twice in the middle of the night the cries woke him. The first time he got out of bed and stumbled into the wall, thinking he was heading into Loo's room. The second time he stayed in the bed and stared at the slices of light across the ceiling from the blinds and scratched his beard until morning.

He'd stopped shaving and his beard had grown wild, spreading down his neck and setting out across his cheeks, as if it were determined to cross the bridge of his nose. It had taken twelve months to get this far, and each day the beard covered more of him. Here in Wyoming, Hawley had noticed, more than half the men had the same look.

At six Hawley lit some Sterno and cooked a can of beans on the bathroom counter. When the brown juice started bubbling he turned off the fan and doused the flames. He clicked on the TV and ate the beans sitting on the bed. When he was finished he rinsed out the can and threw it away and cleaned the spoon and put it back into his kit. He opened a pouch of tobacco and took out rolling papers. He never used to smoke but after Lily's funeral, he'd found the tobacco she'd bought the night before she died. He'd rolled a cigarette, thinking of her hands and how they would move, and ever since then he'd kept it up, just to have the taste of her in his mouth. Hawley lit the paper. He breathed it in. He flicked the ash on the floor. When the fire reached his fingertips, he stubbed out the end, and then he took out his list.

It was only a row of words. *Laundry, Groceries, Pharmacy, Hardware Store*. He was careful about that. Careful about everything. If someone picked this paper up or looked over Hawley's shoulder they would think it was a list of errands. But each item was someone to be eliminated before they came after him or his daughter. He would leave nothing to chance anymore. He would leave nothing at all.

He'd had to bring in a cleaner at the lake. The cleaner took all the money in the licorice jars. The cleaner cleaned things. Got rid of Talbot's body. Brought in a doctor. Paid off the man doing Lily's autopsy. Scrubbed the police report. But the cleaner couldn't clean Hawley. After the funeral was over and Loo was left with Mabel Ridge, Hawley had driven to the nearest bar and then stayed on a bender for two weeks straight. When he woke up, he was on a boat with Jove. His friend said Hawley had called him, though Hawley had no memory of picking up the phone. Jove had found him passed out on a mountain of garbage about to be trucked away to a landfill. That was before Hawley had made up his mind to kill anyone. He was still feeling too sorry for himself.

Over the years, Jove had finally learned to sail, and now he'd been hired to bring the boat they were on from Boston down to the Virgin Islands. On the way they met drop points and delivered various goods that he had stored underneath the floorboards. The yacht was a Bermuda-rigged ketch, with three sails: a mizzenmast, a mainsail and a jib. Jove was good at navigation, and he showed Hawley how to manage both the boat and his sorrow, giving him whiskey when he needed it, taking it away when he'd had too much. Talking him out of throwing himself in the water as they pushed through choppy currents. "Think of that daughter of yours," said Jove. "You want to give her two dead parents instead of one?"

Their route went along the coast past Newport to Little Creek, Virginia, and from there on to Saint Thomas. The crossing took twelve days, and by the end of it, Hawley had sobered up enough to realize that the only thing that mattered was Loo. He needed to keep his daughter safe. And the first step was getting out from underneath Ed King. Hawley's thinking was violent, but Jove talked him into putting the old boxer in prison instead. From the Alaska job he had enough to frame him for the pilot and the girlfriend, which wasn't a frame exactly, since King was the one who had murdered them in the first place.

"Are you sure?" Hawley asked. "I know he's your friend."

"Not anymore," said Jove. "Not after this."

They made their final delivery and dropped the boat off. If there hadn't been all that rain once they arrived, they might have stolen another boat and brought it back up the coast. But instead they caught a flight to the States and Jove went on to Alaska to take care of King and Hawley decided there were other people he needed to get rid of.

He'd meant to leave his daughter only for a week but it had been more than two years now. She was better off without him. Hawley knew that. But he also knew that he owed her this: a life without looking over her shoulder. And he was determined to finish the list to make sure that it came true, even though there were times when he could feel himself slipping, and he'd wonder if he'd last until the end. He'd scratch his beard and hours would pass, the skies darken and go light and then dark again. Sometimes he'd lie to himself.

He'd think: *One day I'll get over this.*

He'd think: *Tomorrow it will be less painful.*

Then he'd scratch his beard some more and another day would be gone.

HE'D SPENT SOME TIME IN Wyoming before, with Jove, back when he was in his twenties. It was after the Indian casino job and they'd both had some cash to spare. They went in on a three-way land deal with Frederick Nunn, whose house they'd robbed when they were first starting out, back when they were nothing but kids stealing silverware.

The land was near the Bighorn National Forest. Hawley and Jove had sold their shares off to a natural-gas company, using banks and intermediaries to keep the paper trail off. But Frederick Nunn's property got declared a wildlife refuge for an endangered species: the black-tailed prairie dog. And then the feds came down and busted Nunn for money laundering and put him in jail, and in the process Nunn lost everything, even the great house in the Adirondacks. When he got out all he had left was the prairie-dog land, and it was full of giant rodents who lived in extensive colonies and tore down all the vegetation and dug their holes and ruined the soil until it wasn't fit for cattle or horses or any kind of farming.

The land had been split into three separate properties. They had flipped a coin for the deeds. Hawley won the first toss, and got to pick first. Jove won the second. They didn't think it would make a difference who got what, just ordered another round of whiskeys from the bar. Jove had even told Nunn about jacking his forks and spoons all those years ago and Hawley getting shot by the groundskeeper, and they had joked about it, aglow with the prospect of wealth, Nunn making a show of forgiveness, Jove and Hawley chipping in the next day and buying him a whole new fancy set of Mexican silverware. But later on Nunn said Hawley and Jove had known about the prairie dogs—that they'd fixed the toss somehow, and that they owed him. And then because Jove was in jail, Nunn started calling Hawley late at night and then every night, saying the dogs were laughing at him. That they could talk to one another. That they knew what Hawley had done. He'd thought of killing Frederick Nunn then. But instead he'd pulled up and moved on to Oklahoma, and Arkansas, and Louisiana, and New Mexico, and Florida, and then after Florida he'd met Lily.

Now, as Hawley drove west on Route 14 in a stolen sedan, he remembered how much he'd liked living out West. The sky so big and open and no one and nothing as far as the eye could see. Snow clipping the tips of the rolling hills, which were covered in scrub grass and packs of wild turkeys and elk and horses and cattle and sage. Trees were so scarce you could tell where the water was from miles away, sets of widow-makers clustered along the riverbeds, their weathered branches twisting out like giants turned to stone.

Then in the distance he caught sight of the gas flares blazing up against the setting sun, trailing dark smoke in the wind. Methane and sulfur dioxide. The stacks holding the drills in place were crossed with metal pilings, like the neck of a crane perched on the edge of a sky-scraper. All that metal looked out of place in the middle of this wild country. As did the men Hawley could see closing down for the day—workmen in hard hats, nothing like the Basques Hawley knew from his days on the ranches, drifting from place to place, living alone in the mountains with the herds, barely a word between them for months, and layers of dirt and sweat so thick on their skin that even the snakes kept off.

There was a twenty-foot chain-link fence with barbed wire running all along Hawley's old property. He slowed down to look and then he kept going. It was the only fence he'd seen for miles. Even on I-90, where eighteen-wheelers roared down at one hundred miles per hour, the cattle were kept back with just a few wooden posts and maybe a single electric wire. The gas company drilling Hawley's land had closed up around the property like it was a prison.

Up ahead, Hawley saw a sign nailed to a telephone pole. On it was a picture of a prairie dog, with crosshairs circling its head. Underneath was written: TARGET PRACTICE! And: NEXT LEFT! And: USE OUR GUNS OR BRING YOUR OWN AT PRAIRIE-DOG RANCH!

Hawley took the left. He pulled through the open gate and drove up the road for half a mile or so. The land started out flat but then veered steeply uphill onto a ridge, a curved slope covered in ragged bushes that flattened at the top like a mesa, overlooking the giant fence and towers of burning gas on Hawley's old property.

Next to a sign marked PARKING was a Jeep with a roll bar and a torn cover and a beat-up SUV. Behind the sign was a three-wheeled camping trailer, the hitch propped up on cinder blocks. The trailer looked like it had been hauled from the ends of the earth. It was small, the sides dented and beaten in, the screens full of holes, an old wooden trough set in front of the door, and, duct-taped to the roof, instead of a satellite dish, was an old-fashioned antenna wrapped in tinfoil.

Hawley turned off the car and waited. Then he heard a rifle shot. And another. His .357 Magnum was on the seat beside him. The shotgun was loaded and set across the dashboard, the rifle covered with a blanket and hidden underneath the front seat. He did not reach for any of them. He waited to see who would come.

A woman, wearing an orange hunting cap and a bathrobe, cracked open the trailer door and peered out at him, then stepped down onto the trough. She was young, with a body made thick with fast, cheap food. The hunting cap was pulled down over her ears. Her ankles were elegant. Her feet bare. Her toenails painted bright green. The robe swung open and revealed a football jersey and a pair of sweatpants cut off at the knee. She motioned to Hawley. He put the handgun in his jacket pocket. He opened the door to the car and stuck his head out.

"They've already started," she said. "Go on through the back."

"Thanks," said Hawley. He left his door unlocked and the keys in the ignition. And then he started off in the direction the girl had pointed.

About one hundred yards ahead were six tables and chairs set up for long-range rifle practice. Sandbags and tripods and scopes. There were two men sitting and shooting, and another standing and staring out into the distance with a pair of binoculars. Hawley watched the man clap one of the shooters on the back, then turn and pick up a beer from the table. Frederick Nunn still had the same mustache, heavy, like a finger bent beneath his nose. And Hawley would have known those hands anywhere, fringed at the top with tiny black hairs. Nunn used to scare people with those hands, flexing them while he talked. Now he wrapped them around the can of beer and tipped it back down his throat and then he swallowed and saw Hawley coming. He swallowed again. He picked up the binoculars. Hawley could feel the glass on him and tried to keep his face neutral. He kept walking straight, even when Frederick Nunn put down the binoculars and picked up one of the rifles.

"Sam Hawley," said Nunn. "I didn't know you at first."

The shooters took off their ear protection. One fellow was in his twenties and wore an army jacket and a pair of ear guards that matched, both desert camouflage. The other was at least ten years older and had cratered cheeks and a western-style vest with leather tassels. The shooters were both drunk. But Nunn was not.

"What're you doing here?" Nunn asked.

"I saw your sign," said Hawley.

Nunn lifted his nose, like a dog trying to find a scent.

"Everything all right?" said the man in the leather vest.

"Yeah," said Nunn. "He's all right. This is Mike, and that's Ike."

"Like the candy," said Hawley.

The men nodded but did not get up. They kept their hands on their guns.

"Don't let me stop you."

"Oh," said Mike. "There's no stopping us." He put his ear guards back on and leaned across the table in his leather vest, setting his eye to the scope. Ike played with one of the zippers on his camouflage jacket but kept his eyes on Nunn and Hawley.

"Fire in the hole!" said Mike. And then he fired. Everyone turned to look. In the distance, Hawley saw a small explosion of fur and guts.

"I thought the dogs were protected," said Hawley.

"Not anymore," said Nunn. "Now they're target practice."

"That's good news," said Hawley, "for you."

"It's something," said Nunn. "People pay me to come try out their guns, before the hunting season starts."

Hawley looked out over the prairie-dog town. There was no vegetation. Only mounds of dirt and holes and craters to fall into. A dead landscape that belonged someplace dead.

"Who's the girl?"

"Just a girl."

"I mean who's she to you?" Hawley asked.

Nunn looked him over. He spit on the ground. "That's some beard you got."

Mike and Ike began shooting, one after the other, misses that sent tiny clouds of dirt up like smoke signals in the distance and occasional hits that blasted blood and innards in tiny splatters across the dried-up earth. Between each bullet Hawley could hear the prairie dogs calling. A chorus of weeps and chattering so loud it drowned out everything but the gunfire.

"Let's go someplace we can hear each other," said Hawley.

"All right," said Nunn.

They walked back to the trailer, but Nunn didn't ask him in. Hawley could see the girl watching them from the window. Hawley didn't say anything. He just stood there feeling the Magnum in his pocket and waiting for something else to happen, something that would let him finish what he had come to do.

"You on a job?"

"Yeah," Hawley said.

Nunn was flexing one of his big hands. He was nervous—Hawley could see that now. Nunn had never been the kind of guy who got nervous. But here he was, staring at Hawley like he was something wild. And maybe he was.

"Who's the girl?" he said again.

Nunn lifted the rifle and pointed it at him. "What the hell do you want, Hawley?"

"Tell her to come outside."

"Not until you answer me."

"You," said Hawley. "I came here for you."

For a moment he wasn't sure if he'd said the words out loud, he was so used to being alone and not talking. The conversation was already the longest he'd had with anyone in nearly three months. At least he thought it was three. He wasn't too sure about that, either.

Nunn lowered the rifle. He sat down on the wooden trough and stared at the dirt. He didn't look surprised. "Was it Rodriguez?" He rubbed his hand back and forth across his mustache. "Or Manley? I bet it was Manley."

"It wasn't Manley."

"Parker, then. He always hated my guts."

"It wasn't any of those guys," said Hawley. "I've got a list, that's all. And you're on it." He could smell it now, the air from his old land. Full of carbon monoxide and clouds of chemicals. The smell of burning things never meant to be burned.

"King," said Nunn. "He on your list?"

"He's in prison."

"Somebody sold him out, I heard." Nunn touched his mustache again. He seemed more thoughtful than frightened, as if he'd been waiting for something like this to happen. "Well, anyway. I was right, you know. They *can* talk."

"Who's that?"

"The prairie dogs," Nunn said. "A scientist came out here from the University of Oklahoma to count the population. Helped them get off the endangered species list. He paid me to study the dogs and the noises they make. They have words and grammar and everything. A whole language."

"Why are you telling me this?" Hawley asked.

"It's just that I thought I was losing it. When I got this dead land. I used to go up on that ridge and listen to them talking and think about blowing my brains out. But they *were* saying something, after all. It felt good to be right about that. They're actually quite intelligent."

In the distance, Hawley could hear Mike and Ike pulling off their shots. And then he heard a phone ringing, from inside the trailer. The phone rang and rang. Hawley waited to see if Nunn would go answer it, but the man stayed where he was.

"Why use them for target practice, then?"

"I got to shoot something," said Nunn.

The screen door opened and the girl came outside. She'd ditched the bathrobe, but was still wearing the shorts and football jersey. The orange hunting cap was pulled tight around her face. She was wearing flip-flops with daisies on them, her green toenails flashing beneath the flowers with each step.

"Phone," she said.

"Right," said Nunn. To Hawley he said, "Wait." Then he stepped on the trough and into the trailer.

Overhead the sky was starting to pink, the sun slipping behind the mountains. In the distance Mike and Ike whooped, and the guts of another prairie dog blew across the ground.

"He's a little old for you," Hawley said.

The girl shrugged and pulled at her hunting cap.

"Why don't you get out of here."

"I've got a deal with him," said the girl.

"Whatever it was it doesn't matter anymore," said Hawley. And he showed her the Magnum.

The girl looked at him and then she looked at the gun and then she opened the door to the SUV and got in. She turned the ignition. She rolled down the window.

"He's got a custom Weatherby in there. Semiautomatic, with a laser."

"Jesus," said Hawley. "Thanks."

"Wait until I'm on the road," she said. Then she pulled the hunting cap off, and her hair came down, and it was green, too, just like her toenails. And even though her lips were chapped when she smiled at Hawley, it was the nicest thing that had happened to him in a long time.

Then she threw the SUV in gear and drove off.

Hawley knew that Nunn was inside watching him. Probably already had the semiautomatic trained on his back. He took the gun he'd shown the girl and tucked it into his jeans. Then he walked toward the screened door and knocked.

"Are you really fucking knocking?" Nunn called out.

"I guess so," said Hawley, and then he went inside. The place was small and cramped but surprisingly tidy. The bed at the back was covered with a quilt, and the miniature kitchen had a propane stove and a row of mugs hanging from a rack. In the corner was a table piled high with old country records—Lefty Frizzell and Kitty Wells—and a record player, the portable kind that came in a suitcase. There were four clocks, one on each wall, all set to the same time. Two Hawley recognized from the great house: a face with Roman numerals instead of numbers, and a Kit-Cat clock next to the door, the eyes clicking back and forth.

Nunn was standing by the stove, holding the Weatherby, and it was just as the girl said, a beautiful weapon with a laser and a scope that looked like something out of the movies.

"Take it easy," said Hawley.

"Give me that gun and I will."

Hawley turned around and Nunn put the Weatherby right between his shoulders. Then Nunn pulled the Magnum from the back of Hawley's jeans. He opened the gun and took out the bullets and put both onto the counter behind him. He motioned to the bed and Hawley sat down on it.

"Right," said Nunn. "Now what happens?"

"You try to change my mind," said Hawley.

"About what?"

"About killing you."

Nunn rolled his lips, so that his mustache moved forward and back underneath his nose, like it was itching him but he couldn't take his hands off the gun to scratch it. "I thought you'd gone off and married some girl."

For a moment Hawley just sat there. But his feelings were as straight as a line. He was not surprised that Frederick Nunn would know about Lily. Hearing this only made him more certain of the job he needed to do. In October, his daughter was going to be three years old. Three short years of being alive in the world.

"You said this was a job," said Nunn. "But I think it's something else."

"My wife is dead."

"So that's it." Nunn lowered the gun and put it across his lap. "You're looking for a way out. Someone to off you? Is that it?"

Hawley wondered if Nunn was right. He closed his eyes and tried to listen, to dig the truth out of himself, but his body was numb. "I've got some errands to run first."

The door to the trailer opened. The man with the leather-fringe vest poked his head inside, his rifle slung across his shoulder. "We're outta beer."

Hawley couldn't remember if it was Mike or Ike.

"Whoah, brah," the man said, eyeing the Weatherby. "Nice scope."

"We were just talking about prairie dogs," said Nunn.

The man blinked once. Twice. Then grinned. "Oh, shit. Don't get this guy started." He stumbled inside and opened the small fridge. He pulled out a six-pack. Hawley could smell the alcohol coming off his skin, a sickly-sweet odor that reminded him of his mother, before she switched to vodka and moved to Phoenix and drank herself to death.

"Getting dark out there," said Hawley.

"Won't stop us. Besides," the man said, "you can hear the little fuckers." He put down the six-pack and picked up Hawley's .357 from the counter. "Nice." He opened the cylinder. "Old school."

"Take it," said Hawley.

"You serious?"

"I've got another one just like it."

Nunn shifted the Weatherby in his arms. "Better say thanks, Mike, or he'll hold it against you."

"Shit, thanks, brah."

"No problem."

Mike loaded the Magnum, sticking each round back into its chamber. Then he tucked the gun into his pants. He handed a beer to Hawley. The aluminum was cold and wet with condensation. The can was a good weight. Miller High Life. Hawley opened it and took a sip.

"What about you?" he asked Nunn. "I'm sure you get real dry talking to those prairie dogs all day."

"Ha-ha," said Nunn.

"Come on," said Mike. "Drink with us." He opened a can and held it out.

Nunn had already flipped off the safety on his rifle. Hawley could tell he was trying to make up his mind—whether to murder him or wait. Nunn was looking at Mike, sizing him up as a witness. One beer. That's all it would take to decide.

Hawley sucked in a breath. He let half of it out. And then he threw his Miller High Life as hard as he could at Nunn's face. It smacked his chin, then bounced and knocked the Weatherby, which went off, a hole blasted in the wall next to the Kit-Cat clock, the boom of the rifle ringing in their ears. The can dropped onto the floor, spraying foam and beer across the tiny kitchen. Hawley grabbed the Magnum from the back of Mike's pants.

"Brah!" Mike said.

"You think you can come to my house and kill me?" Nunn shouted. "You think I'm going to let you do that? I got a *right* to live. A goddamn *right*."

"She's got more," said Hawley.

He shot Frederick Nunn in the head. It was a clean shot. Done and done. The back of the man's skull opened in a dark spray across the walls. Mike started screaming and whacked the Magnum from Hawley's hand with the butt of his rifle. Hawley pushed out the door of the trailer, cutting around the corner just in time to see Ike hustling toward them from the shooting range.

Hawley got the door open to the car, but before he could get inside, Mike had shot out the windshield with the Weatherby and then rattled up the rest of the sedan with holes, hitting the tires. Hawley snatched the shotgun and blew both barrels into the trailer, and it was enough to make both Mike and Ike dive for cover. Enough time for him to run.

Hawley chose the only direction he could: toward his own land. But first he had to cross the prairie-dog town. He covered fifty yards and then a bullet rang out over his head in the gloom, and he flattened, losing the shotgun. He got his elbows up and started army-crawling across the dirt, dragging himself over the holes.

The prairie dogs had all disappeared into their tunnels, but he could still hear them underground. Thousands of little throats straining in a mile-wide game of telephone. And then he felt the earth give and his whole arm broke through into one of the holes and he was up to his shoulder. He tried to pull himself out but another shot rang over his head, and then he felt an even bigger shift in the earth and he was falling through, a chasm opening beneath his body. Dirt and sand was all around him and in his eyes and in his ears and up his nose and in his mouth.

When Hawley finally hit bottom, he wiped the grit off of his face. He'd fallen into a hollowed-out den, seven or eight feet from the surface. Something was moving in the dirt around him, struggling out from the sides and below, biting and scratching. The prairie dogs. At least a dozen of them. They had looked small and cute from a distance. But up close they were giant furry rodents, backing up on their hind legs, with rigid tails and fat bellies and short noses and black eyes and agile, humanlike paws with long fingers and even longer nails. Overhead he could see the darkening sky and some of the prairie dogs were clambering up toward it, and others were trying to find the tunnel out, and still others were crawling across his back and his head, and Hawley pushed himself up and threw the dogs off of him, shoving away until he was sitting against one side of the den and the dogs were scuttling back and forth across the other. They seemed to move and act as one. All of them barking, barking, barking.

Once Mike and Ike found this hole, he was dead. Unless he could get out in time and make it to the fence. Hawley moved to his knees and then to his feet, but when he pulled himself up, the edge crumbled around him. It was like trying to crawl out of a hole in the ice. Hawley dug in with his boots and scraped at the sides and he got his head above the burrow, just enough to see Mike and Ike searching the field about two hundred yards to the west. And then the whole side collapsed, and Hawley dropped to the bottom, and the earth fell down and buried him.

The loose ground pressed on Hawley like the weight of a blanket. He was covered up but he couldn't breathe. He clawed with his fingers and felt an opening. A tunnel left behind by the dogs. He grabbed hold of some roots, shoved his head inside and took in the fetid pocket of air. The walls were tight, but he forced his shoulders through. Then he dug madly and widened the space until he was jammed half in, half out of the narrow tunnel. He could hear the men's voices getting closer.

"Thought I saw something."

"Brah, check this out."

Hawley bent his head to the left. He could see their shadows at the edge of the hole.

"Think he fell in here?"

"Can't see the bottom."

Hawley heard one of them spit. There was the sound of a bullet being chambered and then both men aimed their guns and fired down into the hole. The first missed and the second drove through the layer of soil covering him and split Hawley's calf and nicked the bone. He knew at once it was the Magnum from the force of the blow and how much it hurt and the way it made his leg feel like it had been ripped from the rest of his body.

He bit into his arm to keep from shouting, even though a part of him was aching to scream and let them know he was stretched out in the bottom of this hole. They wouldn't even have to dig a grave to bury him. It would be so easy. It would all be over. But Hawley only bit himself harder. There were more errands to run. So he just lay there in the dirt and bled.

Above, the men were listening.

"There's no cover out here."

"You spooked?"

"I can't see for shit. We should go back to the trailer."

"We're going to make you a fucking ghost, brah!" Mike's words echoed across the prairie and up into the mountains. Then Hawley heard their boots traveling over his head and their voices began to fade. He knew he was safe when the prairie dogs started up again with their weeping.

Hawley stayed squeezed inside the hole like it was his own tomb. He waited for the men to come back. He waited for what felt like hours. He waited with the beetles and worms and millipedes and ants, his mouth gasping at the tunnel, ready to taste the night on his lips, until the pain he felt became not pain anymore, but a creature eating into his flesh, clamping down with piercing jaws each time he kicked against it, and he pushed and punched and tore away at the ground and he stomped the pain beneath him and it was like stumbling through the dark, it was like the murky bottom of the lake that had taken Lily, and it made him dig harder and faster, until his fingernails broke and bled and he began to breathe dirt and sand. The earth was inside and outside and all around him, but he was moving, he could feel his body making its way, and then he touched the grass and he was rolling out of the burrow and onto the open field, every inch of him covered in dust.

It wasn't as dark as he imagined it would be. The sky was clear overhead and the stars so multitudinous that they brightened the landscape to the edges of the horizon. Hawley covered his mouth to stifle his coughing, tried to gather some saliva and rid himself of the grit that had covered his teeth. Then he dug his filthy fingers up his nose to clear his nostrils and scraped the dirt from his ears until he could hear again.

The lights were on inside Nunn's trailer. The windows were open and the men were arguing, their voices slurred. Hawley tore off a piece of his shirt, tied it around his leg, then crawled slowly across the dry ground, past the tunnels of the prairie dogs, until the voices of the dogs and the voices of the men started to meld together, and then he was coming up to the trailer, and he was right underneath the window. He was so close that he could smell the beer that had spilled—the foam and the busted cans across the floor.

"You think my parole officer is going to believe that shit? Some guy showing up out of nowhere and blowing Nunn's head off? We gotta clean this up. We gotta clean all this up."

"Shit, brah. Look at him."

"I don't wanna look."

"So what do you wanna do? Bury him someplace?"

"Fire's better. Fire happens all the time."

"All right, but I'm gonna play him some music first. He liked music, didn't he?"

They put on one of Nunn's old country records. Hawley could hear the slide guitar, and a twangy voice singing. *If you've got the money honey, I've got the time.*

Hawley limped over to Mike and Ike's Jeep. He could get in and drive off before they made it outside. He could leave and not come back. But then there would be loose ends, and he couldn't have any loose ends anymore. Hawley went back to his car. The shotgun was somewhere out on the prairie, but the rifle was just where he'd left it, hidden underneath the front seat. He pulled his satchel carefully through the broken windshield. He opened the orange toolbox and gave himself a shot of morphine. Then he wrapped his leg in a pressure bandage. He checked the rifle and got a few extra mags loaded and left them on the hood of the car. He grabbed his knife, a pair of pliers and two roadside flares. He waited to see if the men had heard him. Then he slid beneath the trailer on his back.

It was damp and full of spiderwebs in the crawl space between the trailer and the ground. Hawley listened to the music and the men talking, and slowly pulled himself along until he reached the propane tank. He cut the lines and redirected them and opened the pressure valve as far as it would go. He lit the roadside flares next and slid them up into the air vents. He crawled back out and got between the two cars, with a clear line to the trailer door. He picked up the rifle.

Through the window, he saw the flames shoot up from the stove. The men did not even notice at first. And then there was a crackling noise in the air, and the propane blew, and the lights went out, and the trailer caught on fire. He could hear both men screaming. The first one, Ike, burst through the door, and Hawley shot him cleanly through the head, and the man's body crumpled and fell against the trough. Then he heard some shuffling and realized the other one was climbing out the back window. He went around the trailer and there was Mike, half in and half out, his leather vest caught on the ripped screen. He was carrying the Magnum. The side of his face was burnt and he was aiming wildly. He shot off all the rounds. Hawley spun the rifle and knocked the piece from his hand. Then he picked the Magnum up from the ground and reloaded while the man struggled and cried out.

"God, Jesus, no, brah, Jesus, no, please."

The man kept talking, kept saying God's name out into the cold night air. Hawley shot him with the Magnum again and again, remembering the power of it going into his own leg, counting the bullets now, one after the next, listening to them strike bone and flesh and the metal of the trailer until the cylinder was empty and he had made enough holes, and the voices stopped coming out of them.

Hawley shoved Mike's body back through the window. Then he went around front and opened the trailer door and lifted Ike and tossed him down into the smoke. The fire had spread to the curtains. Nunn's body was on the bed, a blanket tossed over his face. On the table, the record player was still spinning. Hawley slammed the door. He hot-wired the Jeep and backed it up and attached it to the trailer and then drove the trailer to the edge of the hill. Then he unhitched the burning tin can and began to push. The morphine had kicked in. He couldn't feel the pain in his leg anymore.

The hitch was low and Hawley had to lean down and wedge his shoulder against the metal wall, which was getting hot from the fire. The coach was heavier than he'd expected. Like he was lifting the whole world onto his shoulders. He forced Frederick Nunn and Mike and Ike and even Lily out of his mind. And he thought of Loo. Only Loo. Three years old. Still alive. Still breathing.

The back wheels of the trailer teetered at the edge of the ravine. For a moment Hawley was all that was keeping it there, the metal hitch tugging at his fingers. And then a clod of earth gave way, and he could feel the wheels go and the weight shift and then the trailer left his hands. Hawley stood at the edge of the mesa, the wind across his back, his palms reeking of oil and soot. The coach rolled slowly at first and then it bounced and began to gain speed. The glass burst from the heat. There was smoke coming out of the windows. The coach roared down the slope like a headless horseman, like Cinderella's pumpkin turned to flame and ash.

It barreled across the flat plain, a streak of light through the prairie-dog town, and then kept rolling until it rammed the chain-link fence surrounding Hawley's old place. The blaze lit up the edge of the gas field, and he could see blue sparks as the electricity caught and failed and then the floodlights went out, and the land went dark, and all that was left was the burning trailer, roaring like a monster against its cage.

The Cooler

POLICE CARS SWARMED UP AND DOWN MAIN STREET. LOCAL AND STATE authorities were put on alert. The Coast Guard was upping its patrols. The mayor gave a press conference, and the head of Fish and Game made some comments he later had to retract. Even *The Boston Globe* had sent a reporter to cover the story, and the local headlines were printed in inch-and-a-half type: BULLETS OVER BITTER BANKS.

Someone had fired a single shot into the front door of Mary Titus's house. Disgruntled fishermen, folks were saying, or maybe one of the Moonies, or some hired thugs sent by Nova Scotia or the Japanese. Whoever pulled the trigger, it had brought enough media attention to the depletion of the catch and illegal fishing practices—including a TV spot on the national news—that the EPA and NOAA announced they were temporarily shutting down parts of the Banks until further studies could be performed. Each day millions of dollars were being lost. At the Sawtooth, it was all anyone would talk about.

"They were lucky no one was hurt," said Agnes.

"They were lucky they didn't get *caught*," said Loo.

Mary Titus didn't say anything, because Mary Titus wasn't there. She'd taken a personal day. But Principal Gunderson was sitting at his booth, and he was losing his mind.

"This doesn't happen," he said. "Not in our town."

"It does," said Agnes. "It happens everywhere."

Gunderson took another bite of his kippers. He ate kippers with eggs on toast every morning for breakfast. Kippers and eggs and coffee. Usually people would avoid his table for the smell. But now everyone was gathered around, because Principal Gunderson had started dating Mary Titus (three dates, he said—well, two and a half, really), and that's where Mary Titus had been when her house was shot up—on her second-and-a-half date—eating dinner at Principal Gunderson's house. Not kippers, Principal Gunderson said, because Mary Titus was a vegetarian.

What about Marshall? Loo wanted to ask, as Gunderson spoke about the cauliflower soup he had prepared especially for that night, the curried tofu and broiled pineapple for dessert.

"Mary never even got to taste it. The soup, I mean. We'd only had wine and kale chips when the police called," said Principal Gunderson. "I can't believe someone tried to kill her because of that petition. Though the threat on her life has made her very popular in environmental circles. Even her ex-husband called."

"The guy from *Whale Heroes*?"

"That's him," said Principal Gunderson, and then he took a few more bites of his breakfast, chewing hard and slowly, as if he were imagining the ex-husband between his teeth. "He called ship-to-shore. He wanted to congratulate her."

"What happened? After the cops came?"

"She couldn't stop laughing," said Principal Gunderson, "and I laughed, too. It all seemed so ridiculous. But even after she calmed down, she said she'd never stop fighting. It's very admirable."

"I don't think your brothers would agree," said Agnes.

Principal Gunderson looked worried. He took another bite of his breakfast. "Her son was home at the time. The police were taking his statement when I dropped Mary off. I put the dinner I'd made into Tupperware and left it with them. But I haven't heard anything yet," he said. "About how the soup was, I mean."

"Did they find out who did it?" Loo asked.

Principal Gunderson gave a timid smile. "I believe the police don't have any official suspects yet."

"Whoever it is," said Loo, "they're going to regret it."

"Oh, well, yes, of course, my dear." Gunderson let out a soft belch and then began guzzling his coffee, as if he had suddenly remembered Loo's rock-in-a-sock.

After the lunch rush Loo ducked into the walk-in cooler, the one place at the Sawtooth where they could sneak moments of privacy. She wrapped her arms tightly around her middle and stared at the rows of vegetables. Her breath clouded in front of her face, and that was all she could concentrate on: the frozen air coming and going from her own mouth.

It had been ten days since Jove launched his boat and sailed away from Olympus. She'd thought she'd be relieved when he left but she'd grown fond of him, the way he commandeered their kitchen, cooking giant meals, holding a spoon out for Loo to try. He'd made their home seem boisterous, and made her father behave more like a regular person. Now the house was quiet again and Hawley and Loo were avoiding each other. When they did cross paths, in the kitchen or outside the bathroom, her father looked at her like a beaten dog—nervous and twitching—and it took all she had not to kick him.

She signed up for as many extra shifts as the Sawtooth would give her. She worked and saved money and she wore her mother's gloves and she tried to curb the anger inside of her and she waited for the sanctuary petition to pass, to prove that she was not like her father. That she was a person who could save things. Now her plan had nearly gotten Marshall killed.

Agnes opened the door to the freezer and stuck her head in. "You all right?" She pushed her pregnant stomach forward through the plastic curtain. "I can't have you getting sick, not with Mary out, too."

"Just give me a minute," said Loo.

"Feels good in here," said Agnes. She shut the door. "I wish I could smoke a cigarette."

All around them was the smell of cold meat. The giant fridge hummed.

"He broke up with you, didn't he?" said Agnes. "I can always tell. You've got that look, like you're driving with a broken windshield."

"Can you cover for me this afternoon?"

"Oh, honey," said Agnes. "No."

"What?"

"Don't go over there. You don't want to be that girl. Believe me."

"I just want to see if he's okay."

"No, you don't." Agnes rubbed the side of her belly. "Besides, half the people out there think your father did this, even if no one's saying so yet."

"Why would he want to hurt Marshall?"

"He already beat up that boy at the police station. And Mary's always showing off those stitches in her head. The fishermen might hate those hippies, but your father's the only one who's ever hurt them."

Loo thought of the bruises on Marshall's back from where Hawley had thrown him into the wall. Mary Titus pounding their front door with her tiny fists.

"I don't feel so good."

Agnes found a lunch bag and rolled it open, then held out some saltines from her pocket. Loo pressed her face into the bag, which smelled lightly of onions. She breathed in and out, inflating the paper, while Agnes patted her back. Under the fluorescent light, Loo could see wrinkles across the woman's forehead that weren't there at the start of the summer. She was the same age Loo's mother would have been, if she'd lived.

"Maybe it doesn't have anything to do with you. Maybe he was just trying to scare them off the petition. He's thick as thieves with Strand and Fisk, and I wouldn't put it past those two."

Loo dropped the bag on the floor. She didn't know what to do. She crumbled the crackers in her fist. "This is so stupid."

"Oh!" Agnes said, as if she'd suddenly thought of some answer. She grabbed Loo's hand and squeezed it, and Loo nearly cried. She felt so lost and so grateful. Agnes pressed Loo's palm against her stomach. There was nothing at first. And then Loo felt a struggling movement. A tight, desperate twisting of flesh.

"Feel that?" Agnes said. "He's kicking."

For all the times she had watched and waited for Marshall in the Firebird, Loo had never been inside his house. But she had imagined what it might be like, and he had told her a few details, like the Greenpeace poster his mother kept on the wall in their kitchen, and the misshapen plates and mugs from when she'd taken pottery classes. The house seemed quaint from a distance but up close was run-down, from the peeling paint to the secondhand furniture.

"You," said Mary Titus. She was wearing an orange terry-cloth bathrobe and her hair was wet. She gave Loo a look that must have been close to the one Loo had given her years ago, when she'd first knocked with her petition and bottle of wine. Now Loo was the one standing on the porch, hoping to be let in. And Mary Titus was the one deciding whether or not to slam the door.

"Is Marshall home?" Loo asked.

"My son has nothing to say to you."

"Please. I just need a minute."

The widow scanned Loo up and down, as if she knew what the girl had really come for. "The police are here, so don't get any ideas." She pointed to a black sedan parked on the sidewalk in front of the house. Two men, both wearing sunglasses, were sitting inside drinking coffee. When they saw Mary Titus pointing, one of them waved.

Loo tried everything she could to stay polite and smiling. "Principal Gunderson wants to know if you liked his soup."

"What?" said Mary Titus. Instantly her hand went to her hair, patting it in place.

My God, Loo thought, these men do it to all of us.

"Mom." Marshall was at the top of the staircase, wearing a shirt printed with an image of a whale's tail. Loo could feel her heart thrumming in her chest. They hadn't spoken in more than a month but at the sight of him her body flicked on, like a switch. Marshall gave half a grin. She could not tell what he was thinking. She could not tell if he wanted her there or not.

"The camera crew is going to be here in an hour," said Mary Titus.

"I know," said Marshall. "Why don't you finish getting ready?" He came down the staircase and stood between Loo and his mother.

"For me," he said.

Mary Titus looked at her son. "For you," she said. "For you I'll do anything."

The widow put her hand on Marshall's shoulder. The easy intimacy between them made Loo uncomfortable, and also filled her with longing.

"Leave the door open. I want those officers to keep an eye on things."

"Okay," said Marshall.

Loo watched Mary Titus begin to mount the stairs, her hand gripping the banister like it was a lifeline. She paused at the top and turned. In her orange robe, with her face flushed and shining, she looked triumphant.

"You can tell your father he *missed*."

Then she went into her bedroom and shut the door.

Marshall pulled at the neck of his whale shirt. He would not meet Loo's eyes. "I've got something for you," he said. "Can you wait here a minute?"

"Sure," said Loo.

She stayed on the threshold, afraid to step outside, and afraid to step inside, too, glancing back at the black sedan. The men did not seem very vigilant. One of them was working a crossword puzzle, and the other appeared to be asleep. She looked for the bullet in the door. Underneath the street numbers was a single hole, the edges dug out, the shrapnel gone.

Her finger was deep in the hollow when Marshall came down the stairs. He was carrying a brown paper bag with the top folded, just like the one Loo had been holding over her face in the walk-in freezer. He gestured for her to come inside and then he shut the door, nodding at the men in the sedan before turning the lock.

"It's good to see you," he said.

Loo's skin started to sweat. "I wanted to make sure you were all right."

They stood in front of the door. She wasn't sure if she should touch him or not.

"What's with the T-shirt?"

"My stepfather gave me that spot on *Whale Heroes*," said Marshall. "I guess my life finally got exciting enough for television."

"So that's the camera crew?"

"They want to film me and my mom saying goodbye. Then I'll be on the ship this afternoon. My stepfather says he's going to stay at the Banks until NOAA agrees to the sanctuary. He's got a whole crew of scientists coming in to collect data."

"When will you be back?" Loo asked.

"I don't know. Whenever the show gets canceled, I guess. Listen," he said, "about the petition."

"Don't worry," she said. "Nobody knows it was me."

Marshall shook his head. He put the paper bag down on the coffee table. "My mom never gets enough signatures for any of her petitions to get to ballot. Those names we faked—no one was ever going to see them. They were just to replace the ones I'd lost. I didn't think you'd write out five thousand signatures. I didn't think you'd turn it *in*. I don't know what you were thinking."

She was not thinking, Loo wanted to say. She had only wanted to be with him again. Even now, she wanted him to lay her on top of his Salvation Army couch, peel off her jeans and kiss her thighs. But Marshall just hooked his fingers together behind his neck and pulled. None of this was going as Loo had expected. She'd never wanted to put anyone in danger. She'd meant the petition to be a gift.

"I thought you'd be happy." As soon as the words were out of her mouth Loo felt how pathetic they were, and how sad and desperate she was, staying up all those nights, finding the names and copying out the addresses. With her colored pens she had fooled everyone. She had even fooled herself.

"My mom's happy. You don't even know how much," said Marshall. "But I feel like an asshole, because none of it is real. I had to tell her that I'd turned the petition in as a surprise for her. She thinks that I changed all those people's minds. But eventually someone's going to check those signatures, and the whole thing is going to be thrown out."

Marshall picked up the bag he'd set down earlier on the coffee table. He reached in and took out a hand towel and unwrapped it. Inside was the gun Loo had given him. The Beretta with the slide lock. He handed it to her like a baby, supporting its head. The metal grip felt cold in her hands.

"You should keep this," she said. "In case the shooters come back."

"They're not coming back," said Marshall. "And if the gun is here my mom might find it."

Loo flipped the safety on the Beretta. She flipped it back and forth, on and off.

"Did the police take the slug?"

Marshall nodded. "They found the casing, too."

"Then they can match it," said Loo. "Track the gun. Find out who really did this."

Again he would not meet her eyes. "Publicity is the only thing that works. That's the one thing my stepfather's right about. Now, even if the petition tanks, there will still be a chance for this to go through with NOAA."

"You shot up your own house?"

"I emptied one round," said Marshall. "And after all those years of people slamming doors in our faces, everyone's calling us heroes."

"You can't lie about this," said Loo.

"But I should lie about the signatures?"

"This is different. It's my dad's gun."

"Your father didn't do anything. He's not going to get into trouble."

Marshall twisted the towel he'd used to hide the Beretta, then threw it on the couch. "But if the sanctuary doesn't happen, my mom—I don't think she could take it."

Loo thought of the bloody money in the back of the toilet. She touched Marshall's arm. "Tell them it was an accident."

"It wasn't." Marshall picked up the brown bag from the table. He put it in her hands. "It's my fault this happened. I'm the one who lost the signatures, so I'm the one who had to fix it. And I'm going to keep fixing it until it's done."

The bag was still heavy, even without the gun inside. Loo reached in and pulled out a jar of homemade maple syrup, the golden color shining like amber through the glass.

"Look," he said. "I just want things to be okay between us."

"Okay," said Loo. "Okay." As if saying it twice would make a difference. But it was definitely *not okay*. It took everything she had to not break all of his fingers. She slid the gun back into the bag, next to the jar of syrup, and walked out of house and past the policemen, clutching the paper sack tightly in her hands, like a secret, like a dead heart.

Bullet Number Eleven

HAWLEY SHOT HIMSELF WHILE CLEANING HIS COLT IN THE MOTEL ROOM he was renting. He'd had too much to drink and the trigger got caught and the chambered bullet he'd forgotten to take out went straight through his left foot. Once he was through cursing and yelling, he pulled off his boot, peeled down the sock and there it was—a clean hole right in the skin between his ankle and toes, coming through the other side between the ball of his foot and heel, the skin torn and ragged by the exit, blood pouring out onto the floor. The bullet had made its way past the rubber sole of his work boot and jammed into the crumbling tile, right next to the mini-fridge.

Hawley howled as he stood and tried to put weight on it, then punched the wall and hobbled into the bathroom to inspect the damage. He sat on the edge of the tub and turned on the water. He yanked down a towel from the rack and wrapped it around his foot and ripped the ends and tied it tight. Then he opened the cupboard under the sink and pulled out the orange toolbox and started rummaging. He'd been adding more to the prepper's WROL kit over the past few years, trying to be ready for the worst, which just seemed to keep coming. He was out of morphine and fentanyl lollipops, so he cracked a bottle of Percocet. He started cleaning and disinfecting and dressing the wound. Then he climbed into the empty bathtub, his bad leg propped up on the ledge.

The blood from his foot was leaking through the bandages and clouding the bath. All he could think of was how stupid he was. He leaned back. He could feel the tile and concrete, hard against his neck. He reached down and grabbed the bottle of painkillers off the floor. He took another Percocet and waited for the pills to start working, imagining them sliding down his esophagus and into his stomach, the juices breaking them to a powder, and then into a liquid and then the very elements of chemistry, dissolving into his bloodstream, spreading out through his veins to the ends of his toes. Once the pain started lifting, once he was numbed enough to the world, he'd move. But not until then.

It had been over three and a half years since Lily had died. Hawley had finished his errands, hit every name on the list but King. Thanks to Jove, the old boxer was locked away for good, a double sentence for the murder of the bush pilot and his girlfriend. The world seemed safe enough for now, safe enough to sleep again, and Hawley slept so much that his dreams had started moving to the forefront of his life. He dreamt about the weeds at the bottom of the lake, he dreamt about a car with hinges that could fold down into a suitcase and he dreamt about Lily, crawling into his bed, burying her face in his neck and wrapping her legs around his waist. Little by little, the world he passed into when he closed his eyes became more real than the one outside his door. He woke up wanting only to return to that other, vivid place, the hours between seeming dead and pointless. When he did leave his room, things felt off; everyday actions became more and more alien. At the grocery store the cashiers and the people in the aisles buying food and the folks in the parking lot parking their cars and the ones he drove past on the street all seemed to be staring at him, like they knew he didn't belong.

The only times he felt like himself were back in his room locked up and dreaming, or sitting in his car outside Mabel Ridge's house, with half a dozen loaded guns beside him and another batch in the trunk, just in case. For the past six weeks he'd been living in a motel on the back shore and coming out to Dogtown as often as he could. He'd visited with his daughter once or twice, helped her blow candles off a birthday cake at Chuck E. Cheese, taken her to the beach and the zoo. But most of the time he just stayed parked in his car outside, keeping watch from dusk until morning. Sometimes Mabel forgot to pull down the shades, and he could see Loo walking around inside. Those were the best nights. He'd watch his daughter float from room to room, eating dinner, sitting at the table, her face flickering for hours in the dim blue light of the television. On the nights the shades were down he could still see bits of glow around the edges, and occasionally a shadow passing by. It was enough to know Loo was there, only five hundred feet and one wall between them.

The day after Hawley shot himself his daughter came outside and brought him dinner. His heart caught up in his throat when the door opened and he saw her small figure coming down the path. He grabbed the bearskin rug from the backseat and threw it over the guns beside him. She came straight to his car and knocked on the window and he rolled it down.

"Hi Dad," she said, and handed through a plate wrapped in tinfoil. It was still warm. He put it on his lap, and she passed him a knife and fork and a napkin, too. In the doorway, he could see the outline of Mabel Ridge watching them, her arms folded tightly across her gigantic breasts.

"Thanks," said Hawley.

"Grandma says you shouldn't be out here all the time."

Loo was leaning on the window. She was so close Hawley could smell her hair. It smelled just like Lily's.

"Tell Grandma I said tough."

He'd been careful about parental rights, paying large sums to a high-end, discreet and ruthless lawyer. Each time Mabel Ridge went to the courts to get sole custody, he'd shut it down. He'd been generous with child support, but all the real money was locked up tight for Loo. He didn't want the old bat getting her hands on it, or trying to push him out of his daughter's life, either.

"Are you sick?" Loo asked. "You look sick."

"I'm okay." He could feel the heat of the plate through his pants, across the tops of his knees. The Percocet was starting to wear off and there was a puddle of blood beneath the parking brake. Loo's eyes trailed to the passenger seat. At the bear covering the guns. Usually when he came to visit he brought presents, and he could tell she was trying to figure out if there was something hidden there for her.

"What are you going to be for Halloween this year?"

"A witch."

Hawley tried to think of something else to say. Something that would keep her next to the car. But he could already feel his strangeness rising up between them, the same way it emerged whenever he left his motel room, a block of ice between him and the world.

"Come inside, Louise," Mabel Ridge called.

"I could swing by tomorrow," said Hawley. "Take you trick-or-treating."

"I don't think Grandma would like it."

Hawley looked down at the plate in his lap. He wondered what was underneath the tinfoil. It smelled like some kind of pasta. Spaghetti, maybe with meatballs.

"Pretty please," he said.

Loo ran her hands back and forth along the car, like she was testing the metal. It looked like she was searching for hinges, hinges that could fold the car in two. Something in the back of Hawley's mind flashed forward, a memory tilting and sliding, and his stomach gripped as if he were suddenly teetering on the edge of understanding some great secret of the world. And then it left him.

"Okay," Loo sighed. And she turned around and walked back up the path to the house. She opened the door and went inside and shut it behind her. And then Mabel Ridge went to each window and pulled down every shade.

HAWLEY CAME THE NEXT NIGHT at five-thirty. The sun was just beginning to set. He parked his car, got out and then walked up the path. Mabel Ridge had never invited him inside, but he knew every inch of the place. The way the kitchen was set behind the living room, the way the stairs ran up behind the chimney. Two second-floor bedrooms with two windows each, separated by a hall and one bathroom. Laundry in the basement, and a bulkhead door that led out into the backyard and was locked with a chain.

He didn't want Mabel Ridge to smell anything on him so he hadn't had a drink all day. Instead he took an extra Percocet so he could walk on his foot without limping too much. He'd cleaned out the wound again and wrapped it, but his toes and ankle were swollen and he could hardly fit them inside his boot, so he'd removed most of the dressing and covered the bullet hole with a sock. He'd shaved. He'd bought a new shirt. Even his fingernails were clean.

Hawley lifted the heavy pineapple knocker and rapped it three times. He could hear little footsteps tup-tup-tupping, and then the door swung open and there was Loo. She was wearing a white T-shirt with a red circle glued to the front, and a cardboard poster tube spray-painted silver was tied to her head like a crown. At the very top a bunch of bubble wrap was glued in a spiral, stuck out in front like a traffic signal. In her arms was a basket full of apples.

"Trick or treat," Hawley said.

Loo handed him one of the apples.

"Don't you have any Milky Ways?"

"Grandma says no candy."

"The kids are going to love that," said Hawley. "What are you, a periscope?"

"*No,*" Loo said. "I'm a *toothbrush.*" She poked the red circle on her shirt, and made a whirring, machinelike sound in the back of her throat.

"I thought you were going to be a witch."

"She was," said Mabel Ridge, coming in from the kitchen, wearing her apron and goggles and rubber gloves, looking every bit the mad scientist. "Her teacher made this costume for a school play, and now she won't take it off."

Hawley crouched next to his daughter. Her dark hair was cut short, to her chin. A month earlier she'd stuck gum in her hair. Mabel Ridge had tried ice and peanut butter and all kinds of soaps and finally sat his daughter down at the kitchen table, wrapped a towel around her shoulders and cut all of her hair off. Hawley had watched each snip of the scissors through a pair of binoculars. Loo had cried the whole time.

"Boop," said Hawley, and he tapped his finger to the red button on her shirt.

"You don't have to say anything," said Loo.

"All right," said Hawley.

"Push it again," she said, and this time when he touched his daughter she made the sound again, a kind of growling.

"This is for you," said Mabel Ridge, and she handed Hawley a tall white paper hat with pleats on the sides, the kind that chefs wore in fancy restaurants. Then she held up a T-shirt. A piece of red felt in the shape of a triangle was sewn to the front, with the word CREST painted in white.

"I made it for me, but it should fit you just fine." Mabel stood there, waiting for him to balk, and it wasn't until he saw her tight, steely grin that he realized how much the old woman still hated him.

"I'll wear it," said Hawley.

"Let's give your dad some privacy," said Mabel Ridge.

"I need the shirt," he said, and she threw it at him. Hawley took off his jacket and drew the costume over his head. He put on the chef's hat and looked in the hall mirror. He thought of ways to get Mabel back for this. Then he smothered the whole idea. He had to give the old lady credit—it really *did* look like the cap on a tube of toothpaste. And it was enough that he was in the house at all. It was enough that Loo was smiling.

"You look funny," she said.

"I know," said Hawley, but he didn't really know how funny until he walked outside with Loo and started going from house to house and ringing bells. People opened their doors with smiles that quickly faded when they saw him lurking in the shadows of their porch. He was the only parent wearing a costume. No one knew what he was supposed to be. They didn't know what Loo was, either.

"Maybe we need a routine," Hawley said.

But Loo was interested only in the candy. She approached each new house with growing confidence, until she was dashing ahead and leaving Hawley behind on the sidewalk. He hadn't been around so many people in months and it made him nervous, the children in their costumes, shrieking and running past in the dark. Witches and fairies, clowns and skeletons and a whole cast of cartoon characters that Hawley didn't recognize. The other parents clustered in groups, grinning and nodding. Pumpkins glowered on doorsteps. And Loo's tiny hand slipped into his, her fingers gripping his thumb as they made their way down the street together. Toothpaste and toothbrush.

Hawley's foot was throbbing by the time they started back. He could feel the sock soaked with blood, and the side of his boot was starting to show a bright stain across one side.

"You're leaking," Loo said.

"It's just some paint I spilled," said Hawley, and when she kept staring, unsure, clutching her bag of candy tight in her fist, he said, "Look," and turned his boot and dragged it along the sidewalk, one way and then the other, until he'd made the letter *L* in red on the concrete.

"For Loo?" she asked, delighted.

"That's right," said Hawley, though he'd been thinking of Lily. "And now it's time to go home. I promised your grandma I'd have you back by eight."

"One more house," Loo begged.

"You've got enough candy," said Hawley.

"But they have so many pumpkins." Loo pointed to a bungalow at the end of the block. "Please? Please?"

Hawley knew it was the candy and not him she wanted, but it still felt good. "All right," he said. "Last one."

There was already a group of kids at the door. A ghost, a punk girl and a hot dog. As they got closer, Hawley could see that the kids were teenagers. Fourteen, maybe even fifteen. Their costumes were haphazard. Their pillowcases filled to the brim. They snatched at the candy bowl like they were aiming to empty it.

"That's enough," the man at the door was saying.

The punk girl hefted her bag onto her shoulder, but the ghost and the hot dog kept grabbing at the bowl.

"I mean it." The man took a step toward the teenagers. He was dressed up as a policeman, his cap pulled down on his forehead. He was wearing a badge and mirrored sunglasses. The hot dog looked up and dropped the candy in his hand, while the ghost hooted and then they scattered down the walkway.

Loo hurried into the space they'd left behind, holding up her pillowcase. "Trick or treat," she said. That's when Hawley noticed the handgun snapped into the policeman's holster and the nightstick and can of pepper spray dangling from his belt. That's when he saw the cruiser parked in the driveway.

The policeman held on to the glass candy bowl and watched the teenagers laughing and hurrying down the street. Then he turned to Hawley.

"And what are you?" he asked. "Some kind of superhero?"

"Toothpaste," said Hawley.

Loo gave a big smile. "Push my button," she said.

"I'm a little afraid to do that," said the policeman. He peered at the bubble wrap stuck on the end of the poster tube. "Is something special going to happen?"

"I'm going to brush your teeth," said Loo.

"I've had a lot of candy tonight, so that's probably a good idea," said the policeman. He turned his mirrored sunglasses toward Hawley, and his expression could have meant a thousand different things. He bent down and pushed the red patch on Loo's shirt, and as soon as he did she started up with her growling.

"That's great," said the policeman. "Who made the costume?"

"Her grandmother," said Hawley.

Loo took a step toward the policeman, angling the top of the poster tube, as if she were getting ready to shove the whole thing inside his mouth.

"That's enough, honey."

Loo stepped back. She held up her bag again.

"Those damn kids nearly took it all," the man said as he dropped a candy bar into Loo's pillowcase. He leaned down. "Don't ever become a teenager."

"Are you a real policeman?" Loo asked.

The man laughed. "I left the suit on after my shift. I was hoping it would keep the eggers away. They get my car every year."

"Little pricks," said Hawley.

The policeman glanced down at Loo and then back at Hawley, eyeing him carefully. "They're only kids," he said. "I did worse in my day."

"Dad," said Loo, "you're leaking again."

And he was. As they were talking a small puddle of blood had spread out of Hawley's boot and made its way onto the policeman's porch.

"Is that paint?" the policeman asked.

"Fake blood," said Hawley. "We were playing around earlier. I guess some of it spilled onto my shoe."

"A bloody toothbrush?"

"Root canal," said Hawley.

"That would have been something." The policeman wrapped his arms around the bowl of candy and looked at the puddle on his porch. His sunglasses reflected back all the darkness of the world.

"Happy Halloween," said Hawley. "Sorry about the mess."

"Thanks for the candy," said Loo.

"You're welcome," said the policeman. He stood on his porch, watching the two of them walk down the path. Hawley tried not to limp, and only glanced back once they'd reached the corner. Under the streetlamp, he saw that he'd left footprints, tracked all the way down the policeman's stairs and along the sidewalk. Beside them were the small footprints of his daughter, the soles of her sneakers caked in his blood.

. . .

WHEN HE GOT BACK TO the motel later that night, Hawley brought a beer into the bathroom and started unlacing his boot. Maybe it was enough, he thought. To see Loo now and then, to be on the edges of her life. He'd been lucky to have as much of her as he did. He didn't know how to take care of a child. And after Wyoming and Texas and New Orleans, he didn't think he deserved to, either.

His foot looked inflamed. He could barely get his toes free, and had to yank the laces out entirely. The wound probably needed sewing, or at the very least to be cauterized. Hawley ran the tub and emptied a bottle of peroxide over the bullet hole and watched the edges of his skin foam white and burn.

Properly this time, he bandaged the wound, packed the wrappings tightly and bundled layers of dressing. In the end his foot looked like a mummy's. He didn't even try to put a shoe back on. He just cut the leg off an old pair of sweatpants and slipped that over his foot and then tied the ends and wrapped a plastic bag around it and then duct-taped the whole thing for good measure.

The room was splattered with red. What a mess he'd made, Hawley thought. He wished he could erase his entire life, starting with his father's death and then every step that had led him here to this crap motel room, every bullet, every twisted turn of the road he'd followed—even meeting Lily, even having Loo. Hawley wanted it all gone.

He popped another Percocet and washed it down with beer and then he started searching under the bathroom sink until he found a bucket. He filled the bucket with soap and sponges and paper towels, and then he went under the kitchen sink and found a bottle of turpentine there, and also a bottle of bleach and a pair of rubber gloves. He brought it all out to the car and then he drove back to Dogtown.

The porch light at Mabel Ridge's house was out but there was still a pumpkin burning by the door, its jagged smile illuminated. Hawley parked in the street. He filled the plastic bucket with supplies and crept onto the path, dragging his bound-up leg behind him.

One by one, Hawley began to erase his own bloody footprints, from the sidewalk to the house. First his. Then Loo's. It was difficult to get the stain off the pavement, and even harder to get it off the wooden stairs to the porch. He added some bleach to the bucket, and took a scrub brush and leaned his full weight against it, going back and forth, back and forth. Then he'd stop and check his work with a flashlight. Then he'd start again.

He'd been out there for maybe twenty minutes when the porch light clicked on and the front door opened. Mabel Ridge leaned against the doorknob, dressed in striped pajamas. Hawley stopped scrubbing.

"What the hell are you doing out here?"

"I'm cleaning your porch."

"I nearly called the police."

"I just need to finish this," said Hawley. "It won't take long." And he went back to pushing the scrub brush back and forth.

"Is that blood?"

"It's paint," said Hawley. "I was painting and I got some on my shoes and I tracked it here so I wanted to clean it up before it dried."

Mabel Ridge stood over him. "It looks like blood."

Hawley was still wearing the Crest T-shirt that Mabel Ridge had made. His pupils were fixed from the drugs. But he didn't feel high. He didn't feel anything.

"I think your car got egged."

"Goddammit!" Mabel Ridge came out onto the porch. Then she went back inside and flipped on more yard lights before going to inspect the damage. Hawley had noticed a few broken shells as he came up the driveway, but now he could see that the old Pontiac had been fully covered, at least two dozen yolks smeared across the windshield.

Mabel Ridge went around to the side of the house and unspooled a hose. She turned on the water and began to spray the car. "What kind of soap are you using?"

"All kinds," said Hawley. "I wasn't sure what would work."

"Well, if you've got any dish soap, bring it over."

Hawley carried his bucket and sponges and the liquid soap over. He refilled the bucket with water and added some soap and helped Mabel

Ridge clean the car. It wasn't what he'd planned on doing. But Hawley didn't have much of a plan anymore for anything.

"Is Loo awake?"

"It's the middle of the night," said Mabel Ridge.

"So she's asleep?"

The old woman eyed Hawley's foot, the bandages and plastic bag sealed with tape. "Look," she said, "I don't know what kind of trouble you're in. But don't bring it here."

"There's no trouble," said Hawley.

Mabel Ridge stared at him. "Are you drunk?"

"Nope," said Hawley.

She went inside and came back with the basket of apples Loo had offered him earlier.

"Why don't you eat something."

"Thanks," said Hawley. He chose one and took a bite. The fruit was crisp and juicy. The skin stuck in his teeth, the tartness coating his tongue.

A group of teenagers with masks walked by on the sidewalk carrying backpacks. Rubber faces hung on their scrawny necks, a collection of adolescent horrors—dangling eyeballs, rotting flesh. One of the boys reached into his bag. Hawley could see the egg there in the teenager's hand, white and delicate and waiting. Then the boy lobbed it through the air toward them.

"Trick *my* treat!" the boy yelled.

Mabel Ridge turned the hose on them. The kids cursed and ran.

"Effective."

"I don't need any more nonsense tonight," Mabel Ridge said. "I just want to clean this up and go to bed."

"Let me get this last bit off the driveway," said Hawley, and he was back on his knees, sponging the asphalt.

Mabel Ridge watched him work. "You're not doing her any good skulking around like this," she said. "You need to move on. She's got a home here. It's what Lily wanted."

Hawley stopped scrubbing. He looked up at Loo's window. The

room was dark, but he could see the curtains with giraffes printed on them that Mabel Ridge had made for her third birthday, which he had missed. His daughter was behind those curtains and she was sleeping and she was dreaming and she was safe.

The old woman turned off the water. She started coiling the length of the hose, wrapping it around her elbow. "I think you should go now."

"I will."

Mabel let out a sigh of relief. She put the hose away. She climbed the stairs of the porch, then turned back and looked at him kneeling in the driveway. "Good night, then."

"Goodbye," he said.

He took his bucket and sponges to his car and drove back to the motel. When he got there he pulled out the car mats and washed them down and then scrubbed them and then he scrubbed the inside of the car, too, until any trace of his blood was gone. Then he cleaned the walkway that led to his room. He made it to the front door and then through it and closed the door behind him. His fingers reeked of disinfectant. His clothes were all wet and the sponge was black.

Now there was no trace of Hawley outside. No footsteps leading to this room. But there was still the mess inside. Hawley threw out the sponge he'd been using and got another from under the sink. He dumped the dirty water and filled the bucket again, until the suds were foaming over the top. He could barely feel his foot anymore. He could barely feel his hands, either. Even his fingers seemed distant, as if he were no longer washing the floor but sitting on the bed across the room, watching himself wash the floor.

This job was easier. The motel carpet seemed built for the aftermath of violence. Before Hawley knew it, he had erased what was left. The blood was gone. Every speck of it scrubbed out of his life, except for what was still pumping through him.

Hawley went into the bedroom and pulled out the box he'd kept of Lily's things, the scraps and pieces left behind, after Mabel Ridge had packed up the rest and driven away with Loo in the car seat. There was a photograph he wanted to look at. The one he'd taken on their honeymoon in Niagara, with Lily smiling and the waterfall rushing behind her in a cloud. He found it in an envelope. It was a Polaroid, the edges thick, the layered colors starting to blur.

He needed pictures now. He was starting to lose the details. The way Lily's waist fit into the crook of his arm, how he could feel the pulse in her neck when he put his lips against her skin. For months he'd been able to pull these memories out and burrow inside them so completely that he could conjure every aspect of her. The sight, smell, taste, touch, even the sound of her voice. Hawley would lose himself for hours, imagining her in bed beside him. But now the images were fogging around the edges, like an old movie narrowing the lens on a scene that he was still trying desperately to slip through.

Hawley turned on the faucets and filled the tub. He rummaged through the bathroom drawer until he found some rubber tape he'd bought to seal the drains. He tore off a piece and taped the Niagara picture to the bathroom wall, underneath the showerhead, where he could see it. Then he pulled his shirt off. He got his good leg out of one side of his jeans and then took a pair of scissors from the medicine cabinet and cut the rest away so he wouldn't have to redo the bandages on his foot. He picked up the Colt from where he'd left it on top of the toilet and lowered himself into the bathtub, keeping his bad leg out of the water, propped along the edge.

He opened the cylinder and checked the bullets, even though he had loaded the gun only a few hours before. He closed the cylinder. Then he opened it again. The brass fittings on the ends of the bullets shone in a ring. A circle of six circles.

He looked up at the picture. It seemed crooked. Was it? He shifted forward in the tub and reached for the wall, dripping on the tiles, measuring the photo with his finger to be sure. And as he was measuring he remembered another photo that he had, that he liked even better than this one, and he realized *that* was the photo he wanted to be looking at.

Hawley got out of the tub and hobbled into the bedroom. He opened the box again. He found the photo strip. It was from their first week together, taken on the boardwalk at Myrtle Beach. His face was hardly in it. Only one eye and the side of his beard. Lily was trying to make him laugh. The first shot she was sticking a finger up her nose. The second she'd blown up her cheeks like a balloon. In the third Hawley was out of the frame completely, and Lily looked surprised, the edges of her mouth starting to soften, because in between those last two pictures, Hawley had taken her hand and threaded his fingers tightly with hers. And in that captured moment, as the light flashed inside the booth, he'd felt a flash inside his own body, striking a spark that turned the rusty gears of his heart, gears that had been frozen for so long Hawley had forgotten they'd even existed, until the parts in his chest groaned and started to move.

Hawley taped the strip to the bathroom wall, too. Then he went back and pulled everything else he had from Lily's box. A pink razor blade, the small bag of cosmetics she always carried around but hardly ever used, some old brown prescription bottles with her name on the label from when she had strep throat, her comb and brush, still tangled with strands of her hair. He carried it all into his crummy bathroom, and arranged the objects around the sink and in the drawers. He hung her green kimono from one of the hooks. He slid her toothbrush next to his beside the sink. Set her lipstick by the mirror. He arranged her shampoo and conditioner along the edge of the tile. Then he got back into the tub. He closed his eyes. He opened them.

It was as if she had only just stepped out of the room.

The water had cooled but was still warm enough. He wet his hair and then used some of Lily's shampoo and ran it through with his fingers until his head was white with foam. Lily had always taken showers at night, and she would climb into bed smelling like freshly washed berries. He paused for a moment, inhaling and exhaling her scent. Then he pushed himself down under the water until his lungs burned.

He came up sputtering, as he always did, full of shame and guilt and self-disgust. He looked again at the pictures he'd taped to the wall. He looked at Lily's brush on the edge of the counter. He looked at the half-used bar of almond-milk soap he'd placed by the sink, the dragons sewn into the back of her robe on the door, her perfume bottle and its tiny glass stopper.

He was ready now. He picked up the gun. He pressed the barrel to the soft flesh beneath his chin.

The phone rang. Hawley sat there in the tub, listening to it ring. He'd conjured Lily so well that he could almost hear her bare feet padding across the rug beyond the bathroom door, the click of her lifting the mouthpiece from its plastic cradle.

Hello? she said. *Hello?*

The phone kept ringing. Urgent and echoing. And now Hawley imagined her voice on the other end of the line, reaching out at last, after all the times he had asked her to come and she had not. Hawley put down the gun. He scrambled out of the tub and went into the living room. He picked up the phone.

"I'm sorry to wake you," said Mabel Ridge, then coughed as if Hawley had been the one to ring. "Louise had a nightmare. Too much candy, I think. And now she won't go back to bed." Her voice was like Lily's, or what Lily might have one day sounded like, if she had lived to let the years pass and take their toll. Mabel Ridge cleared her throat. "She wanted to talk to you. I told her it was too late to call. I told her you were asleep."

"Not yet," said Hawley.

A muffled sound of the phone being passed. Voices low and far away, the mouthpiece pulled across a length of fabric. And there she was.

"Hello," said Loo.

"What's wrong?" Hawley asked.

"You're not outside."

"Not tonight."

"But you're *always* outside."

Hawley did not know how to answer. All this time he had been watching her window, it had never occurred to him that she was watching for him, too. He could hear Loo's breath, heavy and expectant, blowing hard into the mouthpiece, and for a moment all he could think of was the sound of the whale's spout—the blast of air and water as the giant rose to the surface, the salted spray that had rained down upon him in Puget Sound and filled him with terror and longing and a sense that he could right the path he was on. He had not realized that he'd been waiting for this sound until he heard it. He knew only that he had been waiting—for something that had never arrived, that had failed him, that had made him rage and murder in the silence it had left. But now here it was again. His daughter, still breathing. And so was he.

"I'll come now."

"Right now?"

"Yes," said Hawley. "Put your coat on. And get your toothbrush. Your real toothbrush."

Hawley wrapped the phone cord around his arm, tighter and tighter, waiting to hear what she would say. Instead he heard the sound of footsteps. A door open and close. Then a clattering as the phone dropped to the ground. Hawley called Loo's name. He pressed his ear tightly against the receiver, straining to listen. Something dragged across the floor. Shuffling. Thumps. A noise like Velcro being ripped apart. And then she came back to him.

"I've got my shoes on," Loo said. "I've got the candy, too."

Everything That's Happened & Is Happening & Is Going to Happen

WHEN LOO HEARD THE KNOCK ON THEIR FRONT DOOR, HER FIRST thought was of Marshall—she hated herself for this, but it was. It had been a week since he'd left to join his stepfather's boat. But today was her birthday. She was turning seventeen. And she felt light, thrilled, as she hurried downstairs, making up a story in her head with each step: that Marshall would be standing there with a present, saying that he'd changed his mind, that the petition didn't matter, that she was more important than his mother. Instead she found two policemen on the front porch, their faces dour. One of them was Officer Temple, who had pulled Loo over in the Firebird. The other had red hair. Even though it was sixty degrees, they looked chilled, their uniforms buttoned up to the neck.

"Your father home?" Officer Temple asked.

She should have known that it was only a matter of time before the gossip about Hawley would lead the police to their door. The bullet, she thought. Could they have traced it to the Beretta? She swallowed hard. "He's out fishing."

The policemen exchanged a look.

"We need to ask you some questions about Thomas Jove," said Officer Temple.

"Oh," Loo said, relieved. "What about him?"

"There was an accident," said Officer Temple.

"What kind of accident?"

"The Coast Guard just brought in his boat. It was floating out by the Banks. The guys from *Whale Heroes* called it in. The sails were up, but no one was on board," said the red-haired cop.

"I don't understand," said Loo, "where did he go?" She imagined Marshall in the middle of the ocean, climbing onto the *Pandora*.

"He might have fallen off." The redhead coughed. "Or been hit by a wave."

It took a moment for her to realize they were saying Jove was dead.

"But he could swim," said Loo.

Officer Temple gave the redhead a nudge. "It's easy to get turned around, especially at night."

And there it was in her mind, already a memory: Jove's lifeless body drifting beneath the waves, getting caught in a dragnet, bundled with lobsters and crayfish and eels and skates and lifted out of the sea, the creatures around him flapping their fins, their mouths gaping, their gills sucking open and closed.

"We heard at the Flying Jib that he was staying here," said the redhead.

"He's friends with my father."

"When was the last time you saw him?"

"Three weeks ago. At the launch." Her voice faltered. "I christened the boat for him."

"We can't find much information beyond his registration with the harbormaster," said Officer Temple. "Do you know where he used to live? How long he knew your father?"

"He never said," said Loo. She could hear the truck coming down the street, its distinctive rattle as familiar as Hawley's own voice. Her father slowed as he reached their house. He'd left before she got up that morning, and now Loo saw him take in the police car and the men on the porch. He pulled across the end of the driveway, blocking them in.

"It's Jove," she called as he got out.

The policemen turned and walked toward Hawley's truck. Loo watched his face as they told him. Hawley listened and ran his fingers through his hair. Officer Temple asked him something and he shook his head. Then he asked him something else and Hawley nodded.

The police walked back to their cruiser and got in. Hawley opened the back of his truck and grabbed three bags full of Chinese takeout. He carried the bags up the steps and set them on the porch.

"I'm going to the station," he said.

"I'm coming, too."

"Like hell you are." Then Hawley softened. "They're only going to ask me some questions."

Loo reached out and took hold of his sleeve. She did not want to be left behind again. The policemen had rolled down their windows. They were watching them both. She could hear the static of the radio, the squawk of strange voices.

Her father gently removed her fingers. He squeezed her hand once, then let it go. "Stay here," he said. "Start packing." And then he walked back down the driveway and got into his truck. He pulled into the street and the cops followed, creeping slowly behind, lights on but siren silent.

Loo had not heard Hawley say those words in more than five years. But they were hard-wired to her nervous system and she felt a shock all the way down her spine, as if she'd been shot through with electricity. She carried the Chinese food to the kitchen, then went straight to the closet and grabbed their old suitcases. The ones they had crisscrossed the country with long ago. She threw one bag onto Hawley's bed and the other across her own and undid the latches. Back when they were on the road, Loo and her father could pull up stakes and be away in under an hour. It was a game they played. Who could pack the fastest. Hawley had always won, until he taught Loo his trick: to always take the same things. Everything else got left behind. She would run around and grab the items from her list: toothbrush, comb, underwear, socks and her planisphere. It had been years, though, and Loo was out of practice. Everything seemed important enough to take.

Would it be cold where they were going? Would it be warm? Cold, she decided, and filled the suitcase with long underwear. There was no room left for any pants or shirts or shoes. She turned the suitcase over and started again. Hangers came out of the closet and her clothes were strewn across the bed. She could not bring herself to choose between them. In the end she packed only a pair of jeans, a T-shirt, a sweater, her new telescope, her mother's gloves, the Carl Sagan book, Mabel Ridge's scrapbook and the planisphere. She brought the suitcase downstairs and put it next to the door.

It was only after seeing her belongings set firmly on the threshold that she began to have second thoughts. She'd grown used to living in Olympus. To the beach outside their door, to seeing the same people year in and year out. She loved their house, and even the Sawtooth had become a place where she felt that she belonged. She was supposed to be working a lunch shift, right at that very moment.

She considered calling in sick. The summer tourists had all left town and once that happened the Sawtooth was usually half-empty. But there was a paycheck waiting for her in Gunderson's office. If she hurried, she could get there and back in half an hour on her bicycle. So she pulled on a sweater and left Hawley a note, then rode her bike downtown and chained it to the fence. She opened the door to the Sawtooth and the first person she saw was Mary Titus.

Marshall's mother was wiping down a table near the back. Loo watched her replace the silverware and set the napkins. In her apron she looked less triumphant than she had wearing her orange robe. None of the fishermen would eat in her section. They were all crowded around the bar.

"Where's Agnes?" Loo asked.

"She started having contractions, so Gunderson drove her to the hospital," said Mary Titus. "I'm filling in."

"Did anyone call her boyfriend?"

"Brian?" Mary Titus plucked a fork from a bouquet of silverware clutched in her fist. "He walked out on her two months ago."

Loo glanced at Agnes's section of the restaurant. It made her uncomfortable to know that she'd been too caught up in her own misery to notice anyone else's. In all the weeks and months they had worked together, Agnes had been carrying her own troubles. And she had never missed a shift. The child she was delivering now—all alone, her feet in the stirrups—would share a birthday with Loo. I will send him a card, Loo thought. I will mail him one every year.

"You better get to work," said Mary Titus. "Nobody here wants me to serve them."

"I can't stay," said Loo. "I just came to pick up a check."

Mary Titus folded a napkin and slipped it under a fork. "You'll have to wait, then."

The crowd at the bar was full of fishermen out of work. They were all waiting for the ban on the Banks to be lifted. Joe Strand and Pauly Fisk were there, too, and they waved Loo over.

"The principal just called," said Fisk. "He's on his way back with cigars."

"It's a boy," said Strand.

"I know," said Loo.

Fisk sipped his beer. He looked at all the empty tables. "We gotta find a way to break up Gunderson and that damn tree-hugger."

"He likes her," said Loo.

"Maybe your dad can help," said Strand. "He's good at breaking things."

"You don't know what you're talking about," said Loo.

"You think?" he said, rubbing his jaw.

"Ah, don't be mad," said Fisk. "He was just doing what any father would do, scaring your fella a little. Teaching him and his mom what principles mean." Fisk tapped the visor of his Hong Kong hat, then pointed his fingers in the shape of a gun.

"That wasn't him."

"Sure," said Strand. "But tell Hawley we owe him, just the same." And then he raised his own finger-gun and pretended to shoot Mary Titus.

"That's not *funny*," said Loo, but it got big laughs from the rest of the bar, and soon others were pointing more fake weapons and finger-pistols. They hid behind menus and pints of beer. They added sound effects. *Bang! Boom! Ping! You missed her! Ten points! Twenty!* Fisk picked up an imaginary submachine gun and strafed Mary's section like he was Rambo.

While target practice went on, Mary Titus continued setting tables. But when she finished folding the last napkin she snatched a carafe of hot water off the burner and threatened to pour it over Fisk's head. Loo stepped between them. She took Mary's arm.

"Let's head out back," she said.

"Troglodytes!" Mary screamed.

"We need to talk. Come on."

"I'm taking this with me."

"Suit yourself," said Loo.

The woman threw a withering look at the bar and filed through the kitchen and into the walk-in freezer. The door sealed shut behind them, blocking out all the noise from the cooks and the customers. Then it was just the two women facing each other, their breath creating a thick fog between slabs of meat.

"Don't tell me you're pregnant," Mary Titus said.

"I'm not," said Loo.

"Thank God." Marshall's mother lowered the carafe. The throat of the pitcher was still steaming.

Loo glanced around the tight room. There was no place left to go.

"Your petition for the sanctuary," she said. "It's fake."

"What are you talking about?"

"Marshall didn't submit the paperwork. I did."

Mary Titus's cheeks flushed, as if she had been the one to tell a secret instead of Loo.

"You're lying," she said.

"Do you really think that many people suddenly cared about a fish? I forged the names. All five thousand of them."

Mary Titus clung to the shelf that held the butter. It looked like she was going to be sick, but now that Loo had started, the truth kept coming, words tumbling one after another from her mouth.

"Marshall shot up your front door. For the publicity. And that's why he's out on that boat right now. Trying to make this happen for you, in case the petition's thrown out." Loo cleared her throat. "I just thought you should know that it wasn't any of those fishermen who put a bullet in your house. And it wasn't my father, either."

"You," said Mary Titus. Her fingers went tight on the carafe of hot water. "You. You. You."

There were bubbles against the glass. Loo could see them rising, could see the steam and the heat heading her way and even the blistering burns that would tear into her skin and the scars that would follow—as if this had all happened before. She knew the water was coming even before it began to come and so she stepped to the side, and instead of scalding her face, the hot liquid splashed directly onto the floor. They both stared at the bright spot on the tile, a circle in the middle of the grime, as if a witch had just been doused and melted away, leaving behind nothing but a cloud of steam and heat.

The freezer door opened.

"What the hell is going on in here?" said Principal Gunderson. "We just lost five tables."

"We need a minute," said Loo.

"George." Mary Titus was staring at her arm holding the carafe as if it wasn't her arm at all.

It was the first time Loo had ever heard anyone use his first name. Principal Gunderson paused, strips of plastic curtain on his shoulders. Mary Titus's eyes were shining and on the brink of tears, just as they had been that night long ago when she'd told Loo about her first husband. And Loo realized then, for the first time, the real reason why the widow wanted to make the Banks a sanctuary. It wasn't to save a disappearing fish—it was because the father of her only child had drowned there.

It was like looking in a mirror. The same flickering hope in Loo, the same desperate need to be loved, was right here in Marshall's mother. And it was in Principal Gunderson, clutching Lily's waist in that old prom photo. And it was in Agnes, pressing her feet into the stirrups, listening for her child's cry. And it was in Hawley, mourning with his scraps of paper in the bathroom. Their hearts were all cycling through the same madness—the discovery, the bliss, the loss, the despair—like planets taking turns in orbit around the sun. Each containing their own unique gravity. Their own force of attraction. Drawing near and holding fast to whatever entered their own atmosphere. Even Loo, penning her thousands of names way out at the edge of the universe, felt better knowing others were traveling this same elliptical course, that they would sometimes cross paths, that they would find love and lose love and recover from love and love again—because, if they *were* all going in circles, and Loo was Pluto, then every 248 years even she would have the chance to be closer to the sun.

Principal Gunderson crossed the frozen room, past the meat and baskets of icy vegetables, and wrapped his arms around Mary Titus. "It's all right," he said. "Whatever it is, it's all right."

Mary Titus clung to him and wept, as if her husband had died all over again. Principal Gunderson said nothing and stroked her hair. Loo watched them embrace and take comfort in each other and felt ashamed and jealous and ashamed that she was jealous.

When Principal Gunderson finally glanced over Mary's shoulder, his face full of questions, Loo said the only thing she could think of that would make everyone feel better. "We're leaving town. Me and my father. So I guess I quit." Then she stepped outside the freezer and watched the clock on the wall as the cooks wove around her and steamed clams and shucked oysters and rang the bell for pickup.

After a few minutes, the door opened and Principal Gunderson and Mary Titus emerged holding hands. Their faces were pink. Mary Titus looked ragged, but Principal Gunderson seemed energized.

"This is over now, whatever was between you two," he said. "You should shake hands."

Mary Titus and Loo stood their ground, eyeing each other like children forced to apologize. Sorry but not meaning a word. Until at last Loo held her palm out. And Marshall's mother touched it with her cold, damp fingers.

"You ruined my life," said Mary Titus.

"You're welcome," said Loo.

Principal Gunderson released a small belch into the air. "I have your last paycheck," he said. "Why don't you come with me, and we'll let Mary get back to work."

The widow wiped her eyes with the hem of her skirt, just as she had long ago in Loo's kitchen. It had seemed so important to wound her. But now Loo's hard feelings had been washed away, like the grime on the floor of the freezer. She watched Mary Titus set the empty carafe back on the burner and return to her empty tables.

"You certainly know how to keep things interesting," said Principal Gunderson, as he dug around in the register. "I just hope you use that strength of will for good. I think it could take you to extraordinary places." He pulled out an envelope. "We're going to be sorry to lose you."

"Really?" Loo asked.

"Of course," he said. "You're a bright student. And not everyone can handle the Sawtooth. It takes a lot. Physically, I mean. And mentally. The ladies who work here—they're Amazons." He slid some extra cash into Loo's envelope and passed it over. "So are you."

The paper was heavy and thick beneath her fingers, like an announcement or an invitation. "I didn't mean to screw everything up."

"Nobody ever does."

She tucked the envelope into her jeans. "I guess I should say thank you."

Principal Gunderson shut the cash register slowly until the drawer caught and the bell let out a muffled ding. "Just take care of yourself, my dear."

Loo shifted on her feet. She didn't know what to do next, and so she held out her hand again. Gunderson shook it.

"Do you know where you're headed?"

"Not sure yet."

"I never thought you were going to stay long."

"Because of my dad?" Loo asked.

"No," Principal Gunderson said. "Because of your mother. All she ever talked about was leaving this place."

LOO RODE PAST THE PIER where Hawley had danced on the greasy pole. Past the impound lot. Past the beach where Marshall had stolen her shoes. When she finally got home her father's truck was in the driveway. She hurried inside and found him in the kitchen. The bags of Chinese food were still sitting unopened on the counter. Hawley was at the table looking grim.

"What did the police say?"

"That Jove got washed overboard. They have his boat docked at the marina. They said they didn't find anything unusual but I wanted to be sure so I snuck inside and checked it," said Hawley. "Jove was on a job. Sailing to a marker offshore to make an exchange. I went through the hold. I looked everywhere, even under the floorboards. But there weren't any goods in the cabin and there wasn't any money, either. And there should have been a lot of money."

Loo felt a cold unease spread across her skin. She remembered the conversation she'd overheard the first night Jove had showed up at their door.

"You think someone might have killed him."

Hawley chewed his lip. "They're still searching. The Coast Guard is dragging the area where they found the boat."

"This isn't your fault, Dad."

"It is," said Hawley. "Everything that's happened and is happening and is going to happen."

Loo got the whiskey out of the cabinet over the sink. She poured her father a shot and set it beside him. He took the glass and drained it.

"We should go out there," said Loo. "Look for him."

"He's already dead."

Hawley poured himself another whiskey. "Whoever hired him asked for both of us. They knew my name." He rubbed his face. He cupped his hand around his drink. Then he looked straight at his daughter, and she remembered all the nights Hawley had stared out their windows and polished his guns.

"Maybe nothing happened," said Loo, her voice tight. "Maybe it was just an accident."

"Maybe." Hawley stood up and walked to the counter. He started pulling out the containers of Chinese food. "We should eat. I got all of your favorites."

"It's cold."

"Then we'll heat it up."

Loo watched him take down plates from the cabinet and pull silverware from the drawers, like it was any kind of normal evening. She swallowed hard. Tried to stifle the choking feeling at the base of her throat.

"You think whoever did this might come here."

"I just want to be careful." Hawley spooned fried rice and moo shu chicken into pans. He lit the burners, and then he rolled a cigarette and lit that, too. "We won't make it to the fair tomorrow. But we'll find another one somewhere else. Ride the Ferris wheel."

Loo tore open one of the fortune cookie bags. She cracked the shell, pulled out the tiny paper fortune.

"What's it say?" Hawley asked.

"Land is always on the mind of the flying bird."

"Open another one."

Loo smashed a cookie against the table. *"The early bird gets the worm, but the second mouse gets the cheese."*

"That's more like it."

She watched her father cook. His hair was threaded through with lines of silver. The skin on his fingers rough and cracked. Someday, he was going to be an old man, and she would have to take care of him. But not now. Not yet. The smell of hoisin sauce and cabbage filled the room. She wondered how long it would be before they had a kitchen again.

"The things I did before," her father said. "They weren't right. I was young. And I didn't understand what a life can mean in this world." Hawley stirred the pots. He let out a cloud of smoke. "Now I have you and I know better. But the past is like a shadow, always trying to catch up."

"So what do we do?" Loo asked.

"We eat," said Hawley, setting down their plates. "And then we run before it gets us."

A HOUSE IS HARDER TO leave than a motel room. Still, Hawley seemed like he'd been planning this escape for years. He had an envelope ready with Loo's birth certificate and their passports. He talked with Joe Strand and Pauly Fisk about finding a renter. Then he called Mabel Ridge and asked if Loo could spend the night with her. His daughter had never seen him be so polite.

"I'm not going over there," Loo said after he hung up the phone.

"There's things I need to do," said Hawley. "And I won't be able to do them if I'm worried about you."

"What things?"

Hawley lifted the edges of the tablecloth and picked up everything inside, the plates and glasses and silverware, and dumped it all into the garbage can. "I don't want to lie to you. So please don't ask."

"I'm not a little girl anymore."

"I know," said Hawley. "But I need you to be a kid for one more night. I'll come and get you first thing in the morning. We'll go away for a few months. It'll be like a vacation. Then if everything checks out, we'll come back."

"But I yelled at Mabel. I smashed her dishes."

"She's your grandmother," said Hawley. "She'll forgive you."

He went upstairs and packed. It took him only ten minutes. He dropped his bag and his orange toolbox by the door, and then he started to gather his guns. The Colt, the Smith & Wesson, the Luger, the Saturday night specials, the shotguns, Loo's rifle and the set of derringers. Hawley piled them all on the kitchen table, along with his case of suppressors and bags of ammunition, hemming and hawing the same way that Loo had struggled to decide which pair of jeans to put in her suitcase. In the end he left none of them behind.

While he finished, Loo went upstairs. Out on the roof the shingles were cold. There was a breeze coming directly off the shoreline, and it smelled of seaweed and sand. It smelled like home. Loo pulled her arms into her sweater and hugged them close. She wanted to know where this exact spot was on the map, so she could put her finger on it when they were gone and remember.

She had already packed her telescope, but in Carl Sagan's book, she'd read instructions on how to find longitude and latitude, using a clock set to Greenwich Mean Time and the North Star. Holding her arm out, and starting at the horizon, she counted how many fists fit in the sky until she reached the bright spot of Polaris. Each fist equaled approximately ten degrees, which meant they were somewhere between forty-two and forty-three degrees north.

The front door opened, and she watched as Hawley carried a box out to the edge of the sidewalk, where she'd dragged the garbage earlier that night for pickup. He set the box right by the cans. He looked up at the sliver of moon. The light from the window cut across his face, dividing his body into sections of shadow and radiant strips of white, like something that had been taken apart and reassembled without all the original pieces.

Loo crawled back inside. She went down the staircase and peered inside the bathroom. The door to the medicine cabinet was open and reflected her own face back at her. Hawley had cleared the shelves. The lipstick, the compact powder, her mother's toothbrush and all of the old prescriptions with Lily's faded name on them were missing. The perfume bottle was gone. The cans of pineapple and peaches. The shampoo and conditioner from their places on the side of the tub.

Hawley came back inside with a garbage bag in his hand. He started taking down the pictures from the walls. The receipts and scraps of paper, the scribbles on parking tickets, the grocery lists. The picture from Niagara Falls.

"You're throwing everything away?"

"Not everything." Hawley turned to her. "Is there anything you want?"

Loo scanned the counter, the tub, the empty towel racks. The walls looked so naked without her mother's belongings. The room suddenly larger and full of possibility.

"The bathrobe."

Hawley unhooked the kimono with the dragons from the back of the door. He opened it like a coat, and Loo slipped her arms inside. She'd done this dozens of times over the years growing up, but this was the first time the robe fit her. The sleeves fell from her arms, the green silk still bright.

She reached for the photo strip next. It was the only picture she'd ever seen that had both Hawley and Lily together. Her mother making faces, her father moving out of the frame. She pulled, and the tape ripped the bottom corner, so that a part of the picture remained in place. She held the photo out to Hawley. Her father eyed the tiny triangle of black-and-white left behind.

"You keep it."

Loo took out her envelope from the Sawtooth. She put the picture in between the bills. She counted the money. Principal Gunderson had slipped an extra hundred dollars into the stack. When she looked up, her father was still staring at the torn piece of photo left on the wall.

"Dad?"

"Get the jars," Hawley said. He turned away and finished taking down the rest. He stuffed everything inside the garbage bag, and then brought it outside.

Loo opened the back of the toilet, placed the heavy ceramic lid on the seat, then slid her hands inside the water and pulled out the licorice jars. She set them side by side on the counter. She looked for something to dry them off with, but Hawley had thrown away all the towels. She wiped the glass with some toilet paper, then brought the jars into the living room.

Hawley was on his knees in front of the bearskin rug. "Give them here," he said.

She thought he would open the jars and count the money, but instead he laid them end to end across the rug then started rolling them up inside, tucking the tail and moving toward the head, so that when he was finished, the bear's chin rested on top of the bundle.

"How did you know that I knew," she asked, "about the money?"

"I put a piece of Scotch tape on the back of the lid." Hawley tied the feet together until the money was rolled tight. "Okay, this is everything." He stood up and scratched his beard. Then he handed Loo the card that Lily had bought after she was born, the one that had hung in all their bathrooms, all these years. A cupcake with a single candle flickering. Loo opened it. The inside was still blank.

"Happy birthday," her father said. Then he wrapped his arms around the bear, and passed it into Loo's arms.

By the time they reached Dogtown it was nearly midnight. Hawley pulled up in front of Mabel Ridge's house but he did not get out of the truck.

"I can't believe you're leaving me here," said Loo.

"It's just for tonight," said Hawley.

Loo looked at the pineapple hanging on the door. She thought of their visit, long ago, when they'd first moved to Olympus, Hawley in his new shirt, Loo in her dress and chewed-up hair. "You wanted her to take me again," she said. "That time when you punched the radio."

Her father shook his head. "I didn't know what I was going to do."

"What if she'd let us in?"

Hawley and Loo sat there breathing together in their seats. The clock on the dashboard was an hour behind. They had never fixed it for daylight savings. Loo reached forward and pushed the buttons and spun the dial, moving the numbers out of the past and into the present. In that moment, it seemed like the most important thing she'd ever done.

"I wanted you to have family besides me," said Hawley. "A normal life."

"But we've never been normal," said Loo. "*I've* never been normal."

"Don't I know it."

Loo pulled her bag onto her lap.

"You have to come back. You have to promise."

But her father only said her name.

Loo got out and slammed the door. The moment she did, the door to Mabel Ridge's house opened. She walked up the path, hefting her bag on her shoulder, the motor of Hawley's truck idling behind her.

The old woman stepped onto the porch. She was wearing striped pajamas, with a hand-woven wool blanket wrapped around her shoulders. It took Loo only a moment to recognize the blanket from the loom. The one with the overshot pattern made of indigo. It was finished. And it made Mabel Ridge look like an Indian queen.

"Welcome back."

"It's just for one night," said Loo.

"That's what he said the last time," said Mabel Ridge. She eyed Loo's robe. "I like the dragons."

"This was my mom's."

"I know," said Mabel Ridge. Then she opened her arms and she hugged Loo with all her might, folding them both inside the woolen blanket. Loo tried to pull away but the old woman's grip only tightened, until finally the girl gave in and hugged her back.

"All right, let's get you settled." Mabel Ridge reached for the bag but Loo snatched it up, and as she did, Hawley's truck pulled away.

Loo turned and watched the red taillights flickering along the dark road. She thought, He's going to stop. He's going to stop at the corner and wait for me, just like he did when we stole the Firebird. Her fingers wrapped tightly around the handle of the bag, ready to run after him. But Hawley didn't even slow down. If anything, he just pressed harder on the gas, the exhaust pipe rattling out one last cough of smoke. The truck turned without signaling a direction, and then her father was gone for good.

Bullet Number Twelve

HAWLEY TOOK THE BOAT AT FIRST LIGHT. PICKED UP SOME SUPPLIES, drove out to the basin, then sat in his truck waiting in the dark, watching the fishermen load their trawlers and draggers and crabbers, gather bait and ice and slip cleats and pull up bumpers and crank motors and set out in the early gloom. After all the men had left, Hawley climbed down the ladder to the floating dock, where Jove's sailboat was tied. He pushed off silently, then started the engine and made his way into the harbor. By the time the sun peeked over the edge of the horizon, he was in open waters.

He'd brought his orange toolbox and the guns. His father's rifle, two shotguns, the long-range sniper and two handguns. The long guns were under the seats, covered by a blanket, the Glock was tucked under his belt and the Colt was in the pocket of his coat. There was a bag of extra ammunition next to the lifesaver and the bailer. He was wearing a bulletproof vest. It was as heavy as the guns. He'd also brought rubber gloves and industrial garbage bags and duct tape, a net and a boat hook, breathing masks and a bottle of Vicks.

Along the coast and near the shallows of Thacher Island, Hawley saw lobstermen checking their traps, hauling the algae-covered ropes up from the bottom of the sea. He passed a few charter boats heading to Jeffrey's Ledge, a high-end yacht from Boston and a whale-watch cruiser powering toward Stellwagen Bank, packed with yawning tourists. Three miles out, the other ships thinned and Hawley turned on the navigation system he'd installed with Jove, fixing his point on the radar.

It was fifteen miles to international waters, but now anyone wanting to conduct business had to go out at least fifty or more. The Coast Guard had doubled its patrols because of the EPA investigation, and it was causing a lot of trouble along the coast. Not only for the fishermen, but for anyone trading drugs or guns or anything else illegal out on the open ocean. At least that's what Pax had said, when Hawley tracked him down for the details on Jove's job. The buyer had been a collector from Reno. As far as Pax knew, the deal had gone through. He'd been paid in advance, and received no complaints from the buyer or seller. He'd received no word from Jove, either, before he disappeared.

The meeting spot had been a marker set 110 miles from shore and about 40 miles southeast of the Bitter Banks. *Easy money*, Jove had said, but now, as the land fell away and the sea got more wild and desolate, it did not seem easy at all. There was nothing in any direction, only the line where the horizon met the sky. It was like sailing through a desert, the water always shifting, the landscape changing with each blow of the wind. Jove's body would be long gone by now—eaten by sharks, or picked up by the current. But Hawley was hoping the marker was still there. He checked the coordinates that Pax had given him. He needed to see the place for himself. Figure out if he needed to make a new shopping list of names. Otherwise, he'd have to take Loo and keep running.

Another ten miles and the sailboat passed a cargo ship the length of an aircraft carrier, stretching across the surface like a giant guarding the edge of the world. Hawley rode the waves from the wake and shifted the motor to neutral. The boat floated easily, rising and falling. Once the freighter was past, he tied off the tiller, then scrambled over the bow to unfurl the jib and then the mainsail, hanging his weight against the rope. The wind drew the battens tight and the canvas filled with air. Then he cut the motor.

He'd forgotten how nice it could be, using only the power of the wind. Nothing but the sound of the waves slapping the sides of the hull and the soft echo of the halyards against the mast. It was humbling to be set against such a landscape, cutting through the miles that stretched above and below, layers of creatures of every size and shape passing beneath the sailboat's fragile hull on their way toward eating one another.

A large swell approached off the port side, and Hawley leaned on the tiller so the boat would face it head-on. The bow rose and then came out of the water, before landing hard with a smack into the hollow left behind after the wave had passed. Deep inside the hold Hawley heard something tumble and then set to scrambling. He drew the Colt and cocked it. The hatch opened and his daughter climbed out.

"Hi Dad."

"You've got to be kidding me." Hawley lowered the hammer, then returned the Colt to his pocket. He pushed the tiller starboard and set the boat into the wind. He let loose the sheets and the sails luffed, the ropes whipping like snakes as the boat drifted, then came to a stop. "How the hell did you get on board?"

"I snuck out Mabel's window after she went to sleep and drove the Firebird into town. If you didn't show I figured I'd just go back in the morning." The breeze was pushing her hair into her face. No matter how she tried to hold it back, the ends kept getting in her mouth. "You know his bunk is full of porn down there."

He'd left Loo at her grandmother's house. Just to be safe. And now it was all for nothing, even the old woman softening and thanking him on the phone. He'd finally done something to mend fences, and now Mabel Ridge was going to be pissed.

"I can't believe you took the car again."

"She promised to sign the title over to me if I came for Thanksgiving and Christmas. So technically it wasn't stealing this time."

"We're going back," said Hawley.

"But we've got to be close by now," said Loo. "And I brought sandwiches."

"I'm still turning around."

"Don't. Not yet. I'll do whatever you say." Loo took hold of her hair firmly with her fist. She pulled an elastic band out of her pocket and tied it back tightly, until all the strays were caught. "I want to be here with you, if you find him." Her face was determined. And so much like her mother.

In the past year Hawley had blinked once, twice, and his daughter had grown into a woman carrying her own secrets. He'd tried to protect her. Now he hoped only that Loo would not end up like him. Hawley took off his coat. He removed the bulletproof vest. "Put this on."

She slid her arms through. It was too big for her.

"I'll sink in this."

"Then you'll wear a life jacket, too."

He dug one of the orange life vests from under the side bench and zipped it open, wrapping his daughter in layers of fabric and foam.

"I look like the Michelin Man."

"That's the deal," said Hawley. "In or out?"

"In," said Loo, and then she climbed up onto the bow and took out her binoculars. "What are we looking for?"

"Anything that floats."

Hawley turned the boat away from the wind. He took hold of the sheets and the sails filled and he pulled until they held the perfect amount of air. The wind was from the southwest. The spray from the waves speckled their faces with salt. Loo cleared the long guns and the ammunition from the deck and stored them in the cabin to keep dry. Occasionally a gust would come up and the boat would heel too far, the side dipping into the water. But as soon as Hawley leaned his weight on the opposite rail, it would steady again.

As the hours passed they took turns steering and crawling down to the tiny head in the hold, a pump toilet that smelled of chemicals and piss. In the galley everything was miniaturized: a tiny sink, the pots and pans held in place with latches on the shelves, each cup and plate secure. Hawley opened the cupboard and found packages of ramen noodles and a giant tub of peanut butter. There were sleeves of saltines and a jar of iced-tea mix and some instant coffee. Under the sink was a tank of potable water, a boat horn, a box containing a flare gun and three bottles of whiskey.

He brought one of the bottles up on deck.

"Where'd you find that?"

"In the galley."

The wind had slowed, so Hawley started the engine again. Loo took the bottle and turned it over, as if she were looking for the price tag.

"We used to drink together when you were a baby," said Hawley.

"Whiskey?"

"Just a drop. It kept you from crying."

Loo unscrewed the cap and sniffed. It was strange for Hawley to think she had no memory of the lake house. What happened had happened to both of them, but was his to carry alone. He would never forget the tug on his finger, the silence and relief when she'd finally stopped screaming. Her tiny hand wrapped tightly around his, her eyes wide and focused and watching.

"I have to tell you something." Loo capped the bottle and slid it underneath the bench. She seemed suddenly nervous. "It's about Mary Titus."

"What about her?"

"People think you did it," said Loo. "The shooting at her place."

"Really." Hawley tried to keep his face serious.

"It's my fault," said Loo. "I gave Marshall one of your guns. For protection. And he shot up his own house."

Hawley pulled on the mainsheet until the sail was tight. "A real winner, your guy."

Loo ducked her head, embarrassed, and Hawley wished he hadn't said anything. He'd been relieved when he heard the boy had left town. But he knew that Loo was still hurting.

"When the police came I thought they were going to arrest you. I thought they'd traced the bullet."

"From the Beretta?" Hawley asked. When she looked surprised he said, "It was the only one missing."

"I should have told you," Loo said. "And I shouldn't have trusted him."

Hawley pretended to think this over. But he already knew everything she'd just said. Everything but Marshall shooting his own house.

He'd been following Loo ever since she was arrested. He'd treated it like any other job, as if his own daughter were a mark he was going to rub his finger against and smudge out. He dug through her clothes and books, looked at the bottom of her shoes to see where she'd been walking. He trailed her to work, watched her dodge the men eyeing her there, marked the sweat on her brow as she lifted platters and scrubbed dishes. He watched her go into Dogtown and come out with leaves in her hair. He'd seen her sitting on the roof and tracking stars through her telescope. And he'd uncovered the scrapbook of clippings about Lily's death, hidden inside a dress in her closet. Saw the ways she was trying to make sense of things, just as he had, taping up his memories in the bathroom. Hawley read every article and clipping, turned every page, then put the book right back where he'd found it.

"The police can only trace a bullet if they have the gun that fired it," he said at last. "They re-create the shot and compare. But I modified the barrel in the Beretta as soon as you put it back in the chest. Believe me. If I wanted to shoot your boyfriend, nobody would ever know it was me."

He didn't necessarily mean it as a joke. But Loo brightened, and Hawley knew he'd said just the right thing. She reached under the seat. She took out the whiskey again. This time, she opened the bottle and took a sip. Then she coughed and spit into the ocean.

"I don't know how you can drink this stuff."

"You get used to it."

She put the cap back on and held the bottle like a club. Like she was going to smash it against the boat, ready to christen the *Pandora* all over again. And then her eyes moved toward the horizon and her face changed. She focused on the water. "I see something."

Hawley grabbed the binoculars. It took awhile for him to find where she was pointing and then he did—something big was floating about a hundred meters north. It was hard to tell from the waves, but it looked like a body.

The engine kicked to life and Hawley turned the throttle as far as it would go. He pointed the bow straight and Loo crawled topside, focusing and refocusing the binoculars. She was hit by spray and wiped the lens on her jacket. As they got closer Hawley could see a mass covered in seaweed; there were arms and some kind of head. It was facedown in the water. And then he saw fur.

It was a giant bear. The kind Hawley used to win for Loo at cheap roadside carnivals. A huge pink stuffed animal filled with shredded foam and sawdust and hung high to lure in marks. Hawley would shoot out a paper star, and the carnies would hand over the prize, and Loo would stagger under the weight, refusing to let her father carry the bear and refusing to let go, shoving the animal into the seat next to them on the roller coaster, hugging the bear as they went up in the Ferris wheel and then strapping the bear into the car to go home. When they moved, there was never enough room to take it along. Hawley always promised to win another at the next carnival to make it up to her, and when he did, they left that bear behind, too. Now this waterlogged body seemed like a manifestation of all those abandoned animals, floating a hundred and ten miles out in international waters, in the middle of the Atlantic Ocean with a rope around its neck.

Hawley took hold of the stuffed animal and pulled it into the boat. The fur was a horrible fleshy color, the cheap, synthetic coat soaked through. Strips of shiny green kelp and brownish gunk caught around the arms and legs. The bear was missing one of its eyes, but the other remained—a clear plastic bubble with a small black disc that moved like a real eye, the iris slowly turning.

"Looks like our bearskin rug went out and got drunk," said Loo.

Hawley nodded. Just hours earlier he'd been rolling all their savings into that fur, wishing he could wrap it around himself and Loo and hide away from the world.

"How the hell did this get out here?"

Hawley pointed to the rope. It was tied tightly around the animal's neck and hung over the side of the sailboat into the water. He started pulling it up. He pulled and pulled and pulled, the rope getting thicker with algae the farther he went, until his hands were covered with green-and-black slime and he saw a ghostly shape rising through the shadows—an old wire lobster trap, filled with garbage.

"It must have washed out in a storm," said Loo.

"No," Hawley said. "It's a marker."

There were two lobsters in the trap, as well as a couple of crabs, but the rest was jammed with junk—bottles and bits of metal and stones and in the middle of all that something square and bright. A silver box, vacuum-sealed in plastic. Hawley pulled the lobsters out first, their tails flapping madly against the air, their claws raised, the antennae long and slippery. They were a good size, big enough to eat, but Hawley tossed them into the ocean, followed by the crabs, yanking each creature through the plastic netting. Then it was just the stones and the broken beer bottles and finally the box.

Loo handed him her knife and he cut through the plastic. It was thick as skin and twice as hard but eventually split in two. Hawley eased the box out. The sides were industrial-grade metal. The kind normally used on gun cases. There was a lock but it did not take long for Hawley to break it open with the knife. Then he flipped the side latches and opened the lid. The interior was lined with black velvet cloth, still perfectly dry. And in the center was a gold pocket watch.

Hawley picked up the watch and turned it over. The metal was cold as ice in his hand. There was an etching of a deer on the cover, its hooves raised in midflight. The deer was being hunted, an arrow in its side. He pressed down on the winding key and the shell flipped open. Set within the face were four smaller dials, marking the year, month, date, hour, minute, second. Hawley took a breath, and once again he was sliding his hand into the pocket of Maureen Talbot's wedding gown and pulling out this same watch, like a magic trick reaching across time. He touched the key and the lid split in two, and there was the star chart, with its tiny flecks of diamond and sapphire, catching the last of the afternoon light. He pressed the heart of the shell against his ear.

The watch was ticking.

The floor of the boat had opened beneath them and he was falling through layers of his own life.

"Dad," said Loo. "Dad."

And then Hawley heard the boat.

It was half a mile off. A cruiser, maybe thirty feet, and the wake behind was wide and open, white froth streaming in lines and breaking the pattern of the waves. The boat was headed straight for them. And it was coming fast. There was no way they would outrun it. Not with the wind dead like it was.

"Go below," said Hawley. "Get the guns."

Loo scrambled into the cabin and came back with guns and the bag of ammunition, and together they started loading.

"Who is it?"

"I don't know."

"What are we going to do?"

"We're going to be careful."

The pink bear was still tossed facedown in the bottom of the boat. It was the same size as Loo. Hawley's hands started to shake. He should have turned the boat around. He should have followed his instincts and hit the road the instant he got home from the police station.

Loo peered through the binoculars. "It looks like two people on board."

Hawley tucked the Glock back into his belt. He grabbed his father's rifle and hid it under one of the blankets. "Take the shotgun and the sniper rifle and stay in the cabin," he said. "Get in there before they see you."

"Maybe they're fishermen," Loo said. But still, she ducked into the hold.

The cruiser pushed steadily toward them. When it was in range it began slowing its engines, the foam diminishing into bubbles. Hawley could smell the briny scent of the waves as they slapped against the sailboat, rocking the hull. He cut the idling motor and shifted his weight, trying to keep steady. Gasoline leaked into the water, spreading slick swirls of color across the surface.

The first man was at the wheel. He was older and had a military buzz cut, broad shoulders and a face dimpled like a potato. A nose like a broken door hanging off its hinges. It had been years since their fight at the diner, but Hawley knew at once it was Ed King. The old boxer wasn't wearing a hat and his head and face and neck were burned bright red from the sun. Hawley could see the flaking on his crooked nose, the ring of white skin by his collar.

The other man in the boat was Jove.

Hawley's friend was still wearing his captain's cap and those special boat shoes. His face was busted and both eyes were black and he was holding on to his side like his ribs were broken. But he hadn't been killed yet. And that was something.

The cruiser slowed and the grinding roar of the engine stopped, and the boat and the men continued to drift forward, the momentum bringing them along the starboard side.

"Sam Hawley," King called out. "We've been waiting for you."

The wind picked up and the mainsail fluttered. Together the boats bobbed up and down.

Hawley said, "Aren't you supposed to be in prison?"

"I got an early release, for good behavior. And a favor or two. People always need favors." The old boxer came over to the railing and leaned on it. He kept an automatic trained on Jove. "You look the same."

"You don't."

King put his hand on his thick waist. He laughed but it wasn't a funny laugh and nobody else laughed with him. Hawley tried to figure things but they were hard to figure.

"Came looking for your friend?"

Hawley's eyes shifted to Jove. "That's right."

"Me, too," said King. "A real good pal he was, sending me away for fifteen years. Just to cover his own mistakes. And yours."

"Nobody forced you to kill those folks in Alaska. So you paid for it. You did your time."

"Like you did yours?" King asked.

Hawley didn't answer.

"So high and mighty," said King. "But you're just another pair of dirty hands. All I had to do was dangle this job. Offer enough money. And wait. And I've gotten very good at waiting."

Jove glanced at the porthole where Loo was hiding. A moment later he seemed not to be looking anywhere, only blinking at the orange streaks that stretched across the sky. His ruined face made all of the holes in Hawley's skin start itching.

"I never thought I'd see you again," Jove said.

King clapped him on the back. "Your friend tried to convince me you wouldn't come looking for him. But I had a feeling you would. So we cut his boat loose near the Banks and let those Whale Heroes call it in to the Coast Guard. Then we came back here. It gave us a chance to have a nice long talk."

The sun had reached the edge of the horizon, and the sky began to fill with pink, turning the clouds a dark magenta. King's eye was twitching against the light, and Hawley remembered the same twitch on the boxer's face at the diner, when he'd been looking at Lily. Back before Hawley had even touched her hand.

King was staring at Hawley now that same way, like he couldn't believe his luck. So many years had passed and the boxer had the same tell. He pressed the automatic to the back of Jove's head. "Let's start by giving me your guns."

Hawley took the Glock from the back of his pants and threw it into the cruiser.

"And the one in your coat."

Hawley removed the Colt and tossed that next. The only weapons left now were the rifle under the blanket and the long guns down in the cabin with Loo. The wind picked up and the boats began to drift. King made Hawley toss a line, then Jove tied the rope to the bow of the cruiser.

"Now the bear. Stick the watch inside and send it over."

Hawley put the timepiece back into the metal case, then back into the plastic. He used Loo's knife to cut a hole in the bear's chest and jammed the bag where its heart should be. The stuffing was surprisingly soft, bits of cotton and rags, though heavy when he lifted it. Hawley swung the bear back and let go. The animal spun in the air between the two boats, hit the bow of the cruiser, and landed with a splash in the water. Jove stabbed it with a boat hook, then dragged the body on board.

King put his hand inside the bear, feeling around. He extracted the plastic bag. He opened the case and palmed the watch, rubbing the gold clamshell with the tips of his fingers.

"Biggest bait I've ever used," he said. "But it was worth it for this." King slipped the watch into his pocket. He led Jove to the edge of the cruiser.

"Time to take your bear and go home, Jove."

"You mean jump?"

"That's exactly what I mean."

Jove lifted the soggy stuffed animal. He climbed over the rail, dragging the toy behind him, then stood on the edge in his expensive windbreaker and ridiculous hat and special loafers he'd bought and been so proud of. He looked at Hawley, his face a mixture of apology and relief. And then King slid the automatic to the center of his back and pulled the trigger. The bullet went through Jove and then it went through the bear, the stuffed animal's chest bursting forth in a snowy cloud of foam and fur. Then Jove and the bear both fell into the water.

There was a muffled cry from inside the cabin. King looked at Hawley and then at the sailboat, but before he could do anything else or shoot again, Hawley dove beneath the seats and pulled the blanket off the rifle.

King spun his automatic and strafed the side of the sailboat. Hawley ducked down, crouching out of sight. He could hear the bullets hitting the wood and the porthole windows shattering. He counted the shots. When the mag was finished King ran for the cabin. That's when Hawley stood and raised the long gun and fired. He watched the boxer collapse and then fall down the ladder into the hold.

He crouched back down and waited.

No more shots.

He leaned over the side of the boat. "Loo!" he cried. "You all right? Loo!"

His daughter slid the shotgun out the broken window and started shooting directly into the hull of the motorboat. There was a pause as she reloaded and then two more giant blasts followed, ripping holes into the fiberglass of the cruiser, opening it up for the ocean to pour in.

It was like they were one person, not two. When he thought, Loo acted. She continued reloading and blasting holes into the sinking cruiser, while Hawley used the boat hook to catch the back of Jove's windbreaker and drag him to the leeward side. He reached under his friend's arms and pulled both him and the bear into the boat. Jove's eyes were still moving, but he was bleeding badly. Hawley pressed his hand against the wound, the blood pumping out with each heartbeat between his fingers.

The door to the cabin opened and there was Loo, carrying Hawley's orange toolbox. "What do you need?"

"Israeli bandage," said Hawley.

Beside them, the cruiser continued to take on water. There was a thud as a wave spun the bow and knocked into the sailboat. The whole deck tilted and Loo dropped to her knees. She threw down the case. She grabbed a sealed package and ripped it open.

"Is he going to die?"

"Probably," said Hawley.

"Fuck you," Jove groaned.

"Ha," said Hawley. "See?"

Together they got the bandage around him. Hawley tightened it as best he could. Something glittered and caught the light. He looked at his daughter.

"There's glass in your hair," he said.

"The cabin windows got blown out." Loo raised her arm and tiny fragments fell sparkling to the deck like crystals.

"I've got to check on King. Stay here," said Hawley. "Keep pressure on the dressing."

"All right," said Loo. She put her hands where his had been and her eyes did not leave the blood running out all over Jove's windbreaker, beading up and streaming off onto the floorboards.

Hawley ducked under the mainsail. The cruiser was foundering, tilted to its side but not yet underwater. The sailboat was wedged against the broken hull. It was close enough to climb across and Hawley did, the fiberglass echoing as he landed. The door to the cabin where King had disappeared was still open. He picked up the Glock and the Colt from where he'd thrown them on the deck. He started down the ladder. The cabin was flooded, food and clothing and garbage floating in the tight space, which was foul-smelling and dark except for a single hatch at the tip of the bow.

Hawley waded through the wreckage toward the opening. When he reached the hatch he found a torn piece of fabric on the hinge. Then he heard music. At first he thought it was coming from a radio, and then he recognized the song. It was Debussy, each note both hopeful and sad, played by man-made gears buried deep inside a timepiece, so that the bearer would know the marking of an hour.

Hawley scrambled through the hatch, stumbling against the rail as the deck heaved and tilted. The old boxer had crawled on top of the roof above the cabin. His shadow stretched across the mainsail of the *Pandora*. A shadow in the shape of every imaginary monster that had ever lived underneath Loo's childhood bed. Every nightmare that Hawley had soothed and rocked away from his little girl and then tucked back inside his own dreams. King's shadow pointed a gun and the boom echoed across the water, and beneath the canvas Hawley saw Loo doubling over. She stumbled and tried to stand and then another blast came and she was rolling over the side of the boat and Hawley saw her fall into the water. His daughter. His Loo.

Gone.

King's shirt was ripped from going through the hatch and his hair was wet from the water but there wasn't a spot of blood on him. Hawley never missed, but he had missed him somehow. King was holding up the handgun he'd shot Jove with and shot Loo with and now he was shooting Hawley with it, too. The bullet hit above Hawley's heart and below his shoulder, and right off Hawley felt the difference, how this bullet did not slide through his body like a visitor but instead tore and split and sliced as if it were building a home for itself out of his insides, as if it intended to stay and put down roots.

Hawley's hands fumbled for the Colt, but King jumped down from the roof and knocked it away before he could pull the trigger, and then the cruiser tilted as the men wrestled and both their guns fell into the water. He could feel the heat of the old boxer winding up and then the man was punching Hawley, first in the stomach and then in the face and then where he had shot him, each blow landing like a burning ember across Hawley's scarred body. He remembered what Jove had told him about the men King fought, how their minds would be sheared into a place of forgetting, a place where they no longer remembered who they loved or why they loved them.

Hawley struggled to his knees and threw himself into King and knocked the older man down. He crawled to the edge of the boat to look for Loo in the water but there was only water, only waves, and then King was on him again and threw one last blow to the side of Hawley's head and Hawley felt his skull crack and then he saw stars. Bright and shining sparks of light that broke into flames and streaked through the night that swept over him.

And the stars began to fall together, to pull and form a body that sparked and shone into a greater brightness and out of that brightness stepped Lily. She was standing behind King, her long black hair dripping wet, as if she had decided not to drown and had instead been waiting all these years for just the right moment to rise from the water.

"Get away from him," she said.

And like a miracle, the beating stopped. The shadow of King moved and Hawley could feel the air on his face again. He could taste the blood running down the back of his throat. He coughed. He listened.

"Over there."

Lily was holding Hawley's father's rifle and she was pointing it at King's chest. She backed the boxer to the edge of the sinking boat. She kept enough distance so that he wouldn't be able to grab the rifle if he lunged or tried to snatch it away. Her finger was on the trigger and her elbow was tucked in tight and the grip was braced against her shoulder and the barrel was steady enough to balance a quarter and the sight was leveled up for a shot to the head. Hawley had taught her that. She remembered. She knew it all, he thought. His girl.

"The watch."

King slipped the gold out from his pocket.

"Throw it in the water."

"What?"

"You heard me."

The boxer glared at her. "This piece is priceless. One of a kind."

"It's a stupid watch." She set her eye to the scope.

King turned his face as if he couldn't bear to look and dropped the watch over the rail, the gold catching the light and flashing, a beating heart lost between the waves, turning end over end until it disappeared into the gloom.

"Your turn."

"I don't know how to swim."

"Then you better hope the Coast Guard finds you. Here." She threw him a life jacket. King slipped it over his head. Pulled the buckle around his waist. He was still eyeing the place where the watch had gone in. Hawley could see him wondering if he should dive for it, if there was a chance to snatch the gold before it hit the bottom of the sea.

"Now what?"

"Now this."

She took aim with the rifle and shot King in the arm. His punching arm. The one he'd used to beat Hawley. The man screamed. He clutched at the wound with his fingers. Blood ran down his elbow and splattered the deck. "What the hell was that for?"

"For the sharks," said Loo. Then she spun the rifle in her hands, took hold of the barrel like it was a baseball bat and swung the butt of the gun with all those kill marks against the side of King's face, a blow as hard as any right hook. The boxer stumbled and she kicked him in the ass with her steel-toed boots as he went over the edge into the water.

Loo hurried over to her father. She wrapped his arm around her shoulder and then hefted him to his feet and dragged him back to the *Pandora*. She cut the rope and pushed the cruiser off their bow. As the boats drifted apart, she kept the rifle trained on King, watching him try and fail to climb on top of the cruiser, which bubbled and sucked as it sank. At twenty yards, Loo started the engine. It caught and sparked. She shifted gears, and the propeller turned, and they were moving away from the toppled cruiser. Loo took hold of the throttle and turned it all the way up and then there was just the rumbling beneath them and the movement of the waves and the sound of the wooden hull cutting through water. Loo tied the tiller in place to keep them on a straight path. Then she went back to Hawley.

"You missed him," she said. "I can't believe you missed."

"Check for an exit wound," said Hawley.

She turned him on his side. It felt like a giant weight pressed against his lungs. Her fingers ran over his back and shoulder. "There's a lot of blood."

"Bullets," Hawley said, "usually go right through me."

"This one didn't."

She looked for bandages. She tore them open with her teeth. She pressed the cloth to the hole in his chest. He knew that she wasn't Lily anymore but Loo didn't seem like herself, either.

"You're not hurt?" he asked.

She tapped the vest he had given her.

Hawley closed his eyes in relief. He pressed against the pain branching through every nerve, threading a thousand needles.

"What about Jove?"

They both looked where Jove had fallen, his body tangled with the giant bear. His face was pale but he was still breathing. Loo checked his pulse.

"I don't know what to do next."

"We'll figure it out." Hawley tried to grab her hand but his fingers slid. She was drenched. Shivering. "Loo," he said. "You did so good. You did everything right."

"I couldn't kill him."

Hawley squeezed her palm. "I'm glad."

There was something wrong with her face. He couldn't tell at first but then he knew.

"Get the bottle," said Hawley.

"You're dying," she said.

"No I'm not," said Hawley.

Loo pressed another bandage against his chest. Then she reached underneath the seat. The whiskey was still there. She unscrewed the cap and lifted it to his mouth. He could smell the animal fear on her breath.

"No," said Hawley. "It's for you."

Loo took a swig. She coughed but she took another.

"There," he said. "Still crying?"

"No."

"Good. Now take us home."

The boat was rocking but Hawley felt still. The world was righting itself, turning sky to water. Water to sky. He'd spent his whole life pushing upstream, struggling and cutting through the current, forcing himself over waterfalls and dams, and at long last he'd finally stopped beating his ragged tail against the rocks and was sliding in the right direction. Moving with the world instead of fighting against it.

Why didn't I do this sooner, he thought.

Loo slapped his face. "Stop *dying*," she said.

"Troublemaker," said Hawley. "Your mother would never approve."

Loo

Night came down. In less than an hour Loo could barely see the shadow of her father in the boat. Across the sky was a multitude of stars. There was no moon.

They had lost their radio and navigation. The system box in the cabin was hit when the portholes were blown out. With Hawley's help she'd used the last gasp of the setting sun to take an initial bearing, but now they'd been traveling for miles in the dark and Loo sensed they'd fallen off course. There was a flashlight in the hold and for half an hour she had held it pressed to her shoulder with her chin while her fingers worked, trying to reconnect the wires, before she gave up and crawled back onto the deck and took the captain's seat and wrapped her hand around the tiller. She did not know which way to turn or if she should turn at all. But a decision had to be made and there was no one else and so she drove blindly into the dark, hoping she was going in the right direction.

Loo covered Jove with one of the blankets. She'd packed his wound and given him some morphine for the pain. His hands were cold when she touched them. She was afraid that he would die before they reached shore. Her clothes were still wet from going overboard. When the wind picked up she started to shiver. She was the only one in the boat without a bullet in her body.

"Lift his shoulders," said Hawley.

Loo got another blanket and pushed it beneath Jove's back so that he was at an angle. "How long do you think he has?"

"Not long."

"I could shoot another flare."

"There's only one left," said Hawley. "Save it until you see some lights. We'll run into the Coast Guard eventually."

"How are you feeling?"

"I'm fine," said Hawley. But when she pointed the flashlight he didn't look fine. His face was pale and his eyes were unfocused. She took his hand and it was as cold as Jove's. She found another blanket in the hold and covered him. She got another pressure bandage and wrapped it around his chest. She checked his pulse. It was weak but it was there, a soft signal beating beneath his skin.

"Just rest for a while."

He didn't argue. He closed his eyes.

Loo got the binoculars from the cabin. She climbed onto the bow, turned left, then right, but it was like looking into nothingness—two black circles of glass. The only thing of any consequence in any direction were the stars.

She had never seen so many. The dome of sky spread out unencumbered and uninterrupted by landscape, by trees or mountains or houses. The heavens fell down like a bell jar, meeting the edge of the earth, a stunning multitude of galaxies and satellites and distant suns so bright she could not find the North Star among them. Even the planets were lost in the hazy spread of the Milky Way. Loo wished she had her star map, with its diagrams and spinning circles, but it was packed in her suitcase, left behind at Mabel Ridge's house. For years she had carried the planisphere with her from place to place, studied its contours in motel rooms and hotel rooms, in diners and libraries, in the back of classrooms and her father's truck, under the bearskin rug and in the bathtub and finally on the roof of her own home. Tracing the patterns of constellations. Memorizing their names. Finding comfort in the way that infinite space could be fixed and charted.

Loo closed her eyes. It was not that different from having them open. The heavens were still there, beneath her eyelids. Tiny sparks. She could smell the salt. She could feel the boat rocking. She listened to the waves and her father's shallow breath and slid her hands across her face. The map was inside of her. She knew these stars. They had been drawn across her own body.

When Loo opened her eyes and looked through her fingers, the darkness seemed brighter. Clearer. She watched the froth of the sailboat's wake disappearing, then lifted her chin and searched through the radiants for the first constellation she had ever learned: Ursa Major. The Great Bear's back branched off from the four stars shaping its body, pointing the way toward the more hidden Ursa Minor. The Little Bear resembled the Great Bear the way a child resembles her parent. A smaller configuration of the same parts. A mirror image with the contents slightly shifted but containing something more powerful than size or strength at the end of its tail, a faithful constant, a guiding principle: the North Star.

Now that Polaris was in her sights, Loo felt her heart calm to a single purpose. Like the moment in Dogtown when she discovered those giant, unmovable, erratic rocks. The stars were signposts, just like the words carved in the stones, and she could find her way by moving from one to the other, just as she'd traveled through the woods from TRUTH to COURAGE to NEVER TRY NEVER WIN.

Loo raised her fist and held it toward the horizon. Starting at zero, she began to count, using her own body as the compass. Ten degrees for each fit of her knuckles into the sky. The North Star set at ninety. They were around forty-three degrees north. And they needed to head west. Loo pushed the tiller hard alee, putting Ursa Minor firmly on the starboard side of the boat.

The sails luffed and filled with wind. On the bench beside her, Hawley shifted.

"I know where we are," she said. "At least, I think I do." The world had suddenly come into focus, and now all of the constellations were making themselves known to her. Perseus and Pegasus. Cetus and Hercules.

She could not see her father's face, only his chest rising and falling. Every moment that he did not speak made her more anxious. She pointed overhead. "That star is Vega, I think. It has a blue color, and it's one of the brightest, next to Polaris. It's part of Lyra, the harp that belonged to Orpheus. He played it to convince Hades to release his wife from the underworld. Are you listening? Dad?"

"I know that story," said Hawley. "He shouldn't have looked back."

She hadn't taken off the bulletproof vest. Underneath her clothes were damp, her skin covered with goosebumps. Her body was bruised and her ribs hurt whenever she took a breath. The impact of the bullets had been absorbed directly into her body. She could still feel the vibration deep inside her bones, the energy of the blast that forced her over the edge of the boat, the wind knocked out of her lungs. She was so scared she couldn't feel the cold and then she did and she was surrounded by white water. Not knowing which way was up or down. Then her father's life jacket had lifted her back to the surface. And with her first gasp of air, she'd felt the opposite of dead. She'd felt real and full of power, the same way she'd felt staggering out of the ocean and breaking Marshall's finger—as if all her fear had been nailed shut tight inside a barrel.

"Your mother," Hawley said. His breath was ragged.

"Tell me something about her," Loo said. "Something I don't know."

Hawley tugged at his beard. "Well," he said. "One time, she shot me."

"What? Where?"

"Here." Hawley pointed to the back of his leg. "It was a perfect shot. But on normal days she couldn't hit a target. I had to scare her to get her to focus. Like when you first started."

"Some trick."

"It worked," said Hawley. "We wouldn't be here now if it didn't."

She adjusted the tiller. Pulled the ropes. "I should check on Jove."

"Loo." Hawley spoke softly. He reached out and took her hand. "Jove's dead. He's been dead for the last twenty minutes."

Loo pulled away. "Why didn't you say anything?"

"I didn't want to scare you."

She got to her knees. She felt Jove's wrist and pressed her fingers to his neck. It was like touching the slabs of meat in the walk-in freezer at the Sawtooth. A solidity beneath the skin. Jove had lost his hat and his hair was in tangles. Loo patted it down, then covered his scarred face with the blanket. She got back into the captain's seat.

"Do you need a drink?"

"No."

"Well, I do," said Hawley.

She found the bottle, raised it to his lips. Watched him swallow. Hawley coughed and wiped his mouth with the back of his hand. There was blood on his lips.

"We should say something," she said.

"Like what?"

"I don't know. A blessing. Like at the christening."

"It won't help him now."

"Not for Jove," said Loo. "For us."

Hawley dug inside his pocket. "I don't know any prayers."

Loo thought of Jove's sleeping bag, the pattern of ducks on the inside and the hole that leaked feathers all over their house. For weeks after he'd left, she'd found tiny clusters of down in the corners of the porch, woven into the fabric of their rug, even in the cupboards, between the plates and the coffee cups. That same sleeping bag was in the hold now. She had crawled on top of it when she slid the barrel of the shotgun out the window, and a cloud of white fluff had ripped loose from the seam.

"Help me with this," said Hawley.

Loo took the tobacco pouch from him. She peeled off one of the rolling papers, tucked in a pinch of thick, sweet-smelling leaves. She licked the ends of the paper, spooling the cigarette together, twisting the ends.

"We can talk about him," said Hawley. "And share what we remember. Then after we die maybe other folks will talk about him, too. Or they won't, and no one will remember him. And his story will end there."

"That's terrible."

"It's just the way it is," said Hawley.

On the port side, there was something riding on the water, bobbing on the waves. A ghost that dove and rose and shook its beak until she saw that it was a seagull. Catching the starlight on its feathers. Another gull circled past and then landed close to the first, leaving a crest on the surface of the water.

"What are the birds doing out this far?" Loo asked.

"They must be following something," said Hawley. "A trawler, maybe."

Loo stood on top of the bench. She scanned the dark horizon. But there was nothing. No lights. No land.

Hawley coughed again. He tried to sit up. "I got us into such a mess."

"It's all right."

"It's not," said Hawley.

The cigarette she'd just rolled was still in her hand. She put it between his lips. She took his lighter and lit the end. The tip glowed red. He blew smoke then glanced over at Jove, hidden beneath the blanket.

"I don't want you to feel responsible if something goes wrong."

"You're my father," said Loo.

"I know," Hawley said. "But I've been in your place before. And you can't save everyone."

The motor rumbled beneath the deck. She could feel the gears turning. Each piece working together to make the engine run.

"Watch me," said Loo.

She used her fist to measure the sky. She counted to Polaris. She pushed the tiller until the boat jibed, the wind whipping around hard and snapping the sail.

"What are you doing?" said Hawley.

"Heading to the Banks. It's closer than the shore. The *Athena* will be there and they should have doctors on board. Scientists, at least. And a radio."

"Your boyfriend, too," said Hawley.

"He's not," said Loo. "Not that. Not anymore."

Hawley threw the end of his cigarette overboard. "Well, I hope you'll keep trying."

"Trying for what?"

"To be with someone."

It was as if he'd been listening to her inner thoughts. As if he knew Loo was afraid that no one would ever love her.

"You told me you weren't going to die."

"I'm not," he said.

"Then shut up." Loo clicked on the flashlight again. She checked his bandages. They weren't holding. She opened another roll of gauze and wrapped it around and around his shoulder. She dug through the med kit searching for anything else that could help. She tried not to look at Jove's body, stretched out beside Hawley on the deck, turning stiff and cold beneath the blanket.

"Roll me another cigarette."

"You shouldn't be smoking," Loo said, but grabbed the pouch anyway. She lifted one of the thin pieces of paper and stuffed it with tobacco, her fingers shaking, just as they had when Hawley first put a gun in her hands.

"There's a list of my deposit boxes in the licorice jars. I put the keys in there, too."

Loo flicked the lighter, cupped it with her hand, and for a moment her father's face was lit with dancing shadows across his jaw and circling his eyes, so that his features looked like parts of a broken mask, and then the flame went out and there was nothing but his cigarette. She watched the ember glow and fade and she inhaled her father's smoke and she was back in the woods behind their house five years ago. She felt the rifle in her arms. She turned her head and listened. Hawley was leaning against a rock in the sun. He was telling Loo to name her target.

"The rest of the money is in a trust. You'll get it when you turn eighteen. The lawyer has all the instructions."

"Shut up, shut up, shut up!" Loo cried.

The motor dropped out and the world went quiet. Loo checked the gasoline. They were low. She decided to save it. The wind was picking up and the sails were taut. When the boat heeled, Loo pressed her own weight against the starboard side. She kept the bow pointed north.

"We should have bought a boat like this," said Hawley. "We could have had picnics. It would have been nice."

"We have one now," said Loo.

"I guess you're right."

There were more birds gathering, gray phantoms bobbing in the water and circling above, riding the air currents, then darting up toward the stars and spiraling downward. The wind was different and the air had changed. It smelled like an island. Seaweed and barnacles. The Banks, Loo thought. They must be getting closer.

"I'm glad you threw away the watch," said Hawley.

"How much was it worth?"

"Too much."

His words were starting to slur. Hawley pulled on his cigarette, then lifted it from his mouth. Released the smoke like he was releasing years of his own life. Then the ash was falling, the paper tip crackling and curling, and the birds all rose from the ocean at once, flapping and calling to one another. Ahead, Loo saw the waves flatten into a slick pool, and then something rose out of that flatness, a crusted, pale hump of earth that split open and discharged a mist of ancient, pressurized air.

"Dad." Loo pushed hard against the tiller. "There's something out there."

Hawley turned to face the water. Whatever the creature was, it had fallen back under the surface. Loo swallowed hard. She had spent so much time focused on the stars overhead that she had ignored what might be below them. Now she imagined the deep distance beneath the hull, miles upon miles of water, and all the life that was living there in the dark. Animals that had no need for light, no need for air, no need to come to the surface except to feed.

A rush of bubbles surrounded the boat. There was a sucking noise, of water being displaced, and a whale broke surface right next to the sailboat, sending a blast of spray directly off the port side. A rush of brackish water fell down over their heads. Loo threw her arms across her father, and when the shower ended she reeked of algae and slippery rocks and Hawley's waders and the powerful joints of mussels and clams that kept the halves of their shells snapped tight together. It was the scent of water meeting land. It was the whale that smelled like an island.

She could tell from the glow of fins beneath the waves that it was a humpback. The rest of its body was nothing but a giant silhouette, a shadow circling the boat and nudging the hull. Loo gripped the tiller. She knew that whales could dive for forty minutes. Live whole lives between each inhale and exhale. But this whale stayed close. As if it were making up its mind about Hawley and Loo.

She took a breath. She let half of it out. She waited. And waited. And then she remembered the whale's heart. The one made of red and pink molded plastic that she had climbed into at the museum long ago. Each chamber had been a separate room where Loo had felt safe and protected, the aorta a tunnel leading to a whole new world. How small everything else must seem, she thought, when your heart is big enough for someone else to crawl through. She put her hand on her own chest. Felt the life inside her pushing back against her own skin.

"Dad," she said. She needed to tell Hawley about this. She needed him to know.

And then all at once the whale's open mouth pushed through the waves, its rostrum crusted with barnacles, the figurehead of a lost and forgotten shipwreck returning from the sunken depths. Loo could see the baleen lining the inner edge of its jaw, like the comb on Mabel Ridge's giant loom. The whale turned and there was its eye, black and shining beneath heavy folds of skin, set above the jagged grooves of its thick, expansive throat. She could not tell if the whale was looking at her. She could not tell if it was thinking anything at all. The creature rolled sideways, a rotating school bus, and lifted its pectoral fin high in the air and then it spun easily and dove, showing the full running slick of its long back, until there was only the fluke rising, the tail's ragged edge flecked with white, bending and scraping the surface of the heavens and then plunging deep, until all that was left was a rippling circle, that widened as it reached the *Pandora*.

The seagulls moved off, heading north. Loo pulled tight on the mainsheet. She set a course and followed the birds and the whale. A hundred yards ahead she saw the spout dimly against the stars. On the next surfacing Loo could hear only the blow. The tight noise of air released.

On the opposite bench, Hawley's cigarette had gone out. Loo scrambled over and pressed her ear to his chest, felt his throat with her fingers. His heart was still there. Still beating. Loo's face and hands came away wet with blood.

She leaned over the side of the boat. She touched her palm to the surface of the ocean. There were tiny things shimmering there in the water. Phosphorescence stirred up from the depths by the whale. Dino-flagellates and phytoplankton sending out an ethereal, muted green pulse that mixed with the reflection of the stars above, all the heroes and legends in the sky. The light was strong enough to cut a path through the swells. Bright enough for Loo to watch the blood leaving her skin. She lifted her head and saw a string of beacons, blinking in the distance. There was a boat. And then another. And then another.

"We're here," said Loo. "We made it."

She grabbed the flare. The plastic piece felt flimsy and light, even after she jammed in the cartridge. The gun was like a toy in her hands. A weapon transformed into a thing of wonder. She climbed onto the bow of the boat. She clung to the mainstay. She tried to get as high as she could, to set her sights in the right direction.

Her father's voice came out of the darkness.

He asked her, "What are you going to shoot?"

"Everything," said Loo. And she raised her arm and pulled the trigger.

Acknowledgments

The journey to this book was a long one and I have many people to thank. My parents, Hester and William Tinti, who continue to inspire me with their steadfast support and love. My sisters, Hester and Honorah, for always having my back and bringing Owen, Phelan, Isabelle and Geno into my life. Helen Ellis and Ann Napolitano for keeping the faith. My One Story family: Maribeth Batcha, Devin Emke, Patrick Ryan, Will Allison, Karen Friedman, Adina Talve-Goodman, Amanda Faraone, Lena Valencia, and all of our supporters, volunteers and authors. The amazing Dani Shapiro, Michael Maren, Antonio Sersale, Carla Sersale, Jacob Maren, Jim Shepard, Karen Shepard, Sirenlanders past and present and our dearly departed Franco. My New York Family: Yuka, Kareem, Maya and Saya. Kate Gray, for oceans and oceans. Ruth Ozeki, Ann Patchett, Richard Russo, Karen Russell and Meg Wolitzer for their generous words. Deborah Landau and all the staff and students at NYU's Creative Writing Program. Ruth Cohen and the

American Museum of Natural History for letting me crawl inside the whale's heart. Rahna Reiko Rizzuto, Dan Chaon, Willy Vlautin, Josh Wolf Shenk, Leigh Newman, Anna Solomon, and all the folks in the Poker Gang, for their early reads, friendship and advice. Joe Lewis and Matthew Cheney for sharing their gun expertise. Brooklyn Creative League, The Center for Fiction, the Ellen Levine Fund for Writers, The New York Community Trust, the Civitella Ranieri Foundation, Aspen Words, Catto Shaw Foundation and Hedgebrook for providing shelter in a storm of doubt. The Borg and the Erratics, who showed me how to draw my boundaries. Lynda Barry for *One! Hundred! Demons!* E. L. Doctorow for singing "Bye Bye Blackbird." Nina Collart for the beach in winter. Amy O'Neill Houck and James Houck for Alaska. *Tin House*, for taking a chance on "Bullet #2," and Otto Penzler and Lisa Scottoline for *Best American Mystery Stories*. A big, giant, round of drinks for the brilliant visionary Susan Kamil, the mighty editor Noah Eaker, and everyone at The Dial Press who wove a red carpet for this novel with their bare hands: Gina Centrello, Sally Marvin, Maria Braeckel, Theresa Zoro, Susan Corcoran, Jessica Bonet, Leigh Marchant, Avideh Bashirrad, Emma Caruso, Dhara Parikh, Allyson Lord, Kelly Chian, Benjamin Dreyer, Caitlin McCaskey, Anastasia Whalen, Michael Kindness, David Underwood, Ruth Liebmann, Sherry Virtz, Ron Shoop, Michele Sulka and so many more—you are a constellation of excellence. The Marsh Agency, Abner Stein Agency, Caspian Dennis, Jill Gillett and Geoffrey Sanford for introducing Hawley and Loo to the rest of the world. And finally, one thousand loaves of gingerbread for Aragi, Inc., an agency that feels like a home, a team of writers and artists who resemble blood relatives, Duvall Osteen, who keeps us all in line, and Nicole Aragi, my tea-drinking warrior, who never stopped believing I would find the words.

THE TWELVE LIVES OF SAMUEL HAWLEY

HANNAH TINTI

Top 5 Lessons from Samuel Hawley

1. NEVER HIDE ANYTHING IN YOUR UNDERWEAR DRAWER.

2. MAKE SURE YOU TAKE OUT ALL OF THE SECURITY CAMERAS.

3. DON'T POINT A GUN AT ANYTHING YOU DON'T WANT TO SHOOT.

4. TAKE A BREATH. LET HALF OF IT OUT.

5. EVERYTHING BREAKS IF YOU HIT IT HARD ENOUGH.

The

TWELVE LIVES

of

SAMUEL HAWLEY

. . .

HANNAH TINTI

A READER'S GUIDE

A Conversation Between Karen Russell and Hannah Tinti

KAREN RUSSELL's debut novel, *Swamplandia!*, was chosen by *The New York Times* as one of the Ten Best Books of 2011, was the winner of the 2012 New York Public Library Young Lions Fiction Award, and was named a Pulitzer Prize finalist. Russell has been featured in *The New Yorker's* 20 Under 40 list, and was chosen as one of *Granta's* Best Young American Novelists. She is a Guggenheim Fellow and a 2013 MacArthur Fellow. She is also the author of two short story collections published by Knopf: *St. Lucy's Home for Girls Raised by Wolves* (2006) and *Vampires in the Lemon Grove* (2013), which was a *New York Times* bestseller. She is the 2017 Endowed Chair at Texas State University's MFA program.

Karen Russell: I'm always curious where other writers begin. What was the first image you had for this book? Did you start with Hawley and his daughter, Loo, in their current lives, or did you begin with the secrets of Hawley's past?

Hannah Tinti: The first spark of this novel came from my desire to write a love story. One of my favorite books is *Jane Eyre*, and the moment Jane meets Mr. Rochester is such an iconic scene—he is literally thrown at her feet. So I started by sketching out my own meeting of two people (which is actually still in the book—when Marshall washes up at Loo's feet from the ocean). Once I had that boy and girl together, I wrote a paragraph for each of their backgrounds, and that included a description of the girl and her father clamming on the shore. Right away, the father began to dominate the story. He was a lot more interesting than the boy or the girl. But what was his name? While walking through one of the old cemeteries in Salem, Massachusetts, where I grew up, I came across one that struck me: Samuel Hawley.

Hawley's name and those brief paragraphs were fragments that I carried around with me for months. They didn't come together until I sat down and wrote about the greasy pole. That was the breakthrough, when the novel fell solidly into place. The Greasy Pole is based on a real contest that I grew up going to and still attend each year when I can. It takes place each summer in Gloucester, Massachusetts, during a celebration of Saint Peter, the patron saint of fishermen. A forty-five-foot pole is attached to a pier and set horizontally above the water, then covered with grease and lard. A flag is attached to the end. The first man who manages to walk the pole and reach the flag wins. These fishermen break their arms and smash out teeth as they slip off the pole into the harbor, all for the simple glory of capturing the flag and being carried through the streets in triumph.

I put the character Samuel Hawley on that pole and began to sketch out a scene. When his turn came to enter the contest, I described him physically for the first time, and realized that his skin was covered with scars. Once the scars appeared, I wanted to know the stories behind them. Hawley's body became a map of the book that I was going to write.

KR: The central conceit of the novel is that it weaves back and forth through time. Every other chapter dives into Samuel Hawley's past life and tells the story of one of his "bullets"—a moment where he narrowly evaded being killed and earned another scar as a consequence. How did this fabulous idea come to you, and how is this structure important for the story you wanted to tell?

HT: I wrote the first bullet chapter to explore Hawley's backstory. I needed to find out how he got those scars. The marks we carry on our physical bodies are full of memory—stories that usually get shared only with the people we're most intimate with. That's what I wanted to uncover. The more I wrote, the more intrigued I became with the idea of telling the story of a man's whole life this way—brief flashes of meaning with many blank years in between that the reader would have to imagine. I began to write short pieces, skipping through Samuel Hawley's criminal past, each story revealing one moment where he'd found a way to keep living, starting when he was sixteen and ending when he was nearly fifty.

While the past drives much of the novel, I wanted it to be in conversation with the present, and for objects and characters to jump back and forth between the two timelines. Each bullet adds another piece to the present narrative—which is held by Hawley's daughter, Loo. In this way, the reader gets to be a detective, picking up clues and slowly filling in the picture. I wanted the structure of the book to be a call and response. The father's experiences in the past and his daughter's experiences in the present are intricately linked—two separate coming-of-age stories that eventually flow together, like a confluence of two rivers.

KR: I love how the story ranges in setting all over the United States. Each time we turn the page, we might find ourselves in Alaska or the desert or the Midwest. How did you decide where to set Hawley's bullet chapters? Did your travels over the years inform the book? And how did you come up with Olympus, Massachusetts, where Hawley lives in the present with Loo?

HT: Early on I decided that, with this book, I would write about places that I knew. Each of the settings are worlds I have visited or lived in, and feature bits of my own experiences. I've stayed at a great camp in the Adirondacks. I got caught in a dust storm in the middle of the Arizona desert. Whidbey Island is a place close to my heart, as is the ferry ride from Mukilteo. I have visited prairie dog towns in Wyoming. And I've walked in midnight sun and watched Childs Glacier calve in Alaska. As for Olympus, Massachusetts—where Hawley and Loo live—that is the only fictional setting in the book. I based it on Gloucester—home of the Greasy Pole, and a place where I lived for a year after college, waiting tables. I called the town Olympus in a nod to Greek mythology. It gave me some creative license and allowed me to shape the world of Hawley and Loo in more mythic proportions.

KR: Hawley reminds me of Clint Eastwood in an old spaghetti western—you're a little frightened of him even as you root for him, but his essential goodness is never in doubt. How did you develop him as a character, and were movies an influence as you wrote?

HT: Movies were definitely an influence. I grew up with *Star Wars* and *Indiana Jones*. But also classic films like the Marx Brothers' pictures and the original *King Kong* (1933). Because of this I tend to write with a focus on visual elements, and I'm very aware of pacing and the reader's experience. I want them to be surprised and have fun and also to be emotionally moved. Like when you're on a roller coaster, screaming with fear and dread and excitement and joy but at the end you get the wash of adrenaline and relief, and you stumble away grateful to be alive, stunned, and maybe even a little weepy, and for a brief period of time the world is brought into a sharper focus.

As for Hawley, he became the beating heart of the novel as soon as he stepped onto the greasy pole. He takes part in the contest not for glory, but to help his daughter. This act opened up the idea of the reluctant hero for me. I started reading myths and looking at heroes in different cultures and finally landed on Hercules (a.k.a. Herakles). Famed for his twelve labors and rewarded by the gods—Hercules set out on his quest after murdering his own wife and children, and later committed more terrible acts. Say the name Hercules, though, and a strong and powerful man comes to mind. A legendary hero.

I took the structure of Hercules's myth and used it as a framework for Hawley. The number twelve also became important, not only because of its connection to the recording of time and the zodiac (which comes into play with Loo) but also because it set a challenge for me as a writer. How could I make a man get shot twelve times, and the reader know that he is going to get shot, and still have each episode feel unpredictable? I spent many years working that out. And over those years I fell for Samuel Hawley, who, despite all of his violent tendencies, is driven by the need to cure his own loneliness. He is on a desperate search for love.

KR: This is a book where some scary things happen. Yet it's also a story about love and connection, especially between a parent and child. No matter what Hawley and Loo are going through, his desire to protect her is so clear to the reader. Can you talk a bit about how their relationship evolved as you wrote the book?

HT: In each of Loo's chapters, she learns something. She starts by shooting her first gun. Then she has her first fight. Her first drink. Her first kiss. Her first job. Her first car. Her first heartbreak. And she also commits her first crime. Her father acts as her protector and teacher, until eventually Loo begins to forge her own path. Samuel Hawley is a classic masculine hero, tough and rugged. But as his daughter's coming-of-age story intertwines with his own, Hawley ends up being saved by Loo—not once but twice—and by the final chapter of the book, she is the one who rises. She becomes the true hero, and Hawley (like Hercules) takes his place among the stars.

KR: In addition to your writing, you're known for your work as the co-founder and editor of one of my favorite literary magazines, *One Story*. How does being an editor inform what you do as a writer?

HT: *One Story* has been one of the greatest joys and most rewarding experiences of my life. Together with Maribeth Batcha, I co-founded the magazine in 2002, and was editor in chief for fourteen years. I'm now executive editor. We're a nonprofit organization, and publish one story at a time, allowing authors to take center stage, and giving our subscribers an intimate, focused reading experience. When *One Story* launched we made the rule to never publish an author more than once, so we have run stories from over 250 different writers from around the world. Editing these diverse voices has been enormously educational, and has made me acutely aware of how a reader maneuvers his or her way through a story. It also makes me hard on myself. I constantly stop and tinker with sentences, and often can see only the flaws in my own work.

While that side can be hard to turn off at times, being an editor has been a great gift. It taught me to respect the magic that happens in the creative process, while also understanding the mechanics behind the page. It has provided a way for me to support and celebrate emerging writers, something I feel very strongly about. And it's introduced me to a generous group of readers who love books as much as I do. I am thankful for the people I have met, and for the authors who have trusted me with their words. Now, with *Twelve Lives*, I'm trusting readers with my own. It's a delicate thing, like handing over your heart. So I'm grateful for everyone holding this book and listening.

Questions and Topics for Discussion

1. The central relationship in this story is the one between Samuel Hawley and his daughter, Loo. In what ways are they similar, and in what ways are they different? How do Hawley and Loo evoke the special bond between fathers and daughters?

2. So much of this story begins at "The Greasy Pole." What did you like about this particular chapter? How does it color your understanding of the distinctive town of Olympus, Massachusetts? How does it shift your perspective of Hawley, as a father and as a man?

3. Discuss the theme of secrets. What are the secrets that drive the action of the novel? How do secrets bring characters together? How do they drive them apart?

4. So many great stories are founded on the distinctions between heroes and villains, but in this novel, the line between the two is not

so easily discernable. Who do you feel are the heroes of this story? Who are the villains? How did this novel make you rethink how you define good and evil?

5. Discuss the structure of this novel. How does the switch between past and present contribute to the arc of the story? How does it deepen our understanding of Hawley and Loo, and connect these two very different coming-of-age stories?

6. In this novel we are taken on a road trip across America. How do the themes of travel and searching play a role in this story? Which setting did you enjoy the most? When Hawley and Loo finally settle in Olympus, how does this new, permanent home impact them?

7. As we get to know Hawley and Loo, we begin to understand that "Loo's mother had been dead for years but she had never been invisible." How does Lily play a role in the novel, even though she is no longer with her husband and daughter? How does her absence drive their actions and motivations?

8. While so much of this novel concerns the stories of relationships between characters, there is also great significance in the relationships between these characters and nature—for example, Lily and Loo's fascination with the stars, or Hawley's interactions with a whale. How does the natural world contribute to the storylines of these characters and help them find their places in the universe?

9. This novel focuses on the love between a parent and child, but there is also romantic love between Hawley and Lily, Mary Titus and Principal Gunderson, and especially Loo and Marshall Hicks. Do you think any of these romantic relationships are successful? Why do you think Lily stays with Hawley? How does Loo's bond with Marshall change her?

10. Objects carry immense significance in this novel, from the watches to the star map to the bathroom shrine of Lily's things. For Hawley and Loo, these objects represent important memories. How do these pieces of the past influence the present? How do characters' memories help or hurt them? Which objects did you remember the most after you'd finished reading the book?

PHOTO: © DANI SHAPIRO

HANNAH TINTI grew up in Salem, Massachusetts. Her short story collection, *Animal Crackers*, was a runner-up for the PEN/Hemingway Award. Her bestselling novel *The Good Thief* won the Center for Fiction First Novel Prize and an American Library Association Alex Award, and was a *New York Times* Notable Book of the Year. Tinti is the co-founder and executive editor of the award-winning literary magazine *One Story*.

hannahtinti.com

Facebook.com/Hannah.Tinti

@hannahtinti

To inquire about booking Hannah Tinti for a speaking engagement, please contact the Penguin Random House Speakers Bureau at speakers@penguinrandomhouse.com.

About the Type

The text of this book was set in Janson, a typeface designed about 1690 by Nicholas Kis (1650–1702), a Hungarian living in Amsterdam, and for many years mistakenly attributed to the Dutch printer Anton Janson. In 1919, the matrices became the property of the Stempel Foundry in Frankfurt. It is an old-style book face of excellent clarity and sharpness. Janson serifs are concave and splayed; the contrast between thick and thin strokes is marked.